CAUGHT BETWEEN

CAUGHT BETWEEN

Jeannie McLean

CAUGHT BETWEEN
Copyright © Jeannie McLean 2020

ISBN 978-0-473-51464-8

The author asserts the moral right to be identified as the author of this work.

All rights reserved. No part of this book may be reproduced, stored in a retrieval system, or transmitted in any form or by any electronic or mechanical means including photocopying, recording, information storage and retrieval systems, or otherwise, without prior permission in writing from the author.

Contact the author on jeanniemcleanauthor@gmail.com

This is a work of fiction.

Cover design by
Design for Writers
www.designforwriters.com

Produced for Jeannie McLean by
AM Publishing New Zealand
www.ampublishingnz.com

Acknowledgements

*Ehara taku toa i te toa takitahi,
engari he toa takitini.*

*My strength is not mine alone,
it comes from the group.*

Without the help and support of the following, this book may never have happened:

To the Rogues: Bronwen, the late Hilary, Katie, Pauline, Rod, Shauna, Ted, Tui – words are not enough to express my gratitude to the most audacious writing group.

Tania Roxborogh for her belief in me.

NZSA for all they offer New Zealand writers, and especially for awarding me a manuscript assessment with Vanda Symon.

Craig Sisterson for providing a platform for New Zealand writers of crime to showcase their work.

Shauna Bickley for always reading changes to the manuscript and productive writerly conversations.

Stephen Stratford for the first full edit and expert advice. Adrienne Charlton for her patience and expertise in producing the book.

Trish, Helen T, Linda, Felicity, Helen R and Heather for their friendship and loyal support; and of course, Xanthe, Siobhan and Steve who have always given me space and time to write.

1. KK

A ride to the playground, Jacob said, all smiles, nods and promises. Skin tight over knuckles as he gripped the handlebars, shunted the bike backwards and forwards. Wound up, keen to get moving.

KK glanced at his mother, waiting, willing her to object. She waved them off with, "Be back at dinner time."

Jacob took the lead, disappeared round the corner into the walkway and KK followed, let the distance between them grow. But Jacob waited at the junction: left to the inlet and past the mangroves to the end of Te Atatu Point, or right to the adventure playground.

Jacob pointed. "Something to show you."

"Like what?" KK pulled up short, his front wheel alongside Jacob's back wheel.

"Come and see."

KK didn't move.

"I heard these guys talking." Jacob pushed his bike back until their wheels almost snagged.

"What guys?"

"Dunno. Guys. Last night. It was dark but I saw them, take this ... thing ... that way."

KK looked.

"Ever seen one of those sex doll things?" Jacob spoke through tight lips, like a ventriloquist.

"No."

"Come and check it out?" Jacob taunted.

KK's bike wobbled.

"Too chicken?" Jacob's grin revealed his crooked front tooth. "It's plastic. Reckon they dumped it because it had a hole in it. Know what I mean?" Jacob's breath hot in KK's ear.

"Yeah, course." KK swallowed, ran his tongue over his dry lips.

"Sure you do." Jacob followed it up with a punch to KK's arm. "Come on, race you."

Jacob took off, body streamlined, head down to the handlebars, elbows tucked into his side.

KK prayed Jacob would lose control, speeding on the wet path. Grazed skin might be enough to let them both go home, honour intact.

Jacob didn't fall and KK pedalled, exerting enough pressure to stay upright but ensuring inadequate speed to catch up. He rode in the centre of the path that ran parallel to the beach as he kept an eye on the bushes and shrubs on the upside. Undesirables sheltered under them, his mother said. One might be there now, ready to jump him.

The path meandered away from the sloping sand and pebble beach. It followed the stone sea wall which arced around the mangrove inlet through a long, ragged canopy of overhanging branches. KK lost sight of Jacob long enough to make him cautious, ready to duck a wet branch flung back into his face.

"Hurry up!" Jacob's yell loud, disembodied, well ahead, round the corner. "It'll be too dark soon!"

"Someone will already have taken it." KK's whisper joined the swish of water lapping over rocks and against the sea wall, and the distant hum of motorway traffic. He wanted to see the doll but wished they'd come earlier. The coastal walkway with its overhanging trees was eerie at any time. Creepier in the twilight.

He dismounted, wheeled his bike – a precaution – expecting Jacob to have his mates hiding in the bushes and they'd jump him, punch him where the bruises didn't show. Payback for some perceived slight. Or just because.

To his left, the grassy reserve and picnic tables held back the treeline, the houses behind obscured; to his right, the beach gave way to the shallow Te Atatu inlet; and ahead, the trees and shrubs closed in, weighed down with age and damp. In the fading light it would be too easy for Jacob to toss a dead fish at him, yell, "Catch it, fuckwit!" and he'd laugh until he pretended to pee himself. The consequences far worse if KK turned round and scurried home, giving Jacob future opportunity to entertain their schoolmates, truth succumbing to the fun of embellishing KK's existing reputation – wimp, wuss.

Jacob waited beyond the canopy, his bike dropped at his feet, a wheel still lazily spinning. He pointed a stick in the direction of the sea.

KK propped his bike on its stand off the path and glanced around. No one was in sight – no dog walkers, no joggers – and if Jacob's friends were going to jump him they'd had plenty of opportunities. Maybe they were waiting until he moved away from his bike then would rush in, steal it. Or get him once he was down by the water, dunk him.

Guarding the bikes like a sentry, he gazed up the channel to the harbour bridge and the Sky Tower in the distance. His mother promised she'd take him up the tower one day.

"Go look," Jacob ordered.

"Me?" KK sucked in his breath, pulling the word back. It was a plastic doll. If he went first, would it either look as though he was braver than Jacob, or stupid enough to be sucked in by yet another of his tricks? There would be nothing there, except garbage floated in with the tide, caught in the shallows. Why would anyone dump a thing like that? If something was wrong with it, why not deflate it, scrunch it up and throw it in the rubbish?

"Jeez, KK, you baby." Jacob pushed into him.

KK stumbled back, his ankle connecting with handlebars, and he bent down to rub his shin.

Sneakers squelched into the sludge, and KK crinkled his nose at the rising stink of mud, seaweed and tidal debris that drifted up. Jacob was carrying the joke too far. Still, it was his sneakers that would need hosing off.

KK stood back from the edge. Jacob, below and a few metres along, balanced on rocks, one foot behind, one in front, as if ready to duel with the human-sized plastic doll lying face up against the retaining wall. He stretched out his arm and poked at the foot with the stick. KK expected it to wobble, as plastic toys sometimes do, but the prong bent ever so slightly into the flesh of the big toe with its fire-engine-red painted nail. Jacob dropped the stick but stayed in his bent-over position, his right arm still extended like a gentleman offering to help the girl to stand.

"Fuck, shit," Jacob gasped, gulped in lungfuls of air as he backed off, his feet slipping on rocks, arms windmilling to keep balance. He took a running jump at the retaining wall and landed on all fours by KK's feet. "It's real. A real dead girl."

Any second now, Jacob's laugh would ring out. *Ha ha, fell for that one, you wanker.*

"Shit, I thought it was …" Jacob's head shook from side to side and he took a step forward, a step back. He coughed and hawked a gob of spit at the ground. "You check." He pushed KK forward.

If it was a set-up, he'd pass the test, if he didn't burst into tears or wet himself first. KK hunched into his hoodie, shoved his hands into his jeans and took tentative steps along the wall until he judged he was level. No way was he going to jump down as Jacob had. He took deep breaths and gazed up. The sky was a low winter ceiling of grey that pressed down on him, that in-between time he usually enjoyed, fading light dusky, city lights in the distance. KK made out the shapes of bushes and trees and mangroves and rocks and Jacob beside him. He licked his lips again.

A quick glance over the edge. She was a pale form against the wet, dark rocks. His eyes moved up from the foot, his brain registering that it wasn't seaweed over the groin. There were hips and stomach and breasts, neck and half-open lips, wet, stringy strands of hair and wide brown eyes. Not doll-naked and smooth. One foot rested on its heel, toes pointing upwards; the other turned. One arm was thrown out sideways, appearing to indicate which way she'd come; the other wedged between her body and the wall. The head was pillowed on rocks and tilted towards the sea view, its eyes unseeing. Wriggly black lines stretched down from her stomach. KK's eyes hovered over the tattoo, the ink unsmudged by water. It was real. Like her.

KK imagined the sound of air seeping from the body like a pricked balloon, and his stomach heaved. He swiped one hand back and forth across his forehead like windscreen wipers, swishing away tears and sweat and the image of the white flesh from his mind. He pulled his hoodie off – until the thought of jumping down, leaning close enough to cover her made his stomach heave again. "We better tell someone."

"No, no one's seen us." Jacob grabbed KK's arm, his fingers hot through the clothes, like a branding iron. "We saw nothing, we were at the playground. Got it?" – where KK told his mum they were going, to the flying fox and mounds and humps to practise wheelies and bunny hops. Not that he ever did if Jacob was with him. Then he sat on his bike, one foot on a pedal, one foot on the ground, made it seem he was about to launch into a manoeuvre.

"But ..."

"Someone else can find her." Jacob released his grip, grabbed his bike and took off, his thirteen-year-old legs churning fast.

KK hauled up his bike and followed, keeping Jacob in sight.

Near the junction, Jacob swerved his bike off the path to avoid the walker appearing in the gloom. Mr Weston, the guy who lived opposite Jacob. The old man, head down as though he hoped to find money or something, didn't notice Jacob until the yaps of his scruffy, short-legged Pekinese made him look up.

"Hey, watch where you're going."

Jacob sped past.

KK slowed, tempted to pick up the excited pooch, cuddle into its warmth and smell its doggy breath. Instead, he steered round Mr Weston, kept his head down.

Jacob was out of sight. KK doubled back and circled the man and dog, the lead in danger of tangling in the bike wheels. "There's a body back there," KK said.

He swung the bike away, headed for home and didn't look back. Too bad if Mr Weston didn't believe him; he'd done his best to do the right thing. Maybe the tide would float her out. How long did it take for fish to eat a whole body?

Jacob waited where the path entered their cul-de-sac. He pushed right up close to KK, hit him in the arm, hard, almost knocking him off his bike, and whispered, "Remember, shut the fuck up." He didn't need to add 'or else'. Jacob was expert at getting himself out of trouble and others into it.

Through his tears, KK pedalled home, down the drive to the garage. He took his time with the bike lock, double- and triple-checking his bike was secure. He stood in his backyard, tilted his head back. A single star glinted through a sliver of a gap in the clouds.

The way Jacob had prodded at the girl's foot. And the panic on his face. Jacob had wanted the girl to be fake but somehow he knew she was there and he knew she was real.

2. TOVA

Tova Tan was travel-gritty and hungry after the four-hour trip on the Intercity bus from Tauranga. A twelve-minute wait for the Herne Bay bus, a stop-start ride along Ponsonby Road, the Friday-night party life getting into swing, and then a two-phase wait at the red lights to Jervois Road. The driver returned her 'thank you' and wave as she got off at the last stop. She checked her phone. 8:20. Wonky-wheel case in tow, it was a sluggish slalom around cars parked across driveways down Clifton Road and into Argyle Street.

She walked in the centre of the dimly lit road to avoid low branches and overhanging hedges still dripping from the usual September dampness, although the rain had stopped. And to check the parked cars, none of which were large and black with tinted windows. Anyone who'd asked had been told she would be back at the end of the weekend, not the beginning. She didn't expect the vehicle to be there but she still checked.

A quick rummage in her shoulder bag, fingers clutching house keys, the gate opened with a push of her knee and the security lights blazed on. So much for sneaking in. She expected Juliette or maybe Jasmine to poke their head out of a window.

The large white villa was silent.

A shower, a relaxing green tea, a decent night's sleep, then the weekend ahead of her, get organised for the return to uni lectures on Monday. After the six-week teacher placement in Tauranga, she looked forward to two days on her own.

She turned the key, paused, savouring the thought of her own place, her own bed. She pulled the wheelie case across the doorstep, past the laundry alcove on the right, kitchen on the left, into the lounge. Smiling, tempted to say, 'Hello home'.

Her smile dropped. The lounge was neat, tidy, but it wasn't as she had left it six weeks ago.

The cushions on the two-seater were centred, not one against each arm. The table that doubled as eatery and workspace was not flush with the wall.

A hurried check found towels on the shelves in the modest en-suite folded unevenly, and the toilet seat was up. The photo on the bedside table was face down. She hadn't left it like that. Turning it over, she caressed the glass with her sleeve and righted it. She put her hand on the duvet, flapped it back. Although the sheets looked clean, she pulled them off, dumped them on the floor next to the washing machine and remade the bed. She imagined the pillow was Jasmine's head as she plumped it into shape.

Now was the time to face Mrs Dunn or she'd talk herself out of it by the morning. It wasn't her business what the daughter Jasmine did upstairs, but the flat belonged to her, rent paid in advance. Tova was not prepared to let this go. She had expressly told Jasmine to keep out of her space.

Tova opened the French doors that led to the garden and shivered in the night air. A suggestion of scent, a memory of its heady summer fragrance, lifted from the shrubs along the back fence, planted when the human Jasmine was born.

No television flicker, no footfalls, no muffled sounds at all drifted down.

"Shift work sure takes it out of me," Mrs Dunn had said when Tova first moved in. "So on my nights off, I'm always in bed by ten-thirty."

Tova wasn't sure if Mrs Dunn was reassuring her that the flat would be quiet or warning her that no noise would be tolerated.

"And don't you worry about Jasmine, she's a responsible teenager. On my night shifts at the rest home, she'll be studying."

Learning about the seedy side of life. Too often, on those nights, Tova was kept awake by laughter and loud music, and the unmistakable sound of the headboard banging against the wall, so vigorous that the few glasses she had vibrated against each other, setting up soft musical tinkling of their own. She never worked out if the night visitor was one energetic stayer or several people, each visiting on a particular night; nor did she care. Once, she had purchased some high-quality ear plugs from the Jervois Road chemist.

It was after 9 pm. She was tired; perhaps the difficult conversation would be better approached in the morning. It didn't need to be confrontational. She didn't want to shame the girl but she had to make a clear statement, citing her rights as the tenant, before time changed her mind. With luck, she could talk to Mrs Dunn without Jasmine present.

She thought back to her first day of teaching practice. "Whakawhenua," the head of department advised. "Stand firm. Start as you mean to go on." Less formally, she also said, "And don't take any teko."

Tova picked up the photo again. She smiled into the eyes of her mother.

"For you, Mum, I must stand up for myself and not take shit from anyone."

3. FINN

"McIntosh, one for you. Another bloody hoax, I bet. It's the weather, people stuck inside, bored." The Henderson Police Station duty sergeant grumbled, didn't look up. "Some old guy rang direct, rambling on about bodies in the sea. He wasn't too keen to give his name, said he'd tell the officer who turned up. Makes me think it isn't genuine. No squad is in the area, can't pull others off their jobs. We're short-staffed as usual, so you check it on your way home."

In a 'detour' sort of way, thought Finn.

The caller had said the body was on the Te Atatu reserve by the sea wall, far end, near where the mangroves start. Te Atatu Peninsula was not in a direct line to his home in Waterview. He'd have persuaded his colleague Ngaire Wright to attend with him except she was on a day's sick leave. She'd have cheered him up, her non-stop chatter taking his mind off things. It had been a long week of patrols, domestic call-outs and nose-to-tails in the wet weather. All week he'd anticipated knock-off time end of Friday shift and a free weekend for once.

"Definitely dead, Sarge," Finn confirmed to the duty sergeant after he had checked for a pulse by torchlight, although the way the body bobbed on the incoming tide it had been apparent. Back on the path, he stood between the sea and Mr Weston, who shuffled forward until Finn was in danger of falling backwards into the water.

"Only one of you?" Weston shook his head, his disgust unmistakable. "I told the woman on the phone she was dead. Obvious to any idiot. The water will ruin what evidence there is if you muck around too long."

"Thank you, sir. You did the right thing, ringing the police." No point in annoying Weston further, telling him he should have given the information asked for from the start. The duty sergeant, juggling staff leave, illness and fewer officers each shift to handle calls, might have given this one more of a priority.

Finn sidestepped, turned away and rang in. "Female, mid-teens. Naked. No clear sign of how she died. Suspicious, I think."

"Yours not to think, McIntosh. Probably a jumper. She's floated there. The bloody weather is enough to make anyone depressed."

"Suicide jumpers don't take off their clothes." Finn talked through deep breaths to foil his fluttering stomach, not blasé yet at the sight of death.

"Secure the scene, keep spectators away. The immediate scene crew will be with you as soon as." The instruction given, then enough of a pause. "Think you can follow that simple order?"

"Shit," he mouthed, head averted from the old guy. He

stabbed at the phone, ended the call. Six years of policing behind him, mostly getting it right, yet his reputation forever defined by his last posting in Manukau.

"Go home, Mr Weston, out of the cold. Nothing else for you to do here." It was the second time Finn had asked him to go since he'd learned the old man's name and address. "Someone will be along to take your statement."

Weston's lips pursed in disapproval, his scruffy dog yapping close at heel as he shambled away. Again Finn wished Ngaire was with him to accompany the old guy home, make sure he didn't trip over the dog in the dark, or cark it from a heart attack, adding to the body count.

Arms folded against the chill, Finn stood at ease, his back to the sea and the body. He tried to hold the idea of a beer and bite to eat while blobbing out in front of *Stargate* reruns, but his mind returned to the body behind him. Not a suicide. An accident? What sort of mishap would land a naked body on Te Atatu beach? Had she been on a boat, drunk, cavorting, fallen overboard? It was winter, too bleak to be out on deck with no clothes on. How had she ended up here?

His mind wandered to the problem he'd been grappling with since his move to Henderson: keep at the study, get through the detective training or stick with general duties? How much would his past come back to bite him? He had the backup of teaching, but after enduring one long, hard year at it, policing had offered another career path. Maybe it was time to do his OE.

'Detective! If that's what you want to be, go for it.' Ngaire had said when they'd talked career paths. 'Dead body after dead body, strung-out relatives, lying crims and pedantic lawyers, not to mention the paperwork.

As for me, I think I'll put my name down to be a dog handler. Way better than dealing with humans.'

Hardly a ringing endorsement. She'd heard the talk, thought him too weak. Policing was a small world, someone always knew someone in each area, but so far she hadn't let on.

He turned to look at the sea, the outline of Birkenhead and Kauri Point wharf across the harbour, but his eyes dragged to the body, so he faced the trees again. Two runners – serious, judging by their lithe, trim bodies, arms going like pistons – approached from the left, eyes shaded by sunglasses and caps, although it was dark and the sun hadn't peeked through the clouds all day. Intent on keeping pace, they didn't see him waving them back until he stood in their way. They complied, receded from view, back the way they came. He suspected that, near their finish line, one would break and sprint to the end.

They provided a diversion. He thought about his own exercise regime – moderate, erratic, a bit of swimming, some weights work at the city gym he frequented less and less, which made him more sluggish, and so the vicious downward spiral spun. If he didn't shake himself out of this lethargy, he'd resort to one too many beers at the end of shifts, and before long, he'd be like colleagues he knew of, taking solace in the bottle.

Twenty minutes later, the first of the police teams arrived. Two patrol cars, followed by a dark-grey Holden Commodore, an unmarked van and an ambulance which proved to Finn that the duty sergeant didn't trust him to get death right. They drove in file through the asphalt car park near the picnic tables, over the gutter onto the grass, and stopped in a row as though a parking warden had guided them. Finn was thankful the ground was firm and hadn't suffered from the persistent rain during the past week. One of the media pack, likely to show up any minute, would go off half-cocked on a 'police carelessness causes damage to coastline' tangent to give the drama a spin if the female turned out to be a skinny-dipper who had a dicky heart and died of natural causes.

First out of the van was a uniformed officer carrying a roll of crime-scene tape that hid his hands like a muff. Following him was a woman in a full dark-blue jumpsuit, her shoulder dipping from the weight of a large, black toolbox. She'd struggle to lift any worthwhile fingerprints off leaves and grass and rocks and the sea-washed body.

He recognised the two fresh-out-of-probation officers from Henderson, Luke Unsworth and Isaiah Cranston, already at the back of the van, dragging out large arc lamps and tarpaulins to hide the body from view. Finn sighed away a twinge of envy. Six years under his belt and only recently he'd made constable-on-trial. They'd been full constables less than a year, on some new fast-track initiative, so Ngaire said, to detective status. Too many cops not applying, put off by the hard slog of full-time work and part-time study. And for what gain? Little extra pay and even more erratic hours than a general duties officer. Both had been shoulder-tapped, Luke because of his law background, and several years of youth pastor work behind Isaiah.

He turned his attention to the three officers from the second car pulling on protective coveralls and booties over their clothes and shoes, then to the Holden. Detective Senior Sergeant Goran Pavletich got out. He commanded attention, an alpha male, a good head shorter than Finn, thick-necked, muscle-toned like a weightlifter, often referred to behind his back as 'Gorilla'.

Finn thought of him more like a sheepdog, always pacing and circling a room, herding his flock into a semblance of order. Hard to work for, too exacting, the gossip said. Not that Finn would get an opportunity to confirm or deny, not with his history.

Pavletich opened the boot, took off his polished leather shoes, placed each one inside and pulled on gumboots. He surveyed the scene, completing a 360-degree turn, then headed towards the group by the vehicles. The officers formed a semicircle around him. Finn imagined Pavletich would have preferred running around, a dog off the lead, free of any confines.

Finn hadn't been called over, and he strained to hear the instructions, who was allocated what role – scene officer, body looker-after, witness interviewers – who was to accompany the detective, who needed to wait until the photographers arrived and recorded the scene. He needed action, resisted stamping his feet to aid circulation, ward off the slow creep of chill up from his boots, through layers of uniform. What were his chances of being included in the investigation?

Pavletich approached at a brisk pace, eyes darting bird-like, left and right. Finn was sure he figured on the hyperactive scale. "McIntosh." No handshake.

"Yes, sir," Finn acknowledged. Pavletich knowing his name wasn't good. Detectives gossip among themselves, like everyone else, so Finn played it safe, going for respectful. He'd wait for Pavletich to indicate how he preferred to be addressed.

"Fill me in, McIntosh." The detective stood beside Finn, copied his stance of legs wide, arms folded, back to the sea.

A surnames man.

"Deceased female, reported at 17:58 by a Mr Weston out walking his dog. He lives in Rewarewa Road, the street behind." Finn couldn't bring himself to use the detective's surname; too same-level colleague, too close. And he'd got used to calling his previous boss 'sir'. He solved his dilemma by avoiding use of any part of the man's name and waited for more questions to answer.

"You checked the body?"

A trick question? Finn scratched behind his ear, delayed his reply. If he said yes, would he end up disciplined for corrupting the scene? If he said no, would he be accused of a lack of initiative? Honesty was the best policy, though sometimes it wasn't. "I felt for a pulse. Otherwise kept clear of the body. Female, about fifteen or so. Weston showed me where he stood. No people have come this way other than two joggers who didn't stop. Too dark now for people to be out."

"Hell, I hate these young-kid cases. A local? Know of anyone missing fitting her description? Did she jump? Is she a floater?" His questions fired at Finn.

"I doubt it." As soon as he spoke, Finn regretted it, realising the questions were likely rhetorical.

"The Met Service will tell us if the tide brought her here. Bloody water will have ruined the scene." Pavletich thumped Finn on the back, one clean palm-slap. The jolt pushed Finn forward, requiring a mini soft-shoe shuffle to steady himself.

"Good idea, gumboots." Finn lifted a foot to show the cuffs of his trousers were wet but the detective had already jumped down to the rocks and didn't look back.

4. TOVA

She'd never been invited to enter the two-storey villa from the street entrance, and she'd never used the internal stairs. It didn't seem right to pick 10 pm and the Dunns absent to start.

In jeans and a fleecy sweatshirt rescued from the laundry basket, wishing she'd thought to find a torch or bring her phone for its light, Tova hurried to the back of the house and up the wooden stairs before she changed her mind. She hesitated at the top. The ceiling-height glass bifold doors, wide open to the spacious deck, revealed the darkness within.

"Mrs Dunn? Jasmine?" Tova followed that with three short raps on the glass. She expected Jasmine's petulant, 'What do you want?' Or her mother, one merlot too many, snoring on the couch. Tova edged into the room and flicked on lights.

At some stage, internal walls had been removed, allowing for indoor-outdoor flow, popular in renovated villas. Tova admired the restrained taste in décor, white and chrome dominating, but the owner hadn't stayed committed to the minimalist look. Surfaces were cluttered with photos of Jasmine: baby Jasmine, toddler Jasmine, cute first-school-uniform Jasmine, ballerina and piano-playing Jasmine. Mrs Dunn beamed beside her daughter in several photos, the likeness between them striking. Same colour light-brown hair, although Juliette's, fashionably cut and styled, had the look of regular hairdresser visits. Same big dark eyes and wide-mouthed smile with even, white teeth, signalling expensive dental work. Juliette must have been quite young when she had Jasmine. The mother could pass, at a quick glance, for Jasmine's older sister. Tova wondered if that was the look Juliette aimed for.

Jasmine smiled back in all but the school photo, taken in Jasmine's first year at high school, where she stared blankly at the camera. No others chronicled the transition from pretty child to sulky teenager, the only mode Tova had ever seen Jasmine in on the few occasions their paths had crossed.

She called out again, half hoping a neighbour would arrive to investigate the knocking and the lights. They would find a comatose Mrs Dunn together.

Get a grip. You're nearly twenty-three, a soon-to-be-qualified teacher.

TV remotes were lined up like paperweights on top of a neat stack of magazines. In the *House and Garden* kitchen, no glasses or plates sullied any surface. She tiptoed into the hall and hesitated before pushing doors and peeking in. The main bedroom, more white and chrome, was tidy, the bed made with a lace bedspread. A jarring note was a ruby-red, heart-shaped cushion, centred, back-dropped by several pillows sheathed in white, frilly-edged cases. The next room was Jasmine's, her discarded school uniform tossed on the dishevelled duvet, shoes at odd angles on the floor. Her school backpack slumped on a desk facing the window, school texts and refill pads beside the laptop.

Tova knocked on the bathroom door, self-conscious at her wavering, "Hello?" What if one of them was enjoying a hot soak by candlelight?

The large white tiled room was empty. She sniffed, sniffed again. Household cleaner. Maybe Mrs Dunn's idea of a fun Friday night was to clean. She'd run out of Jif and dashed to the supermarket. Letting out the strong smell might explain the open windows, but Tova doubted she would leave the house unsecured.

She gently edged open the door to the third room and realised she was holding her breath, thinking of an excuse if Juliette or Jasmine were woken by her presence.

It was an office. Tova couldn't remember if Mrs Dunn had told her what she did at the rest home, but judging by the set-up, she brought a lot of administration work home with her. With its back to the window, a large office chair faced a long, wide desk, dominated by two computer screens. At one end stood a narrow photocopier; at the other, a three-drawer filing cabinet. Neatly aligned file boxes, spines facing out, filled the shelving built along one entire wall. The first thing Tova thought was she would have turned the desk around so that while working, the occupier could see out the window into the garden. The second thing was that the loose papers on the desk and on the floor by the chair suggested Juliette was in the middle of some task. So, where was she?

Returning to the kitchen, Tova chided herself for checking the walk-in pantry. What forty-something woman would hide from her?

Except for the state of Jasmine's room, the messy desk in the office and the oversupply of photos in the living area, it could have been a house readied for an open home, everything tidy, the house smelling lemon-fresh. Tova closed windows, turned off lights, shut doors and hurried out, reproaching herself for overreacting. There'd be an explanation, one she hadn't thought of.

Back in her own flat, one look at the remains of the plastic-packed tuna sandwich bought in a rush before boarding the bus and it landed in the kitchen bin. She filled the jug for her usual bedtime green tea. Two teabags left in the container. Her mother's favourite bone china cup and saucer were not in their usual place beside it but in the cupboard with the plates. Tea made, she cradled the cup, appreciating its warmth as she searched for logical reasons.

Mrs Dunn might have swapped a work night. That didn't explain the open windows. Jasmine went out and forgot to lock up. More likely, but doubtful on a raw and drizzly night. Tova found her phone, still in her bag, entered her password and checked if she'd received a text message. Nothing.

She texted: *Mrs D. Im back. Where r u?* Then she backspaced, deleted the last three words: they sounded over-familiar. She retyped, *Hope everything OK. Its raining so closed your windows. Tova.*

It was too late to wake up neighbours she didn't know. They'd think her an over- anxious busybody. Her mother's strong stage-presence voice carried from the great beyond and Tova smiled. Believe in yourself, trust your instinct.

Instinct told her to ring the police.

Putting the cooling teacup aside, she picked up her mobile again. She focused on it so long the screen went to sleep.

What would the police say? 'Wait until morning.' They'd ask questions. She wasn't ready for that. She put the phone back in her bag, away from temptation.

She unpacked the teaching resources she had spent hours researching to engage her students and stacked them on the pinewood table, a Trade Me ten-dollar bargain with its *I Luv Sandi* surface decoration encased in a large heart, along with other doodles of indeterminate meaning. Washing sorted, in readiness for first thing the next morning, and the case stored under the bed.

She resisted the urge to do a room-by-room vacuum, rid the flat of the last vestiges of Jasmine and her visitors using the flat in her absence. The irony didn't escape her. Jasmine had no compunction using the flat, but here *she* was, worried about making too much noise.

Bedtime, it was close to midnight.

It was the weekend to have lunch with her father. If she was the slightest bit off-colour or listless he'd ask if she ate well, had her eight hours' sleep, play the Dad-hand, outwardly concerned. He'd tell her again he would buy her an apartment as he had for Richard. Why persist in renting a dingy flat?

If he started with the, 'We can't continue like this. It's been over twelve months. You have to forgive,' she'd tell him this was her last lunch until she'd worked things out her way. She had no reserves of emotional energy for herself, let alone for him, not after teaching in a decile three school full of high-energy, loud, excitable kids. Too many troubled children tore at her heartstrings, and she had existed in a perpetual state of near-exhaustion.

Some time later she tipped the cup of cold tea down the sink and went to bed.

5. FINN

Right on midnight, the crime-scene crew packed up their black boxes and clipboards and shed their protective clothing. The tarpaulin remained, even though the body had been removed. First light would bring the next lot of investigators and search teams looking for any explanation as to what happened.

Numb and hungry, Finn had been replaced once to relieve himself, which he did further along into the trees, out of sight of the reporters with their telescopic camera lenses, and of the growing cluster of onlookers. All that activity in spite of the dark and the on-off drizzle and nothing to see.

"Better not be skiving off for a fag," his replacement said. Just his luck to get landed with the smart-arse Unsworth.

"I don't smoke," Finn said as he walked away. A few hours standing around in the dark with the likelihood of more rain might be what Unsworth needed to dampen his usual cockiness. But Finn hurried, more from worry about being caught with his zip undone than concern for his fellow officer.

"The girl did herself in, I reckon. We could have all gone home hours ago. Pavletich trying to make his mark, is he?" Unsworth said on Finn's return.

"Not our call." Finn shrugged, hoped that would shut down further discussion. He, too, wanted to go home. Pavletich had paid him no more attention, and the officer in charge of the scene had left him on guard duty for hours. Deliberately, Finn thought.

So far, so mediocre with Pavletich. And no chance now to make an impression.

The detective moved away from the site back to his car, opened the boot and swapped the gumboots for his shoes. "McIntosh!" he yelled and waved him over.

"Pissed off the new boss already?" Unsworth muttered.

Pavletich was in the car, the engine running by the time Finn stood by the driver. "Report to me first thing in the morning."

"Yes, sir." Shit. What had he said wrong this time?

6. TOVA

Saturday dawned bleak and damp. Tova longed to doze, maybe read in the warmth of her bed for another few hours but by 6.45 she was listening for sounds from upstairs. Jasmine rarely surfaced before midday on weekends, and Juliette was probably enjoying a lie-in after a late night out.

Tova showered and dressed in record time, not lingering under the hot water, her day planned. Breakfast, cleaning, food shopping, confronting – not necessarily in that order.

A quick check of her mobile. No texts. The few who might care had been told she was returning on Sunday night: long-time friend Sarah who had texted days ago about a Sunday night catch-up; half-brother Richard who, left alone for the last six weeks, might have miraculously turned into a thinking adult. The rent was paid so it hadn't seemed necessary to inform the Dunns. No need to tell her father of her return date: she hadn't told him she would be away for six weeks, figuring he'd find out without her help.

No reply from Juliette.

Breakfast consisted of a bite of dry toast, with a coating of apricot jam scraped from the sediment and sides of the jar. The rest went in the bin. The tea from the last teabag tasted stale. Teabags added to her shopping list.

The washing, cleaning and vacuuming up six weeks of Jasmine using her flat filled time but didn't require deep thought, and she rehearsed what to say to Mrs Dunn.

At 9 am, she was on the upstairs deck, her heart rate up, its thudding syncing with her loud knocking. Drizzle drove her back to her flat.

Something wasn't right.

Using Google maps she rang the rest home. The ringtone gave way to the answerphone. "Please ask Juliette Dunn to ring me. She has my number. It's Tova."

How to track down Jasmine? Staff might be at Jasmine's school for Saturday sport, but no one would be at reception. No point in leaving a phone message. And she had no idea who Jasmine's friends were, let alone where they lived.

At the front gate she looked first right, then left, then right again, as if the Dunns might appear. No one answered her knock at the neighbours to the left. The house on the other side was protected by a high wall and an intercom, and from what she could see of the upstairs, the house was closed up. She recalled Mrs Dunn mentioning that those neighbours spent the winter months in Europe.

She would wait, use the time to get a head start on her assignment. The blank laptop screen beckoned, and she had every intention of typing *Final Teaching Practicum Report* but her fingers keyed in *What is the worst that can happen? Last year was ... last year.*

She held down the delete key.

She glanced over to the photograph of her mother. "Tell me what to do."

What would you want to be done if it was you?

Tova rang the police.

7. FINN

'First thing', Finn understood, was Saturday, 7.45 am, upstairs to the end of the corridor and the corner office at the Henderson Police Station.

He was awake three hours earlier, couldn't sleep, going over and over the night before until he was sure he'd followed procedure.

He cursed himself for not swinging by the supermarket, having arrived home to find, as suspected, no milk and two thin-crust slices left in the bread packet. As he had to get dressed to go out for supplies, he might as well head to the gym, then get a decent full breakfast and cappuccino at the café next door.

He hadn't been swimming for over two weeks, and it took the first ten laps for his under-utilised muscles to give up protesting. Half an hour later, he towelled himself dry and headed for the equipment to give other muscle groups a workout. Fifteen minutes on the rowing machine left him panting like a dog in need of shade and water. He would like to have lifted some weights but all stands were in use. He showered, resolved to get to the gym three times a week, and headed to the café, keeping his eye on the clock. He couldn't afford to be late for his appointment with Pavletich and had no intention of mentioning it was his weekend off.

Finn was ten minutes ahead of schedule, but Pavletich was already in his office, opening and closing drawers, answering the phone, making calls. The walls were paper-thin. It seemed too much like spying on mates in the shower, so Finn examined the dark-patterned carpet and peered at the wall opposite, an aged pastel lemon.

Pavletich knew his name, so he must also know that Finn had reached the heady height of constable-on-trial, the first study hurdles behind him. So far he'd been tagged on the end of minor investigations – a spate of car thefts, a dairy robbery – barely tolerated by the more-experienced detectives.

He'd said nothing to annoy Pavletich, he was sure, so the summons had to be to invite him onto the team. He rehearsed his acceptance when offered a place on the investigation. A simple 'Yes, sir, thank you' sufficient. Clear, to the point, professional.

The command to "Come in!" delivered at 8.18.

"How difficult is it to get the facts straight from one old geezer desperate for his fifteen minutes of fame, McIntosh? The first on the scene wasn't Mr Weston, it was two kids on bikes."

Finn processed Pavletich's sarcasm, thankful the spittle didn't reach as far as the words. Shit, shit.

"Or so he told a reporter. Weston reckoned he didn't know who they were. Might be making it up, of course. Get back to Weston and go over his story. Find the two boys on the bikes, confirm if they exist or not."

"Sir."

"Routine, McIntosh. Crime scene are back there doing a thorough search. So far no evidence of anything other than she did it herself. The severe lacerations on her back most likely caused by scraping on the rocks, hard to tell in the light last night. No one fitting her description has been reported missing, so she's still unidentified. No more staff will be assigned unless the autopsy tells otherwise. So I'm stuck with you to do the ploddy legwork. Fill in the forms, write it up, paperwork perfect. Think you can manage that?" Pavletich threw a manila folder at him, Frisbee-style. Finn grabbed it but not before loose pages fell to the floor.

He bent down to shuffle them back into the folder and prayed for the floor to swallow him. Much like he so often did when he misinterpreted one of Emily's moods. The floor didn't open then, and it didn't now. He straightened up and backed out like a lowly servant.

"Why didn't you tell me about the two boys on the bikes?"

"You didn't ask," Weston said.

"You mentioned them to a reporter."

"She was interested."

Finn forced an apologetic smile. "You didn't recognise them?"

"And give that Hemona another reason to make our life hell?"

Finn stared out the large picture windows of the Weston's two-storey house – a seventies brick-and-tile with a wide concrete driveway and manicured lawn – and dredged up his interview-technique training from too long ago. The 80:20 rule had been drummed into them: let the witness tell their story most of the time, listen and paraphrase back what had been said to ensure understanding. Listen, defuse the ire in the cantankerous man. Easier said than done. He sure wasn't following Weston so far. "Go through it again, please, and tell me what happened from the time you left to go on your walk."

Weston took the armchair and Finn sat on the heavy red-leather three-seater. Notebook ready, he prepared for a long-winded, shaggy-dog story.

Mrs Weston, spry and smiley, said she was on her way out for a walk, then lunch with friends. She stroked her husband on the arm, told him to behave and left the room.

"The kid who told me about the body lives on the corner, the weatherboard house with the tidy garden, can't miss it. He's polite, says hello, pats Scruffy if he isn't with the ratbag Hemona boy. That one lives opposite, next to the walkway." He pointed it out. "The house that looks like a hurricane hit it, there's so much rubbish in the yard. Give him a good rev up, cheeky little bugger. And while you're at it, tell his parents our cul-de-sac was lovely and quiet until they moved in. Cars coming and going at all hours – drug dealers, I reckon, in their flash cars, Mercs and BMWs." He slid a glance Finn's way. "Drug overdose, was it? That Hemona boy involved?"

"Mr Weston?" Finn interrupted his tirade. "What happened next?"

"I thought he was pulling my leg."

Finn waited.

"I walked all the way to the mangroves; gives Scruffy a decent run. On the way back, where the path is right on the sea wall, there she was, in the bend. Looked like a log at first. Thought I'd have to get down, pull it up, stop rubbish banking around it. I'd wait forever if I expected the council guys to come clean it up. But up close ... Well, I knelt down to double-check, in case my eyes were tricking me in the dark." Weston's hand moved, making the sign of the cross.

"I'll arrange for Victim Support to talk to you if you like." No matter how tetchy the old guy was, finding a body was still a shock.

"What the hell for? I'm not the victim."

Finn held back a sigh. Time to put an end to the interview. He transferred both pen and notebook to his left hand, stuck out his right, ready to thank Weston for his help.

"Don't you go telling that Hemona I said anything." Weston ignored Finn's outstretched hand.

After several apologies, none of which appeased Mr Weston, and armed with the boys' addresses, Finn stood on the footpath looking across at the Hemona house, Weston's description of it accurate. The name Hemona was mentioned around the station at regular intervals. A ute was in the driveway. It might pay to get an assessment of the home and occupants before knocking on their door.

Sheer bloody-mindedness made Finn get in the squad car and wave like a royal as he did a lap of the cul-de-sac, sure that Weston was watching. He cruised the length of Rewarewa Road to the Te Atatu Road intersection, taking note of the walkway entrance, the high fences separating most houses, people inside seemingly oblivious to his presence.

Mindful of Pavletich's order to get confirmation of the boys' existence, he did a U-turn, drove back to where the road curved into the cul-de-sac and opposite the nice boy's house.

A woman – pale, windblown hair, dressed in tracksuit and Kathmandu fleece jacket, the standard parent uniform for soccer game sidelines on Saturday morning – opened the door on his third knock. "Yes?" Surprise and query. She looked beyond him, left and right, checking which neighbours were watching. A common reaction when confronted by a policeman in full uniform, padded out with vest and fluoro jacket, a touch of formality with the police hat on. She eyed the red ring binder under his arm.

"Constable Finn McIntosh, Henderson Police. I understand a young boy with a bike lives here."

"Why?" she repeated, the vowel drawn out, not willing to admit it until he gave her more information.

"I'm making enquiries about a body found on the beach last night. A witness mentioned seeing two boys on bikes. May I speak with your son?"

"A body?"

That was news to her. Her eyes grew wide. She must be one of the few people in the area not privy to the neighbourhood drama. There had been a sizeable crowd watching proceedings the night before, but in the absence of firm details, a less than thirty-second sound bite on news sites: "An as-yet unidentified body of a young female was discovered on the Whau West Walkway in Te Atatu. Investigating officer Detective Senior Sergeant Goran Pavletich of Henderson Police said once the formal identification was carried out and cause of death confirmed, more details would be released. He asked anyone who had any information to contact the police."

"Mrs ...?"

"Nell Kalgour. And Karl, my son. Everyone calls him KK." She held herself still, that moment before truth dawns.

"Mrs Kalgour, do you know anything?" Finn kept his voice steady.

"KK seemed upset when he came back from playing with Jacob. I thought they'd had a falling-out again."

"Jacob? Jacob Hemona?"

"Yes. He's here. He comes for lunch after soccer."

At the sight of the police officer, the boys stopped talking. They were side by side, hamburger boxes, chip pottles, cans of Coke in reach between them, feet dangling over the low back deck, dressed in muddy soccer gear.

"Bit of a treat. They lost 4–1," Nell Kalgour explained, as if Finn might moonlight as the healthy-food police. "KK and Jacob." She indicated which boy was which as Finn moved to face them, although he would have guessed right. KK had inherited his mother's pallor and thin, straggly, reddish hair. Jacob watched him with deep-set large brown eyes, eyebrows hidden by a long black fringe, the fading purple around his bruised mouth evidence that the blow hadn't happened in the game.

KK collapsed his McDonald's bag and sat ramrod straight, his face growing paler by the second. Jacob shuffled his bum and moved one arm behind KK's back. Finn would have put money on it that Jacob had prodded KK a warning.

"I'm Constable McIntosh. I understand you were riding your bikes down by the beach last night."

Neither boy spoke.

"It's important to tell the officer," Mrs Kalgour said,

sitting close to her son. "A body has been found." She looked up at Finn. "Do you know who it is?"

"She hasn't been identified yet. That takes a few days," he lied. Most bodies were identified immediately – they died at home or in a car they owned or were with people known to them.

"We didn't go that way on our bikes yesterday afternoon," piped up Jacob.

"Which way would that be, Jacob?" Finn asked, aware that Mrs Kalgour's worry lines creased deeper.

"Someone said. The cops turned up and everyone went to the beach to look." Jacob shrugged his bony shoulders. Finn recognised an older-than-his-years kid in a hurry to grow up to live life the way it was portrayed on cheap DVDs: gangsters and staunch bros, the go-it-alone code of the heroes and villains, corrupt public officials, cops' fair game.

"A witness said they spoke to a young boy on a bike a few minutes before the body was found. Was it either of you?"

"Nah, not us, eh KK? We were way down at the adventure playground, weren't we?" Jacob elbow-jabbed KK then presented a sly smile to Finn. "Lots of kids ride their bikes along the path. We all look alike to old people."

How does he know the witness was old? "I'd like to speak to KK first," Finn said, planning to divide, and conquer the weaker boy. "Perhaps if you go home, Jacob. Tell your parents I'll be along."

KK's head shot up, eyes imploring his mother to save him from impending doom.

Jacob leapt to his feet, head shaking. "Mum and Dad are out."

"They must have come back. A car's in the drive." Finn waited for the boy to come up with another excuse.

Jacob sent KK a last, long glare, full of promise of dreadful things to come if he spoke out of turn. Finn had seen the same look on the faces of ringleaders each time he confronted a group of youths doing burnouts in the Concourse industrial area, drinking and pissing in the stadium car park or hassling pensioners at the mall.

"See ya." The hand Jacob pressed on KK's arm was far from delivering support. KK pulled his sleeve down, but not before Finn saw the spreading pinky-red of pinched skin.

It was warmer and more comfortable inside. Mrs Kalgour sat close to KK on the couch and the boy didn't squirm away from her. Finn sat opposite, on the edge of the matching La-Z-Boy, elbows on knees. "KK, you told Mr Weston about the body, didn't you?"

The boy's recollection was delivered fast, like a sluice gate releasing the guilt but not the memory. The chronological order was hard to follow and Finn patiently waited until the boy finished to check the facts.

"Where did Jacob touch the body?"

"On the foot, with the stick." KK shrank further into his mother's side, hand trembling as he pointed at his own foot.

"You didn't see anyone other than Mr Weston?"

"No."

The boy told the truth, he was sure of it.

"And you've never seen that girl? Did Jacob know her?"

KK's eyes flickered. He cuddled into his mother, a child seeking warmth and comfort. She smoothed hair away from his forehead then stood and ushered Finn out to the porch.

"You can't suspect the boys. If you need to ask more questions, wait until tomorrow. KK's had a dreadful shock. As have I."

Children younger than KK and Jacob were capable of dreadful things. "Mrs Kalgour, the quicker we get all the facts, the sooner we'll be able to work out what happened. They discovered the body but didn't report it. Why?"

"KK did. You said he told Mr Weston." She drew back in indignation. "Look, you've scared KK. Give him tonight, come back tomorrow if you need to ask any more questions."

Time to back off. He had the information he needed. The boys were real. Official statements would be taken later.

"They seem very different," Finn said, thinking through the dynamics of the boys' relationship, leader and follower.

"We live in the same street, the boys go to the same school. They're on the same soccer team. There aren't too many boys of KK's age living close by, and Jacob deserves better. His parents ... those bruises on his face. You'll see when you meet them. Good luck with that." She shut the door gently.

8. TOVA

Tova disconnected the 111 call before it made it to the second beeps. Memories flooded back. Ringing emergency would mean police cars on her doorstep within minutes. Was it really an emergency? The officer last year had given her a lecture about nuisance calls and taking police away from genuine problems. Implying she was adding to that cost. She wasn't sure she could cope with another accusation of wasting police time.

Sticking to her plan for the day, Tova grabbed a shopping bag, dropped the list into it and made the mistake of glancing at the photo of her mother.

What would you want to be done if it was you?

Tova picked up her phone and googled police non-emergency number. She knew there was one, had seen billboards advertising it but she couldn't recall it. As soon as she saw it – 105, and the rider in bold: **Report any situation that doesn't require immediate police or Emergency Services attendance** – she pressed the numbers and wondered if she could report Mrs Dunn missing without involving herself.

What was the worst that could happen? Mrs Dunn, when she turned up, would think her over-anxious but would be polite, thank her for her concern. If the police followed up, they, too, would say she'd done the right thing – better to be safe than sorry and other platitudes – but she would see they had checked up on her, think not a lot had changed in a year, she was still trouble.

She looked up to the ceiling, hoping to hear the Dunns moving about upstairs. The dial tone gave way to a click as someone picked up. Tova cut the call. She'd be asked for her name and address. More likely, they had Caller ID, see her number, trace her through that.

Ten minutes passed while she argued with herself. The prevarication was hardly the behaviour of a responsible, almost-qualified teacher.

She rehearsed what she'd say, brief and factual. I'm worried about my landlady. Her house was left open and she hasn't come home.

She opened the keypad on her phone. And stabbed the numbers in before she changed her mind again.

9. FINN

Jacob's house was shut up, the ute he'd seen parked across the footpath, nose-in to the drive, was gone. Finn wasn't disappointed, probably wouldn't get a much different story from Jacob. If the girl had topped herself, it was a case of the boys being in the wrong place at the wrong time.

Gentrification was yet to come to this part of Te Atatu, but most of the neighbours kept their older-style houses and yards tidy. From the footpath, he gazed at the Hemona residence. It needed a paint and gutters replaced. The patchy grassed area at the front didn't merit lawn status. He walked the length of the fence – waist-high, slack wire netting, minus a front gate. Two vehicles, one behind the other, took up much of the long gravel-and-weed drive on one side. Finn took down the licence plates. Judging by the grass growing around the wheels, neither had shifted in some time. A wooden fence separated the house yard from the public walkway along the other side. The public side was painted in green patches where someone had attempted to camouflage the graffiti. The house backed onto the reserve and beach beyond.

Back in the squad car, he rang in and asked for a rundown on the Hemonas. The duty sergeant grunted at the mention of the name. Jacob may have engineered his father out of the way until Finn gave up. More likely, Mr Hemona spotted the police car, and absence was in order.

Finn headed towards the Te Atatu township and onto the peninsula road back to the motorway. He pulled over when his mobile rang, in case of a smart alec with a smartphone, keen to upload to YouTube a police officer using his mobile while driving. No thought the reason might be a matter of life or death for some poor sod.

"McIntosh, you're out and about. Follow this up." Pavletich, loud and curt. "Central logged it, say they're sitting on it, awaiting further information. Reckon the woman who reported it might be overreacting, peeved that her upstairs neighbours didn't tell her what they were up to for the weekend. Two missing women, one too many for us, but there are no other recent reports of AWOL females."

The address given was in Herne Bay. He liked driving along the North-Western Motorway, across the causeway, catching glimpses of moored boats at the inlet, the harbour bridge in the distance and the kitesurfers at Point Chevalier. Extensive road works defined by orange traffic cones, red-and-orange graffitied barriers and sandbags that blocked sections of view detracted from the area's beauty. His mood lightened as drivers slowed when they spotted the squad car.

He recognised her. And she remembered him, clipped off her "Hello", and kept the door half closed.

Tan. He hadn't made the connection. Why would he? Different part of the city and that surname was common enough in Auckland. It was definitely her: Chinese in appearance with olive skin, 157-centimetre woman of slim build. His eyes flicked to his open notepad, checked what he'd scribbled down and tried not to stammer. "A Mrs Tan rang ..." He glanced at her hand holding the door. Fingers manicured, nails unpolished. Wrong hand to see a wedding ring.

"Ms Tan," she clarified. "I don't use my mother's surname now, for obvious reasons. I thought you'd know that." Straight, thick, black hair fell around her face and shoulders, shimmering as she moved a few strands behind one ear. No rings on any finger. *Exquisite* popped into his head, a word he'd never had use of before. She held his gaze, her dark eyes, deep set, accentuating high cheekbones.

Finn imagined how she saw him, cumbersome and awkward, a giant in comparison, the heavy uniform adding bulk to his already solid build. To douse the inappropriate twitch in his crotch, he reminded himself of her record: assault on a police officer, obstructing police in their enquiries, resisting arrest, offensive language, making a false claim.

Not that he believed the charges, misrepresented at best, lies at worst. Did she know he'd questioned the lead officer's tactics, resulting in removal from her case and a stand-down citing flawed judgement due to personal issues? Reinstated with a warning to sort his life out, which would happen faster if he transferred out of Counties Manukau.

Ten months since he'd last seen her, that sound bite on the evening news still burned in his brain. He had been slouched on the couch, second beer poured, the first hour of his three forced days off work. Emily not at all sympathetic. She took the opportunity to kick him while he was down. Sitting at the other end of the sofa, dabbing a sodden tissue at her tears and runny nose, she as good as said he bored her, his best mate didn't, and she was leaving.

He'd focused on the woman staring at him from the screen. The camera had been right in her face, journalists jostling to get closer, calling out questions she didn't answer. She forged ahead, her sad, tired eyes glistening. It was as though she pleaded only to him and she was fixed on walking out of the TV and into his lounge. With a face like that, she had to be innocent. The newsreader returned and Emily swore, said he could at least have tried to persuade her to stay. She flounced out of the room, slamming the door, and all he felt was relief.

The only woman to make any impression on him other than Emily happened to be unsuitable in so many ways. For too long, whenever he thought of Emily, the image of Tova surfaced. The two entwined in his mind, one wrong for him and the one in front of him so much more so. If he ever let a therapist get anywhere near him, he would probably hear about 'subconscious emotional associations'. He tried not to think of Emily too often.

Maybe Detective Senior Sergeant Hammond Harris had been right. After all, most people never experienced any level of investigation, let alone two less than a year apart. No, there was nothing wrong with his judgement but a lot wrong with Harris's techniques.

"I'm following up on your call."

"Is there a red flag against my name, ring Detective Harris immediately if I contact the police about anything? And he sent you. I should have known I'd be treated like this." She spoke calmly and took a step back, about to shut the door.

"Wait, Detective Harris has nothing to do with this." Finn fumbled in a pocket for Pavletich's business card, held it out to her. "Detective Pavletich, Henderson Police sent me."

He'd written his own name and work contacts on the back of the card, ready to leave it in the letter box if no one was home. She read both sides then held it between two fingers, positioning it to flick into the nearest bin as soon as he left. "I never did know your name."

Finn had been too low-ranking for Harris to acknowledge his presence, not that he was about to admit that. How to assuage her anger? Would telling her that he had criticised Harris's methods achieve that? No, too personal, he'd come across as creepy.

"I can ask if another officer is available, if you'd prefer," he offered. "It might take a while, though." He tried not to think of Pavletich's reaction if she took up that option, wasting another officer's time.

"Are you really here about my neighbours?"

"Yes," Finn checked his notes. "Mrs Juliette Dunn and her daughter Jasmine, I understand. How long have they been missing?" He wished he'd phrased it better, as though she had been too hasty.

"I'm not sure, exactly. I returned last night after six weeks away. It wasn't that they weren't here that worried me, but that the house was wide open in the middle of winter. They still weren't back this morning."

"You did the right thing ringing the police," Finn

said. "Your landlady will thank you for looking out for her. Do you know her well?"

"No."

"So they may be on holiday?"

"She wouldn't have left the windows open, would she?"

Finn thought of the number of calls the station received to go round to people's homes to check if they'd locked the back door. He kept his mouth shut, detecting the slight rise in Ms Tan's voice. One of Harris's accusations of her, quick to anger. "OK, describe them." He smiled, friendly, wondered if he should suggest they go inside her flat, decided not to push it.

"Juliette is late thirties, I think, much taller than me. Jasmine's a bit shorter than her mother, but not much." She used her hands to give an indication of Juliette's height and he estimated she must be about 170 centimetres.

"How old is the daughter?"

"Fifteen, sixteen."

Finn kept the pen steady as he wrote down the age in his notebook. "Perhaps I'll have a quick look upstairs."

She led the way round to the back garden. He stepped ahead of her at the foot of the stairs. "Did you come this way last night to check?"

"Yes." She frowned slightly.

"Understandable. Take me through what you did."

"The doors were unlocked and windows were open. I called out but no one answered. I checked each room. They weren't home. I closed the windows, shut the doors."

Concise, logical. "Did you notice anything unusual?"

"Other than the house deserted? No."

He supposed his question deserved her sarcastic response.

"Except ... Mrs Dunn, or someone, has been cleaning recently. The place smelt of Jif."

Reasons for that. Cleaning on a Friday night in anticipation of entertaining over the weekend, or indicative of a lonely life. He thought of her previous encounter with police. Attention-seeking? He hadn't seen signs of it then, or now, although he was no expert on mental health. He knew what to do, advise her to ring the police if the mother and daughter hadn't turned up by Monday. And go out of her life again.

But for the information that Jasmine Dunn was fifteen.

"Wait here." No need to break in, the door was unlocked and he had reasonable cause to enter. If the Dunns appeared, Tova's concern would be his excuse.

The house was still. His "Police. Mrs Dunn?" carried. Elbowing doors ajar, keeping fingers off, he peered into rooms, bedrooms, a study, office. One door was locked. A faint but identifiable suggestion of cleaning products was stronger in the bathroom. He retraced his steps to the lounge and stood in front of the group of photo frames on top of the low bookcase, eyes lingering on the girl in school uniform. She had the same eyes, same shaped face as the girl on the beach. The hair colour was different. He took one last look around, imprinted the scene on his mind, picked up the photo and headed back to the deck and Tova.

"The locked door. Is that the internal access down to your flat?"

Her eyes fixed on the photo he held. "Why do you want that?"

Finn persisted with his question. "Did you use those stairs to check up here, or return to your own flat?"

Her chin lifted. "Are you accusing me of breaking into the place?"

"No," he said, surprised. "I'm noting ways in and out of the house."

"Why? Has something happened? Is that why you're taking the photo?"

The photo would be up on news channels and websites and shared on blogs within hours, to trigger memories, times and places. Some would be worth following up, most not. The girl's death was no accident, he was sure, and by the smell of the too-clean house, he would put money on it that all surfaces had been wiped down.

"That's not recent," Tova, beside him, tapped the glass. "She's changed her hairstyle, and colour, since that was taken."

10. TOVA

Tova followed the constable's instructions without comment or complaint, back down the stairs and into her flat. She sat at the table, he stayed by the entrance, scanning the room while he took out his mobile. He could have made the call from anywhere – in the back yard, up on the deck or out the front beside his car. He spoke quietly into his phone while keeping her in view.

He had recognised her as soon as she opened the door, she knew, and he had remained politely cautious, doing his best not to turn his back to her. She wanted to tell him her side of the story but she reminded herself that Detective Harris had been considerate too, at first.

He finished the call. "Officers will be here soon to examine the house. Nothing to worry about, Ms Tan. Routine in missing-person cases, looking for something to suggest where Mrs Dunn might have gone."

"And Jasmine," Tova added.

"Yes, and Jasmine." He didn't look at her when he said it.

"What's happened? You know something. Where she is. Is she all right?"

"Do you mind answering a few more questions?"

"I don't know any more." She'd been through the process before. He would interpret her replies in light of what he knew about her. What he *assumed* he knew.

"Can we go somewhere quiet, private? What about a neighbour's place? The scene staff will want to have a good look around. In here, too. You said you'd been away, so they'll want to check." The policeman paused, licked his lips. "It's routine, won't take long."

"I don't know the neighbours." Where else would he suggest? A café? A park? The patrol car?

He came up with another option. "We can talk at the station."

Clever how he ended with the last place she would ever suggest. He would have more control there.

She let the silence lengthen.

"I thought you might prefer a female officer to take your statement. It will take less time if we went there rather than wait for her to come to us," he said with a mix of sympathy and understanding. *Because* he knew her history.

It was time she buried her paranoia. The few times she'd seen him during her mother's investigation, he'd always been polite. There was something he wasn't telling her, but it did seem to be linked to the Dunns' disappearance and not to her. He was taking her seriously.

"Afterwards, I'll arrange for you to be driven wherever you want to go. Do you have somewhere to stay?"

She nodded. And didn't add the details.

"Good." He sounded relieved. "Pack a few things in case it's a day or two before we let you back in."

Tova nodded again, feeling like one of those toy jiggle animals people had in their cars. She grabbed her backpack, stuffed a change of clothing in it, made no comment when he held the rear passenger door of the police car open for her.

She checked off landmarks as he drove: Cox's Bay and the tennis courts, Meola Road past the soccer grounds, left onto Pt Chev Road, a wait at the traffic lights before taking the motorway on-ramp, heading west. She got up the courage to speak her mind as they crossed the causeway, approached the Rosedale Road off-ramp.

"I've changed my mind." What had she been thinking, agreeing to go with him? Lulled into some sense of security because he was vaguely familiar? "I don't like police stations." Like a little kid, working up to a tantrum.

"Anything you can tell us about the Dunns may help us understand what's happened." He stayed in the middle lane, made no sign of slowing and they passed the exit.

"I don't know what Jasmine has done. I don't want to get involved." It was the only reason for the disappearance that made sense. To protect her daughter from whatever juvenile trouble she was in, shoplifting or drugs likely, Juliette had whisked her away in such a hurry she forgot to lock the house.

"Why do you think she might have done something?" He flicked a glance at her in the rear-view mirror. She held his gaze, she wouldn't be intimidated again.

"I said I've changed my mind." Irritated by his failure to listen, Tova flared. "My complaint against Detective Harris still stands, you know." Warning him that she knew her rights.

"I'm very sorry for what you went through."

He made it sound a minor thing, like going through a tunnel, from darkness, to light. By now, he expected she would have put her mother's death behind her and come to terms with all the lies.

"Detective Harris didn't fully investigate my mother's death, in spite of the information I gave him. He twisted the circumstances to fit his theory that she killed herself." Why was she talking about her mother? And to him of all people, a police officer?

"I don't work with Detective Harris any more. I transferred to Henderson midway through your case."

Was that supposed to appease her? She shrugged, *I don't care. You're all the same.* Childish and illogical.

At the Lincoln Road off-ramp, he spoke again. "You'll be treated well, and quickly, Ms Tan."

She stared out the window, filled her mind with reading street and shop signs and the huge side-of-the-road billboards, the mind-junk deflecting any thoughts of her mother or Jasmine or Juliette, or him.

Through the automatic doors, past the staff behind the protective, glassed-in reception area and the two men being attended to, busy with their own problems, no one taking notice of her being ushered up the stairs. Grateful he parked out the front.

He guided her to the main entrance. She pretended she was a willing visitor as he led her into a conference room with a large oval table and several chairs arranged around it. It was nothing like the poky interview rooms she had spent time in before.

"Take a seat, I'll get you a drink."

She had no reason to be nervous, but memories of her last experience were hard to shake, and she took a seat facing the door. He returned holding a polystyrene cup, along with a pen and an official sheet of paper. "Water is preferable to the coffee we have here," he said as he placed the cup down in front of her.

He sat down opposite her and slid the paper and pen across the table. "This is for your contact details, in case we need to get hold of you."

In the designated NAME line, she wrote Tova Tan, the signature still unfamiliar after all these months. She filled in her mobile phone number and her address in Argyle Street. She left 'Alternative Contact' blank. No one, her friend Sarah, or brother Richard, least of all her father, would appreciate being brought to the attention of the police again. Besides, make them dig out last year's form if they needed to know.

A female officer entered and went straight to the chair beside Finn. She sat down, then inspected Tova, assessing if she measured up to expectations.

Another officer in the room felt like two against one.

"Constable Ngaire Wright," she said. Dark-brown hair, with kinks and waves suggesting recent release from a tight ponytail, framed the officer's dark olive-skinned face.

Tova kept her eyes steady on Wright's face, willing a kindred bond, part-Māori together, hoping the officer saw beyond her being Areta Amahua's daughter, the popular actor whose avoidance of discussing her Māori heritage was well known. "I have no connection to anything Māori," Areta had once said.

Under the intensity of Wright's gaze, Tova looked away first. No hint of a connection there. She moved the still-full cup of water to the left and centre. The last thing she wanted was to knock the flimsy paper cup over.

Finn began the questions.

"I don't know if they had other family," she replied to his first query. "There isn't a Mr Dunn, as far as I know. I've never asked. No, I don't know any of their friends. I don't know if they were friendly with the neighbours, either." She sounded like an arrogant, selfish young thing with little interest in anyone else. "I was their tenant," as if that absolved her.

"I'm a sound sleeper," Tova replied to the question if she heard anything from upstairs, omitting to mention the quality earplugs that she returned to the bedside table each morning when she woke, rested and refreshed, even on Wednesdays, Thursdays and Fridays. It didn't seem right to gossip about what Jasmine might have been up to.

"I'm busy with university or work. I don't see Jasmine much. Mrs Dunn works at the rest home a few blocks away, three nights a week. They will be able to help you more than I can."

Constable McIntosh wrote her answers down on a page in his ring binder. She wanted to correct the way he held the pen and had to stop herself from reaching over to reposition his fingers.

"There is this more recent photo." Tova dug out her mobile from her bag and turned it so he saw the screen. "Mrs Dunn, with Jasmine, earlier this year, taken the first weekend I moved in." She'd been snapping close-up photos of leaves and twigs and dandelions in the back garden for creative writing exercises. Mrs Dunn joined her, asked if she had settled in; Jasmine sidled up to them and at one point grabbed the camera. Later, Tova deleted all the girl's selfies but saved the photo Jasmine took of her with Mrs Dunn, spoilt by shadowed faces and their feet cut off. And the one she had taken of mother and daughter, in spite of Jasmine's objections that it was stink. Tova had always meant to get a printed copy for Mrs Dunn.

He and Wright stared at the screen, and Wright whispered behind her hand to him. Tova heard the faint words, "You do it."

"Ms Tan." Constable McIntosh put his palms down on the table, examined the backs of his hands for a pause too long. "I'm sorry." He paused. "But a body was found last night in Te Atatu." Another pause. "We have reason to believe it is that of Jasmine Dunn."

He needed lessons in how to impart such heavy and heady news: eye contact, then straight to the point. Do it fast, like ripping of a Band-Aid.

"Jasmine? Jasmine?" Repeating the name as though she doubted the observational skills of the police, convinced they often misidentified bodies. "A car accident?" People were always dying in car crashes – the modern form of natural selection, her ex-boyfriend said, weeding out the idiots. If that had been scientific fact, he would have joined the ranks long ago, instead of suggesting she let him back into her pants whenever she had the misfortune to run into him.

The officers exchanged glances.

"Are you able to continue?" McIntosh sat forward.

"Sure." Get it over with, get out of there.

"When did you see Jasmine last?" Wright took the lead, polite, conversational tone but a shift had occurred. Finn avoided Tova's gaze.

"Six weeks ago," she answered. Don't give them the satisfaction of adding 'Why?'

"You seem sure."

"I am. It was the Sunday morning I left for Tauranga."

She wasn't likely to forget in a hurry. Jasmine had accosted her, blocked her way as she hurried up the path with her wheelie case on the way to the bus stop. "Okay if I move downstairs into the flat while you're gone, look after it for you?"

"No thank you, Jasmine. Please move or I'll miss the bus." Tova had eased past the girl, ignoring the swearing that followed her up the street.

"Ms Tan," Wright said, bringing Tova's attention back, "did Jasmine and her mother get on?"

"I suppose so. I don't ... didn't ... often see them."

"You're not that much older than Jasmine. Did she ever confide in you about problems with her mother or with school friends, male and female?"

"No." Tova wasn't sure if Wright expected her to agree or disagree with the age comment. Older by six or seven years, but worlds apart from the brash, over-confident Jasmine. She thought about reaching for the cup, taking a sip, decided against it in case her hand shook. Stay calm. It will be over soon enough.

"You didn't keep Jasmine company on the nights her mother worked?" Wright asked the same questions, varied the phrasing.

"Like I said, I didn't socialise with either of them."

"No arguments, disagreements, no matter how trivial? Landlord-tenant issues?"

Tova had no intention of revealing her suspicions of Jasmine's nocturnal activities. They'd twist it somehow, accuse her of aiding and abetting Jasmine. Or blame her for not taking on the role of responsible adult in Juliette's absence.

Both officers watched her. It was last year repeated. Questions that seemed logical, interspersed with meaningful gazes between them, long pauses. Why question her if Jasmine had died of natural causes? What was the statistic Detective Harris had spat in her face last year? More than ninety per cent of murders were committed by someone known to the victim. To the police, she was that *someone*. They'd made up their minds, especially the female. She had history, Jasmine was dead. The two must be linked. Like last year, Harris too quick to join the dots between an argument and her mother's death. No apology when her alibi stood firm.

Tova couldn't picture her landlady harming her daughter, no matter how provoked. She'd never heard a raised voice against the girl, but who knew what happened behind closed doors? Tova was well aware that people were capable of all sorts of extraordinary behaviour.

Not suicide, not an accident, unlikely to be natural causes. What did that leave? They hadn't said murder, they didn't have to. There was the bleach smell in the house. The police had said the body was found at Te Atatu. What was she doing there?

"Her mother. Does she know?" A surge of sadness engulfed her. Whatever Jasmine's faults, her mother loved her. Tova shivered as though an ice-laden draught had breezed in under the door and swirled around her.

"We've yet to locate her." His words kind, no hint of suspicion. Good cop, but still one of them.

Tova had experienced worse cops but the fixed stare pointed to Wright's knowledge of her history: emotional, volatile, prone to outbursts, cop attacker. Did she think there's a pattern here? How many people were involved in two suspicious deaths within a year?

Tova kept her eyes straight ahead and thought of the long, aimless walk she'd taken through Tauranga's streets the previous Sunday and the promise she had made herself. Don't let the past define you. Look to the future. How hopeful she had felt then.

Constable McIntosh cleared his throat. "Thank you for your help, Ms Tan. We have to ask these questions. I'm sorry it has taken longer than expected. It isn't easy, I know."

Tova registered the sideways glance Wright gave him. It wasn't meant to be easy, the look said. Maybe Wright treated all witnesses like this. But it felt personal.

"There's one more thing you can help us with," Wright said. "We need a positive identification. In the absence of her mother or any other known relative at this stage, would you be willing to identify the body? It will help us proceed with the investigation."

Another black mark if she refused? They would check her reaction, compare it to the norm and if necessary, throw it back at her.

Seventy minutes later, Wright turned into the hospital grounds off Grafton Road, a large sign with a white arrow and lettering on a black background indicating the direction to Te Arai Kapua, Auckland's mortuary.

The officer waiting at the entrance, introduced by Wright as 'the officer in charge of the body', no name given, acknowledged Tova with a nod and led the way into the glass-fronted building with its discreet 'Lab Plus' sign. A softly spoken staff member greeted them and led them through locked, coded doors, security cameras above them.

"Seems odd, doesn't it, to have this level of security in a morgue?"

No one answered, and the woman ushered them into a fluorescent-lit room. "Do you want the procedure explained?"

"We've been here before." Wright indicated her fellow officer. She turned to Tova. "I suppose you have, too. Last year, to identify ..."

"What?" the woman said, looking at Wright to Tova and back again.

"No." Tova eased the confusion with a quick thin smile at the woman but offered no explanation.

"There's no easy way to do this, so, if you're ready ..." The woman wheeled in a stainless-steel trolley through a far door. Jasmine's body, sheet-covered, her head visible. Her usually spike-gelled, hairdo was flat, listless, her face a dull, wax-like sheen.

Tova asked Constable Wright to drop her off on K Road, at the top of Queen Street.

"OK." Wright's shrug suggested it made no difference to her, and she pulled over into a five-minute loading zone.

Halfway out of the car, she turned to Wright. "I have never been to the morgue. My father's lawyer identified my mother. He said it wouldn't help me to see her like that." *Like that.* Areta had been in the water at Half Moon Bay, close to Malcolm Tan's suburb, for several hours, her stomach full of sleeping tablets, whisky and bay water in her lungs, according to the autopsy. Verdict, suicide, after a major argument with him. "Ironic, as the police used that against me, said I was hysterical and threw around accusations because I hadn't had closure."

Wright's raised eyebrows didn't stop Tova, even though she was probably living up to Wright's preconceptions – like mother, like daughter, emotional, unpredictable.

"I'm used to the police not believing me, so why should you be any different?" Hours spent failing to convince Detective Harris that Areta wasn't the type to demean herself and stalk Malcolm. Her mother didn't drink alcohol, there were no sleeping pills in the house, so where was the proof she'd bought any?

"I believe people who tell the truth, the whole truth."

Clutching her shoulder bag and pulling the backpack after her, she shut the door, not giving in to the temptation to slam it. The Walk sign flashed. She hurried over the pedestrian crossing and glanced back. The police car was still in the loading bay, Constable Wright watching her.

Tova walked as far as a bench seat on Queen Street with Myers Park as a backdrop. She wedged the pack between her legs and contemplated where to spend the night: her friend Sarah's couch, and they could stay up late, putting the world to rights with a bottle of Chardonnay. Or her brother's. He would object but he'd let her in. She didn't consider phoning her father.

Tomorrow. One night to herself, work out what to do next. She checked how much cash she had. Thirty-three dollars; too little for a night's accommodation and something to eat. She'd have to set aside her self-imposed financial restrictions, cut into her next fortnight's expenses. That didn't mean she could be extravagant. Taking out her phone, she googled budget city accommodation.

11. FINN

"No good time for murder, is there, McIntosh?" Pavletich didn't break stride, paced twelve steps to the right, twelve to the left, hands clasped behind his back as he waited for the team to arrive.

Finn took the question as rhetorical. He braced himself against the wall of the Crime Room, easing his leg muscles, overworked for the first time in weeks by the swimming and walking and standing he'd done in the last twenty-four hours. He'd turned up for work, ready for a usual shift of 'go here, go there, complete that report', only to find his name on Pavletich's list. He double-checked it wasn't a forgery; he really was on the team.

"So much for shovelling clay and getting the retaining wall finished this weekend, keep the wife happy. Instead, we'll be knee-deep in all sorts of human crap and misery sorting this out. It's too much to hope someone confesses before the media stirs up the usual police ineptitude stuff. With any luck, they will get sidetracked with Ms Tan."

Inspector Dal Smith entered the room. Experienced, a career cop, one of the handful still in the job over fifty. Dalrymple Smith, a little pompous, like his name.

"Sit down, Goran, and keep still. You'll give me motion sickness or yourself a heart attack." Smith let out a belly laugh, but he was the one to sit. "Your body on the beach. Murder, is it? And I hear the Tan woman is involved. Have you told Harris yet?"

Pavletich kept up the pacing. "Murder it is. She didn't stab herself in the back and drive to Te Atatu to die." No sarcasm, more thinking aloud. "And no, I haven't told Harris yet." *And nor do I intend to until I have to*, evident in his tone.

Smith seemed to notice Finn for the first time. "Ah, you'll be McIntosh?"

"Yes, sir." Finn straightened up. Another boss who knew who he was.

"The move from Counties Manukau working out?"

"Yes, sir." Finn wanted to take Smith's words at face value and not read into what he might or might not know. He was well known for turning up at briefings then disappearing. One wit had likened him to a regal visitor, venturing out for occasional appearances, smiling and waving from doorways. Some admired his leadership, allowing his detectives to get on with it. Others said he was past it, good only for shuffling paper around. Finn wondered when he had last seen the front line but he seemed to know what went on around him.

"Different styles, Hammond more traditional, Goran more lateral. I suppose you've worked that out for yourself." Smith held his gaze.

"Sir." Acknowledging he was being spoken to, giving Smith nothing.

Unsworth appeared at the doorway, glanced Finn's way and winked, then presented a solemn expression to the room. Too full of himself, Finn thought, recalling the whispered comments in his ear a few weeks earlier when Unsworth was selected over Finn to work on a spate of gang-related burglaries. "Chosen for my good looks, obviously. Or my brains – law degree trumps teacher training any day, mate." A degree he often complained about, saddling him with a crippling student loan.

Isaiah Cranston, close behind his colleague, eased into the room, nudged the door shut with his foot and stood to attention. Finn wouldn't have been surprised if he'd saluted. He imitated Pavletich – hands linked behind his back. Instead of making Cranston look serious and professional, it pushed his torso forward and emphasised his stoop.

A loud knock, the door opening at the same time, and Ngaire Wright entered, smiling apologetically. "Auckland traffic," she said, an excuse no one questioned. She circled the room, decided on the vacant chair next to Smith and sat down, giving her superior a wide smile. At first Finn thought her sick day the day before, spent at a specialist's to find out why she wasn't falling pregnant, had yielded good news. But the smile stayed fixed a moment too long.

"Right, you lot are my Suspects Team." Pavletich shut the door, trapping in the wheezing and clanking of the old wall-mounted air-conditioning unit that didn't produce the desired respite from too much body heat in too small a room. "The inspector informs me that staff are spread thin with too many current cases. You lot are all I can call on for now, so we hope for a quick result. Find Mrs Dunn and we may well have our answer. She and her daughter argued, things turned to shit. I have teenagers, I understand how they can wind you up."

Finn found it hard to imagine anyone getting to Pavletich. He ran a finger under his uniform collar to loosen it, grateful he hadn't told Ngaire before the briefing that he reckoned they'd be told culprit caught, case closed. Finn put his money on the mother, flushed out of her hiding place. Or maybe a jealous boyfriend about to be charged, no doubt screaming, 'The bitch asked for it!' as his defence. A tidy-up of the paperwork and then back to normal duties, bringing an end to his too-short foray into homicide.

And gone was the plan to shrink the pile of long-overdue reports by the end of his shift, after which he'd go home, conscience clear, and get onto the truckload of washing piled up in the corner of his room. If he had energy and inclination left over, he'd hit the gym.

"You all know Inspector Smith." Pavletich didn't wait for the mumbled acknowledgements to die down. "He's giving us the benefit of his experience."

Finn kept his eyes forward, unsure if Pavletich was being sarcastic or implying that Smith had what the team lacked.

"Operation Firecloud. The facts so far. According to the preliminary forensics, the deceased, Jasmine Dunn, was killed from behind. Under the abrasions caused by the rocks, they found a single, deep, downwards-angled stab wound from a long-bladed knife that entered between her shoulder blades and pierced her heart. The murder weapon is yet to be found. No evidence of being killed at the scene. No water in her lungs, dead before she hit the water. It's doubtful she floated to Te Atatu so looks like she was dumped there. Maybe the killer or killers hoped she'd float away. She was found at around six pm yesterday. Judging by the condition of the body, she died sometime Thursday night, early Friday morning. She lived at home with her yet-to-be-located mother. Jasmine was sixteen years of age and sexually active; she'd had an abortion recently. Any signs of recent sex has long been washed away. There was no indication of rape, no bruising or trauma to the genitals. She had one identifying mark, a tattoo, 'Just Do It', starting from her navel to her inner left thigh. We have yet to speak to Mrs Dunn so the body has been identified, a facial visual, by the tenant living in the flat below, Ms Tova Tan."

Pavletich made eye contact with officers around the room, pausing at Finn, holding his gaze for a second longer than necessary. "Two teenage boys saw the body first but they didn't report it. A Mr Weston did."

Finn willed himself to sit still and not show any discomfort.

"That's a summary of what we know so far; you'll get copies of the full report. As we learn more, check those facts over and over. Keep the details in your heads. It makes the difference between a quick resolution and a complete botch-up."

"Are the boys suspects?" Ngaire asked.

"One's a Hemona." Pavletich quietened the murmurs. "So he's of interest, given his family background, but forensics said she wasn't murdered at the beach. There are indications that Jasmine may have been killed at her home in Herne Bay. Initial tests show few fingerprints. That's suspicious in itself. Ms Tova Tan reported her landlady missing several hours after she first noticed the Dunn house was open to the elements. Didn't check with neighbours either."

"That wouldn't be the Ms Tan related to Areta Amahua, she of 'the wacky actress, the married lover and the crazy daughter' fame?" Unsworth slid a glance Finn's way. Trust Unsworth to be up with the gossip.

"The rumour mill is obviously running hot," Pavletich said. "Ms Tan is the daughter, but get your facts straight before you make another comment like that. Chat to McIntosh, he has first-hand knowledge, worked on the case before transferring here."

No avoiding talking about it now. Thanks, boss.

"Ms Tan is to be treated by the book," Pavletich warned. "The last thing we want is a repeat of the media circus that hit the Howick branch last year."

"Once the media find out Ms Tan is involved, they'll not pass up the opportunity to rehash the whole Amahua mess again," Ngaire said. "Don't they realise the damage they cause? No matter what euphemisms they use, everyone accepts she killed herself. And again, they'll rake over Areta's animosity towards her whānau and the whole tangi debacle. It will undo years of positive work we do with disaffected Māori youth." Ngaire wasn't inclined to outbursts, but it was obvious from her flushed face that her feelings ran strong, and went some way to explain her barely concealed animosity towards Tova in the interview.

"Focus on *this* enquiry," Pavletich ordered. "If the mother didn't do it, she might know who had motive." He moved around the room as he talked, halting by the inspector. "Is there anything you'd like to add, inspector?"

Smith blinked, cleared his throat as though he'd taken forty winks, but he had been listening. "I'll see who else we can rope in to help if you don't surprise us all with a quick arrest." He laughed as he stood, creating a minor breeze that lifted a few strands of his comb-over. "And Goran, talk to Harris, learn from his problems in Howick."

"I don't recall the Dunns being mentioned last year, so I can't see that Ms Tan living in their house can have any bearing on the Amahua case."

"Hmm, you might be right," Smith muttered. "According to Harris, Ms Tan is trouble. Take her witness statement then leave her alone. Keep her role in this confidential for as long as you can. You'll need to sort this fast." Smith moved his arm, somewhere between a salute and brushing a pesky mosquito away, as he left.

Pavletich roamed the room. Finn avoided looking at anyone.

"Sir." Wright broke the silence. "I'm sure you're way ahead of me, but Jasmine was killed in the bath, right?"

"It looks that way."

"That explains her nakedness. It's pretty difficult to put clothes on a wet body. And a downwards angle suggests the killer came from behind. If Jasmine was in the bath, someone slight in build could have done it?"

Finn didn't like Ngaire's line of thought.

"It is possible." Pavletich stopped his pacing. "You're thinking of Ms Tan. Why?"

"She lives there. Opportunity. She killed the girl, cleaned up, then spent time working out a plausible story." Ngaire held up her hand in a 'stop' gesture as she detected movement from Finn. "Her cooperation when interviewed was at best passive, gave nothing away. Her past behaviour. She didn't act at the morgue as I expected. No tears, and she was stroppy afterwards, didn't want me to know where she was staying for the night. I found her ..."

Beautiful, Finn added in his head.

"Too self-controlled, evasive. She puts up a façade," Ngaire said.

"What's the motive?" People in the room turned to Finn again. Sweat ran down from his collar, down his spine, under his arms. He didn't realise he'd said it out loud.

"Underneath that serene exterior, she's an emotional mess, and Jasmine pushed the wrong button. She reminds me of a ninja warrior woman, creeping around in the dark and assassinating whole towns of bad people. Beautiful to look at, dangerous to know." Wright bowed, acknowledged the laughter.

"It's too early to speculate." Pavletich divvied up tasks. "Wright, get onto the tech guys to build up Jasmine's profile, Facebook, Twitter, Instagram accounts, emails in and out, text messages, phone calls. I want to know everything about Jasmine, especially who got her pregnant. And in spite of what Smith says, Ms Tan requires further investigation. She has a history of lashing out. Maybe Wright is onto something. Find out if Jasmine upset her. McIntosh, double-check her alibi, make sure she was out of town until Friday night."

"I could do that. Better to have someone unconnected to Howick," Unsworth said. "Don't want to give Ms Tan another reason to claim police harassment." He winked at Finn. *I'm doing you a favour, keeping you away from the crazy lady.*

"It doesn't call for her to be interviewed again at this stage, but do a thorough check that she was where she said she was." Pavletich came to a stop behind Unsworth's chair. "Fair point, though."

Finn looked away.

"Wright, get onto that." The walkabout started up again. "Unsworth, with your charm, you're on door-to-door. You might get lucky with home-security cameras in the area. Cranston, get hold of the rest home, talk to Mrs Dunn's colleagues, friends. Someone must have some idea where she might go. McIntosh, you think Jacob Hemona knows more than he is letting on? Probably trying to steer you away from his father. Hemi Hemona has a long history of domestic violence, car conversion, a bit of thieving, receiving stolen goods. Nothing that suggests he's a killer. Talk to the boy again. Seeing a body might be enough for him to wish his father would go straight, and he'll dob him in. If we clear a few burglaries at the same time that will be a plus."

Like a well-timed cue, the three knocks on the door came as Pavletich paused for breath. One of the office staff poked her head round, passed him a piece of paper.

"It appears Ms Tan gave us incorrect information," Pavletich said as he read the contents, then waved the slip of paper like a fan. "Mrs Dunn doesn't work at the rest home and never has." His frown lines deepened. "What does that mean?"

The question hung in the air. *A number of things. Or nothing.* Finn's chest tightened.

"Looks like Ms Tan does need pressure put on her," Pavletich said.

Finn wanted to wipe the smirk off Unsworth's face.

"McIntosh, you know her background, use it. Find out why she lied."

The knock on the door was more forceful than the first. The office woman came right into the room and passed a mobile phone to Pavletich. He put it to his ear.

"Pavletich ... When? ... Where? ... Who's there now?"

Pavletich checked his watch. "It will take me thirty, forty minutes to get there."

He lowered the mobile. "Juliette Dunn has been found."

The details were sketchy. Mates, heading off to O'neill Bay for a spot of fishing had their day spoilt. They came across Juliette with her head bashed in, strangled with her own tights and half-buried in the sand. But for them, her body might have remained undisturbed in the dunes for days, if not weeks or months.

No one spoke for several minutes after Pavletich hurried out.

"There goes the murder-suicide theory," Cranston said.

"Now, surely, we can rule out Ms Tan," Finn said.

Wright wagged her finger at him. "Not so fast, Finny."

12. TOVA

Tova scrutinised the international backpackers across the street from the conveniently placed park bench. Third listing in her Google search, its closeness to city attractions its claim to fame. She spent half an hour watching people entering and leaving the main entrance, making sure she didn't book a room in Auckland's sleaziest dive.

The last thing she wanted was chit-chat with chirpy international travellers in a dormitory. She asked for the cheapest single room at the same time the attendant's mobile rang. He gestured for Tova to wait. She couldn't help but listen in while he arranged his evening, starting at the Occidental in Vulcan Lane and which hook-up bars to move on to. Tova turned to leave, still plenty of time before nightfall and several more backpackers to choose from.

"Sorry," the attendant said, sounding anything but as he pocketed the phone.

Tova was tempted to say the Occidental was a bit out

of his league. She decided against it, didn't want him to think she was angling for an invite to join him.

Fifty-nine dollars on her debit card later, he placed the room key on the counter and pointed in the direction of the lift. The narrow room, crowded by the double bed, required sliding-door access to the ensuite. Her Argyle Street flat positively palatial in comparison. The view from the single window was of the building opposite or, if she looked down to street level, of a rubbish-bin-lined alley. She kept her shoes on to avoid walking in whatever created the brown-edged patches layering the fading maroon carpet. It was for a night, or two. She would cope.

The room lacked the one thing she wanted – tools to make a cup of tea. No stale sachets of instant tea, powdered milk and sugar, and no jug. In fact, no microwave, no fridge, no sink. Tova guessed at a considerable mark-up on the food in the café downstairs to offset the budget room prices.

She locked the door behind her, took the stairs to the foyer then walked the length of Queen Street.

The weak afternoon sun had long given way to grey skies and a drop in temperature. She quickly tired of looking in windows at clothes and shoes and bags she had no intention of buying. Somehow it didn't seem right to be thinking about retail therapy. Her aimlessness wasn't helping her to decide the next move. Ring Sarah for consolation? Start flat-hunting? Both, but not yet.

She zipped up the dark-blue fleece jacket she was seldom without, given the changeable nature of Auckland's September weather. She didn't want to return to the hotel room so waited in line to buy a grilled chicken wrap, the healthiest option she could find at the

McDonald's at the bottom of Queen Street. She headed towards the Ferry Building and found an unoccupied bench on the waterfront. Ignoring the view across to the North Shore, Tova started on the takeaway. A late lunch or early dinner? Either way, she hadn't eaten much all day, and she was ravenous.

Ferries came and went, people got on and off, but her mind dwelt on her mother's quick and easy laugh. She and her mother had often strolled from their apartment near Albert Park, along to the Viaduct area. They would outdo each other with outrageous imaginings of the lives of passers-by. Areta entertained with tales of the foibles of her current leading men or women, laugh at fluffed lines and behind-the-scenes carry-ons.

Tova hunched into her jacket, thought of the last time Areta had nuzzled into her neck and hugged her tight, refusing to heed the 'Oh, Mum.' She smiled at the memory, grateful that Areta's features remained clear in her mind. Arohanui. E kore e miti te aroha mōu. The Māori saying she'd learned since Areta's death came to mind. Goodbye, my love for you will never wane.

Then she remembered the lies.

"Ms Tova Tan?"

Her mouth full of chicken and salad, all she could do was nod. Standing either side of her were two police officers. It had to be about Jasmine.

"Won't keep you long, Ms Tan." One folded his arms and tucked his hands under his armpits as though seeking warmth; the other stepped a few metres away and spoke into the walkie-talkie attached by a cord that disappeared under his thick vest.

His conversation over, Phone Call officer nodded to his colleague, who spoke. "Detective Sergeant Pavletich wants to ask a few more questions. He said you'd know what it was about. Someone will pick you up from Central. We'll drive you there."

Last year she was more trusting. A lot had happened since. She asked the officer's names, typed them into Notes on her phone. One of her mother's many warnings, 'Never get into a stranger's car', flashed into her mind. Should she text Sarah, tell her what was happening? Don't be paranoid, her next thought.

Folded Arms invited her to get into the patrol car with the enticing, "It's warmer in than out."

She accepted, but not to avoid the dropping temperature. The trio drew attention: pedestrians slowed their sauntering and gawked, drivers took their eyes off the road and passengers rubbernecked out their windows, dreaming up stories why two officers were speaking to her.

Silence on the drive through the city to the station near Victoria Park, Phone Call Officer in charge of the vehicle. A patient driver, he kept a safe distance from the car in front and signalled all turns well in advance. The glass-and-metal building with its imposing royal-blue sign came into her view as they passed Victoria Park, through the lights by the supermarket, then a right turn, another and he squeezed into a vacant space in the Police Vehicles Only area outside the building.

Escorted by Folded Arms Officer, Tova walked slowly through the landscaped approach, taking in the wooden benches, manicured raised garden beds and the New Zealand flag flapping on its pole. All designed to welcome. She wanted to turn and run.

After thirty minutes of waiting in the reception area, Folded Arms giving no indication he could be engaged in small talk, not that Tova made any attempt to do so, an officer – young, tall, slightly stooped – appeared out of a side door.

"Here he is," Folded Arms said. "Constable Cranston will look after you now, Ms Tan. Thank you." The politeness not so much in recognition of anything she had done, more bringing to an end his responsibility.

Cranston indicated the way, walked a pace behind her, apparently unable to trust her to follow, back out the automatic doors, back the way she had come. He clicked a remote in his hands, and the sidelights of a squad vehicle ahead flashed. He held open the rear door, didn't put his hand between her head and the vehicle as she got in. She was helping with enquiries. Not a criminal, yet.

Constables McIntosh and Wright greeted her in the Henderson Police Station foyer. They stood in front of the glassed-in public counter; cut their conversation with the woman behind a computer as she was shepherded in. McIntosh smiled, put his hand out.

Tova held back. He wasn't her friend. "Did you have me followed?" Too brusque, a defence. She wished she had declined to accompany the first two officers or refused to be driven back to Henderson. What else could she tell them? What did they *want* her to say?

"We circulated your description," Wright said.

Tova's eyebrows rose a fraction. They found her from that? Light olive-skinned Asian-featured female, early twenties, slight build, one fifty-six or -seven centimetres, shoulder-length dark straight hair, last seen wearing skinny blue jeans, a cream shirt and a navy polar fleece –

a description of hundreds of females in the central city at any given moment.

"You were so quiet, we were worried you might go into shock, and you hadn't let anyone know where you were staying." Wright's words projected concern but her steady gaze conveyed no sympathy.

Tova wondered if she wasn't weepy enough for Wright, her dry eyes a sign of a callous, cold heart. Guilty by lack of emotion.

"We have new information and need to clarify a few of your answers. We normally follow up anyway," McIntosh said, avoiding her glance.

Did he think the same as his colleague? They'd be trained to say the right thing while thinking the worst. His kindness wasn't personal. It was his job.

"So where's the detective who wants to speak to me?" Her tone was short. She wanted it done with, and if Wright added rudeness to the list of her shortcomings, so be it.

Was it deliberate, sandwiching her between Wright, who led the way up the stairs, and McIntosh, a few steps behind?

They passed the conference room she had been in earlier and guided her into a smaller interview room.

Wright introduced Detective Goran Pavletich, already seated, facing the door. Wright took the chair beside her superior and directed Tova to the chair opposite. McIntosh stood at attention, blocking the only exit.

"Thank you for agreeing to help us with our enquiries into Jasmine Dunn's death," Wright said, sounding as if she read the words from a script.

Tova's gut twinged. It was natural to be apprehensive. Of course the police wanted to talk to her. She lived in the downstairs flat, she knew Jasmine. Whatever Jasmine was or did, she didn't deserve to be killed for it. *I'm helping*. Where were the people helping her last year? Tova sat back, breathed in, ready.

"You have a part-time job with a modelling agency called Star Power. Correct?" Wright asked.

"What does that have to do with Jasmine?" Tova kept calm, thankful her complexion camouflaged flushed cheeks. People made assumptions about the type of modelling she did. The chain-store catalogue work was legitimate, and it offered weekend and night assignments that fitted with her studies and teaching practice. Showcasing lingerie paid well, she never needed to seek her father's financial assistance.

"You didn't fill in the next of kin on the contact details form." Wright's glance drifted over Tova's face, down to chest level and back up, to lock eyes. She made ticks on the page in front of her, firm, strong movements that suggested disapproval.

"I didn't think it necessary."

Wright's glance at Pavletich was enough for Tova. Cops were all the same, jumping to conclusions. Her father had warned her at one of their lunches: 'Everyone thinks wealthy Chinese control the drug gangs. I am wealthy. Given the chance, the police will use you and Richard to get to me. Do nothing ever again to bring attention to the family.'

'Is there reason to suspect you?' Tova had asked, irritated he lumped her in with her half-brother, annoyed at his hypocrisy and incensed at herself for not ignoring his summons to lunch.

Malcolm Tan had glared at her. She read his stony expression: *How dare you question me?* 'They don't need a reason, they are naturally suspicious. Be assured, all my businesses are legitimate.'

The police wasted their time. She knew little about her father's work.

"Did your father visit you at the flat?" Wright asked.

"What?" She hadn't expected that question. She added a firm, "No," remembering the advice her father's lawyer drilled into her last year: 'Keep answers brief. Don't elaborate. Speak with conviction.'

"Did he visit Mrs Dunn?"

"No." Why did they think he might?

"You own a car." It was a statement. They knew she did.

"Yes." The questions headed off on tangents. Why?

"Where is it?"

"In Howick. At my father's home."

"When did you last drive it?"

"I've never driven it." One of a long line of useless, expensive gifts to buy her affection. No one could ever accuse her of being a spoilt daddy's girl, living off her father.

"Did you travel back from Tauranga alone? Did you know anyone on the bus? Did anyone see you come home, go into the Dunn house?"

There were lengthy pauses after her monosyllabic "Yes," "No," "I don't think so," answers.

"You were concerned about your neighbours but you didn't investigate straight away, and you waited until the next morning to ring the police?"

"That's right." She didn't explain further. One thing she had learned, too much detail provided more to twist and distort.

She imagined they deliberately kept the room stuffy, quick confession-inducing. She craved a cup of tea to ease her dry throat. She didn't ask for one, and they didn't offer.

Her unease grew exponentially with each question. Her actions had seemed reasoned, and reasonable at the time. The longer the pauses, the more glances that darted between Pavletich and Wright, the more Tova wished she hadn't agreed to the interview. She wished Sarah was with her. That couldn't be misconstrued, a friend by her side. If she had rung her father, he'd bring his lawyer, and the police would have questioned why the need for one.

Pavletich asked for the third time if she had spoken with her father since her return to Auckland.

"I've told you I haven't. Besides, what has he to do with any of this?" She made no attempt to hide her exasperation.

The officers took fifteen-minute breaks but they never left her alone. Pavletich read through the papers in front of him and received two phone calls. After he gave his name, all she heard was "Hmm," and "Okay."

In turn, each officer joined Pavletich in the corridor, their murmurings too low to distinguish words. The faint aroma from the takeaway in her bag reminded her how little she had eaten all day. McIntosh brought her a glass of water. She was tempted to swat it away, the thoughtfulness not enough to compensate for the grilling she had endured.

Then a bathroom break. Wright walked with her along the corridor. Out of politeness in the unfamiliar surroundings? The constable swiped a card to allow entry.

On her return to the interview room, they took up the same positions.

"Ms Tan, Jasmine Dunn and her mother Juliette Dunn have been murdered." Pavletich rested his elbows on the table, hands clasped as if about to deliver a prayer for the dead.

"Both of them?" In her lap, her fingernails dug into her palm.

He watched her, reading her stillness, waiting for the tears. If only she had inherited her mother's effusive manner, instead of her father's reticence. Except for that one-time anomaly, she was the stereotypical, undemonstrative Chinese. Her friend Sarah made a big thing of it, giving Tova smoochy, sloppy kisses at every opportunity. "Break down your reserve, people think you are frigid and stand-offish."

Wright scraped her chair back. Tova's shoulders tensed. She didn't want the constable to leap up, sit beside her in fake commiseration. Wright stretched her legs, stayed watchful.

Tova eased her fingers, stiff from clenching and rolled her eyes to the ceiling, a trick she'd learned to hold tears at bay.

"Why were you in Te Atatu last Thursday night?" Straight into it, no asking if she needed a few moments.

"Me?" *Who killed who* was slithering around her mind and she had to push it aside and focus on Pavletich's question. He didn't give her time to remind him she was in Tauranga that night.

"A late-night delivery driver rang the Roadwatch line, reported your BMW being driven erratically on Te Atatu Road."

"There must be a mistake."

"You'll want to hope so." He scratched his cheek. "Another inconsistency in your statement. The story about Mrs Dunn working at a rest home. Is that the cover you came up with to tell your friends?"

"Story?"

"You must have known we'd find out her line of business. Why lie?"

Tova bit her lip, copied Pavletich's tactic and let the pause lengthen. She wasn't going to echo him again.

"Were you one of Juliette's girls? I can't imagine your father too pleased about that. Maybe this was his way to deal with the problem."

"I don't understand." Her scalp itched, the skin taut.

"You claim you didn't socialise with Jasmine," he said.

"I didn't."

"Yet her fingerprints have been found in your flat."

She needed fresh air.

"I'll go now," Tova said, a direct, simple statement discounting other options she'd thought of: You can't keep me here. Stop asking about my father, I'm not like him. Am I under arrest? I'm a witness. Why are you mean to me? I want my mum.

"It's been a shock, I expect," Pavletich said. "We can resume the interview Monday, at 11 am. You might like to bring a support person."

Unsteady on jelly-like legs and clutching her shoulder bag close, she walked out, head high.

13. FINN

Finn stretched and yawned, took a furtive glance at his watch and caught Pavletich lifting a pizza slice to his mouth. The triangle tipped and a chunk of pineapple slid off, dragging a fine strand of melted cheese with it. The day had started early, it was heading for a very late finish, and there had been the stress-inducing interview with Tova a few hours earlier. He wondered where she was, how she was.

Pizza boxes, paper and iPads littered the table, and the heady aroma of pizza supreme overlaid the too-long-in-the-same-clothes body odour emanating from the five of them.

"Good work, team, we have a development." Pavletich's pause got their attention. "Juliette Dunn has been telling porkies. Cranston's been digging into her background."

Heads turned to Isaiah. He cleared his throat. "Juliette Dunn doesn't work at that rest home and never has."

Tova said ...

"On our door knocks, two of the neighbours were adamant Dunn mentioned she worked there."

Finn resisted leaping up and shouting, 'See, Tova was telling the truth.'

"Dunn lied to *everyone*," Cranston emphasised the last word. "The boss thought her house was too flash for someone on a rest home worker's wage. He got me checking to see if she rented it. The property search showed that a Ms J Evans-Roger owns it." Pause. *What, there's more?*

At Cranston's pace, midnight would come and go.

"Evans-Roger is Juliette's maiden name. She owns a number of inner-city properties, Freeman's Bay, Newton, one in Grey Lynn. Massage clinics."

Unsworth's slap on the desk made Finn jump. "There's your motive. A neighbour did them in. Had enough of Dunn lowering the tone of their suburb."

"Be serious," Wright said. "Juliette's death was brutal." Her expression was sombre. "So, which Dunn was the main target?"

"Juliette, I'd say," Pavletich said. "She's older, has more years on her to earn a reason to be killed, probably has links to the fringe elements. Doesn't explain Jasmine, though."

"What about a sex angle?" Wright asked. "Between Michael Tan and Juliette? There's a connection there, I'm sure. A lover's quarrel gone too far? Or jealousy? Maybe Ms Tan tried to recruit Jasmine into lingerie modelling and ..." Frown lines appeared across her forehead, the pieces not fitting.

"All theories worth looking into." Pavletich licked his fingers and picked up more pizza, the topic of conversation not putting him off his food. "There's no evidence Jasmine was raped. That's not usual. Of the few female teenagers murdered each year, most have been."

Wright was quick. "More reason to think Ms Tan was involved. She could have done it. We know there are unexplained hours in her alibi."

Finn didn't need reminding. He'd read the Tauranga police email. They'd spoken with the owner of the small bed and breakfast Tova had stayed in. The reporting officer had been diligent. He'd quoted the B&B owner. 'Ms Tan was quiet, she didn't engage in chit-chat, not like the usual trainees I have.' She hadn't seen Tova from about 7.30 on Thursday night until 6.45 the next morning at breakfast. Over ten hours with no sightings of her.

Like most people who don't share a bed, me included, Finn thought.

Guilty of being an introvert? Finn understood how investigations progressed. Early stages, cast-the-net wide discussions, no theory discounted. Pay close attention to the way those caught up in the enquiry behaved. Never take anything or anyone at face value. Always ask why. Add impressions and intuition to the mix of facts, interpret them, run with scenarios until the hard facts point them in another direction. Process of elimination.

Ngaire kept on. "This is how it could have happened. Tan drives up from Tauranga, kills Jasmine, then Juliette, dumps the bodies, one at Te Atatu, one at O'neill's, then drives back to Tauranga."

"We'll have a better idea if that theory is feasible once Tauranga get back to us again," Pavletich said. "They're following up whether she had access to a car in Tauranga, hired or borrowed, and they'll check with the bus company that she was on the bus the whole way. I should have their findings by Monday at the latest."

"If Ms Tan killed them, she'd have needed help," Finn said, getting it out before one of the others ran with Wright's premise. "Juliette Dunn was at least twice Ms Tan's weight and several centimetres taller. I can't see her overpowering the woman." He didn't mention Jasmine. Ngaire had already suggested Tova was capable of that killing.

"There's the druggie brother, or the father. It's all on Ms Tan's file." Pavletich wiped his hands, removing traces of cheese. "Let's hear about the argument first. Unsworth."

Unsworth peered at the iPad in front of him. "One neighbour, a woman across the road, mentioned it. She recalled hearing lots of swearing several weeks ago between the daughter and the Asian girl who lived in the downstairs flat. It stuck in her mind because she seldom saw anyone from the house. She often heard loud music during the week, and she intended to speak to Mrs Dunn about it or ring Noise Control ..."

"Who started the argument?" Finn asked.

"Hard to tell, the neighbour said."

"Let's say Tan did," Wright butted in. "She was annoyed, stewed over it for weeks, snuck back, killed Jasmine. The mother heard it or saw it happening, so she had to go, too. We know Tan has a temper."

Finn sighed.

"The neighbour did say *they* were arguing. I haven't had time to check if any other neighbours heard," Unsworth admitted. "The neighbour also mentioned the vehicles and you told me to check that out."

"I'll follow up, sir." Finn inwardly cringed; he sounded like a schoolkid eager to please.

"OK, McIntosh," Pavletich said. "Ms Tan didn't lie about the rest home, but she didn't tell us Jasmine had been in her flat, and she hasn't told us about the argument."

Finn saw Wright take the micky, miming the classic thinking pose of frown combined with thumb and index finder on her chin.

"Now, back to the big news of the day. Unsworth, the vehicle." Pavletich directed their attention to their colleague.

Unsworth read from his notes. "A black SUV has been parked in the street at odd times in the last several weeks, according to one neighbour. He was vague on exact dates, but he remembered part of the registration. Good Neighbourhood Watch, useful for us."

Not *neighbourly*, though. High fences, alarms, sensor lights kept baddies out. They also made obsolete the chats over the back fence that went a long way to help neighbours keep an eye out for each other.

"Transport ran a check on cars of that make and colour with those letters in the number plate." Unsworth made the most of his spotlight moment. "Did you know black is the most preferred colour for SUVs?"

"Get to the point," Pavletich said.

"I checked Auckland addresses first. Fifty-six matches. One of those cars is registered to Mr Malcolm Tan."

Wright let out a loud, knowing, "Aha!"

"Visiting his daughter." The retort came out before Finn remembered what Tova had said.

"Spying on her. There's a motive," Wright chipped in. "Her father found out what she was up to and put a stop to it. She'd dishonoured the family. Isn't that big with Chinese?"

"In which case," Cranston said, "Tova Tan would have been the one killed. Besides, honour killings are more common in Indian cultures, not Chinese."

Cranston, not a complete bootlicker.

"No father wants his daughter, estranged or not, earning her living that way," Wright said.

"There's no evidence that Ms Tan is," Finn countered, speaking directly to Pavletich. "No Amahua or Tan on Mrs Dunn's books."

"Don't be so naïve, McIntosh. The girls don't use their real name. Look at the car she owns. She didn't buy the latest BMW on what she earns."

"Good." Pavletich was on the move, walking around behind them.

"In Juliette's line of work, a number of people might have grudges against her. Jasmine saw or overheard something, maybe." Finn reached for the last slice of pizza in front of him, fingers touching cooled, brittle dough. He examined the congealed meat, the drying cheese sauce, and he pushed the box away while his mind raced to picture a logical scenario. *A disgruntled customer, one who didn't get the time of his life?*

"Possible, McIntosh. We'll certainly be burrowing deep into Dunn's life." Pavletich ceased his pacing and swayed into his second-favourite stance, feet apart, hands behind him. "I also want to consider Ms Tan's father, Mr Bloody Malcolm Tan. What do we know about him?"

No need to respond, the question rhetorical, Pavletich about to launch into the details. Wright yawned again and faced the door, in readiness for a quick escape.

"He keeps out of the public eye. Why, something to hide?" Pavletich asked. "Did he set his daughter up in that flat? If so, why? He owns apartment buildings, with penthouses."

Pavletich sat down in the seat next to Finn and leaned so far back his chair was in danger of tipping over. "OK, the motive has to be a powerful one if killing two people is the solution. As McIntosh pointed out, it will pay to look into Dunn's business. Maybe a client has a grudge."

The others, red-eyed and sallow-skinned in the fluorescent light. As tired as he felt. *Can we sleep on it?*

"If we don't get a result soon, there'll be longer nights than this," Pavletich's exasperation clear.

"Money, drugs and sex, that's what gets people killed," Wright offered. "Any record of affiliation with any gang?"

"You thinking it's a turf war? Maybe one of the gangs wants in on the cash-heavy brothels and Mrs Dunn wasn't easily persuaded." Finn was surprised the idea came to him, considering his bone-weariness. "Surely the few houses Mrs Dunn ran are minor league, though, not worth killing for."

"Maybe Tan runs gangs, under our radar. He's a rich Chinese, isn't he?" Unsworth said, with a hint of venom, not hiding he had something against the rich. Or the Chinese.

Wright took over. "Presumably Tan had a mistress because he didn't get on with his wife; Areta was dead and he hadn't found anyone to replace her yet. Maybe he was getting some action from one of Juliette's girls. Maybe he no longer wanted to pay for it. Or it's a drug deal gone wrong. Tan supplied Dunn's girls and Mrs Dunn objected or wanted a bigger cut." Wright barely paused for breath. "Maybe Tan discovered his daughter worked for Juliette, an extension of her so-called modelling." Wright sat forward, eyes shiny with excitement. "No, I know! This explains Ms Tan's flashy car. She was the one selling Dunn's girls drugs. Anything to suppress hunger, keep them slim. Those type of models are heavy into drugs, aren't they? And Father Tan went round there to sort the Dunns out, blamed them for the downfall of his daughter."

Silence while they all thought through Wright's jumble of ideas.

"Ms Tan a dealer? Can't see it, we'd have heard. Concentrate on the following. Why was a car registered to Malcom Tan seen in the street several times? Get those dates verified. Was the Tan vehicle seen there before Ms Tan left for Tauranga?" Pavletich yawned, throwing his head back. "Was Juliette Dunn training up the daughter? She was a good-looking girl. Check if any online memorial page gets set up for either Dunn. Check the posts, see if any stand out. Jealousy among Juliette's girls? Put on a bit of pressure if you have to. Get me that staff list. A client list might be harder to come by, even with a warrant, but give it a go. Was Dunn in debt? Check with the other divisions, see if they have anything, the Serious Fraud Office, the Criminal Proceeds Recovery people, anyone likely to hold information. What about the private guys, any had cause to sniff around Dunn or Tan or anyone connected to either of them? If Tan is dodgy in any way, what a coup to bring him down." Pavletich's eyes flashed, a fleeting display of pleasure.

"There's always the opportunist. Any known burglars with a history of assault in the area?" Pavletich shook his head, giving that idea little credence. "OK, home time. More leg work tomorrow, more door knocks. And clean up the mess. I don't want stale pizza stink tomorrow."

They all glared at the door long after Pavletich had left.

"How the fuck are the four of us going to cover all that on a Sunday? He mightn't have a life, but I sure do." Unsworth grabbed pizza boxes, crushed one on top of the other, scattered crumbs, fuelling his frustration. "And what about you, McIntosh, you with all the *first-hand knowledge*. I heard you were kicked off the Amahua investigation?"

Unsworth obviously listened to the gossip.

Now was Finn's chance to put his version of events. It still felt raw, his suspicion that his own superior officer leaked his disciplinary file with the accusations of insubordination, failure to follow instruction, lack of collegiality, lack of the resilience needed to do the job.

Front it. "The officer in charge of the investigation was old-school, you know, the policeman is above the law. He also thought intimidation of a witness was a useful tactic. I objected. He didn't like that. I transferred before the investigation ended. End of story."

"You'll never be a decent detective, Mcintosh, if you can't put a bit of heat on someone, especially someone making your job difficult." Unsworth not prepared to let it go.

"Guys, everyone's tired, let's clean up and go home." Wright rescued a handful of unused serviettes, used them to wipe the scraps into a neat pile and brushed them into an empty box. "I'm sure the boss knows the full details, and he's still picked Finn to join the team. Let that be enough, Luke."

Ngaire to his rescue. He hoped she didn't give in to her softer side too much and expect him to shake Unsworth's hand or bro-hug.

"Give us the insider intel on the Tan family, Finn, oh font of all knowledge." Cranston's grin and mock bow took any sting out of the words. He moved the crumpled boxes to one end of the table, threw his arms wide, gestured to them to sit.

"Keep it brief," muttered Unsworth.

Ngaire pulled him into a chair, sat beside him, a show of all is forgiven.

"I don't know much about Malcolm Tan," Finn admitted, sitting beside Cranston, grateful the conversation was off him. "He was never a focus in Amahua's case, as Harris was sure it was suicide from early on." Didn't stop him implying to the media they were investigating if Tova, in one of her rages, had killed her mother. One of his underhand tactics to shut Tova up. He'd been present when Harris goaded her, threw out the question: 'Had she killed her own mother?' Tova pushed him away. That was the defining moment for Finn.

"Tan's company builds and owns apartments and commercial premises. He's got money, his name was linked to the casino development. Nothing on him, then, other than water-tightness issues in some of his properties."

Ngaire cut in. "No wonder Mr Tan doesn't get on with Tova. His low profile ruined by his daughter's wild accusation of Areta being murdered and police incompetence, his affair with Areta made public, all topped off with the social media morality brigade about Areta's right, or otherwise, to disown her whānau."

The real Ngaire was back, her show of kindness short-lived. Any child she might have would have to be tough.

"We can't link the two situations," Finn said, determined not to let Ngaire goad him to anger. "Yes, Ms Tan was upset last year, said some things she might regret. It doesn't follow that she's capable of murder."

"We think that about most people, until they do it," Cranston contributed.

"Something triggered it," Ngaire said, "like an argument. Ms Tan admitted she argued with her mother the day of Areta's death, which was possibly a factor in her suicide. She argued with Jasmine, too."

"That's quite a leap."

"Is it, Finn? Who else has she argued with?"

Unsworth had his eyes closed.

Cranston frowned as if he was really trying to come up with possibilities.

"Areta's whānau," Ngaire answered her own question. "Can't be a coincidence that Ms Tan spends six weeks in Tauranga where Areta grew up."

"Maybe as part of her healing process, she decided to spend time getting to know her extended family, finding out about her roots, her whakapapa. That's a good thing, isn't it?" Finn failed to see where Ngaire's thoughts were leading.

"A highly emotional time. And she came back to Auckland, all wound up, and Jasmine pressed her buttons and ..."

"We're going round in circles," Finn said, looking at his watch.

Unsworth took his cue, gave him a thumbs up and pushed back his chair. "You were right earlier, Ngaire, when you said sex and drugs and money. That's why the Dunns were murdered. My money is on Malcolm Tan being at the centre of it, with his daughter's help. Nothing to do with Areta or her whānau. That background info just explains why little Miss Tova is so screwed up."

Ngaire stood. "Background that is helpful to know. Read up on it. Impress Pavletich with your in-depth understanding of the main suspects."

"If it gets me on interviewing either of the Tans, I'll do it." Unsworth headed for the door.

Ngaire was a step ahead. "Help Finn and Isaiah get rid of the rubbish." She blew them kisses as she left.

Keep an open mind drummed like a mantra in Finn's head. He stood under scalding water until the skin on his fingers wrinkled and his chest turned blotchy red.

The shower was meant to cleanse away the day's negativity and induce sleep. It didn't work. At three am, Finn was wide awake.

If he'd still been with Emily, she the avid reader and relayer of gossip about the international and domestic pseudo-famous, he'd be up to speed with the goings-on of the Tan household. Without her to assist him, he pulled on a long-sleeve T-shirt, arranged the pillows against the bedhead, logged onto his laptop and settled back to follow Ngaire's advice and read up on the Tans.

His finger paused above the National Intelligence Application database icon. All he needed was a quick read of Richard and Tova's record of activity with the police and see if Malcolm Tan had ever come to their notice. He was expected to work 24/7, but he wasn't confident of Pavletich approving retrospective authorisation. Just his luck to be the team member picked up in the regular audit looking for improper use of the NIA.

He clicked on Google's search bar, typed in Malcolm Tan's name, added New Zealand businessman when the name proved to be more common than expected. Skimmed through entries dealing with his property portfolio and an ongoing legal battle over weather-tightness issues. Strictly business, no personal, private details given. Finn paused on the women's magazine listing with Tan and Areta's names in bold, then clicked.

The article, written after Areta's death, speculated on her depression at the decreasing number of decent roles as she aged. A short paragraph, midway, designed to titillate, spoke of her long-term relationship with the influential but married Chinese businessman Mr Malcolm Tan, the existence of a love-child, now in her early twenties, and the sadness Areta must have experienced at the situation. Mostly supposition slanted to explain her suicide, without ever using that word. Accompanying photos of Areta, stills from television shows, a red-carpet moment, an unkind one of her leaving a café in loose, casual clothes and scowling at the camera. He saw the likeness to her daughter, the clear skin, the thick dark hair, the defined cheekbones. Small sidebar photos of Mr Tan, taken from his company's website, and one of Tova, from the Star Power site in bikini pants and midriff top, apparently summer nightwear, her hair scraped back and piled high on her head.

A black-bordered box, taking up most of the second page, dealt with the controversy of her funeral and the division between the immediate family wishing Areta to be cremated, the extended family, in spite of the years of disconnect with Areta, insisting it was important the deceased return to the land, literally, in accordance with Māori custom.

The 'immediate family' could only refer to Tova.

The case had been gossiped about as all investigations were, the same way teachers talked about students, nurses about patients and lawyers about clients. In the confines of the workplace, among colleagues, but gossiped about nonetheless. He cringed at the memory of laughing along, one of the boys, how they'd all like to get into Tova's pants.

He watched the short video of Detective Harris's final press statement, opening with assurances the police had thoroughly examined every angle, including the possibility of any close family member being responsible in some way, big or small, for Areta's death. Recollections flooded back. Days of speculation, people taking sides. Tova was innocent. No, she was guilty. One lateral-thinking reporter had more than his fifteen minutes of fame; he first likened New Zealand's fascination with all things Areta to Australians' divide over their Lindy Chamberlain and the dingo claim, and then with America's debate over O J Simpson's guilt or innocence. Harris closed his statement, confirming the coroner's verdict, accidental death.

Lastly, Finn did a search on Tova. He flicked through what he already knew, read and reread another magazine entry on Areta, devoting space to the estrangement between father and daughter, starting when Tova learned he had a Chinese wife and legitimate son, Richard. A close school friend of Tova's was quoted, and Finn wondered how close the friendship actually was. No such qualms for the reporter.

He found only one statement made by Malcolm Tan, saying he had no comment to make and he requested privacy while he dealt with personal matters.

Didn't sound like father and daughter would plot anything together, let alone murder. Finn bookmarked the article, a useful point to counter Unsworth's suggestion of their collusion.

He clicked into the Star Power website. The images of her in lacy underwear relayed on a loop through his mind until he fell asleep.

And woke, minutes later, Tova on his mind.

Finn stretched and checked his phone: 6:30. Only a few hours' sleep. Hardly enough, even with regular caffeine shots, to get him through the day ahead.

14. TOVA

Loud noises woke her, again. The first were at two am, voices fading as their owners moved further along the corridor, and Tova listened to the slurred, "Goo-nigh, see ya t'morra" and doors slamming. By six, early-morning risers shut doors, butted against corridor walls, she assumed with their high-end backpacks, and chatted about their plans, oblivious to the idea there were guests wanting the luxury of a sleep-in. She tossed onto her left side and wished she'd thought to bring the earplugs with her. To get back to sleep, she counted backwards from one hundred, reached seventy-three, had a mind blank and lost count. The feeling that things would worsen before they improved was strong. She repeated a phrase often heard in schools to encourage girls. "You are a strong, capable female, a 'wahine toa'. Face your fears."

Giving up on the sleep, she listed off positive thoughts to counter the unwelcome police involvement in her life again: I'm healthy; the feedback from the placement in

Tauranga was encouraging; I'll get a job out of Auckland next year; Or move to Australia where no one knows me.

Too much like running away? She hadn't succumbed last year, so why do so now? Bunching the pillows, she pulled herself up into a half-sitting position and manoeuvred the laptop to her knee. She needed more information before she met with Pavletich again.

While waiting for her laptop to power up, she glanced at her phone. One text from Sarah, sent late the previous night. *Whr r u? Im worried.*

Im OK. Talk ltr. Without thinking of the early hour, she pressed Send and regretted it as soon as her phone rang.

"Oh my God, are you really okay? The news said the murder happened in the house. You're not still in your flat, are you? You can't stay there on your own." Sarah paused for breath. "What if the murderer ... I'll come get you. I've been worried sick. You should've called. You weren't there when it happened, were you? Where are you? You need someone with you. Have the police spoken to you yet? Oh, Tova, have they been, you know ..."

Tova half-listened to Sarah's rapid-fire questions. In the hope she had misunderstood the detective, she typed in the search bar the name of the rest home where Mrs Dunn said she worked. She clicked on its web page. No staff list and no Juliette in the grainy staff photo.

"The police have been okay."

The detective's words, 'her line of business' and 'one of Juliette's girls', didn't require a higher level of reasoning to interpret. She stared at the keyboard, typed in Juliette Dunn then paused, 'brothel' dredging up from some recess in her mind. It didn't sound politically correct. She added 'massage parlour' to the two words already typed and drew a match. The Juliette was a Ms Juliette Evan-Rogers, quoted in an article, dated three years previously, on the legal and professional nature of her brothel business and the service she offered. No accompanying photo. Tova scrolled through several pages on Auckland prostitution and prostitutes. It didn't escape her that a number of the posed photos wouldn't have been out of place on the Star Power website.

"What are you doing? Are you on your computer?"

"Checking out the Dunns online."

Jasmine Dunn. The first item listed her as a valued player in a school netball game two years ago. Next, a mention in last year's school musical. Her Facebook page was public. One click and a portrait shot of Jasmine – staring at the camera, hair tousled, fringe in her eyes – confronted Tova. Scrolling down, most of the photos were selfies – Jasmine experimenting with hairstyles and eye shadow, updating her profile photo every few days.

"How can a teenager have two hundred and fifty-seven friends?" Tova muttered.

"Not everyone is as uncommunicative as you," Sarah said. "The police will be delighted that's all she has."

"What do you mean?"

"They'll have to sift through them, won't they? That's how they'll find out who she didn't get on with. If you watched cop shows, you'd know that."

Had Jasmine told her friends about her use of the downstairs flat? Tova wished she had mentioned the terse words exchanged with Jasmine before the police found out from someone else.

"You still there, Tova?"

"Mmm."

"Are you sure the police are treating you right? It's not the same cop, is it?"

"I'm a lot wiser now." But she hadn't been forthcoming with the detective about her BMW. Her father had a choice of his own cars, preferring larger, more ostentatious styles. Richard often complained of all the power sitting in the garage unused, yet he was relegated to driving one of his father's superseded castoffs. His recklessness in borrowing the BMW while Tova was out of town didn't surprise her. The anglicisation of his Chinese name, Li Cha De, was apt. Her half-brother, definitely a dick.

"Something weird's going on." She didn't dispute that her car had been in Te Atatu, but there had to be another explanation other than Richard being involved in Jasmine's death. She wouldn't put it past him to loan it to some dodgy mates in return for drugs. She would have to go see him.

"Weird like what? They aren't dragging up last year again, are they?" An edge of concern crept into Sarah's voice.

"They asked me why I'd moved into the flat. I said you kicked me out."

"I didn't kick you out." The diversion worked and Sarah went off on a tangent. "I wanted you to stay."

And be the spare wheel. Sarah and Tom had ratcheted up their relationship to seriously-considering-getting-engaged and he moved in, forcing Tova to flat-hunt, two fixed criteria non-negotiable: it had to be cheap enough to stretch out the small inheritance from her mother, her student loan and the money she earned from her erratic modelling, and had to be near a frequent bus route, as she refused to be seen as the rich Chinese girl driving a flash car. Richard had been incredulous when she told him she'd refused her father's conscience-salving gift. 'He's given you a fucking car. Take it. Sell it. Buy some crap Japanese reliable shit, pocket the difference. If you can't bring yourself to do that, give it to me, then I wouldn't have to drive his hand-me-downs.'

"It might be a good idea to contact that lawyer you have." Sarah brought Tova back to the present.

Mr Victor Zhou, her father's friend since they met at school. With his shaven skull and quiet manners, he resembled a Buddhist monk, one playing dress-up in a business suit. Tova found him unctuous. He stood too close by her father's side, and he dipped his head as he spoke.

"No," she said, too quickly. Mr Zhou kept Malcolm Tan informed of everything he learned about Tova's life. She had accused him last year of breaking client-lawyer confidentiality. With a pompous shake of his head, he had told her that did not apply to the father-child relationship. If she contacted Zhou, her father would see it as a sign that Tova needed him. "I don't need a lawyer. A character referee, maybe. Tell the police I'm an ordinary person."

"You want me to lie?" Sarah said, her serious tone overshadowed by snorts and giggles.

Tova's smile receded. She had an image of Mrs Dunn showing her through the flat, and her eyes pricked, tears imminent. Fortunately, Sarah was on the end of the phone and not in the hotel room. One sympathetic hug from Sarah and she'd end up weeping.

Tova rubbed her eyes. It came back to her. "Richard told me about the Dunn flat." She struggled to recall the whole conversation, interspersed as it had been with frequent requests for money and sarcastic remarks about her easy life. "He saw it advertised, or someone told him. Now I think about it, he was a bit vague." She remembered smiling, pleased with Richard telling her about that flat in Herne Bay, not wanting anything in return.

"That's right. You said you wouldn't live in a dingy student dive, and he said in that case, smooch up to your dad for a waterfront apartment."

"And let him share it with me."

Sarah's laugh almost drowned out her next words. "Shows you what a dick Richard is."

Tova hated the persona Richard presented to the world. Black, low-slung jeans, baseball cap backwards, a well-practised swagger copied from the D-grade American music videos he watched for hours. She loathed his fuck-this, fuck-that language. None of it hid what he was – a weedy, wasted Chinese boy in need of some serious bodybuilding and a better attitude. He was her brother. Half-brother. Criticising him was her blood right, but it grated hearing someone else do it, even Sarah.

"He's not that bad."

Sarah struck back. "You warned me to keep an eye on my wallet whenever he was around. And you were the one who asked if he'd turn into a decent human being sometime this century."

Often enough, Tova had railed against Richard's partying and series of sleazy girls, down to the gangsta manoeuvres he thought made him the man. And how he ignored her advice – don't do drugs, don't drink yourself comatose, don't surround yourself with parasitic hangers-on. "Sorry, he is my brother."

"Half. He takes advantage of you. You're not responsible for him, you don't owe him anything. Stop protecting him," Sarah said. "Please come and stay. You don't have to hole up in some backpackers."

"Thanks." But that's what she wanted to do: see no one, not think. "Maybe. I'll let you know." Tova cut the call. And remembered she hadn't packed her meet-her-father outfit. She quickly searched bus times.

Another ten minutes and she dragged on jeans, T-shirt, jumper. At the last minute she grabbed her jacket. It was sure to be another Auckland winter's day, chilly and damp. No one was on the desk in reception and Tova ran out. She'd be back in an hour or so, plenty of time to decide her next move, check out, go to Sarah's, or hide in the room another night.

A brisk walk up Queen Street to K Road and the Link bus stop, time to buy a takeaway cup of tea before the 8.40 bus arrived.

Twenty minutes later, the bus dropped her off at Jervois Road, opposite Bayfield Primary School. It was a short walk down to Argyle Street. She pulled her jacket collar tighter, headed towards her flat and tried to ignore the increase in her heart rate. She had every right to go and get her own things.

With luck, the rain would keep the neighbours inside.

15. FINN

The slow phase of the traffic lights at the Waterview intersection gave Finn time to think.

Arriving at work before the expected time of nine am, Pavletich's concession to calling them in on Sunday, left him vulnerable to try-hard accusations, even if he did have paperwork to catch up on, so a quick swing by the Dunn house was a good idea, check his hunch. If he uncovered nothing, at least the drive back to Te Atatu always rewarded him with views across the harbour to Birkenhead, a reminder of beauty in the world.

He flicked the indicator and edged right, squeezing in between cars, grateful he was in his own nondescript Mazda instead of a patrol vehicle when the guy behind beeped his horn.

Finn parked around the corner on Masons Avenue and retrieved his waterproof parka from the boot. With head down against the drizzle, hands in the parka pockets, he hurried into Argyle Street, keeping an eye out for parked cars likely to harbour security guards from the firm the police used on occasion. Although the initial search of house and yard had been done, it remained cordoned off and locked, in case developments warranted a more thorough investigation. Eventually, it would be released to the next of kin. As of late yesterday, Wright had yet to locate any family. Finn was confident the house stood empty.

He searched for a spare-key hiding place: under a garden gnome, above the door sill. He found it, third look lucky, in a magnetised box the size of a cigarette packet behind the security light. He hoped no neighbours rang the police.

The house already leached abandonment. Slivers of daylight seeped through the closed curtains, allowing Finn to make his way along the hall. The forensic team had Jasmine's laptop, but the school bag, books and strewn clothing were as he had seen them the day before.

He hesitated by the study door. If he was right, Pavletich might praise his initiative. If he was wrong, Pavletich didn't need to know that he had been in the house without authorisation. Mrs Dunn's computer was gone, to be examined in detail, but he expected the file boxes were still there, on the assumption that anything on paper was also on the computer. The brief paragraph in the report listing the items removed in the study had given him the idea. Phone, computer, two external hard drives. No mention of what the file boxes contained.

The first noise didn't break Finn's concentration although he was aware of it, next door perhaps, or further along the street. He'd taken down each file box, flicked through the contents and, as he'd expected, most held hard copies of accounts going back several years, all related to Juliette's known brothels. He returned those to the shelves. Four remaining boxes contained papers with no obvious connection to those businesses. Three boxes each contained ownership or lease documents relating to a city apartment and a page or two listing names – mostly, but not exclusively, female – a mobile number beside each one. The fourth box held an enlarged map of the CBD, a real estate agent's business card clipped to it. He sat back in Juliette's office chair and stared at the boxes. His hunch, triggered by comments made in the briefing the day before, had been spot on.

The second noise, the gentle closing of a door downstairs. Finn listened to the tread of steps on the internal stairs, the clunk of the door bolt released. He rose in slow motion, fingers spread to catch any papers that fluttered with the sudden movement, and braced himself, his weight on his right foot and fist bunched.

The door eased open. Finn registered a sneakered foot, jeans. He lunged, noticing too late the dark-blue fleecy jacket.

The intruder staggered, lost balance, hit the wall with a thud, emitted a cry. Tova fell to the floor.

His instinct was to scoop her up, hug her close, say 'Sorry' several times. "You shouldn't be here," he said instead and folded his arms.

"You scared the hell out of me!" She pulled herself up, one hand to her chest, her face regaining colour.

"You broke in."

"I live here," Tova said, defiance in her eyes. "How can I break in to my own home?"

"It's a crime scene. You were asked to stay away. Why are you here?" He sounded like Pavletich with his quick-fire way of speaking.

"I need some clothes."

"And your clothes are here, upstairs?"

"I heard a noise, came to investigate."

"That was stupid. What if it had been the Dunns' killer?"

"Stupid?"

One glance at Tova's clenched teeth and he stumbled over his words. "I meant, dangerous. What if he came back to check he'd left nothing incriminating?"

Her face paled. "He? You know who killed them?"

"A figure of speech," Finn said. "We don't know. All the more reason for you not to be here."

He followed her downstairs and watched as she entered her bedroom, pulled a knee-length, shift-style dress off a hanger and lifted a pair of black, high-heeled shoes out of a shoebox.

"Going on a date?" An appropriate question under the circumstances, so why did he wish he hadn't asked?

She flung a none-of-your-business glare his way. Easing past him she extracted two reusable shopping bags from a kitchen drawer and folded the dress into one, the shoes into the other, and both into a large shoulder bag she'd left on the table. "What were you doing in the study?"

"I can't discuss an ongoing investigation. You'll be informed when you can return here to live." It came out more officious than he intended. Why did this woman turn him back into a gawky teen?

Tova obeyed his request and relinquished her spare house key, placing them on the table, ignoring his open palm. She refused his offer of a lift to the backpackers, pointed out the rain had stopped.

He watched her leave, the bulging shoulder bag swinging.

He had to tell Pavletich about the incident. The fact that she had crossed the cordoned-off barrier to retrieve a stylish dress was likely to confirm to Pavletich that she was an up-market working girl. He imagined Tova in the classic-looking dress and his mind wandered, remembered the clingy black number Emily had worn to the police dinner the year before. Heat rose on his face as he remembered, when they got home, unzipping the dress, slipping it off her shoulders, seeing it slither to the floor.

Whom did Tova plan to meet? Where? It was part of the job to know about everyone involved in a case, he told himself, not the whiff of jealousy.

With the house locked, Tova's keys secure in a zipped pocket and the spare ones back where he found them, Finn returned to his car. He'd tell Pavletich the truth, admit he'd been back to the crime scene without permission. Fifty-fifty as to whether the reprimand due would be overlooked once the boss heard what he'd found. Explaining Tova's presence as innocent, to an already-suspicious Pavletich, he wasn't so sure about. What if Pavletich thought he'd aided and abetted Tova in some way?

As he started the car, he realised he had yet to ask about her argument with Jasmine.

16. TOVA

An hour after swishing away from Constable McIntosh, Tova paused inside the Cordis Hotel foyer, headed for the ladies room where she swapped her ballet flats for the high heels and shoved her jacket into the shoulder bag to join the rolled-up jeans. She smoothed down the high-necked black dress she always wore to lunch with her father and double-checked that no bra strap had slipped beyond the capped sleeves. The roomy bag jarred with the demure look, and she carried it low at her side as she headed for the restaurant.

Scratch the surface and *dutiful* daughter revealed herself not far below.

Malcolm Tan expected her promptly at midday, and Tova turned up every month.

She attended, she told herself, to remind him she managed well without his help.

Her father sat at his usual table, midway, with his back to the wall, from which vantage point he scanned the room for business associates before they saw him, giving him the advantage. Easier to catch the eye of any passing wait staff, too.

"Your usual, Ms Tan?" Tova allowed the attentive waiter to pull out her chair. It would be too easy to get used to such service.

Nothing was said until her non-alcoholic fruit punch with its decorative umbrella swizzle stick appeared.

"You missed last month, didn't let me know." He spoke softly, although the tables either side of them were as yet unoccupied. Her father, a regular at the Eight restaurant, brought considerable business its way and the maître d' ensured their privacy as long as possible.

Tova caught his disappointment and a quiver of guilt shimmied up her spine, her mini rebellion seeming rude and childish. "I'm sure your spies keep you informed."

"You did not think to tell me of the tragedy at your house?" Malcolm Tan sighed. "Mr Zhou was kind enough to let me know as soon as I returned."

Tova fiddled with the already straight cutlery and did not meet her father's eyes. Of course Victor Zhou knew; everyone did. It was all over the news.

Her father always referred to his lawyer, business partner and friend of many years as Mr, one of her father's many affectations, as if he were Chinese royalty instead of born, raised and schooled in the well-to-do Auckland suburb of Howick. The man who excused her behaviour to Detective Harris, pleading she was consumed with grief, incapable of acting rationally.

"You've been away?"

"Yes, an unexpected business trip to Guangzhou. I left last Tuesday, returned last night. Why, did you try to contact me?" A tremor of hope.

"No." It came out louder than she had meant.

Her father blinked in surprise. "You can't go back to that house. Let me help you."

She looked away from the concern on his face. She didn't intend to return to live at Argyle Street. She wouldn't accept his offer, either; she had to maintain her independence, for her own sake and for his. He would realise this when she told him about the police's interest in him.

"Have you seen your brother recently?" Malcolm asked.

Their lunches had two main topics of conversation. Richard, before they ate, and Areta with their after-meal coffee. Her father had once explained the wisdom of getting the difficult and distasteful out of the way so that such matters didn't spoil the enjoyment of good food.

He would find out soon enough that it must have been Richard who had taken her car, a car linked to the crime scene. If she told him that, she'd have to tell him everything. And then he would give his advice and expect her to follow it.

"You know I haven't. I've been in Tauranga for the last six weeks."

"I'm worried about him. He mixes with the wrong people."

"You need to speak to him." Not that he would, not while she played intermediary, assuaging her feelings of responsibility for the mess her half-brother found himself in.

Tova cut the conversation short by getting up and quickly walking towards the food on display before her father asked if there was anything in particular to raise with his son. She took her time, stopped by each of the eight separate food booths and admired the variety and appetising presentations. She selected what she always did, a fillet of snapper and a scoop of steamed vegetables.

Her father had followed in her wake, made his choices and returned to the table before her. He studied the food on her plate and encouraged her to go back for more. His head-shaking strengthened her resolve. She didn't need him to look after her.

They ate in silence. She was unwilling to talk, and he liked to savour the tastes of the food piled onto his plate.

Tova declined dessert, and her father sighed as she checked her watch. Why did she put herself through the pleasure and pain of remembering Areta? Because they had both loved her and now gained comfort in talking about her. That they had in common.

"You get more like your mother every time I see you," he said after the waiter placed his espresso and her flat white in front of them.

She should have let him do the talking, ease the tension, reminisce about happier times when the three of them were a family. She liked those stories, but not today. "I don't see how. She was a Māori sprinkled with Pākehā and I'm half-Chinese."

"In temperament, I mean," he said, indicating no annoyance at her deliberate misunderstanding. "You have her determination, her stubbornness, as well as her warm heart."

Tova let out a soft breath of disagreement.

"In time, you will grow less angry."

It annoyed her more than usual, his belief that he knew her.

"I might apply for teaching jobs in Tauranga next year." It was the first she had mentioned what she had been thinking for some time.

He took a sip of coffee.

"I'll be able to visit the marae at Matapihi, get to know my Ngai te rangi whānau and learn about my whakapapa." Using Māori words still sounded odd. Like almost everyone in the country, she knew common words but seldom used them beyond the 'Kia ora' to welcome students, 'Ka kite ano' as they left each day, 'Ka pai' for their occasional successes. "I'll learn te reo Māori."

He lowered the espresso cup to half-mast.

Tova had never heard Areta speak any Māori, although she discovered her mother had been a fluent speaker. He never spoke Mandarin to her, although he often used it when on business calls. They always spoke English to each other. Until the day, thirteen years old, she found out he had a dual life, complete with wife and son in another suburb. Then she didn't speak to him at all until their mutual need to remember Areta.

Her father's eyes narrowed. "Your whānau? This would not please your mother."

"She lied to me." Tova swallowed, held back the tears, a mix of anger and sadness, and her own guilt. She had once questioned Areta's disinterest in things Māori, probably brought on by some discussion at school. Areta's reply, 'I'm what is called an urban Māori, long disconnected from my ancestors' iwi', gave her the impression that generations of Areta's family had lived in the city.

"She had her reasons. Respect that."

"I want to know where I belong." Her Chinese features encouraged some people to ask where she was from. Others spoke slowly to her, and a few were quick to mutter she should go back where she came from. Her father's world was not the world she wanted to live in, one where making money was paramount. He thought nothing of investing in projects with no regard for social responsibility, building small but expensive apartments while living in comfort in a spacious home.

The conversation was going off its usual course, and she wasn't sure how to articulate her thoughts. She was still feeling her way.

"You may not like what you hear about your whānau."

"I'm not asking for your permission. Besides, everyone forgave Areta for what she had done." She was unclear as to what that was exactly, some argument among teenagers, adults got involved, Areta in the wrong. It was blown out of proportion, someone had said, and no one willing to apologise first.

"For what *she* had done?" Malcolm's cup clattered in the saucer. He snapped the table napkin from his lap, took his time to fold it and placed it on the table. The waiter, observant, was quickly by his side.

"We will leave now. Thank you, excellent, as always."

Tova watched her father slip a generous tip into his palm. The waiter bowed low as usual.

She gathered up her bag, stood by her chair. There was one last ritual to get through.

"Can I give you a lift anywhere?" Malcolm always asked.

She always refused.

Their exit was unhurried, allowing time for the car to be waiting at the entrance. Malcolm stopped by a table, shook hands with the diners, didn't introduce her.

A slow walk through the foyer, more handshaking with a woman in a well-fitting suit, a gold-leaf lapel badge proclaiming her the maître d'.

The valet had the car door open, a faraway look on

his face, used to customers' last-minute discussions and protracted goodbyes.

"The police will wish to interview you about the girl. Do not speak to them alone. They will bring up the past. Mr Zhou will accompany you. He has been advising Richard on one or two matters. He is willing to help you."

She said nothing. She waited until he had driven away, down Symonds Street, out of sight.

17. FINN

Finn returned to Henderson later than he had intended, what with Tova and a detour to food and a toilet stop at the McDonald's in Grey Lynn.

"The boss is with the top brass, briefing them on progress, begging for more staff." Unsworth's tone suggested the futility of the attempt as he stood beside Finn staring into Pavletich's empty office. "You're to follow up with the Hemona boy."

Finn turned to head back down the corridor and out to the vehicle bay.

"Hang on, I'm with you. Watch and learn, the boss said."

He knocked loudly on the Hemonas' door, the noise possibly heard in the next street.

"You again. This is harassment, waking me up." Repeka Hemona, hair tousled, eyes sleepy, a faded dressing gown over trackpants and T-shirt, and about to slam the door shut on Finn.

"It's past midday, Mrs Hemona."

"Hemi's not here. He's gone away on business."

So Hemi had the wind up, making himself scarce.

"It's Jacob I want to talk to."

"You can't believe that guy across the road. He's half-blind and senile."

"Jacob told you last night that he saw the body?"

"Thought he was making it up."

"Appears not."

He saw it in her face, deciding the best course of action: weighing up removal in a police car and hours later left to make their own way back home. Muttering, she stood back, pointed at the bedroom door.

He instructed Unsworth to remain out front, a lookout in case Hemi returned or Jacob climbed out a window. He'd learn that a lot of policing involved standing around and waiting. Ignoring Unsworth's scowl, Finn entered the house.

The boy lay in bed, blankets pulled up to his chin, the pretence at sleep pointless as his eyelids flickered with the effort of keeping them shut. Finn was tempted to pull the bedclothes back and heave the boy to his feet. He knew better than to do that. He stayed by the door and signalled to Repeka.

"Get up!" she yelled.

Jacob took his time getting out of bed. He was fully dressed, trackpants, long-sleeve T-shirt, socks. He eyed the door while he fidgeted, adjusting his clothes.

"Sit down." Finn stood ready to block him if he tried to run.

Jacob slumped back onto the bed, back to the wall, sat cross-legged. Repeka tugged at the curtains covering the large window facing the street. Before she was satisfied they blocked any prying eyes, Finn glimpsed Unsworth leaning on the squad car, head down, eyes on the mobile in his hand. Catching up with some online study? Playing a game? Whatever he was concentrating on, it wasn't what Finn had asked him to do.

He faced Jacob. "You're not in trouble. You're a witness. I'm checking the time line, that's all. I know you saw the body about six pm on Friday."

Jacob leapt up. "Fuckin KK. Can't shut up."

"Zip it, Jacob." Repeka moved fast, pushed him back down.

"Stand back, Mrs Hemona." Finn drew himself up to full height, planted his feet wide, elbows out, waited until she complied. "Know what else I think, Jacob?" It was inference on Finn's part, KK hadn't actually said it. "You'd seen the girl there before that."

Jacob shrugged, piss off, not talking to you.

Finn turned towards the door, hoped Jacob didn't call his bluff. If he had to take him to the station it would be hours of waiting for a lawyer and more paperwork.

"OK, wait." Jacob rubbed his hands down his trackpants legs, licked his lips, getting ready to spin a story that kept him out of trouble. "Does she have to be here?"

"I'm here to protect you in case he gets physical," Repeka said.

Finn let that go. "When did you first see the body?"

"In the middle of the night."

He had expected Jacob to admit he saw her earlier, after school, then rode off to get KK.

Time for Unsworth to come in, be a witness? Or take the boy to the station? His gut said let the boy talk, get some intel to work with before wasting Pavletich's time.

"He's lying," Repeka said. "Wants you to think he knows more than he does, trying to please you."

Finn almost laughed at the absurdity, but the boy's words rang true.

"I am not. Two guys brought her." Jacob, head low, spoke into his chest.

"What two guys?"

"I dunno. They had a fancy car. I wanted to check it out, sit in it maybe, but Dad biffed me one, shamed me in front of those guys, told me to get my arse inside."

"Did you?"

"Nah, I hid. Dad pissed me off." Jacob raised his chin at his mother, his eyes wide and angry.

Repeka stepped forward and Finn waved her back. He continued. "Your father knew these men?"

"Don't think so," Jacob quickly said.

A lie.

"Then what?"

"It was real dark, and freezing. The big dude dragged something out of the back seat." Jacob scratched behind his ear, moved his hand towards his crotch, thought better of it as he caught Finn's eye.

"What sort of thing?" Finn struggled to read the boy's body language. Distrustful of his mum but not scared of her. Angry at his dad. Uncomfortable in the presence of a cop. And something else.

"Like I said, it was dark but it looked like a ..." Jacob's head was so low strands of his hair touched his knees. "A girl. It couldn't have been, could it? I figured it must have been a doll. You know."

"A doll?"

The boy avoided eye contact, *wish I was anywhere except*

here. Embarrassment, that's what it was. Finn caught on. "You mean a sex doll?"

Jacob's eyes flicked to Finn, away again. An unspoken yes. Finn wondered if he had known about sex dolls at thirteen.

"The guys went down the walkway to the beach, sort of whispering, sort of yelling at each other. Then they came back without the doll and drove away."

"Your dad was with them?"

A glance between mother and son. "Nah, just those guys."

Another lie.

"You decided to go check later that afternoon. Did you take KK because you were scared what you might find?"

"I wasn't scared." Jacob's head lifted. "I didn't think it'd still be there, but if it ... she, was, KK would freak." The bravado subsided and he hunched over, hands clasped between his legs.

Finn had the urge to sit beside Jacob but any show of kindness would be brushed aside, interpreted as weakness. "Can you describe those men for me?" he asked.

"How can he, he didn't see anything," Repeka said.

Repeka's warning to her son wasn't lost on Finn.

"How likely is it that she was there all that time and no one else saw her? Did you think of that?" Repeka was winding up.

Not improbable. Friday had been miserable, heavy rain, enough to keep even hardy walkers and joggers away from the walkway until it eased in the late afternoon.

"Don't you see, Jacob wanted to get his dad into trouble. Payback for telling him off about something else." Repeka moved up close to Finn.

There might be a bit of truth in that, but Pavletich needed to hear from Jacob about the two men. And he was sure Mrs Hemona knew more.

"Maybe. He can tell his story down at the station. He'll be treated right, and we'll soon work out which bits are truth, which aren't."

"No bloody way." Finn could feel Repeka's breath on his face. "I'll say you forced your way in. You scared him, intimidated him. He said stuff to get you to stop."

Finn grabbed her swinging arm before it connected. She aimed a kick. He spun her around, pushed her arm up her back. Jacob squirmed back further on the bed, up against the wall, out of the way.

Repeka's stream of obscenities brought Unsworth running. Finn already had her handcuffed, ensuring that they made it back to Henderson without being strangled from the back seat. The boy squeezed up against the car window. Finn double-checked the child lock was on.

18. TOVA

Tova took off the heels, eased her feet into the more comfortable flat shoes, pulled on the warm jacket. She would change into the jeans later rather than re-enter the hotel and use the foyer toilets.

She checked her phone. A missed call from Sarah. 'Tom's okay with you staying a night or two. We have wine. Ring me.' A glass of Chardonnay with Sarah on her tiny deck in Newmarket appealed, but it wasn't like it used to be. Fiancé Tom had commandeered her old room for his study. He'd give her advice – take advantage of her rich father and his impressive list of contacts from politicians down, order the underlings to back off, leave her alone, she was a victim, too.

One missed call from Richard she didn't listen to. She headed off for K Road. Fifteen minutes later she reached the ten-storey, white-concrete apartment building at the Hopetoun Street end of Beresford Street, one of many owned by Tan Enterprises.

'It is too much to expect Richard to travel from

Howick every day and have time to devote to his studies,' their father had said, handing over the apartment keys to a beaming Richard. Later, Richard bragged to her that at last his father treated him like an adult. She expected Malcolm had a minion or two in the complex keeping him informed of Richard's activities. As he remained blinkered about his son, they were obviously too scared to tell the truth.

Tova pulled out Richard's spare access card to get into the building and took the lift to the third floor. His one-bedroom corner apartment more spacious than most in the complex with its balcony and drawcard of a harbour bridge view, even though the eye focused on Spaghetti Junction and the ear on motorway noises. She had helped him move in the week the mid-year varsity intake started, the first and last time she had seen the flat clean and tidy. Today she resolved not to tidy away the evidence of his squalid habits, remove takeaway boxes, toss empty bottles into the recycle bin, wash the plates he used as ashtrays, clean the bathroom.

Halfway down the long, fluorescent-lit corridor, Tova heard the head-banging rhythmic pounding emanating from Richard's apartment. Big Sean, a rapper her brother favoured, lyrics indecipherable, except for the expletives.

A few minutes was all she needed to confirm her suspicions. If she knew Richard as well as she prided herself she did, he would prove her right: he had found a way around his constant cashless state, dope for him and a hoon around in her kick-arse car for any one of the lowlifes he mixed with.

She knocked on the door at the same time as sliding the access card into the slot. She doubted Richard heard either over the booming music.

Her entry blocked.

In the second it took for that to compute in Tova's mind, she was lifted off her feet, shoved against the door, came face to face with a Sumo wrestler, his giant torso too thick for the tight, white T-shirt he wore. Clean-shaven, face slick with sweat, his greased black hair scraped back off the forehead. He arched his back, avoiding a head butt and preparing to deliver one. A deep belch rolled up and out, a stench-ball of onion, garlic, red meat and indeterminate spices. Her stomach churned.

She scrabbled for a hold into hard neck muscle and dug at his eyes and raked fingernails down his cheeks. She aimed a knee to his crotch. Like kneading marshmallow, her knee disappeared into folds of flesh. Her dress rode up and she wished she'd taken the few minutes to change into jeans.

A gloved paw worked down to her thigh and lingered.

Her yell little more than a squeak, fear constricting her throat.

"For fuck's sake, what's going on?" Another man, similar in size and appearance, stood in the doorway to Richard's bedroom.

"It's her." The hulk swivelled but kept her pinned against the door.

"We were told to leave her alone. You don't have to beat the crap out of everyone, Oso."

Her attacker stepped back from his efforts to crush the life out of her and let her go. Her hip hit the hard metal door handle as she slid down. Winded, she slumped on the floor. His final gesture connected his boot with her cheek. Not a full-on rugby 'I'm gonna get this ball over the goal' type of kick, but bruise-inducing enough to suggest she stay down.

Without taking her eyes off the two men, Tova groped for her shoulder bag, calculated the distance to the bathroom and the time to scramble there, lock herself in, phone 111. Her bum against the wall, she levered into a squat. Both legs wobbled as she dived for the bathroom.

For bulky men, they moved fast. In Charge guy grabbed the thin material of her dress. What if it ripped? He yanked her onto her feet. "It's all your fault, shoulda done what you were supposed to." He motioned for Not So Nice guy to follow him out. "I'll give you one last chance."

Not So Nice guy grunted, feinted a jab to her face.

She seized his arm with both hands, his skin moist, sweaty. He let out a roar and shook his body like a dog shedding water. Her grip loosened, tears clouded her vision. Frustration welled, and this time she let out a scream.

"Shut the fuck up!" A slap for emphasis. "See where disobeying the Boss gets you?" He patted her bruised cheek and slammed the door on his way out.

The men left a black hole of silence that seemed to last forever, but it was no more than the two seconds between one track finishing and Big Sean launching into his next.

Tova bent from the waist, head down, sucked in breaths until her jelly-like legs supported her upright. She pushed the door shut and one turn of the flimsy snub lock. It didn't make her feel safer.

The bedroom smelt. Days-old pizza, sweat and urine overlaid the usual reek of unwashed sheets, discarded clothes and well-worn sneakers. The wooden blinds let in narrow slats of light, enough to make out the body in the bed. Those silly, school-based movies, the teenager's shape imitated by pillows and rolled-up sheets came to mind.

Tova stood beside the bed, hesitating to lift the duvet, its thickness hiding any sign of life.

"Please, please, please," she begged to no particular god.

The body moved, a head appeared. Big Sean's screeching drowned out her own squeak. Richard was almost unrecognisable.

She did her best with the first-aid gear in the bathroom: tissues and water and a tube of Savlon with the expiry date long past. She sponged the already-purpling, swollen right eye, blotted at the blood congealing under his red, puffy nose and dabbed the oozing cut lip, assuring him his teeth were still intact. There was little she could do for the odd angle of his red, swollen pinkies.

"The bugger bent them right back!" Richard wailed.

No police, Richard said. A drug deal gone sour? Money owed?

She was tempted to leave him to it. She headed to the bathroom, time to think and examine her own bruises as she worked each leg into her skinny jeans, her hip jarring with the movement. "You need a doctor."

Tova rang Sarah, who answered on the sixth ring, just as she expected it to switch to voicemail.

"Hello." Sarah breathless, as if she'd been running.

"I need help. Can you come get me?"

Tom's muffled voice in the background.

After a short pause, "Sure."

"Sorry, sorry, did I interrupt? Were you two ..."

"Not any more. Where are you?"

At Dickhead's. "I'm at Richard's. He's hurt. I need to get him to A & E."

19. FINN

Finn took the stairs two at a time, leaving Repeka Hemona to be processed, assault on an officer not her first-ever charge, and Jacob twiddling his thumbs in a waiting room, a constable keeping an eye on him until a social worker turned up. What to mention to Pavletich first, the boy's revelation or what he'd found in the overlooked file boxes in Juliette Dunn's study?

A detective he'd been assigned to when he first joined Henderson turned the corner, bumped into Finn but continued down the stairs without apology. The jolt got Finn thinking. Why did he reckon he knew better than the expert scene crew who had examined Juliette's study? His detective training so far amounted to reading manuals and attending a few courses. If his information sent the investigation off on a time-wasting tangent, what would that do to his career? Decision made, say nothing about Juliette, check his facts first.

Pavletich came out of his office, saw Finn before he could retreat. He strode forward, poking the air. "So much for Ms Tan saying she has nothing to do with her father. Unsworth informed me they meet on the third Sunday of each month for lunch, twelve o'clock to one o'clock."

So that was where she was going.

"Why are you grinning? That's today, in case you've completely lost touch." Pavletich checked his watch. "Bugger, get a move on or you'll miss them. Get onto the Cordis, confirm they did meet, see who else they talk to. She's misled us about their relationship and I want to know why."

Shit. Pavletich still locked onto the Tans as suspects. He had to speak up.

"There's a real estate agent I think we should …"

"Take Unsworth with you," Pavletich said, talking over Finn. "At least he knows what's going on."

How? He was on door-to-doors, and Tova said she didn't speak with the neighbours.

"Didn't you hear me? Get going." Pavletich's scowl lines deepened as he backed into his office and shut the door.

20. TOVA

Richard's damaged face and hands wrapped in the cleanest T-shirts Tova unearthed did not permit him to jump the queue at the Ponsonby Road A & E. Ahead of him was a snotty, whiny kid, a pregnant woman scrolling through her phone, a rugby-uniformed player holding his head and a rheumy-eyed old man with the tremors.

Tova left Sarah browsing through months-old magazines and accompanied Richard into the surgery. "A play fight?" the doctor's scepticism at Tova's explanation of Richard's injuries obvious, through tone and raised eyebrows. She was young, not much older than Tova, but with a weariness to her that said, 'I've seen it all. You can't fool me.'

"That's right."

"The police involved?"

"No need. Mates, mucking around." Did doctors have to report incidents and injuries, as they were supposed to with suspected child abuse?

Richard moaned as the doctor examined his eye and nose. The volume increased as his fingers were taped and bandaged.

"He'll need someone to help him for a few weeks."

"OK."

The doctor pushed her office chair closer to Tova and stared at her bruised cheek. "Perhaps Richard can wait outside while I examine you."

"I'm fine. It's just a bruise." Tova leaned back and avoided eye contact. She couldn't deal with softly spoken kind words and cool fingers. It would be too easy to curl up on the narrow bed and confess all.

"He didn't hit me, if that's what you think. I tried to stop them, got in the way. Stupid thing to do, eh? Should have left them to it." Tova smiled, hoped she was convincing.

"I'd get some new mates, if I were you," the doctor advised Richard.

21. FINN

By the time he confirmed a vehicle was available, tracked down Unsworth - at his computer collating reports - and they drove into the city, the Cordis lunch session was over.

"Ever been here, McIntosh," Unsworth asked as they waited at reception, having asked to speak with the maître d'.

"You have, by the sound of it."

"Once or twice."

Obviously more often. Splurging out on upmarket restaurants was no way to reduce his student loan.

"I get the impression you know a bit about Malcolm Tan? Met him here, have you?"

"I don't know him," Unsworth's indignation strong. "I'd have said, wouldn't I? Disclosure and all that. A neighbour must have said something during one of the door knocks."

Hadn't Tova said she didn't know any of the neighbours? Before Finn could ask more questions, a voice behind them.

"Constable Unsworth, official business?" The maître d', a dark-suited woman, shook hands with Unsworth first. After introductions and a quick explanation of the reason for their visit, Finn let Unsworth do the talking.

His friendly 'you know me, help me out' approach did not dent the professionalism of the maître d'. She cited the hotel policy's strict rules around clientele confidentiality, confirming only that Malcolm Tan dined there often, his daughter joining him once a month. "There are no security cameras in the dining room, our clientele would not tolerate that. Cameras cover only the entrances and exits. You are welcome to the tapes, once you have a warrant. However, I look forward to seeing you here again soon – and bring your colleague." Her handshake was firm, and final.

Like the maître d', Finn too was immune to Unsworth's charm and refused his request to drive back to Henderson.

"She's got a good memory. I don't go there that often," Unsworth said as he got into the passenger seat.

Finn shrugged, none of my business. *But ...*

Unsworth pulled out his mobile, angled the screen away from Finn.

Finn focused on the road, except for occasional glances at Unsworth, impressed at his use of both thumbs. He wasn't on Tinder, no swiping left or right. Whatever he was doing, it required concentration. Finn was grateful. It left him free to wonder why Tova hadn't said she met her father each month.

"We're here." Finn turned off Lincoln Road and headed towards the police station. Unsworth took his eyes off the screen and looked up, as though doubting Finn.

"I'll go tell the boss we got confirmation Ms Tan is in regular contact with her dad," Unsworth said, unclicking his seat belt. As soon as Finn parked, he was out of the car and heading into the building. Keen to get to Pavletich first so Finn couldn't mention that the maître d' recognised Unsworth as a frequent diner at the Cordis?

In itself, not a red flag, eating out, but all cops knew that eyes from within were on them, checking they lived within their means.

"You're overreacting," Finn muttered aloud. Unsworth was young, on a decent wage, no commitments, leaving discretionary dollars available to spend. If Finn didn't have a mortgage to pay, he too could be out wining and dining.

22. TOVA

Tova accepted Sarah's offer, "Come back to mine," but the physical warmth of Sarah's flat did nothing to ward off Tom's frosty attitude. She ignored the way he took Sarah off to the bedroom, and shut her ears to the one-sided argument. She didn't push her luck and ask Tom to help Richard to use the toilet. She unzipped his jeans, pulled them down.

"Tattoos now, Richard?" Tova asked, more to drown out the sound of peeing than any interest in the black ink that snaked from hip to groin. "If you must get a tattoo, why a sports logo? Since when have you been interested in any sport?"

"I don't care what you think," Richard mumbled as he pushed past her. "I didn't do it for you."

She turned her back on him and let him fumble around until he figured out sitting down proved his best bet.

"You can stay. He can't," Tom said as she and Richard reappeared from the bathroom. "We're going to a movie and a meal afterwards. By the time we get back, he'd better be gone."

Sarah hugged her and mumbled, "Sorry, sorry," into her neck.

Tom shut the door behind him with force, his feelings unmistakable.

"You have to tell the police," Tova said. She spooned hot tomato soup into a bowl, aware she would have to feed him.

"No way." His usual cockiness knocked out of him, Richard sounded close to tears. "They'll kill me if I do that."

"They want you to think they will." The exaggeration annoyed her, then she pointed at his injuries. "What have you done to deserve this?"

"I haven't done anything."

"I get attacked and kicked in the face over nothing?"

"I'm so sorry, Tova. They made me ring you."

The missed call. Anger surfaced, then cooled. Having a go at Richard solved nothing. She pressed at the bruise on her cheek, the pain real. "Why did one of them say it was my fault?"

"I told them you'd do whatever I asked," Richard mumbled through his split lip.

Tova snorted. How deluded could he be?

"I had to tell Tupe and Oso something." Richard's tears mixed with the snot and blood from his swollen nose as he used his sleeve. He ignored her offer of a tissue.

Tupe and Oso. Real people, with names.

"It's drugs, isn't it?" Tova didn't attempt to hide her mix of frustration and disappointment.

"They'd keep me supplied, on the cheap." Richard cradled his head on his arm. "All I had to do was ..."

Something illegal, Tova was sure.

"It sounded easy, move into the flat, keep an eye on that Dunn woman." His chin quivered. "Tell them who visited her, if she changed her routine, copy stuff from her computer, emails, spreadsheet, put it on a flash drive for them."

"Spy on her?" Tova's voice rose. Until now their lives had been separate. No friends in common, no reason to meet unless she was salving her conscience, or he wanted money. No guesses why Richard was picked to spy for them: he was gullible enough, enticed by a drug payout, but as far as she knew, he had little aptitude for computers other than to play games.

Then it struck her. "Mrs Dunn refused to rent the flat to you, but having me there solved your problem. Is that what happened?"

Richard studied his thick bandages with a look of puzzlement as if struggling to recall.

"What on earth made you think I'd do your dirty work for you?"

"I didn't expect anything from you." Richard looked straight at her for the first time that evening. "I told Tupe that to get him off my back until I figured out what to do." The whine disappeared and his eyes bored into her. "Served you right, anyway. You owed me, after what you put me through last year. All that crap in the news about your precious mother and my father. Did you ever think how it made me feel?"

Of course she had. She'd tried to make it up to him. Kept an eye on him, didn't expect loans repaid, carried out late-night rescues from dicey bars and did her best to downplay his lifestyle to his father.

"And did you come up with another plan?" She

feared the answer – he broke in, got caught, somehow the Dunns ended up dead.

"Jas was a looker, so I thought I'd have a go there, persuade her to tell me what her mum was up to. I thought it would be easy, she was always slagging off her mum."

"Jasmine?" Tova's throat dried.

"Jas and I ended up ... you know." As quickly as the spark had flared, the fight went out of him.

"You and Jasmine?" A fleeting image of the two of them in her bed making all that noise together. She stopped herself from hitting him.

"Jas said you'd never find out." A moan escaped from Richard. He winced at the effort, his lips parted, and Tova hoped the tears running down his face seeped into his cuts.

"Did you give her drugs?" Tova could think of no other reason the girl would be interested in him. "She was fifteen."

"Sixteen now. She had her birthday a few weeks ago. And I liked her, I really did."

"Some defence that'll be." He hadn't answered her question. "And why are those guys threatening you now? Didn't Jasmine give you what you wanted?" That needed to be rephrased. "I mean, if she provided the information those guys were after."

Ever so slowly, Richard shook his head. "I didn't ask her. I couldn't."

"Which is when the thugs came back?" Tova guessed.

"Last week. Tupe told me no more supplies until I kept my end of the bargain."

"Why not steal her computer?"

Tupe and Oso had no qualms about assault so a bit of theft didn't seem a problem.

"Mrs Dunn couldn't know anything was going on. Tupe said if she found out, they wouldn't get paid and I'd have to cover their expenses."

It was a waste of her time to 'Oh Richard' him. He closed his eyes – his childish, ineffectual avoidance technique. She resisted the temptation to tip the cooling soup over him. Instead, she moved the bowl out of her reach. If Richard wanted any, he could lick it up.

"Things all happened at once last Thursday. Jas rang first, she wanted to see me. Then Tupe had this job for me. It sounded easy, drive some guys somewhere." Richard's swathed hands, like swollen slugs, covered hers. "They said they'd wipe my debt. I'd never have to see them again." The whine returned. "I had no choice."

Tova touched her cheek, her skin cool in spite of the warmth of the room, the discomfort of the bruise strangely reassuring. She eased her bottom, stretched, and pain shot through her hip. Concentrating on the discomfort delayed the inevitable moment she found out that 'somewhere' was Te Atatu.

"You used the BMW?"

"Yeah, how did you know?"

"Good guess," she muttered.

"I'm stuck with Dad's old SUV. You never use the Beemer, so what would you care?"

Three days ago, she wouldn't have.

"After the job, I was supposed to dump the car, torch it."

"Torch? As in burn?"

"I said I had, on some back road near Piha." A sob caught in Richard's throat. "It's such an ace car."

"You didn't do it, did you?" Tova picked up on his use of the present tense. He cared more about a hunk of metal than he cared for his own well-being. "And those thugs found that out." She shook her head, regretted it. The two codeine she'd taken had yet to have any effect and her head throbbed. "Where's the car now?"

"In the garage, at home. If Dad had seen it missing ..."

"Your father is the least of your worries," Tova interrupted. "The police think I drove the car." She rarely swore but in her head, she linked together the swear words she knew in English and Chinese and a few in Māori she'd learned from a student in Tauranga. Their grating sounds didn't ease her panic. "Did you tell that Oso where it is?"

"I can't remember. He bent my fingers, I blacked out."

"Go to the police, tell them everything." She surprised herself saying that. They'd have to keep him out of harm's way, at least until the two guys were caught.

"Tupe's given me a few hours. Can't you get into the house and see if what they want is still there?" In spite of the danger he'd put her in, he still expected her to bail him out.

"I can't get in, not even if I wanted to, which I don't," Tova said. "A cop saw me there this morning, told me I wasn't allowed back."

"A cop? Like, guarding the place?"

"No, he was in the study." But he hadn't taken anything away with him. Maybe he hadn't found what he was looking for. "Even if I get back into the house, it doesn't mean I'll find what you want." She regretted it as soon as she said it.

"What will we do?" Richard asked.

"We? There is no *we*."

How long had they been talking? The movie would be over soon, not long until the deadline for Tom's ultimatum.

23. FINN

The station workroom tables faced each other down the centre, laptops perched on each one, some desks tidier than others. Finn yawned, mesmerised by *Where's Finn?* floating wave-like across his screen. He tapped the keyboard, woke up his unfinished report and scowled at it, willing it to write itself.

He was onto his second coffee from the machine in the hallway. As usual, too much milk diluting the caffeine for all the kick it gave.

"How much longer do you reckon the boss will be? He said five o'clock. It's gone nine and I'm shagged." Unsworth, at the desk beside Finn, rested his head on his laptop.

"Wakey-wakey, everyone." Pavletich appeared at the door. Keyboard taps ceased, voices lowered, then silence; chairs squeaked as they pivoted to face him. "Beddy-byes when we're up to speed." Pavletich stood by the free-standing whiteboard, twirled a black marker in his fingers.

Recording responses meant taking notes and dragging out the meeting. Finn yawned at the thought. But it might be the only way he'd remember everything that was said.

"We're making progress. That's good. Forensics has finished with both murder scenes, and door-knock information has given us some leads about comings and goings at both locations." Pavletich put the marker down gently. "Right, let's get started on suspects."

Don't pick me first. Memories of being singled out in high school, answers eluding him. If only Pavletich had been available to hear his theory about Juliette and her property-buying in private. If he was way off beam, he'd prefer that not to be common knowledge.

"McIntosh, bring everyone up to date about the two boys."

Finn groaned. They'd all have heard the sex doll story by now. Laughter the best way to stave off succumbing to the horror of what people did to each other.

"Karl Kalgour can definitely be eliminated as a suspect," he said. "Pretty sure Jacob Hemona is telling the truth about what he believed the body to be."

"Wish I'd been there to see your face when he tried that excuse," Unsworth called out.

"The boy is thirteen."

"More worldly wise than you, obviously."

Pavletich held up his hand for quiet and the laughter died down. "We're following up on Jacob's information. Hemi Hemona was definitely seen around Te Atatu up to Thursday night. No sign of him since, but we got a response to the trace we put out. The Bay of Plenty force sent word they called in a few favours and they have a lead. One of Hemi's cuzzie bros was not too keen to have him back in the Tauranga area. With any luck, Hemona will return to us by tomorrow."

More laughter, as if Hemi had a choice. Pavletich spun on one foot, turned and paced the room. "Cranston, any ID on the two men Jacob Hemona mentioned?"

"Possible partial, sir." Cranston flicked over a page of his notebook. "Last Thursday, two men visited Mrs Dunn's Grey Lynn brothel around midnight. They spoke to Mrs Dunn, and not long after, she left with them. Unusual, the duty manager said, her boss normally stayed until about five the next morning. The men weren't regulars; she was busy at the time, didn't take much notice. Big and not European was the best she could do." He shrugged. Standard level of assistance in some circles.

Ruling out Richard Tan. No point in stating the obvious, thought Finn.

"Anything more on Mrs Dunn?" Pavletich didn't break stride.

"She did say Mrs Dunn took turns to stay a night at each of her businesses. She didn't work the floor but kept an eye on the girls and the accounts. A decent boss, bit of a snob, used the Mrs title although she had never been married, lived in a fancy house in Herne Bay, pretended to be something she wasn't, worried what the neighbours would think of her occupation and the effect on her daughter if they found out."

"We'll have what's on the security cameras in a few hours. We had to wait for the search warrant, Juliette's manager was worried about client privacy."

Finn looked away from Cranston. One officer doodled on the pad in front of him and Wright let out a yawn. The investigation was getting nowhere fast.

"There was one thing. The woman told me, then retracted it, said she might have got it wrong, out of context. Said I was to forget she mentioned it."

"Spit it out, Cranston."

"A few weeks ago, she overheard Juliette say to someone on the phone that the deal was strictly business, there'd be no freebies."

Pavletich stopped his pacing. "What deal?

"She didn't know."

"It may be nothing, or something. Either way, I want to know. Check her phone records, pin down the time of the call, find out who she was talking to."

Finn pictured the business card in the file box.

"Moving on," Pavletich said, cutting into Finn's thoughts. "Next, Ms Tan."

"Ms Tan's alibi checks out." Ngaire sounded disappointed. "Technically, she had ample time to complete the return trip in the time frame but she didn't have a car; there's no evidence she borrowed or hired a car or that someone else drove her to Auckland. She is who she says she is. Final-year university student, training to be a teacher. Part-time underwear model to pay her way. Nothing to suggest she worked for Mrs Dunn, although we're still waiting for a staff list. It's confirmed she has been in Tauranga for the past six weeks, she attended the school meeting and was at work the following day." Wright tapped the desk. "But, there is the spat with Jasmine."

"That was weeks ago. If it was spontaneous anger, she would have whacked Jasmine then and there. A few terse words is hardly a reason to murder two people." Finn kept his eyes on Wright and hoped Pavletich wouldn't say it often took less.

"Nothing else has come up yet suggesting Ms Tan wanted either of the Dunns out of the way," Wright admitted.

"OK, McIntosh, contact Ms Tan, tell her the meeting tomorrow is postponed but she's not to leave the city. We might need to speak to her again. Right now, we have more important things to follow up."

Wright waited until Pavletich had moved off, his back to them, then nudged Finn and whispered, "You haven't spoken to Ms Tan yet about her fight with Jasmine, have you?"

"Come on, Ngaire. One minute it's a spat and then a fight. Big difference."

"Watch out, Finny. I've seen the way you look when her name comes up. The boss will have, too."

Heat rose up Finn's neck. Was he that obvious? He sat up straighter, gave her a puzzled frown, pretended he didn't understand and paid attention to Unsworth, who had the floor.

"We checked everyone with access to Tan's vehicle seen in Argyle Street – him, his son, his wife and any of his employees. The son uses it the most. Traffic confirm it is at present parked at Malcolm Tan's Howick home."

"No CCTV verifying which Tan was the regular visitor to Argyle Street?"

"Not so far," Unsworth said.

"Dig deeper on Mr Malcolm Tan. Is he a regular at one of the Dunn establishments? Does she attend any functions he does? Do they have business connections? Do they belong to the same clubs or gym, read the same books, both breed Siamese cats? Get the idea? Dig up everything on Mr Tan."

One of the ring-ins from Central put up his hand. Pavletich waved impatiently at him to spit it out.

"Do you think Tan had a thing for young girls? Maybe the mother found out he was giving it to her daughter. She objected. He lashed out and ... whammo."

"Whammo?" Pavletich's exasperation clear. He moved behind the offender's chair. Standing close, he simulated wrapping his fingers around his throat and shaking the life out of him. A few laughed. The offender turned round, flushed red.

"Sunshine, I was informed you had experience and the ability to think." Pavletich's voice carried, heads turned. "Which part of 'dig up everything' was hard to follow?"

The constable mumbled, "Sir."

"Anything yet on Jasmine's social media accounts? Any names of interest cropping up?" Pavletich didn't dwell on the incident, and everyone's attention turned back to him.

"Tomorrow, when the kids are in school," Wright said. "The mobile in her school bag is with the techies, should have the list of calls in and out by tomorrow. It has given us a list of friends to interview. One of them is sure to know if Jasmine had a regular visitor the nights Mrs Dunn was working and, if so, what they were doing."

A parent out of the way, an attractive girl. By the smiles and winks and mutterings of 'Playing music, cards, tiddlywinks', Finn wasn't the only one thinking it was obvious what the girl had been up to.

"Which brings us to Richard Tan." Pavletich's gaze fixed on Finn.

"Richard Tan is a definite person of interest," Finn responded. "Jacob Hemona is not too reliable, keeps changing his story about where his father was on the night. He's sure a young Asian male drove the car to and from Te Atatu. Uniform didn't find Richard at his flat this afternoon or at his usual haunts on K Road, or at the casino. Counties Manukau officers were to check at his father's home. They haven't got back to us yet."

"Why doesn't he tell the lazy sods to get their A into G?" Unsworth murmured, shoulder-to-shoulder with Finn.

The whisper carried in the lull.

Pavletich strode up to Unsworth. "I don't care how short-staffed I am. If you slag off the work of other officers again, I'll send you back to front-line duties, and I'll make sure you stay there. Comprendez?"

Unsworth's face flushed. He wasn't one of Finn's favourite people, but having himself been on the receiving end of a superior's temper, he sympathised. Bawled out was bad enough. To have it done in a crowded room of colleagues was humiliating. It took weeks to get over. It had for him.

He willed Pavletich to get on with the summing up so home time wouldn't be far away and he'd get in at least five hours sleep.

"Before the interruption," Pavletich moved away, back near the door, "I was about to add that we have yet to positively identify the occupants of the car. What we think is that Richard Tan drove the BMW. The two men who collected Mrs Dunn are likely to be the as-yet-unidentified male passengers. Jasmine Dunn was in the back seat, possibly dead already. And Hemi Hemona is involved. Jacob Hemona is our only witness so far, and he's possibly lying, which means triple-check his statement. By tomorrow, I want Richard Tan. I want to know who those two men are. Standover men, by the sound of it, so there's likely a link to Mrs Dunn's business and Mr Malcolm Tan. I'll give the organised crime and Asian liaison crew a hurry-up, see if they have any possible links. Good work, team. Go home, enjoy the hour or so left of Sunday. Sleep well; see you bright and early."

People clapped, some more enthusiastically than others. Finn tapped fingers against his knee. Even that sucked up energy he didn't have. Papers shuffled, laptops powered off, chairs scraped back.

"Can I speak with you, sir?" A quiet talk, just the two of them in Pavletich's office, in case his suspicions were unfounded.

"I'm buggered, McIntosh. If it's important, raise it at tomorrow's briefing." Pavletich waved as he walked down the corridor to his office.

Finn waited until everyone had left before starting up his computer again. It took its time until all the icons fired up; it was as slow as he felt. He opened his emails, clicked COMPOSE.

He tried to order his thoughts before typing. The information in the file boxes wouldn't match what was on her computer files: The way they had been ordered and colour-coded with red and green tags, he was sure she was into dodgy accounting with fabricated accounts on her computer and the real business turnover accounts kept off the work premises. He was also sure that the phone number Cranston hunted down would match the one on the business card in the file box.

He typed, deleted, retyped until he was satisfied with the few lines on the screen. Finn didn't admit he'd been back to the house; Pavletich would figure that out. The find might progress the investigation and overshadow his returning without permission. It was a risk he had to take, even though there was a chance that what he found had no bearing on the case at all.

He reread the email, clicked SEND. The date and time on it would make it clear he had stayed behind. Another point in his favour?

Finn stretched, tilted his head back and yawned. Too easy to fall asleep in the chair. Save a lot on travelling time.

24. TOVA

"I can't sleep, need more painkillers." Richard slumped down beside Tova, curled up on the couch, dozing.

He needed a shower, too. It would have to wait; let her father deal with it. She wasn't ready to give him any sympathy.

"You'll need all your energy to tell your father what you've been up to. You better hope he can convince Mr Zhou to find a way to lessen the barrel load of charges you face."

"I'm so sorry, Tova."

Sorry didn't cut it. She stood up and faced him. "Did you kill Jasmine? Did you?" Her voice rose above Richard's wailing and masked the sound of the front door opening and closing.

"Did he what?" Sarah asked, as she and Tom appeared in the doorway.

"Take the painkillers the doctor prescribed," Tova said, thinking fast, coming up with an answer that might make sense.

Sarah rushed to give her another hug. Tom stayed by the door, keen to usher them out.

"I can't turf him out into the street, can I?"

Tom raised his eyebrows, a look that said it was exactly what she should do.

"It's late. We'll go first thing in the morning."

"It's not too late, it's not even midnight. Besides, the cops are twenty-four seven. I'll ring them for you," Tom offered. Sarah hovered behind him. What had Tom already said to her? Sarah's eyes were red-rimmed, as though she'd cried all the way through the comedy they went to.

"They'll trace the number to you if you ring. Then you'll be more involved. Don't worry about it, Tom, I'll get Richard to his father in the morning. He can sort it out."

"A taxi, then?"

"Once the police know what happened to Richard, they'll ask how we got to Howick. A taxi driver would have to say where he picked us up." It took concentration to keep her voice low and steady. She was too close to losing it with Tom.

"I'll find a taxi in the main street." Richard wilted over the table. Did she have the strength to carry him?

"Don't be silly, you won't be able to cope with Richard on your own." Sarah grabbed the car keys, brushed past Tom. "Don't bother waiting up."

With Richard propped between them, they shuffled to the lift, down to the basement car park and buckled him into the back seat of Sarah's car.

"I'm sorry for all this," Tova said. "I didn't mean to cause trouble between you and Tom."

"I'm the one who should apologise. You're my oldest friend. And it's my flat, after all."

Tova tried to give Sarah a thank-you smile. She feared it was more of a grimace, her face muscles heavy with fatigue. "Head for Howick."

"Where exactly?" Sarah manoeuvred the car out of the building, turned into Broadway and headed up Khyber Pass to the on-ramp.

"You've never been there, have you? I've only been there a few times myself," Tova said, "delivering Richard home without his parents seeing the state he was in. Visits unofficial, of course." Not trusting her memory, Tova read out directions from Google maps on her phone. By the time they were on the Southern Motorway, Richard drooped against the window, already fast asleep, the seat belt tight against his chest, holding him in place.

"Who're you texting?" Sarah asked, alternating her concentration between the road and glancing at Tova.

"Work. I said I'd do that bikini job on Tuesday. I'll have to cancel." The bruise on her hip easy enough to hide, pose side-on to the camera, but no amount of make-up would conceal the large, purple, misshapen circle that decorated her cheek and right eye. Tova pulled out Constable McIntosh's business card and keyed in the number.

"Now who?" Sarah asked.

"The police."

"Good. Tell them to meet us there. Tom and I were worried you might try to keep them out of it." Sarah let out a nervous laugh as if she'd been silly to think such a thought.

Sorry hve food poisoning. Unable to make appointment Monday. Pls let Detective know. Will confirm when better.

Tova clicked back to the map.

Sarah exited the motorway and followed the Pakuranga Highway signs. It took less time than Tova remembered to reach the Mellons Bay turn-off. Maybe because she didn't want to arrive at her father's. The road wound down to the coast with few street lights. Tova indicated the high concrete wall surrounding the buildings on the corner.

"That is one house?" Sarah slowed and hunched over the steering wheel to get a better view through the windscreen, admiring the three-storey white edifice rising behind the wall. "Oh my God it's ..."

A monstrosity, thought Tova, with its mishmash of architectural styles: ground-to-roof Greek columns either side of the imposing front entrance, black metal grilles across the downstairs windows matching the colonial railing running the length of the top-storey balcony, the whole shape of the house spoilt by the add-on of the zigzag fire-escape stairs. The house was out of kilter with the surrounding single-storey wooden houses more suited to a beachside suburb.

"Go to the end of the road, there's a car park," Tova directed. The dashboard clock glowed: 23:48. Neighbouring houses were curtained against the inhospitable September night, and the beachside parks were empty.

"The main bedroom faces the sea. If we go in the front, the security lights will come on and someone might see us. There's a gate by the vehicle entrance." Her simple plan clear in her mind: sneak Richard in, make him comfortable, get away unseen. She was far too tired to face her father now. A text in a few hours telling him to go check on his son would suffice.

It took both of them to carry Richard's dead weight from the car, across the road, to the wrought-iron detail of the impressive automatic gates, replicated in the smaller gate to the side. Beyond, a wide expanse of concrete driveway fronted a four-vehicle garage.

Tova pressed in the four-digit code, trusting it hadn't been changed since Richard moved out. The metal gate swung silently open.

"For a skinny guy, he's bloody heavy," Sarah puffed.

"Shorry," Richard mumbled through his thick lip. He tried to lift his feet higher.

"Shhh, both of you," Tova said, the swish-click of the gate lock too loud, the sound carrying in the still night. Sarah inclined too far to the left. Richard's body sagged, putting more of his weight into her. Steadying herself, feet wide, Tova tightened her arm around his waist.

BOOM BOOM. Explosions of light.

"What's that?" Tova flinched, shielded her eyes. A shadow staggered towards them, growing in size and brightness, shaping into a human fireball. An acrid smell, burning fabric and skin and hair. And its scream high-pitched as it folded forward.

"Get out of the way," Tova yelled, diving sideways, dragging Richard with her, pulling Sarah along. Richard stumbled, legs entangled and they collapsed like dominoes.

Gasping, her lungs filling with smoke and stench, the weight of the world on top of her, Tova squirmed out from under the pile and tugged at what was in reach: Richard's bandages, Sarah's hair, desperate to pull them further away from the burning mound.

25. FINN

Finn headed straight for bed, not detouring to the kitchen and fridge as he often did after a long day at work. Roadworks on the Lincoln Road interchange to the North-Western Motorway meant a detour through Glen Eden and Avondale to Waterview, adding an extra twenty minutes to his normal seventeen-minute commute from station to home. The seventeen-hour shift, with the prospect of a repeat the next several days if they didn't get a lucky break, was enough to put him off his usual supper, scoffing leftover casserole, washed down with a cold beer. Too tired to think of food, too tired to think, period. His fingers fumbled with shoelaces, belt and buttons, and he left his clothes in a jumble on the floor. He fell into bed and his head sank into his pillow.

He dreamt of Tova. She walked towards him, svelte in a clingy black minidress. She morphed into Jasmine Dunn, arms out like a sleepwalker. Then she switched into Tova again, mouthing 'No, no, no.'

A shark with Pavletich's face rose out of the water, jiggling to the 'da-da, da-da, da-da-da-da' of the *Jaws* soundtrack.

Finn groped for his mobile. Still heavy with sleep, he swiped the phone to take the call. That ring tone was assigned to Pavletich.

"Sir?" He glanced at the bedside clock: 4:22.

"McIntosh, fire at Malcolm Tan's in Howick. Ms Tan, her brother and two others. One critical injury, three moderate. They've been taken to Middlemore. Security is watching them, making sure they don't concoct some bullshit to tell us. The Counties people can deal with the fire, but make sure we're in the loop about the findings. Find out what those Tans were doing. This has to be connected to our murders. Get out to Middlemore Hospital first thing. Persuade the doctors to let us interview as soon as. Detective Sergeant Harris is in charge at the Howick end, he'll meet you there."

Pavletich barely paused for a breath.

"Have you seen the latest online? Some smart-arse has come up with 'The Brothel Murders' – nothing like sleaze to sell the news. That slant doesn't help anyone. Play it down. The Dunns are victims first and foremost, and it's our job to get them justice, no matter what."

"Sir," Finn said, by far the safest response, unsure if Pavletich even expected a comment.

"And take Wright with you. Cheer her up."

"Pardon?" That didn't sound right, Pavletich giving permission to cheer Tova up. Did that mean Tova was a moderate injury, not critical?

"You still asleep, McIntosh? Pay attention. Wright puts on a good show but she's unsettled. If she's thinking of quitting, persuade her not to. She's too valuable to lose." The call cut out.

Finn pushed aside the odd request by Pavletich and went straight to his laptop. Tova was the priority. He pulled up the *Herald* site first, clicked onto 'Latest' and skimmed the first entry.

FOUR INJURED IN BLAZE AT PROPERTY MAGNATE'S HOWICK HOME

Four people escaped an explosion that ripped apart a garage housing luxury vehicles at the Mellons Bay Road home of Malcolm Tan, best known for his property company's association with Auckland's 'leaky homes' crisis. The injured, one in a critical condition, have been taken to Middlemore Hospital.

A neighbour, Erika Chan, says she and her husband were woken about 11.40 pm by the sound of a loud explosion, and they ran to their neighbour's house to help. "One of Mr Tan's cars must have caused the fire. He'll be devastated. He loved those cars."

Three Fire and Emergency appliances and crews attended the scene to bring the blaze under control. The fire attracted a large number of onlookers, one saying that he saw the fireball from his home a kilometre away. One eyewitness said, "It wouldn't surprise me if someone had set fire to the place. Malcolm Tan is into all sorts of property deals. He must have trodden on a few toes in his time."

Crews remain at the scene to ensure any remaining hot spots are extinguished. Fire and Emergency investigators are in attendance to examine the charred remains of four luxury vehicles, believed to be a Porsche, a Mercedes, an Audi and a BMW. The spokesperson would not be drawn on the cause of the fire, saying, "It is too early to speculate."

Unconfirmed reports state that the injured are Mr Tan's son Richard, and his estranged daughter Tova, from a liaison with Areta Amahua, the actress who drowned last year. At that time, Ms Tan assisted police with their enquiries into the actress's death. The other occupants of the home, Mr Tan and his wife, are understood to be unharmed.

Finn hesitated over the link to the police communications site. He couldn't quite face seeing his old boss's name attached to the case. Walking away from the laptop, he headed to the bathroom.

A hot shower did little to perk him up. He scoffed down two pieces of toast and half a cup of instant coffee, texted Wright and was on the motorway back to Henderson in less than an hour. He signed out a squad car and headed to Wright's home on Hillsborough Road. Finn wouldn't fancy living on a road that suffered bumper-to-bumper traffic most of the day. Wright said the panoramic views over the Manukau Harbour were worth the slow commute to and from work and time forever lost waiting to turn into or out of their driveway.

Wright would have had as few hours sleep as he had, yet she smiled as she blew kisses to her pyjama-clad husband waving goodbye. "He looks spunky in those PJs, don't you think?" She sounded dreamy and Finn pushed away the thought of how she and her husband spent some of those hours. He already knew more than he cared to about their struggle to conceive.

"On the grounds I will be criticised whatever I say, I will pretend I didn't hear the question," Finn replied.

Ngaire laughed and gave a Queen-like royal wave out the window but her husband had already retreated.

At 7.15, Monday morning traffic flowed, a never-ending river of vehicles. The advantage of the patrol car was that drivers gave way to it. Finn eased it into the steady stream and resisted the temptation to flick the siren on to get to Tova as quickly as possible.

"Any update?" Ngaire asked.

"Speculation about the cause of the fire on the news reports, everything from spontaneous combustion to an insurance scam."

"I meant about those injured."

"Not yet," his reply curt. Get the hint, Ngaire, and shut up. He didn't want to think what that might mean. No news wasn't necessarily good news.

"Bet Pavletich thinks there is a God or karma or whatever he believes in."

Where was she going with this? They were over Mangere Bridge, they'd be at the hospital in minutes.

"You know Pavletich invested in an apartment development, so the rumour goes, and they've turned out to be leaky. Whose construction company but Tan's? Pavletich and the other owners are tied up in a legal wrangle. The apartments are proving expensive to fix, can't sell them, can't rent them out while they're undergoing repairs. See, karma, his own home damaged."

He had heard that but believed Pavletich too professional to allow a personal disappointment to affect his judgement. Nor would he stay on the case if his ability to remain impartial was jeopardised.

Ngaire was on a roll. "It must affect how he thinks of

the father. If he takes down your Ms Tan or her brother in the process, well, too bad."

"She's not *my* Ms *Tan*," Finn snapped back. "What have you against her, Ngaire? You accuse her of murder when it's obvious she didn't have the opportunity, let alone a motive. Now you're willing to let her suffer for whatever it is you think her father *might* have done. You're normally a clear-thinker, but not where Ms Tan is concerned."

"OK, calm down, Finny. I might have overreacted. I shouldn't lay all Māori problems at Areta's feet, and I know I shouldn't blame the daughter for the mother's actions." Wright's sigh was loud, theatrical. "I admit to a smidgen of envy. Look at her – she's young and petite and rich, and I bet there are two or three kids in her future. What am I? Old and dumpy, mortgaged to the hilt, and infertile. I guess I was feeling mean. If I can't have what I want, then everyone else has to suffer, too."

Finn usually let her talk it out, muttering 'Hmm' or 'Oh' at intervals, satisfying her that he was attentive. Ngaire always bounced back. She would apologise for boring him and turn up a day or two later with a thank-you six-pack of beer. Now, he didn't want to listen to her theories or her problems. He cut her short before she unburdened herself any more. "Pavletich is wasting his time on her."

"Finny, look at the whole picture," Ngaire said. "Dysfunctional families will turn on each other – set one against the other, means to an end, as far as Pavletich is concerned. Mr Tan is dodgy whichever way you look at it. That seminar I went to a while back. At lunch, one of the Central guys was moaning about Asian youths getting into trouble and their parents trying to buy them out of it. He gave an example of a rich Chinese property developer's son, lawyered up to get off a possession charge. Who does that remind you of?"

"A father helping his son."

"Sounds to me like a man used to throwing money around to get what he wants."

"Ms Tan has distanced herself from all that."

"Don't be so naïve, Finny. The apple doesn't fall far from the tree."

Finn had been to Middlemore Hospital a few times. Once in his teens after a concussion-causing rugby tackle, once to interview two mob members who almost succeeded in slitting each other's throats, and once as part of a team interviewing a family about unexplained injuries to a six-month-old baby. The place was under constant construction, repairs or renovations; the Accident and Emergency department grew bigger and bigger each year but still failed to cope with increasing daily demands. Each time he visited he had to rethink his bearings.

Finn parked in one of the reserved spaces opposite the entrance. Two other marked police cars were there.

"Looks like Detective Harris might be here already," Ngaire said. "Could be interesting, him and Ms Tan in the same room again. Her complaint about how he conducted the investigation into her mother's death is still open." She undid her seat belt but made no move to get out of the car.

"You know about that?"

"I know you and Harris have history, too." Said with kindness. She would know. Station gossip is a hard thing to avoid.

"You never said anything."

"Thought I'd wait until you told me." The conversation was getting too heavy, even for her, and she offered, "Stay here if you want. I'll go find out what's what."

Pavletich could have sent any of the others with Ngaire. So it was a test. Or an opportunity to put the past behind him.

"I'm coming with you, Ngaire. I'm a big boy now."

As he and Wright walked through the automatic doors, a female constable approached them. "You must be the two from out west. The hospital is short for space but they put three of your four victims in the short-stay unit, with a security guard as requested."

He bit back asking which three, or where the fourth person ended up. His feet clomped heavier than normal in his big boots as he followed behind, the corridor not wide enough for three abreast. Ngaire and the constable exchanged names and time-filling chat, Finn doubting the constable's "Detective Harris will be pleased to see you."

He was in the glassed-walled office behind the nurses' station, deep in a phone conversation, mobile cradled to his ear. His black suit, crisp white shirt and thin, sombre black tie made him look more like an undertaker than a cop. As he listened to the speaker on the other end of the phone, he gestured with his left hand, pointing and splaying fingers. Interpreting the signals, Finn figured that the call was important but they could go ahead, left down the corridor, come back in five minutes. That suited Finn, delay the inevitable.

A security guard stood at the closed door. "Any visitors?" Finn asked.

"The parents of the boy, Mr and Mrs Tan." The guard referred to a notebook. "They stayed with him for fifteen minutes. The mother cried a lot, real upset. Anyone would think her boy was at death's door. He isn't as badly injured as the other guy."

"How long did the Tans stay with the daughter?" Finn, more abrupt than he meant, veered the conversation back to what he wanted to know. The guard shuffled his feet and looked as though he wished to be anywhere but there.

Finn took pity on him, gave him a smile, aware most guards held down two jobs if not three to make ends meet. Most had minimal training to cope with what was literally thrown at them most nights. The last thing this one needed was for a cop to pull rank.

"They didn't." The guard shook his head. "It sounded like the husband and wife argued about it. Hard to tell, as they spoke Chinese." He flicked over a page in his notebook. "A Mr Zhou did, verified by Mr Tan. He came about an hour ago. Wanted to speak to the young man but he was in surgery. Spoke to the girl then left."

"What did he say?" Wright asked.

The man shrugged. "Said he was her lawyer and I had to wait outside. He couldn't have said much, he was only here for a minute, if that."

"Any other visitors?"

"The boyfriend of the one who has gone to the plaster room. Didn't last long, said he couldn't stand hospitals."

"I'm Doctor Patel." A woman hurried towards them, speaking as she approached and glancing at a watch pinned to her lapel. "Sarah will be back soon if they were able to set her broken arm. We've waited a few hours for the swelling to go down. It's a nasty break. Both the radius and ulna were broken above the wrist, consistent with putting her arm out to break her fall. She has epidermal burns to one lower leg where the burn victim fell against her. Her jeans offered a little protection and the ambulance turned up in time." The doctor, matter-of-fact, as though accustomed to police officers at the hospital, wasted no time on pleasantries. Everyone is busy, her manner suggested. "Tova has a non-displaced rib fracture. Consistent with a heavy object falling on her. No burns of any significance. I asked how she and her brother came by their other injuries. It helps to know."

"Other injuries?" Finn asked.

"A cracked cheekbone which looks clean and no deformity, so no surgery required. The bruising makes it look much worse. Plus a severe contusion to her left hip. Both are a few hours older than the rib fractures."

"Did she say how she came by those injuries?" Wright asked, her notebook out.

"She did, a play fight between her brother and his mates and she was in the way." The doctor paused, choosing words carefully. "Unlikely, given her brother's injuries. One broken finger, maybe, but one on each hand? We've had to reset the break on the right. If he follows up with physiotherapy, he should regain most, if not all, movement." Doctor Patel checked her watch again. "I know you have a job to do, but go easy on her, she's had quite a shock."

Wright and Finn entered the small, two-patient ward and positioned themselves either side of her bed. He drew in his breath at the sight of her damaged cheek. Her olive skin appeared paler against the white sheets, and she looked fragile and vulnerable.

"Hello again, Ms Tan," Wright said. She made no comment on injuries and offered no sympathy. Finn was relieved he hadn't told her about the 'food poisoning' text.

"Why are you here?" If Tova felt intimidated, she showed no signs of it, defiance in her eyes, although her voice was a little shaky. "Isn't this out of your region or zone or whatever you call it?"

"We heard you and your brother were involved in a serious incident. And we'd like to know if it's somehow connected to our case," Wright said.

"It was an accident."

"Prone to them, aren't you? Your second within a few hours." Wright folded her arms across her chest and stared at Tova.

Finn usually let Wright lead the questioning. The innocent responded well to her confidence and direct approach. The less-than-blameless lied and soon enough tripped up in their own deceit. His role was to exude testosterone and tackle anyone if he had to, but now he took over, sensing that Wright's approach would shut Tova down.

"The doctor explained Richard's injuries," he said, and gave her a few seconds for that to sink in.

Tova looked at him.

"We'll come back to that." He really didn't want her to continue to lie. "Do you feel up to telling us what happened at your father's home?"

Beside him, Wright sighed, moved her weight to her other foot.

"Sarah and I were taking Richard to his dad. We were on the driveway, near the gate. I thought it was fireworks to start with. Then the explosion and that man was on fire. The smell ... He fell onto us and ..."

"We have progress," Harris called from the doorway.

Tova clutched at the sheet covering her, pulled it up higher, and Finn caught the change in her expression, now anger added.

"You rest," Finn told her and let Wright precede him to the corridor. He shut the ward door and suggested the guard take a ten-minute break, go for a walk, get a coffee, they'd be here when he returned.

"Well, well, McIntosh. Still in uniform, I see. How's it going out west?" Harris extended his hand.

Finn hesitated and then shook the offered hand. Wright followed suit, gave her name.

Harris didn't seem to notice Finn had not answered his question. "First, the investigator says the fire destroyed the four vehicles in the garage. Security light and alarms cut, accelerant used. Second thing, the burn victim has a name, Osovale Vavau. Lives in Kingsland, works as a bouncer at one of the clubs on K Road, has a history. Word is, does a bit of enforcing on the side."

Wright raised her eyebrows at Finn. Too much of a coincidence – Vavau, one of the two men they were waiting to ID?

"How is he, this Vavau?"

"Critical, last I heard, McIntosh. I don't accept Ms Tan's story about him strolling past. Mind you, I don't believe anything that woman says."

Finn did his best to remain poker-faced. He concentrated on counting his breaths, *in for four, out for four.*

"Goran thinks there's a link between his case and this fire, and he's pissed off with me because my men didn't get round to checking out the Tan place as he'd asked. Spread too thin, we were, yesterday. What with boaties in trouble on the Manukau, two motorway head-ons, a missing kid at Rainbow's End plus the normal day-to-day cases, checking on that car was way down the list. I had to listen to him sound off at me about valuable evidence destroyed. There's only so much I can do, we're short-staffed too." He sounded contrite.

"OK." Finn accepted the confession at face value. It was Pavletich's problem.

"Oh yes, another thing. Goran wants you to deliver Ms Tan to the station for questioning. The doc said there's no need for her to be kept in, so I guess that means now." He jabbed the air. "And this happened on my turf, so I better be kept informed about what she does and says." Harris walked out but not before Finn saw him grin.

"Does anyone get on with him?" Ngaire waited until Harris had disappeared around the corner to ask.

"Those who are like-minded."

"His loss, you're our gain, Finny."

Finn headed for the Burns Unit, leaving Wright to get Tova discharged and make sure the charge nurse had the phone numbers to ring as soon as Richard Tan was out of surgery and able to be interviewed.

"Cardiac arrest. Died on the operating table. Overweight and a smoker. Add burns to seventy-five per cent of his body, plus the hit in the back by that piece of flying metal." The nurse giving the details added, "I'm sorry."

Forty minutes later, Finn, back at the car, watched Wright and Tova walk towards him. Seeing them side by side emphasised Tova's slimness and Wright's solid frame. The uniform didn't help.

"How is that man?" Tova asked.

Finn could lie or put her off. Neither was the right thing to do. It was band-aid moment again. Tova would find out soon, and he sensed she wouldn't thank him for pussyfooting around her.

"Mr Vavau died."

Tova's lips moved. No sound came out. What little colour she had drained from her face. Finn moved towards her, ready to catch her if she fainted.

"That complicates things," Wright said. "Don't suppose he said much before he died?"

"Didn't regain consciousness."

Wright, gentler than she was sometimes known to be, directed Tova to sit in the back of the car and slid in beside her. The brown paper bag holding Tova's painkillers rustled with the movement.

He drove out of the hospital and into the heavy traffic, half paying attention to the road, half listening to Wright, acting like a mum keeping a child's mind occupied with her chatter, distancing them from the likelihood of a throw-up or meltdown. "That's what I like about my job, two days never the same. I haven't been to Middlemore Hospital in yonks; sure has grown. Your friend Sarah will be out tonight, maybe tomorrow. You can look after each other," Wright said.

A quick flick of his eye to the rear-view mirror: Tova, eyes closed, head back against the seat.

"My gear, my laptop is still at the backpackers. I should have checked out yesterday but with everything that's happened ..." Tova opened her eyes, caught him looking at her.

Wright tapped her watch, gave Finn a 'can't be late for the boss' look. Finn ignored it, veered out of the motorway lane to head west and took the Khyber Pass off-ramp to Queen Street. He parked on the yellow lines outside the backpackers, turned off the ignition and watched as Wright and Tova entered the hotel.

Just when Finn thought there must be a problem, they returned. Wright tapped the boot, waited for Finn to open it and placed Tova's bag inside.

"The room had been cleaned and relet. The guy on the desk was peeved when he saw Tova, made a big thing about checkout times and rules to be followed. I persuaded him not to charge Ms Tan for the extra day. He had to go get a key to the storeroom and … Sorry, too much information."

Finn did a U-turn, headed back along K Road and onto Great North Road to the North-Western Motorway. The exit to Waterview tempted him. After facing Harris again and seeing Tova in the hospital bed, what he needed was a beer, but it was only mid-morning. What he'd get was a mug of none-too-appealing coffee at the station and Pavletich on everyone's case. He glanced in the rear-view mirror again.

"Ms Tan, the guard said your lawyer visited, spoke to you in Chinese. What did he say?" Finn hoped for kind words.

"Mr Zhou ordered me not to speak to the police without him present."

The rest of the trip was in silence.

26. TOVA

Tova hadn't intended to sound rude. Constable McIntosh had blanched when he saw her in the hospital. Surely that was genuine, not what she expected from a police officer. Constable Wright's chatter most of the drive back to Henderson made it hard for her to concentrate on how to get through the interview without making it worse for Richard. If Wright had stopped talking and if he had said something kind, she might have told him what Mr Zhou had said: 'You are foolish, like your mother. Do not speak to police until I am present.' Why had he mentioned Areta?

She was still thinking about Mr Zhou when Pavletich, Wright and McIntosh sat opposite her, placing identical ring binders on the table in front of them. They dispensed with niceties. No offer of coffee or water, no sympathy for her injuries.

Pavletich launched straight into his attack. "People who lie make me suspicious. You've lied to me, Ms Tan."

His gaze was intense. If she hadn't lied to the A and

E doctor, things might have turned out differently. She'd repeated that lie to the hospital doctor, but it was the same lie. She'd lied about Oso, said he was a guy out walking his dog at the wrong time, but guys like Oso had mates far scarier than the police. They would come after Richard if she dobbed them in. The rest, omissions perhaps.

Now I'm thinking like Richard.

Pavletich ran his fingers along the table edge like a pianist feeling the keys before launching into his pièce de résistance. "You failed to mention that Jasmine had been in your flat. You also said there was no bad feeling between you and the Dunns, yet we have a witness who says you and Jasmine were yelling at each other the day you left for Tauranga. You didn't think that might be relevant?" Pavletich eased back in the chair and folded his arms. "My officers tell me you wish to wait for your lawyer."

Did she? Once out of surgery, Richard needed Victor Zhou by his side, making sure he didn't incriminate himself further. She would do this interview alone, show Mr Zhou and her father, and herself, that any attempt at harassment would not overwhelm her and not provoke her to say things she didn't wish to.

Even if Mr Zhou was available, it might take him some time to arrive. She'd be left in the bare, unwelcoming room. Or, like last year, made to sit it out in a holding cell. And until she understood his comments about Areta, she was in no mind to wait obediently for him.

"I'm not under arrest? I can go when I want?"

"Yes, Ms Tan, you're volunteering to help us with our enquiries, clarify some details, help us understand what happened at your father's home. Let's start with your argument with Jasmine."

"She was unhappy with me. I didn't give permission for her to use my flat while I was away." Tova kept it brief, having learnt well from Mr Zhou. She stopped herself adding, 'And that's the truth'. It would sound anything but. Soon she would have to stretch to soothe the constant ache under her ribs. "I'm convinced she used it anyway."

"That accounts for the fingerprints," Finn said.

"We'll cross-check with more neighbours," said Pavletich. "See if any heard what was said."

Wright picked up a pen, drew a number 1 on a fresh blank page in her folder, circled it, as if it was to be the first point of many.

Pavletich pressed on. "You lied about Oso Vavau."

Tova willed the detective to stop tapping his fingers on the table. The beat was impatient, irregular, a novice drummer. It was annoying. Perhaps that was his intention.

"He was no passer-by, Ms Tan. We now know that Richard did odd jobs for the Vavaus. Is this what happened? Richard used your car to dispose of Jasmine Dunn's body, and Oso was there in the garage giving it a new paint job, new number plates, ready to sell it on, or stripping it down for the parts. What went wrong? You didn't intend for Oso to die, did you?"

"We didn't know he was there," she replied calmly. "He's no friend of Richard's."

"What was the relationship?" Wright asked, her pen poised.

"Richard owed them money." Informing on her brother made her feel sick.

"So he had a motive to get rid of Oso?" Pavletich sat up straight and shot a glance at his officers.

"Pardon?" Just like Detective Harris, making the few facts he did have fit the scenario he wanted. Richard drove the car. That was all he did. "Richard doesn't know how to blow up a car." Was she sure of that? How-to guides were easily found on the Internet.

"It's amazing what you can google," Pavletich said. "Easy enough if you know how – rig the car to explode when the ignition is turned on. Did Richard know Oso was picking up the car?"

"It wasn't Richard. He hasn't been back here since before ..." Tova's ribs ached and she pushed her chair back.

Instantly Wright was up, her baton pulled from her belt. McIntosh lifted out of his chair, in position to hurl himself at her. Pavletich remained seated but pushed his chair back away from the table.

"Sudden movements are not a good idea, Ms Tan," Wright said.

Her reaction told Tova they knew of her response last year to Harris's constant goading, lunging at him.

"My ribs," Tova said. The painkillers she had taken at the hospital had worn off.

Pavletich signalled for her to sit again. "Will you be able to continue?"

The last thing she wanted was to drag the interview out.

"Your brother's injuries are a Vavau signature," Finn continued, taking her silence as agreement. "Did they say they'd wipe the debt if he did a job, used a vehicle untraceable back to them? Was that it? Richard didn't follow orders, didn't get rid of the car?"

Good cop again, full of kindness and concern. He played the part well. Wright was the female presence in case she became hysterical, needed to be restrained. And this time Pavletich was competing with Wright to be the bad cop. Last year, it had been Detective Harris who promised he'd look into her claims that Areta might be dramatic but never suicidal. His attitude changed after the meeting with Victor Zhou. Tova having a lawyer challenged him in some way.

She had to have faith in them. She had no one else. McIntosh wasn't like Harris, she was sure of that, and he appeared to trust the other two. Even the dislike for her evident in Wright's manner was more honest than Harris's original concern ever was.

"Oso was already there."

"Did you see the other man, Tupe?"

"No." Which meant he was still out there, able to hurt Richard.

"According to the fire investigation people, it's possible someone tried to rig one of the cars to explode." Pavletich watched her closely. "Your car, apparently."

"It wasn't Richard. He couldn't bring himself to destroy it when his life depended on it, even though he was terrified of those two men and what they would do to him if they found out."

"Nasty types, that's for sure. If Oso was rigging the car, he wasn't as clever as he thought, wired it up to the accelerant but didn't leave enough time to get out before the whole place blew up."

"He didn't deserve that." A long jail term, Tova thought, not incineration.

"It could have been your brother. Or you," McIntosh said, and Tova noticed the sudden jerk of Pavletich's head.

"The thing is, Ms Tan," Pavletich turned back to look

at Tova, "Oso Vavau wasn't known for his powers of higher reasoning. Scaring people, intimidating, bashing them up, yes, but a technical job involving wiring and petrol and timing? I doubt Oso thought of that all by himself. He was acting on orders. Whose?"

McIntosh, less combative, reworded Pavletich's question. "Help us and we'll keep you both safe until Tupe Vavau has been located. Did your brother ever mention if the Vavaus were working for anyone?"

He's right. The sooner Richard faces up to his role in the Dunns' deaths, the better. He wouldn't see it that way. He'd follow the unwritten code of never dob in a mate even though those mates had thrashed him.

"Richard never told me who their Boss was. I don't know if he was sure there even was one. He thought they used that as an extra threat, you know, like kids, saying their father was better, bigger – a greater fear."

"Murder is an escalation for the Vavaus. We can't see a reason for them to kill the Dunns unless they were doing someone else's bidding." Pavletich paused. "We have to look into the possibility that Richard worked alongside them willingly. Things went wrong after the Dunns died."

"No," Tova said with confidence. "Richard saw the immediate solution, do the work, reduce his debt. He was too scared to question what they asked him to do."

"Why didn't he borrow the money?"

"He knew I didn't have that sort of money. Asking his father would mean admitting he was taking drugs. The people he hangs around with are always broke."

"You took Richard to Howick," Pavletich said.

"To his father," Tova said, aware of the sudden change of tack.

It was Wright's turn. "Ah, yes. This is the father you said you had little to do with. You use his surname, have lunch with him every month and he bought you that expensive car." She sat back. "You were the link with the Dunns. I'm not sure the debt story holds up. Did Malcolm want his son to join the business, learn from the Vavaus, but Richard was too wasted, ruined the plan?"

Tova indicated she wanted to stand. Both Wright and Pavletich nodded permission; McIntosh looked concerned. She held on to the back of the chair; some basic barre exercises might calm her. She imagined the cops' startled reaction if she did. Guaranteed to confirm she was capable of aberrant behaviour, when she needed to satisfy them that she wasn't involved, nor was her father.

"I've already mentioned this to Constable McIntosh. Using my father's surname gives me more anonymity than if I used Amahua." Advice she had acted upon from Mr Zhou. Sarah's Tom and her university tutor had agreed. Losing her temper wouldn't convince them. She spoke more slowly, in an attempt to lower her heart rate. "How my mother's life ended is what people think of every time they hear that name. They wanted to talk about it. I didn't."

It was still hard, the emotions too close to the surface. She hurried on. "I meet my father for a few hours once a month. We reminisce about Areta, remember the fun times, keep her memory alive. And he complains about Richard." How did that sound to the police? "Richard has been stupid, he drove my car, but that's all. And it's ridiculous to suggest my father has anything to do with the Dunns' deaths."

"Is it?" Pavletich asked. "So many things point back to Malcolm Tan. He has financial interests in many businesses – import, export, construction, property development. We hear he has a significant investment in the new casino."

So they'd found that out. She knew from conversations overheard, Malcolm preferring the silent business partner role. She stretched again, breathed in as she did so, pressed her hand against her ribcage. "Like I said, I have little to do with him." Which had been the case since she found out those business trips were to Howick, to his legitimate wife and son. She recalled fights with her mother: *How can you let him treat you like that?* Areta's answer, always the same: *I love him, he loves us. It's how it is.*

"Areta opposed his interest in the casino, didn't she?"

"What has that to do with the Dunns?"

"I don't know yet. Maybe nothing," Pavletich admitted. "Areta's objection must have caused a rift with Malcolm."

"They disagreed on its benefits, that's all."

"You accused your father of killing your mother."

"I didn't mean literally." Would she ever be able to let go of the feeling that someone else had to be held responsible? Areta would never have done that to herself. To her.

"There's a lot of opposition to the new casino," Pavletich said. "Not only the gambling but also the high-end escort business it brings. Investors need to know it will make them money. Perhaps Juliette Dunn's city brothels were seen as competition."

That line of argument suggested that someone only had to be patient, let her brothels fail, up against the glitz and glamour the new casino could offer. She didn't voice her idea. Nor did she feel inclined to admit she'd already linked the knowledge of Mrs Dunn's real source of income and Richard's confession about the flat to Tupe and Oso.

"You're wrong. My father had nothing to do with Juliette or Jasmine's death."

"Maybe not directly, but someone was yanking Tupe and Oso's chain. By your own admission, you know little of his business dealings. How can you be so sure?" Pavletich eased back in the chair.

"Go after this Tupe guy, instead of wasting time with me." Tova was tired and sore and hungry and wanted out from the claustrophobic room, a tension headache building up behind her eyes. "May I go?" She had lasted so well, why did she ask permission now, end on a childlike note, not the self-assured exit she'd hoped for.

"One last question." Pavletich coughed to clear his throat. He sounded tired. "How well did your brother know Jasmine Dunn?"

Too well. Not well enough.

"She recently had an abortion. Does your brother know anything about that?"

Tova's ribs hurt with her sudden intake of breath. "I found out last night that he knew her."

Pavletich indicated to the other officers to stand. At the door, he turned back. "The police in Tauranga inform us you're related to Hemi Hemona. You failed to mention that, too."

She'd read that name on the news app, a 'person the police wished to speak to' in connection with the murders.

"I don't ..."

Pavletich scowled at her. "Like I said earlier, holding back information isn't helpful."

"That's the truth. I don't know who he is." She hugged herself and winced at the pressure. She focused on the ache, let it overtake the flash of resentment towards Areta for never warning her about any relatives.

"The Amahuas and Hemonas grew up together. That's another link between you and my case. What else aren't you telling me, Ms Tan?"

Tova held his gaze. *Whatever I say, he'll twist it to suit his own ends.* "I've told you the truth." What would he think if she admitted not only did she know little about her mother's upbringing, but she had rarely asked Areta when she had the opportunity?

"We'll see about that. You can go for now. We'll be comparing the statements from your friend Sarah and her fiancée, and from your brother. Any further surprises or lies and I'll charge you with obstruction." Pavletich stood. "Make sure we know where to find you. McIntosh, get the details."

Wright, like a one-woman entourage, trailed in Pavletich's wake.

"I'll stay with my friend Sarah in Newmarket." Tova repeated the address. He wrote it down. "Can I go now?"

"I'm sorry, it's not easy," Finn said. "Are you all right?"

"Yes, of course I am," Tova said, although the bombshells Pavletich had dropped weighted her down, too much to process. She had no intention of falling for his kind face and sympathetic words, being familiar with the tactic, assign the right officer to break down her reserve.

"I know the way," she said, but Finn walked down the stairs with her, waited while the woman behind the reception counter returned her overnight bag. No unauthorised gear of any kind beyond the reception,

Tova had been told, and she had dutifully surrendered hers. It contained clothes, nothing incriminating if they rummaged through it.

"I'll need to get back into my flat to clear my gear out. You have my key," Tova reminded Finn.

"Right, so I do. I'll organise it. Tomorrow, or the next day." Finn paused. "Depends on what the boss says."

"If you're offering Ms Tan a lift, McIntosh, this boss says there's a perfectly good train service from Henderson. Buses, taxis too." Pavletich appeared from behind them, sounding cross.

Tova turned her back on both of them and headed for the exit, giving no indication she heard Pavletich shout out, "McIntosh, concentrate on your job. Get to Te Atatu. Speak to Mrs Hemona about Areta Amahua. Take Wright."

27. FINN

Finn was sure Pavletich had raised his voice on purpose. Tova kept on walking, head high, didn't look back, paid no attention at all to Pavletich's rant. "Do a bit of PR work, too; check on that Kalgour kid while you're there."

Finn grunted. He'd had in mind a quiet café, if such a thing existed in hip-hop Henderson, buy Tova a decent coffee, do his bit for police public relations and defend Pavletich's angle of questioning. And hint at two things: if she was related to Hemi Hemona, own up; and if Pavletich asked to speak to her again, bring her lawyer.

The café option a no-go, Finn went looking for Ngaire. He found her with her laptop, fingers poised over the keyboard.

"Come on, help me out, speak to Mrs Hemona for me," Finn pleaded. "She'll take to you better."

"Scared of the bad lady, Finny?"

"Hardly." Not scared, wary.

"Tell me your version of what happened between you and the interesting Detective Harris first, then I'll decide."

He persisted with his persuasion. "I'll let you drive."

"Tempting, but the boss wants these reports. How about you type them, I'll check your spelling and grammar, and then you tell me the details on the way to Te Atatu."

"Ah, no." Less than a second to consider the offer. Out and about trumped any time inside, and he wasn't ready to spill his guts to her. Fingers crossed Unsworth was too busy, too.

Luck was on his side. He collared Cranston before Unsworth reappeared from the toilet. Cranston drove, leaving Finn free to gaze out the passenger window. As they passed a bus stop on Lincoln Road, he caught a glimpse of Tova reading the timetable. She wouldn't have to wait long; buses into the city were frequent. He resisted the urge to wave.

"Can I run something by you, in confidence?" Cranston drove just below the speed limit, slowed right down before the traffic lights flashed to amber and pulled to a stop more than a car length behind the car in front. Finn wondered if he was always this cautious.

No. There's enough on my mind already without adding your problems. "OK," Finn agreed. Hear him out.

"It's Unsworth," Cranston said. "I recognise the signs, saw them often enough in my pastor work."

"Signs of what?"

"I've known him a while and lately, he's been different. More irritable." Cranston sounded genuinely worried.

Cranston could be describing them all. "It's a murder enquiry, long hours, getting nowhere fast."

The lights changed and Cranston set off slowly. More time to talk.

"No, it started before the case. He's lying, too. I asked what he was doing on his mobile the other day and he shut it down, said he was checking the news. He wasn't. He was on a gaming site."

"He's gambling?" Finn had little experience of the gambling addiction but he knew the basics. Unsworth fitted some of the characteristics, competitive, impulsive.

"He often used to ask for a few dollars to get him through until payday. He's stopped doing that. Last week he invited the wife and me out for a flash dinner."

"He must be on a winning streak." Which wouldn't last.

"I'm worried he's gone to loan sharks."

More fool him. What did Cranston expect him to do? Nothing either of them could, or should do, unless Unsworth's work suffered.

Cranston took the Te Atatu exit, got to the right-hand turn down into the Hemonas' street when he said, "I hope I'm wrong."

Finn asked Cranston to stop at the Kalgour house, get the easy visit over first. The response to his knock was a loud wail. "KK, if that's Jacob's mother again, I'm not home."

"It's Constables McIntosh and Cranston," Finn called.

Mrs Kalgour opened the door, her eyes red and puffy from rubbing. "Did she ring you?"

Once inside, sitting at the kitchen table, it took Finn ten minutes to understand what had happened. Cranston took notes, trying to keep up.

Finn did what he was trained to do, repeated the gist of the story, made sure of the salient facts in the correct order. He'd have to check Mrs Hemona's version, but his gut told him that Nell Kalgour hadn't embellished her account of their altercation.

"At approximately 3.30 pm, you were at the Hemona house to pick up Jacob for soccer practice as he wasn't waiting with KK at the school as you expected. His mother spoke to you. She accused KK of spreading lies. She said Jacob was bullied as a result and she was keeping him home for a few days. She threatened you, saying if you didn't shut KK's big mouth she would come round and do it for you."

"You left out the swearing." Mrs Kalgour grinned and colour returned to her cheeks. "And she can't figure out why I've never wanted to be friends."

While his mother had been recounting events, KK had been studying his shoes with great concentration. "Jacob told his mates what he'd seen at the beach. I didn't blab."

KK's voice wavered and his mother stroked his arm.

"I'll have a word with her." The hair on the nape of Finn's neck rose at the thought.

"I don't appreciate her yelling at me in the street. And after all I've done for her boy. Poor kid. With parents like that, what chance does he have?"

Finn didn't reply. Jacob's best chance was to make a conscious decision not to follow in his parents' footsteps. It took a strong kid to make that choice.

He was tempted to accept the offer of tea, coffee or water. He rarely took up such hospitality. It wasn't done for police officers to ask to use the bathroom and officers seen going into public toilets always raised suspicions, one way or the other. Pity any poor person who had entered just before them.

"If she didn't call you, why are two of you here? What's happened? You don't need to take KK to the police station, do you?" Mrs Kalgour's eyes filled up.

"Nothing like that. We were in the area, thought we'd check on KK."

"That's considerate," she said. "We took your advice and told him not to speak about it to anyone except us. KK says he hasn't. The other day a reporter tried to speak to the boys after school. That's why I've been driving them."

"Yeah, he wanted Jacob and me to show him where we saw the body. *I* didn't."

Finn picked up on the emphasis KK put on the I. "Did Jacob show him?"

"He must have. He told me later that someone had put flowers where the body had been."

"Flowers?" Finn hadn't heard if anyone was assigned to check. Some killers were unable to stay away, like arsonists hanging around to admire their creation. Some returned to relive the excitement, a few to seek forgiveness. Finn recalled hearing about a killer, caught by a signed card left at a murder scene, the one name police couldn't place as a relative or friend. The chances of that happening now were nil, the way total strangers placed flowers at tragedy sites. The Lady Diana public outpouring of grief syndrome put paid to that.

Cranston engaged Mrs Kalgour's attention, got her talking about the neighbourhood, while Finn took KK aside. "Have you remembered anything?" he asked.

"No, sorry. Mum reckons I'm getting confused with what I saw, all mixed up with what I've seen on TV and what Jacob's been saying."

No gain in pushing the kid.

"We're sure to get a result soon," Finn's parting words to Nell Kalgour. "You needn't worry any more."

The afternoon wintry sun had long since lost any warmth. Leaving Cranston with the vehicle, Finn took the walkway to the beach. If the local community cop was keeping tabs on the site then he'd wasted only his own time. If that hadn't happened, a visual record of remembrances at the site might earn him a brownie point with Pavletich.

Ragged crime-scene tape, arcing from branches and the post holding the rāhui sign, fluttered in the light breeze off the sea, announcing to any ghouls where the body had been found. He'd seen such signs before where a person had died and knew the local iwi would have declared the area temporarily prohibited, including asking that no fishing be conducted in its proximity for three days.

That hadn't stopped a number of people. A short row of cellophane-wrapped flowers of the type for sale at most dairies, plus a pot plant and a miniature teddy bear with a balloon attached, now deflated, clustered near the path, within the tapu area.

A figure squatted just outside the makeshift cordon, her head bowed. Praying?

"How long have you been here?" Finn calculated the route, bus speed and traffic and the time he'd been at the Kalgours'.

Tova twisted round, overbalanced. He reached out to help her up, half expecting a short, sharp electric shock when he made contact, like the one he often received off his car door.

"Ten minutes or so. Why?" She ignored his helping hand, rose to her feet and took a step back.

"Weren't you taking a bus into the city?" Finn compounded his nervousness with another short, sharp query, his tone accusatory.

"An impulse decision," Tova explained after a moment's hesitation. "The Te Atatu bus came along first. I had the crazy idea that I'd find the Hemonas. Fortunately, Google let me down." Tova held up her phone as proof. "Not one Hemona listed for Te Atatu in the White Pages, so I had no way of finding their address. Just as well – I had no idea what I'd say. Mum refused to speak of her whānau for a reason, I guess."

Tova looked so small and sad. What she needed was a friend to give her a hug, not a police officer to question her. The best he could do was give advice.

"Talking to any Hemona is not a good idea," Finn said. In his experience the Hemonas weren't good people. And if any familial relationship existed, he hoped it would turn out to be too distant to be material to the case.

"I figured that. Anyway," Tova continued, "it wasn't too hard to work out where Jasmine Dunn ... It's been on the news and in the papers. I thought I'd say goodbye. Her mother can't, so I ..." Her voice trailed off.

"But you didn't like Jasmine."

"I didn't wish her dead, though. She must have been so frightened and all alone. Like Mum, at the end. It's helped me sometimes; I spend time where Mum died. I like to think she knows when I'm there. So maybe Jasmine knows too."

Should he say something comforting? Would that overstep the boundary between officer and witness? Where was Wright when he needed her?

"Sounds crazy, I expect," Tova said.

No, he understood that need to stand at the last place the deceased had been, a farewell of sorts. A jumble of ideas floated in his mind about perpetrators returning to the scene of the crime, alongside his gut feeling that she was innocent and wanting to walk away before she revealed too much. But it was his job to find out as much as he could, report it to Pavletich.

"OK, don't glare at me," Tova's irritation obvious. "It was spur-of-the-moment. You're not going to make anything of it, are you, like tell your boss?"

Finn glanced around, relieved they were alone, not wanting anyone to witness the petite woman tongue-lash the big cop.

"Sorry, you're doing your job, I know, but everything I say or do gets twisted to suit."

"Ms Tan, I ..." Finn chewed his bottom lip. What could he say?

"Oh, never mind," Tova dismissed him. She pointed to the meagre line of flowers. "Not many, are there?" Not considering the number of Facebook friends Jasmine had. Maybe it was too difficult for them to get to Te Atatu.

From what had been found out so far, Juliette had few friends and the Dunns lacked relatives. Most likely, compassionate locals put them there.

Her mobile pinged. "Go ahead," he said when she hesitated. "Then go home, Ms Tan. We've had a difficult afternoon, it's getting late; it'll be dark soon." He meant it kindly and inclusively, all in a trying situation together, as he had been taught.

He watched while, head down, she pressed keys and took longer to read the text than the short, illuminated passage called for.

Tova spun round, brandishing her phone at him. "Life should be much easier for you now. Richard's text says he's been arrested. I suppose it's too much to expect you'll tell me the details."

He remembered the notes on her file. Cool, reserved, but quick to react. Proof she was capable of a *crime passionnel*? Wright would think so. Loyalty, a quality to be admired. That's what drove her anger, he decided.

"The charge is accessory to a crime." No reason not to tell her, not if Richard had been permitted to contact her. Pavletich had told him and Wright the bare facts immediately before interviewing Tova. "He'll get bail if he agrees to cooperate, surrender his passport, stay at an approved address and be available at any time for further interviews."

For the second time, she turned her back to him.

"I'll leave you to say your farewells," Finn said, hoping Tova would at least look at him. She didn't. "OK, I have to go see Mrs Hemona, do my job." A job he didn't particularly like right at that moment.

Finn retraced his steps along the path, back up the walkway beside the Hemona house. He'd forgotten to take any photos.

"Did that Kalgour bitch call you? Her kid's a lying little shit." Mrs Hemona stood well within his eighteen-inch personal zone. Aggression her best form of defence. "He's fallen out with Jacob, and this is his way of getting his own back. He wasn't there. How would he know if I went to the beach that night?"

Finn willed his face not to let on it was the first time anyone had said anything about *her* being at the beach. He was grateful Cranston stood beside him, a witness.

"You sure KK said that?" Already the two versions didn't match. Finn eased one foot forward, ready to wedge his foot in the gap if she did try to slam the door.

"Of course I'm bloody sure. Jacob told me. I'm not putting up with these people thinking they're better than me. I told her to mind her own fucking business."

"You admit you verbally assaulted Mrs Kalgour? Did you threaten her son with physical violence?"

Mrs Hemona's demeanour changed as soon as Finn used the jargon. From hostile to simpering in one move. "I was upset. No big deal. Look, I'll go and apologise, if that's what you want."

The last thing Finn desired was Repeka Hemona going anywhere near the Kalgours. "Let things cool for a few days. I'll have a word with the deputy principal at the school about the boys, get her to work out some sort of mediation."

Finn had guessed right. Mrs Hemona back-pedalled fast. "Don't you waste your time. KK's mum and me, we're real good friends, we'll work it out. Kids, eh?"

Finn realised, in spite of the commotion, Jacob hadn't appeared. "Where's Jacob? Can I see him?"

"He's in his room. He's too upset to talk. His best friend, turning on him like that."

Mrs Hemona maintained the indignant, hurt-parent role. Tiny beads of sweat appeared along her hairline, and she positioned herself, her weight against the door, foiling any attempt to barge in.

Finn permitted her the one modest victory. He'd get to Jacob. First, he needed the information Pavletich wanted. "We've learned that Hemi is related to Areta Amahua."

She shrugged. "His whakapapa is a long one." Repeka's chin lifted. "If you dig deep enough, he's related to every Māori in the country, one way or another. Doesn't mean he knows them all."

"He grew up with her." If she continued to deny the connection, he'd want to know why. "You and Hemi were at her tangi last year."

"Oh, her," Repeka said. "His cousin or something. Seem to remember he said she was a stuck-up bitch, out to help herself. Not one to keep in touch with the whānau, you know."

He had the answer Pavletich wanted, and more. The Hemonas knew Areta, and Repeka as good as admitted she was on the beach that night.

"I'd appreciate it if I could speak with Jacob."

"Fuck off. You've harassed my family enough."

The defiance didn't surprise Finn. Harassment, racism, sexism, ageism, whatever 'ism' helped put the blame anywhere but where it belonged. He'd been put through a number of seminars on how to be politically correct, not that they were referred to as that. 'Diversity awareness' the latest term. He and most of his colleagues were fair and unbiased and kept to the law, no matter who broke it. Faced with any confrontation, his stomach tightened, developed a hard knot. One ill-considered word, comment or wrong look undoing his career in seconds. It was like walking a tightrope in a strong southerly.

"A quick word with him, that's all. Or I can interview him at the station."

Repeka stomped away, yelling. Finn was sure she'd weighed it up: face more wasted hours at the station or have Jacob interviewed in his own home, where she had more control over her son, and the police.

She didn't shut the door, and he heard the mutterings coming from Jacob's room. For all he knew they were bolting out the window. He was about to signal to Cranston to check the side of the house when Mrs Hemona returned with a reluctant Jacob.

"See what you lot've done? KK gave my poor Jacob a beating and kids are calling Hemi a murderer."

Jacob's shoulder dipped under the pressure from his mother's hand. He sported a black eye and a cut lip. No way had KK inflicted those injuries on his taller, stronger former friend. His father had been gone two days, so that left his mother. Jacob had paid for shooting his mouth off.

Finn glared at Repeka long enough so she realised he didn't believe her. He pulled out his mobile. Let her wonder who he was ringing. Once through to Pavletich, he'd move away so Repeka couldn't overhear him passing on that she might be more involved than previously thought.

"A mother has a right to discipline her kid," Repeka said and snatched at his phone. She stopped in mid-grab. "What the fuck is she doing here?"

The screech in Finn's ear was loud enough to burst his eardrum, her expletives clear. He staggered back, dropped the phone back into his pocket as Repeka shoved him, a blur of hair flying, arms pumping, dark clothing rushing past Cranston and heading straight for the squad car parked on the road. And Tova beside it.

"Get in the car," Finn yelled at her as he too pushed past Cranston.

Tova's expression changed from surprise to bafflement to unease in the space of a few seconds as the raging woman headed straight for her. She tugged the door handle.

He'd locked it. Finn fumbled in his pocket for the remote. He heard the click and Tova tumbled head first into the back seat, turned and slammed the door shut. He pressed the remote button again as Repeka, still screaming, thumped on the window. "You bitch!"

"Step away from the vehicle," Finn ordered, surprised that Repeka's shriek hadn't shattered the window glass. He signalled to Cranston to approach the enraged woman from the side while he kept out of reach of a sudden kick to the crotch.

Repeka charged. Finn sidestepped, extended one leg. She tripped. He grabbed, pushed her against the vehicle, left cheek crushed against the glass. He moved his forearm across her back to pin her and twisted her arm up and behind, Tova wide-eyed in the car, and a gathering crowd on the opposite footpath.

"Keep still."

"My lawyer will do you for harassment, bringing her here." The words were barked out through clenched teeth with extra grunt behind 'lawyer' and 'harassment'.

He tightened his grip. The last thing he wanted was for her to break and he and Cranston to have to chase after her. Not a good look, not with spectators.

Tova clambered out the far door and had the sense to back off across the road. The closest onlookers shuffled, created a space, not looking at her.

"Support is on its way," Cranston called.

Finn looked across the car roof at the gawkers, recognised Mr Weston holding his yappy dog in his arms, a satisfied smirk on his face. Two onlookers had mobiles upright, videoing the spectacle.

Wright and Unsworth arrived first, the sirens drowning out Repeka. "Your phone was on, Finny. We were already on our way when Comms put the emergency through." Wright raised an eyebrow at the sight of Tova but headed for Jacob, who was leaning against the door jamb. He didn't look too worried. Used to his mother in handcuffs.

Two other cars turned up. Overkill, thought Finn. One of the spectators was sure to be thinking the same. Probably the one with the camera, already tweeting why it took several officers to arrest one woman.

Finn dug out his mobile, still live. He phoned Pavletich, gave him a brief update. "Repeka as good as admitted she and Hemi knew Areta Amahua. And I'd say Jacob suffered a hiding for telling KK that Repeka was one of the people on the beach the night of Jasmine's death. Did Richard Tan mention that?" As much as Finn didn't want to say the next thing, he had to. "Mrs Hemona certainly knew Ms Tan, too."

"So, our Ms Tan did take the bait? Good. Now we're making progress." Pavletich spoke so loudly that Finn held the phone away from his ear. "Bring Ms Tan back, too."

Cranston and Unsworth remained to secure the house and mind Jacob until the social worker turned up. And take statements from onlookers – procedure, most often of varying use as reports were always conflicting – making Wright available to accompany Mrs Hemona in the back of the car, while Tova, at first reluctant, agreed to return with him.

"Not much of a choice," she said. "Go back with you and face more questions, or refuse to cooperate and make your boss wonder why."

The drive back to Henderson was quick, green lights most of the way, the tension in the vehicle high. Finn was relieved when Ngaire agreed to process Repeka, which left him alone for a moment with Tova.

"I've seen Mrs Hemona before," Tova said. "I'm trying to remember where."

"Central tell me several boutique brothels in the suburbs have shut up shop, and not because their services are no longer required." An hour later, Pavletich was addressing the assembled team, including Inspector Smith, who seemed almost animated at the progress. "As-yet-unsubstantiated rumours are circulating that someone is buying them out then closing them down. No one is saying who, so this buyer, or buyers, must have money and influence. Another link to our two murders," he added unnecessarily. He stopped pacing, adding gravitas to his words. "They say it's connected to the new casino."

Finn's gut tightened, anticipating what was coming. Back to Malcolm Tan.

"So I want pressure on the Tans. It's almost impossible to get past the lawyer to the father at this stage, so go for the weakest link: Richard. He's been bailed to his father's address against our request to keep him on remand. The daughter is sticking to her story that she knows nothing of her father's dealings. The Tan lawyer confirms that. It is also verified by statements from people inside Tan's business. No one is talking – there has to be a reason everyone is keeping schtum." Pavletich sounded peeved and he commenced pacing. Finn willed his boss to stand still. The constant movement might help Pavletich's thinking processes but it broke his own concentration.

"The CCTV from the Grey Lynn brothel is poor quality, grainy," Pavletich went on. "Shows two big men going in at 11.45 pm on Thursday and coming out within minutes, both with their heads down like they know to avoid the cameras. One of them looks like Oso Vavau, but without a facial it's hardly a positive ID." Pulling out a vacant chair, he dropped into it, rubbed his face and slid a hand over his scalp. "No rest, you lot. Get out there. I'll re-interview Hemi, and I'll deal with his missus, see what that throws up."

Chairs scraped and squeaked as they were shunted back. There were mutterings about long hours. As he passed Finn, one of the ring-ins joked how to explain to his wife he was paid to go into brothels. Someone laughed.

Finn hung back for Pavletich to end his conversation with the inspector, tried to look as though he didn't hear Smith's, "The media are loving this, Goran. Like ten-year-olds with a new dirty word. You'd think we were back in last century, the way they're plastering 'brothel' in their headlines. Get a move on, get a result, shut it down." Smith ignored Finn as he left the room.

"I'm relieved your story matches hers, McIntosh," Pavletich said, expressionless, when he'd listened to the summary of Finn's afternoon activities.

Was that a joke or a warning?

"She'd left her happy thoughts for the Dunn spirits and then she confronted the Hemonas, didn't she?"

"Is that what she said?"

"No, McIntosh," Pavletich shook his head, rolled his eyes at Finn's naïveté. "She said she was freezing and went looking for you, hoping you'd give her a lift. She has more to tell us. No matter how we look at this, the Tans keep popping up. In the absence of any other leads, we'll stick with them. Find out where Ms Tan recognises

Mrs Hemona from. She says she doesn't remember yet. Drive her home, she might open up more in her own surroundings. She's covering for her father, like she has been for the brother. Get hold of Wright, take her with you. She's more objective."

Ngaire wasn't upstairs, wasn't by the coffee machine. He asked one of the female officers to go look in the toilets, and although he didn't expect her to be there, he checked the back car park smokers' area.

Ngaire answered her mobile on the third ring. "I've snuck off home." Finn knew more about her life than he did about members of his own family. To Ngaire, the confinement of a police car was as good as a confessional.

"I'll be fine, Finny. The usual. I let it get to me today. A touch of 'it's not fair'. The Hemonas have a kid they don't want, and I want a kid I can't have."

Practice didn't make him any better at consoling her, the month before, the time before that. So he reverted to his comfort position, work. "You and I are to talk to Ms Tan." Put the heat on was Pavletich's none-too-subtle message. Ngaire was better at that.

"If I go, you won't get much out of her that we don't already know. I annoy her but you don't. Besides, I need some time out."

Pavletich had made it clear: everyone on the team remained on duty or on call, which to the boss amounted to the same thing, twenty-four seven until they had the case wrapped up. Ngaire must be feeling the strain if she was willing to break the rules.

"My advice is talk to her somewhere neutral, buy her a coffee maybe," Ngaire said. "The formal interviews haven't got us far, so go for the casual approach, it can't hurt."

Ngaire's suggestion made sense, except it wasn't normal procedure. Two officers were usually present at interviews.

"Finny, I'll cover for you, if you cover for me. No one will know. Pavletich will forgive you if she tells you something that'll help us."

He was still deciding when Ngaire said, "Be yourself, Finny, she'll respond to that," and she cut the call.

Unsworth was in the locker room, his back to the door, mobile to his ear. Shit, the last person Finn wanted to see.

"What do you want?" Unsworth spun round.

"Last time I looked this was common space," Finn retorted, then wished he'd said nothing, he was reading too much into Unsworth's anger, suspicion spiked by Cranston's disclosure. He went to his locker, changed out of uniform and into his civvies.

"Sorry, mate. Under a bit of pressure," Unsworth muttered. It wasn't like Unsworth to say sorry.

Finn took his time lacing up one sneaker, then the other. "Everything all right?" he asked, not sure he really wanted to know the answer.

"Nothing I can't handle." Unsworth's actions told a different story, a kick aimed at the locker by the door as he left.

Shit. He didn't have time to check on Unsworth, Tova was waiting back in the interview room.

"Not more questions," Tova said as Finn appeared at the door. "I'm going home." She looked him up and down, and Finn tried to recall if she had seen him out of uniform. He guessed he didn't look his best in his usual off-duty gear, a much-loved faded sweater and jeans well past their use-by date.

"I'll drive you," Finn offered. "All part of the service."

"If you promise not to interrogate me on the way."

Finn didn't answer in case he stammered. She must already think he was a bumbling idiot.

"OK, you have a job to do and I need a lift to Newmarket." In her own quiet way she took control. "Which way?" She followed him out of the building. He reached the car first and held the front passenger door open, then worried she'd think he was a chauvinist. It was all too fraught and they weren't even on a date. It had been easier with Emily, the rhythm of their life and behaviours established. He remembered she'd said that was one of the problems.

Finn waited at the traffic lights to turn onto the motorway. He was aware of the driver in the lane beside him, edging forward before the lights turned green. The woman in front, head dipped, on her mobile, missed the change of lights. Always a cop, on- and off-duty.

"Are you hungry? I am. I haven't had time to eat today." Finn saw the Point Chev off-ramp ahead and cleared his throat, to bolster his confidence and to get her attention. "Do you mind if we stop for half an hour? I know a good Indian place in Point Chev." Finn kept his eyes on the road and slowed the car, in anticipation of her agreeing. Or not say no before he needed to take the exit. Was it open on Monday nights?

"I like Indian," Tova said without moving position.

A warm glow bubbled in Finn's belly.

"Anything to delay getting the evil eye from Sarah's boyfriend."

Finn's bubble burst.

"Namaste." The sari-clad waitress greeted him with the traditional gesture, head slightly bowed, long, graceful fingers pressed together. "We haven't seen you here for a while, Finn."

He waited for the, "Where's Emily?"

Emily had raved about the cheap, casual restaurant with authentic Indian cuisine. A number of their mutual friends were now regulars. A quick glance around and he recognised no one. Two women sat at a table in the centre, holding an animated conversation, seemingly oblivious to their surroundings. A middle-aged couple by the wall stared into the distance, each nursing a glass of red wine. The adjacent table was occupied by two adults and two children. The boy and girl sucked reddish liquid through a straw, competing with each other to produce the loudest guzzling noise.

The waitress tactfully didn't let her gaze linger on Tova's eye-catching bruise. She led them to a table for two by the window with a view of the street, fluffed out their napkins, poured glasses of water and said she'd give them time to peruse the menu, and she'd be back to take their order.

Lamb korma and rice for Finn; fish masala with a side of green vegetables for Tova. She said she'd stay with the water. To keep a clear head, Finn asked for a can of Coke. As he poured it into a glass, he tried to think how to open the conversation.

"Does your wife or partner approve of your career choice?" Tova made it clear she didn't understand why anyone would.

Why hadn't he thought of that smooth approach to finding out her status? "My parents want me to be happy. I tell them I am. My ex-girlfriend," he emphasised the *ex*, "in the end wasn't happy with me about anything, which is why she's my ex." It might help to talk of Emily and of the hurt on learning she'd been sleeping with his mate; Tova, polite, would listen. He hadn't even told Ngaire about the double betrayal, although at the time she had guessed something upset him. No one else had twigged, as far as he knew. But he mustn't get sidetracked.

"Do you have a boyfriend?" Too direct, resorting to interview mode. And overstepping his professional role.

Tova took a moment before answering, as if deciding what to say. "Not on my agenda, constable. I'm concentrating on doing well in my studies, and next year, I'll need all my energy to cope with full-time teaching."

Was she warning him off? "Please, call me Finn. Constable sounds too formal." She didn't suggest he use her first name. "While we're here." The silence lengthened. Finn glanced around the restaurant. The waitress was busy with two new customers, settling them at their table. He said the next thing that entered his head. "I'm learning a lot from Detective Pavletich, even though I'm stuck on ploddy jobs."

"Thank you. I've been called many things, never a ploddy job." Tova lifted her glass which hid her mouth. He was sure she was smiling.

"Sorry, I didn't mean that quite the way it sounded."

"I'm sure you didn't."

Finn savoured the euphoric feeling brought on by gentle flirting. In spite of her discoloured cheek, he couldn't stop looking at her. Not a full-on stare, more returning to a fixed point each time he read the menu or glanced around the restaurant.

It took a few seconds to remember what he'd been talking about. "Ploddy, in the sense of routine in any investigation, chasing up information and talking to people, giving me a go at a lot of things. It all helps if

I want to undertake detective training." He was over explaining, saying more than he intended. "Maybe Pavletich is seeing if I'm cut out for it." He should stop. She might think he was after a compliment. Or think, as Emily had, that he'd be a useless detective, the crims would walk all over him.

They sat in silence while the waitress moved glasses and the small vase with its single flower to fit all the bowls and the large urn of rice on the table.

"Questioning me in a restaurant makes a change." She spooned some fish from the bowl to her plate. "Is your boss against Chinese in general, or my father in particular?" She speared the fish and twirled it on the end of the fork.

"Pavletich is being thorough." Finn defended his boss and avoided answering her question.

"You cops all stick together," Tova said through tight lips, annoyed by his answer.

He glanced around. What if she caused a scene? And he'd wasted time with small talk.

"OK, I'll do a deal," she said, placing her fork down.

Finn had no authority to make any concessions with her. Information in return for the release of her brother? Money under the table for leaving her father alone? He was starting to be as untrusting as Pavletich. Emily would have seen that as progress.

"You ask the questions. I'll answer them. Depends on what you ask, of course, and you still drive me to Sarah's and pay for dinner." The flash of anger had subsided.

"Deal." He spooned more rice and lamb onto his plate and thought if Tova didn't eat much more he'd have enough in the doggy bags for two or three nights. He filled their water glasses. With the memory of Emily berating him for being spineless and the vision of Pavletich demanding more information, he dived in.

"Repeka Hemona. She recognised you. You thought you'd seen her before."

"It must have been at Mum's tangi." The frown lines between her brows deepened. "Most of that time is a blur – so many people, and it was all so strange. Thank goodness Sarah was with me, she'd been to a tangi before and had some idea of the protocol, where to sit, when to stand, the open casket, the three days of mourning, people I didn't know wailing over Mum. She said it was customary, the outpouring of grief helps people cope with the loss. She said I should try it but she cried enough for both of us."

She mumbled the last words and Finn reached for a table napkin. Tova gently brushed it aside.

"A lot of the speeches sounded like arguments to me, and Sarah knew that was common, families arguing over the body, something to do with the mana, the level of respect for the person. It was full-on, hard to think." Her eyes closed for a moment, and he worried she was reliving the experience. "Women were always with me. Mrs Hemona must have been one of those women."

"You weren't aware that Areta and Hemi Hemona were related?"

"She has a younger sister she never mentioned, so she was unlikely to chat about cousins." Tova's voice rose above the hum of chatter in the restaurant. The waitress looked their way.

"This rift, was it over her relationship with your father?"

"No, Mum left her whānau long before she met him."

Whatever had happened still had the power to send

Repeka into a frenzy. He stopped himself from reaching across the table to hold her hand.

Tova sat back out of reach, increasing the distance between them, as though she anticipated he might make such a move. "I grew up believing Areta was an only child, her parents long dead, and she had no contact with distant relatives so I arranged for a cremation here in Auckland. Her sister turned up to claim her on behalf of the whole family, saying the rift would heal when her whānau farewelled her. She then had to be returned to the earth and her spirit rest with her ancestors."

Finn knew a little of the tangi ritual. The importance of the living greeting the body in the belief its spirit lingered until burial, and an opportunity to say all the things they wanted the person to take with them. Family and friends left behind came together, the support often lasting days. He remembered reading that Malcolm Tan had not attended the tangi. That must have hurt Tova.

"Ironically, the person who knew Mum best was my father."

"Oh." Not strong enough to break the flow of her thoughts but enough acknowledgement to encourage her to continue.

"So I turn up to lunch to relive our lives with her. I was a horrible daughter after I found out the truth about their relationship." Sadness crept into her voice. "I know he loved Mum and she loved him."

Finn felt a twinge of sympathy for Malcolm Tan, wanting what he shouldn't have. And unless he wanted to end up in a mess himself, he needed to remember becoming involved with someone caught up in a murder enquiry was not a good career move. Not that the opportunity was likely to present itself. It was clear she distrusted cops.

"I was born here, but because of my looks, many people assume I must be a recent Chinese migrant. But in the last year I've discovered there are all these people who see me as Māori." She stared into the distance, thinking aloud. "I feel caught between Mum's whānau, who I don't know, and Dad's world where I don't belong." She held her head high, her eyes shiny. "I'm sorry, I don't know why I'm telling you this."

She was beginning to place a little trust in him.

The silence extended and he searched for the right words to break it. The best he could come up with was, "Please, don't apologise."

"No point in dwelling on what you can't change, Mum often said." Tova gazed out the window, and Finn looked too, at the cars in the street and the few people dawdling past. "That's why I know she didn't kill herself – she didn't dwell on disappointments."

Returning her attention to her plate, she pecked and picked at her food, then created a sculpture of two symmetrical rice cones surrounded by a shallow sea of the masala on her plate. He stared at the rice pyramids as if they might contain the secrets of Areta's life.

Finn wished they were on a date, finding out about each other: were their music tastes compatible, action movies versus romantic comedies, gym-goer or a jogger? But they weren't on a date. He had a job to do.

"Any more questions?" Tova placed her fork carefully on the plate, signalling she had eaten as much as she was going to. She brushed at a few crumbs on the table, a metaphorical sweeping aside of her emotions. Back to business.

He did. The Hemonas. What exactly was her connection to them?

Her eyes appeared deeper and her skin paler. She was exhausted, needed sleep. A few more hours waiting to find out what she knew of the Hemonas couldn't hurt. He'd arrange to talk to her again, first thing.

Finn attracted the waitress's attention and asked for the bill. He left a decent tip. At the door, the waitress repeated her namaste gesture. Tova returned the farewell and thanked her for the delicious meal.

Before Finn had the chance to be gallant, Tova walked ahead, opened the passenger door as soon as Finn beeped the remote. He walked round to the driver's side trying to think of something to lighten the mood.

"Harris said he looked into Mum's background and found nothing to change his findings," she said. "But he didn't. I checked with my whānau. He didn't speak to any of them. Why would he? He had made up his mind about what happened."

He didn't start the car. "The media were at Areta's tangi, weren't they?"

"What's that mean?" Tova swiped the fringe back off her forehead, a sharp, impatient movement.

"Nothing," he said hurriedly. "Sorry." What had he been thinking? If there had been something to uncover, some ambitious journalist would have done so. Maybe Harris had been right: Areta committed suicide and Tova's inability to accept that didn't mean anything sinister had happened.

"A few reporters tried to hustle their way in but they were soon told to leave. One photographer said she wasn't staying, she only needed a shot of the casket. The media weren't interest in the why. They were only after a few sensational photos so they could write up another weepy piece on what a loss Areta was to the acting world. The whānau wanted none of that."

She brushed at sudden tears. "I don't care whether you believe me or not. I want to go to Sarah's now."

He did believe her. But that could only mean the original police case into Areta's death had been mismanaged.

The *Jaws* ringtone sounded and he grabbed at his phone. "It's work. I'll have to take it. I'll be quick." Finn got out of the car, positioned himself behind it out of earshot but where he had a direct line to the passenger door. He considered pressing the door lock, forestalling any escape attempt. Instead, he swiped the call open before it cut to voicemail.

"You and Wright still with Ms Tan?" Straight into it.

Shit. He didn't want to lie. "I am."

"Ask her why Mrs Hemona tried to attack her. Can't get any sense out of Repeka. Looks to me like those two are more connected than we realise."

"Ms Tan has explained that. She thinks the Hemonas had some grudge against Areta."

"McIntosh, I've read the Amahua file. Harris reported he did background checks, came up with zilch. By the way, I've read your email."

Finn gripped the mobile. Was he about to be yelled at?

"The team that searched the house are scrabbling for excuses as to why they didn't double-check the information on the computer was the same as in those files. The financial crime squad are getting onto it. The real estate agent has confirmed Mrs Dunn was interested in buying several luxury city apartments. He says it was all legitimate, but we'll have it checked out."

"Good." Finn paused. Was now the best time to let Pavletich know his thinking? He was still trying to get the ideas in order.

"Got something else, McIntosh?"

Just say it. "What about this for a theory? This unidentified-as-yet Boss of the Vavaus orders the Dunns to be killed. The Vavaus recruit their mate Hemi to help out with the dirty work. He and Repeka see an opportunity to implicate the Tans in those killings because of whatever happened years ago between Areta and the Hemonas. The Tans are victims."

"Harris warned me Ms Tan would try to get you on her side," Pavletich said.

"Hear me out." Finn hurried on, the ideas forming, jumbling over each other in his mind. "What if this is utu?"

"Utu?"

"Reciprocation, balance and harmony, putting a wrong right." Repeating the words from a bicultural lecture he had attended, aimed at officers improving their understanding.

"I know what utu is, McIntosh. How do you figure that? Amahua's dead."

"Utu carries on, doesn't it, down the generations until balance is restored. That will mean different things to different people. It's a possibility. It all fits if Areta's breaking off from her whānau was connected to Hemi." Finn hoped the few details made sense when he said them aloud. "That might explain why Mrs Hemona attacked Tova – Areta's death wasn't enough to restore the balance and now other family members are liable."

"Utu sounds far-fetched to me in this day and age."

Finn imagined Pavletich, phone held up to one ear,

pacing his office, frown lines deepening. "The Tans, Amahua, the Dunns and the Hemonas, not to mention the Vavaus, are all linked somehow."

"If we dig around in the Amahua case, we'll have to work with Harris."

"I understand that." Everything had its downside. Finn shuffled from one foot to another in a vain attempt to generate warmth against the night chill. He peered through the back window of the car, streaked with dew, kept his eye on Tova's silhouette.

"You think you're onto something."

"I do."

"Let me think about it overnight."

A smile broke on Finn's face. Pavletich hadn't done a Harris on him: 'You're not here to think, McIntosh, you're here to do as I tell you.'

"I'll deal with Harris and follow up with Tauranga. Repeka's bailed, but I'll get one of the team to bring her back in tomorrow. This doesn't necessarily mean Ms Tan is innocent."

But it was possible.

"Wind it up with her. We'll get back to her in a day or two if we need to. You and Wright go home, get a few hours' sleep. We'll go after the other Tans tomorrow. You and Wright interview the son. His doctor says he should be up to a few questions. And I'll find a way round Mr Bloody Tan's smarmy lawyer. Said he was tempted to charge me with harassment. Must be the default position of these Tans." Pavletich's laugh rang in Finn's ear until the call was cut.

First thing tomorrow, he'd persuade Ngaire to admit she had gone home. It was too hard to remember every detail of the whole night. And tomorrow he'd raise his concern about Unsworth, see if Pavletich could direct him to counselling.

Finn slid into the driver's seat. "The Boss has agreed he'll look more closely into the Hemonas' past."

Tova didn't open her eyes. "I won't hold my breath."

Finn accompanied Tova to the door of the apartment, in spite of her insistence she did not need an escort, it was a safe neighbourhood and there were security cameras. He resisted the urge to say cameras recorded a mugging, they didn't prevent it.

Sarah appeared in pink Hello Kitty pyjamas. Oblivious to Finn's presence or the state of Tova, she gave a squeal of pleasure and a one-armed hug to her friend. "Sorry, sorry," as Tova gently released her grip, reminding Sarah of her sore ribs.

Tova took a step inside, half-closed the door but didn't shut it. Tom's less-than-welcoming words reached him. "Sarah has to rest. Her car is still out at Howick. She can't drive with her arm in a sling, and I don't want to leave her on her own. You dragged Sarah into this, Tova, so you sort it."

"It can wait, Tom," Sarah's tone conciliatory.

"It'll get stolen. Or its tyres stripped if that hasn't already happened."

Tova responded. "I'll work something out tomorrow, Tom."

"You'll just buy her another one, I suppose, if hers is a write-off."

Finn nudged the door open. It gave him a little satisfaction to see the surprise on Tom's face.

Tova blocked the doorway, preventing Finn from getting up close to Tom. "It's fine. No need to wait. Thank you for the lift."

By the scowl on Tom's face, Finn doubted Tova would get to bed before she was subjected to more yelling. "I'll get a patrol to go check that Sarah's car is still there, if that helps."

"What are they going to do, guard it all night?" Tom took a breath but Tova cut in before he could say more.

"Tom's right. I'm responsible." She turned to Finn. "Can you drive me to Howick? I'll drive the car back. It won't take long."

"You're in no state ..." Not to mention a number of other reasons why he shouldn't spend more time with her.

"Great, see you soon." Tom tossed the car keys to Finn, shunted them out the door and shut it before anyone objected.

28. TOVA

He'd agreed to drive her, she was sure, to have more time to ask questions, but the thought of suffering more of Tom's animosity and Sarah's unhappiness was enough to make her think only of getting out of the flat long enough for Tom to cool down. If she'd thought it through, she could have rung up a tow truck company to retrieve the car.

He was easy to talk to. The first guy she'd relaxed with in months, a cop. Up until now, she'd had a thing about cops, *against* cops. If only she'd met him before Areta died. What might have been? No, it was stupid and time-wasting to think like that. If she had met him earlier, she wouldn't have been interested.

All through school and university, Sarah had despaired for her. 'Give guys a chance,' she said. 'You're so cute and you drive them crazy, Miss Untouchable.'

'I'm too busy.' The excuse had been schoolwork, dance and music practice to please her mother and, if she was honest, her father. If any boys had been interested, she hadn't been aware. At university, it was study and modelling, except for the few times she let her guard down. It was obvious most people wanted to be her friend because of her proximity to a celebrity. Plus her parents had demonstrated that it was better to avoid relationships altogether.

'You have to put yourself out there,' Sarah said. 'You can't study and work all the time.'

'Getting my degree will give me independence, and the modelling pays my bills.'

'Oh, Tova, it's like clothes shopping – you try a few before you buy. I hope when you do fall for someone, he's right for you.'

Not this one, a cop. His concern seemed genuine, but then, he was paid to look interested and listen.

Still, she could be more grateful.

"I know I've been unhelpful at times. Police bring the worst out in me. It's not personal." She eased into the passenger seat, wincing at the nips of pain from ribs to hip.

"I'll take that as an apology, and apology accepted." McIntosh checked his rear-view mirror and did a U-turn on the deserted street. He turned into Broadway then up Khyber Pass and merged into the light, late-night traffic flow onto the motorway south.

"I let Detective Harris intimidate me last year, and I promised myself I wouldn't let it happen again," saying it more to remind herself.

"I'm sorry if you feel all police behave like that. We don't."

"He charged me with assault for pushing him away." Without having planned to, she said, "Are you going to charge me with breaking into Mrs Dunn's house?"

"No. If I did, I'd have to admit you frightened the daylights out of me." He glanced her way, his face and tone serious.

"But you ... Oh, funny." She smiled. Easy to talk to and a sense of humour. She refocused. "I did go back to get some clothes. While I was there, it seemed a good idea to find something that explained why they were killed. Stupid, really, playing detective."

"I was doing the same." The shadows cast from the motorway lights made him look as though he was grinning one moment, grimacing the next. "I had a hunch, and knew the forensic guys would take forever. I didn't want to wait that long."

"A hunch? Did you find anything?" Tova tugged at the seat belt, too snug against her ribs and turned to look at him. Sitting still had tightened muscles. "Tell me, I'm not going to ring a reporter, am I?" If it cleared her father, she wanted to know.

McIntosh chewed at his lip then said, "Double accounts for her businesses, common with lots of cash flow. She was planning on selling her business and providing inflated accounts for that purpose."

"Killed for conning a buyer?" Unlikely to be her father, he was too shrewd a businessman to be conned.

"It's illegal, and people have been murdered for far less." McIntosh glanced at her, moved his gaze back to the road. "She was also buying several pricey apartments in the city."

Like riding a roller coaster. "Tan Company apartments?"

"We're looking into it."

"That's not illegal."

"No."

Coincidence. Her father owned lots of apartments in the city. It was another connection with Juliette.

"So Juliette was dodging taxes and ripping off a buyer, but why kill Jasmine?" Clutching at straws.

"The killer's reason may seem crazy to us but not to them." McIntosh slowed, let a vehicle from the Greenlane on-ramp merge in ahead of him.

"Like whoever killed my mother," Tova said.

He leaned towards her, making sure he heard. "Sorry, we were talking about Jasmine."

She read motorway signs as Finn veered into the left lane, took the Eastern Motorway exit, heading towards Pakuranga. Shuffling her bottom further back into the seat relieved the increasing stiffness.

"After Mum died, I considered leaving for Australia." That desire to run away was strong again.

"But you didn't." He made it sound like she'd made the right decision.

No, but she did change her name, hibernated from people as much as possible. Some people probably thought she had left the country.

"I mentioned to Pavletich what you told me about your mother's case." Kindly said.

Tova's breath caught, she coughed to clear the lump, wished she hadn't as her ribs hurt.

"I can't promise anything."

"I feel I've let Mum down. I haven't withdrawn my complaint against Harris. I haven't pursued it either. I've let Richard down, too."

"Looks to me like you tried to protect him. He made his own choices."

They crossed the Panmure Basin, stopped at the Ti Rakau Drive lights, turned left and then through the green onto the stretch of Pakuranga Highway before she broke the silence.

"Richard told you about the Vavaus?" She was surprised and relieved. He must be growing up. "They blackmailed him, do what they want or they'd tell his father about the drugs." How weak that made him sound. "You have to understand that, for Richard, the son and heir, that was a big deal."

"He involved you. That's premeditated." He stared at her bruised cheek. He took his eyes off the road so long she thought she'd have to remind him he was driving.

"He didn't understand what the Vavaus were capable of." Still excusing him. "He thought all he had to do was get into Mrs Dunn's office and copy everything he could from her computer onto a USB and take copies or photos of any documents she left lying around."

Tiredness overcame her. She caught glimpses out the window of landmarks she had pointed out to Sarah the night before – the large sports grounds, the high school, a line of shops with takeaway outlets, the petrol station. She warned him of the sudden left-hand turn, easily missed, that took them to Mellons Bay Road. He slowed around the curve, flicked his lights to high beam, picking out parked vehicles, houses in darkness, the dull white of her father's street wall and Sarah's car parked opposite in the small reserve's car park.

"Looks in one piece," Finn said as he pulled up beside it. "Not graffitied, no broken windows, still with all its wheels."

The car was warm, a cocoon against the world. Tova made no move to get out, not ready to see the shell where the garage had been, didn't want to think about Oso running towards them or smell burning flesh or taste the acrid smoke in her lungs. "What sort of person orders the murder of two people?" Not so easy to turn her mind off.

"Someone with a lot of money and a nasty attitude," he answered. "The Financial Unit might come up with a name."

She'd been thinking out loud, a hypothetical question about general humanity, not narrowing it down to any one individual. "You never give up, do you?" her accusation loud, and a chill quivered down her spine in spite of the warmth of the car.

He raised his eyebrows in a silent question.

"We're back to my father again. That's what you're thinking, isn't it? He might be many things. A murderer isn't one of them." Tova let out a rueful cry, the idea preposterous.

"I wasn't referring to anyone in particular." Furrows deepened on his forehead as he half-turned towards her, his body pressed back against his door. "Killing Juliette and Jasmine is drastic, a warning to others, an example – this is what happens if you cross me. Maintaining position, saving face." His fingers tapped the steering wheel.

Her father was like that, maintain the façade: live in the right suburb with a suitable wife and son, pretend that Richard had aptitude and interest in following in his father's footsteps, frequent popular restaurants, make the lucrative business deals.

"As that's a concept big in Chinese culture," she said, "that theory suits your assumptions, doesn't it." Tova eased out of the car, determined to maintain some dignity, surprised at the surge of anger that had taken over. *Why can't I keep my mouth shut? Have I learned nothing?*

She had overheard her parents discussing his latest project, investing in the new casino project. How it would provide employment, boost tourism, Auckland a destination for international high rollers.

Areta asked him to reconsider. To Tova, her opposition was half-hearted, not accompanied by her usual theatrics of arm waving.

Malcolm's replies were calm and reasoned, adhering to his belief that was how arguments were won. He walked out, saw her and wished her goodnight. His composure infuriated Tova. She directed her disgust and anger towards Areta. 'How can you live with him? He's promoting gambling and all that goes with it, poverty and heartbreak and broken families. The most vulnerable people, the ones we should all care about, suffer while the rich profit.'

'I want the deal stopped too, Tova. I'll talk to him.'

A week later, Areta was dead.

"Ms Tan?" Finn was out of the car, watching her but keeping his distance.

"You're like your boss," Tova snapped. "You want my father to be guilty, don't you?" She clutched Sarah's car keys so tightly they dug into her palm. Rather than count to ten, think it through, she rode the emotional wave engulfing her. "If you want to speak to me again, call my lawyer."

He rubbed his face. Tired? Or fed up with her.

She was exhausted, too, self-conscious and overreacting. Why was she so angry all the time? She wished he'd leave before she said or did something else she might regret.

"You okay?" He was a step away.

"Yes." She didn't trust herself to say anything more. What if her father *was* guilty? She'd have a father and half-brother in jail. How could she go teaching the following year? She'd have to change her name again, move further away than Australia.

"I'll follow you home, see you get back to your friend's safely."

"No." Too emphatic; she wanted him to go before her resolve broke. "After all that's happened, I should try to persuade my father not to be too hard on Richard. He might even let me stay the night." She had no intention of doing that, but she'd go through the gate, make it look as though she meant what she said.

"That's sensible," Finn said. "You've had a long day. But ..."

"I'm sure my father is already aware you're suspicious of him."

"I was going to say, let your friend Sarah know. We don't want her ringing 111 to say you've gone missing."

"Sure." She dug out her phone, held the screen so Finn couldn't see what she wrote and composed a brief text to Sarah. *Car in one piece.* She gave a dismissive wave, the movement intensifying the ache in her side. Her head pounded and she would have liked nothing better than to have him put his arms around her and tell her everything would be all right.

Pocketing her phone, she headed across the road, tapped in the alarm code, and the gate opened as Finn's car started.

The security lights had been repaired. Opening the front gate triggered the strip lights along the path to the ornate entrance. She glanced across the lawn to where the garages used to be. A tang of after-fire hung in the air, and she ran her tongue around her lips, tasting soot. She thought of her father's precious cars, destroyed by the explosion. It was easier than thinking of Oso and how close Richard, Sarah and she had come to serious injury. Or worse.

No sound of a car engine. McIntosh must be far enough away. She wouldn't catch up to him on the motorway.

She peered towards the house. There was movement on the balcony. Her father? He'd think she had come to see him.

Leaving was easy, out the gate, to Sarah's car. Run away.

Or face him.

The front door with its large brass lion's-head knocker, polished and cool to touch, was ajar, opening into a spacious, dark foyer. She'd been in it once before when her father and his wife were away. Richard had rung for her to pick him up from a sleazy bar on K Road. He'd had too much to smoke or ingest but not so much he'd risk the drive home.

Voices, indistinct. Did he expect her to go up to his spacious suite – bedroom, sitting room, bathroom, not to mention the full-length balcony that had views of the sea? Tova had never been to that part of the house, but Richard often bragged of its opulence, if he wasn't condemning his mother's crass taste.

She hadn't spoken to Malcolm at the hospital. He'd have questions. May as well tell him what Richard had got himself into.

Subtle, inset wall lights gave off enough glow so she didn't stumble into furniture or trip up the stairs. The wide carpeted staircase curved up the left wall, the right side miniature columned balustrade open to the magnificent atrium foyer, affording a breathtaking outline of the crystal chandelier centrepiece. *Expensive enough to buy lunches for every student in a low-decile school for a year.*

In the silence, she imagined her rapid pulse imitated Richard's favourite thump-thump rap beat. Nerves raised her body temperature. She attempted to shuck off her jacket but resorted to a stand-on-the-spot jiggle to ease her arms from the sleeves as she bit her lip against the pain. Looping a finger through the neck tab and with jacket swinging over her shoulder, she took the stairs two at a time. At the landing she paused, listened to the sounds of the house. Silence. She turned towards Richard's bedroom, hesitated at the door, still time to change her mind. She knocked.

"Fuck, it *is* you. Thought the idiot was hallucinating."

Tova spun round. Tupe Vavau was at the Tan's door at the other end of the hall. Feet apart, he aimed a gun at her head. A dull, black, compact pistol of some sort, her knowledge of weapons limited to movies and novels. It looked real.

He'd have a clear shot if she ran back down the stairs.

Richard's room. Could she get in there before he put a bullet in her back? Then what? Wait for Tupe to find her? Or go out the window, a three-storey drop and give Tupe target practice as broken bones prevented her fleeing. Standing her ground was hardly an option.

His Adam's apple jerked as he swallowed. For a split second, she contemplated coaxing him to put down the gun, the way she might cajole a mischievous fourteen-year-old from disrupting a class.

"Keep your hands where I can see them. Come here."

What did he think? Concealed under her clothes she had a knife to hurl or a grenade to lob? She obeyed, arms raised in surrender. The closer she moved forward, the stronger the reek of cigarettes and raw sweat. Facing him, she edged past into the room, eyes on the gun. Her nose twitched, needing to be scratched. Any sudden movement might provoke him.

Standard lamps either end of the cream leather three-seater couch lit the sitting room in a soft glow. Two matching armchairs flanked an ornate nest of side tables. A quick scan of the room revealed no mantelpiece with heavy candlestick holders to use as weapons, no fire irons to use as swords. At best, she might be able to buy time if she heaved one of the small tables at him.

The prod in her back kept her moving towards the bifold doors, already opened to reveal the bed, its bedclothes tossed back as the occupants leapt up in a hurry. French doors beyond the bed were open, letting in the icy night air. It happened in movies, escape via the balcony, clamber onto the roof, run across the ridge, slither down a sturdy drainpipe to safety. And the baddie tripped and tumbled headfirst to the concrete below.

Her best chance: with luck, swiftness and more luck, she might be able to distract Tupe long enough to lock herself in the bathroom.

Tupe pushed her further into the room, and she gasped with the pressure of the barrel jabbed deeper into her side. Tova blinked, bringing into focus the sight in front of her.

Sitting on the floor, propped against the bed, were her father and his wife, both naked. Malcolm Tan had often promised Areta he was trapped in a loveless marriage. Maybe that was true, and it was since Areta's death that he had turned back to his wife. Why was she even thinking about that?

By the way their backs arched and their necks strained, their arms were tied tight behind them. Dark socks pushed into their mouths puffed out their cheeks. Striped neckties bound their ankles.

"Bang." Tupe pointed the gun at Mrs Tan and laughed as she flinched. He shoved the gun into his jeans pocket.

"Don't even think about it," Tupe said, taking in Tova's glance.

Tears streaked Mrs Tan's face, her whimpering muffled by the gag. After a pleading look at Tova, she hung her head. Having her husband's bastard child see her naked adding to her humiliation.

"Give them a blanket, they're freezing." Tova tossed her jacket at Mrs Tan. It skewed across one shoulder and over the woman's knees, affording a little more modesty and a modicum more warmth.

Tova bent to drag the bedclothes over them and caught her father's glance. His face was grotesque, pulled out of shape by the gag, his skin a pallid grey in the dim light. A thin line of blood oozed its way from hairline to cheek to chin, and tiny droplets fell to his neck. He grunted, eyes fixed on something behind her.

Tova twisted round, arms already out to fend Tupe off. He was more than a metre from her, swaying, facing the balcony. He drew his arms down, gunslinger-style, ready to draw.

Beyond him, a form changed shape like a fern unfurling. Tova made out the lowered head, hunched back, the bandaged arms resting on the railing. Richard, on his feet but his knees buckling.

"Back off," Tupe muttered. The warning, plus the gun, enough to stop Tova mid-stride.

"He needs to go back to hospital."

"Your old man assured the docs Richard would be treated by the best Chinese medicine had to offer, so the cops agreed to home bail. Just as well, or the missus here would have been the one to suffer." Each word expelled through hot breath, and Tupe let out a cackle, droplets of spit like an irritant chafing Tova's skin. He backed away, keeping her in sight until he stood on the balcony, too close to Richard.

"I'll help you find what you want if you let them go." She took slow, small steps forward.

"Bit late for that. He knows too much, can't be trusted to shut up. Same goes for you, fuck what the Boss says."

"Don't hurt him." *Bit late for that, too. Try pleading.* "None of us will say anything, I promise."

"Tan promises are worth shit." Tupe drew out the gun.

29. FINN

Without the engine running, the car quickly cooled. He got out, stretched and rubbed his hands together for warmth, thinking he'd give her five minutes, time to talk to Malcolm Tan, ask after Richard, even time to get a drink, use the toilet. Finn was sure she had no intention of staying the night. For starters, she had lowered her glance when she said it, and he doubted Mrs Tan would make her welcome.

His first instinct – wait. Follow Tova if she came out and drove off in Sarah's car. He'd see her to her friend, report to Pavletich that Ms Tan was where she should be, in Newmarket. Even if she saw him, it wouldn't hurt for her to know he was looking out for her. Although the chances were she'd be irate. First he appeared at the Herne Bay house, now he was lingering outside her father's. She'd lay a complaint against him next.

He wished she had driven away. What assumptions would Pavletich jump to, Tova staying with her father?

He stared across at the house, noticed movement, a silhouette on the upper balcony. He waited for the glow of a cigarette, the only reason to venture out. Maybe it wasn't a person at all but a large ornamental ceramic urn, the point of which escaped him.

From his position he could see the side street and up Mellons Bay Road. No one was about. Several parked cars, one near the vehicle entrance to the Tans', a common Toyota. A temporary replacement for the luxury models incinerated? The garages no longer stood, but Tan didn't need to park on the street: there was plenty of room inside the property and Finn was sure he wouldn't lower his standards.

The guttural shout rose above the indistinct murmurs drifting out from the Tans' balcony and into the night. Definitely not Tova; didn't sound like Mr Tan.

Finn stepped back to the edge of the berm, craned his neck up towards the balcony. The figure still there, bent, leaning on the railing, maybe protecting a match against the wind. Except there was no breeze.

Someone else was on the balcony, not Richard, the new person too big, took up a lot of space. Was he witnessing a fallout between Malcolm Tan and one of his men? Tupe Vavau?

Finn rang for backup. It was a guess about Vavau, but Tova was inside and someone was angry.

He tried the small gate. Locked. He'd get no thanks for heroics, not a lone, unarmed officer against a known criminal. If it *was* Vavau doing the shouting. Do a recce from a safe position, ascertain how many people inside, relay the information. How long before backup? Five minutes?

30. TOVA

Surprise her only weapon. She screamed. And sprinted to the balcony and open air, to the noise-carrying stillness and the fire escape at one end. She dragged in a breath and shrieked, the drawn-out "Help!" reaching a crescendo before she needed to draw breath again. Louder. Enough to wake neighbours. *Come on, Richard. Dad. Join in.*

Tupe's headlock reduced her scream to a squeal. She bit down, tasted sweat. She kicked back, aiming for his balls. He tugged tighter, lifting her feet off the floor. His free fist giving short, hard jabs to her head.

Richard fell into Tupe, his weight too light to push Tupe over, but enough to unbalance him. Tupe stumbled, righted himself, grabbed Richard around the throat, driving him back to the balcony edge.

Richard's cries rasped out, his bandaged hands fumbled, seeking a hold.

Tupe thrust Richard up.

Tova lunged, grabbed at denim, gripped air.

Richard's shriek, her own screams, as if "No!" on repeat might rewind the scene. Then the thud, like a sandbag landing, dropped from a height.

A second to crawl to the railing, look down. Move, move, she willed the still body on the ground. She had to reach him. Take the outside stairs? Go back through the house?

A moment of indecision.

It was enough time for Tupe. Her head jerked back, scalp tightening as he clutched at hair, knocked her legs from under her and dragged her along the balcony to the stairs.

She hooked a foot between two struts of the railing, anchored herself, ignored the pain. Tupe yanked. Splitting her in two.

"Let her go."

She twisted towards her rescuer.

Tupe's hold loosened.

Malcolm Tan edged forward, arms outstretched, pleading.

"No, no, he'll shoot." Her warning too late.

Tupe recoiled, then the thunder craaack.

Her father's look of surprise, then his hands covered his chest and he crumpled to the ground.

Someone was beside Malcolm, reaching down. Another gunshot.

Tova jerked up as Tupe tugged her to the stairs.

But not before she'd seen Finn McIntosh rise, call to her. And fall forward.

31. FINN

Tova's screams sent adrenaline coursing through his veins. He jumped at the gate, gripped the top, one foot using the security pad to launch up, scrabble and slide over and down. A clumsy landing then sprinting across the lawn to the house.

Her screaming louder, terror and rage and pain, and he flew up the stairs, swerved right, following the yells, ignored the pale apparition blindly hugging the wall. It wasn't Tova.

The bedroom door open, the room freezing, his mind racing. The couch his first shield, then the bed, moving to the open doors.

Tova, dragged, legs scrabbling. Another figure rose right in front of him, crying out, blocking his view.

Finn had never been shot at, never had a gun pulled on him. He'd listened to real-life cases, watched training videos in the comfort of a conference room, took the practice and drills seriously, but reality was deafening and disorientating.

Malcolm Tan, near his feet. In spite of the commotion, he registered Malcolm's nakedness, yelled, "Vavau, put the gun ..."

Ringing in his ears, discordant bells and cymbals, fast followed by a searing heat to the side of his head. A dull ache radiated from above his ear, and his fingers pressed around the lobe, touched wet and sticky lumps of skin and hair. No gaping hole. A bullet graze, not enough to stop him, the blood pouring out from surface veins. Precious seconds lost.

The ringing in his ears drowned out any sound of car engines, the cavalry arriving. They'd be there, blocking Tupe's escape.

"Suspect, armed, with hostage, heading for side exit," Finn called out, letting Tupe know he had a line of police waiting for him. He'd have no choice but to surrender.

Finn banked on Tupe being stopped by the backup crew, not able to turn to take another shot. He skittered down the steps, ignored spikes of pain from his head, and jumped the last two metres. Buckled over. The deep breath he drew in gave momentum to the rising vomit. As his gut emptied, he caught a glimpse of Tova, half-dragged, half-carried, as Tupe disappeared out the driveway to the street.

There were no shouts of warning, no bulked-out figures in blue blocking the driveway, no sirens, no flashing lights. Nothing to indicate help was out there.

32. TOVA

Tupe's gun jerked against her bruised cheek. She went limp, a dead weight. He didn't even break stride.

She shivered as if feverish. Richard's howls drummed in her head and beat time with the pain pulsing from her ribs. Could he have survived the fall? Bile rose. *Calm down, think. Options?*

No chance against the gun. And Tupe, wired, unpredictable.

Easy to exit the hard-to-get-into property, a swipe of the panel by the gate and it opened. He pushed her to Sarah's car, tugged at the passenger door, the gun in her back. "Open it. Don't fuck me around. You drove this heap here." He fumbled at her jeans. Twisting away from him, she reached into her back pocket and touched the edge of her phone. Her fingers retracted, as though scorched by its cold casing. The keys, snug in the other deep jeans pocket, hadn't dislodged in the struggle.

He slumped on top of her into the seat, using his hip to push against her until she clambered into the driver's position. It took her two attempts to slot the key into the ignition.

"Drive. Fast. No lights."

"Where to?"

The extra prod with the gun indicated 'out of here'. She reversed out of the parking space blind and relied on her memory up the rise of Mellons Bay Road until the windscreen wipers cleared the night dew. She hoped any speeding police car hurtling around the corner saw her first.

"No funny stuff or I'll shoot before you have the door open." Tupe, skin glistening with sweat, took his eyes off her to glare at the dashboard and fiddle with the dials. "Does this wreck have a heater?"

She glanced at the petrol gauge. Damn. Near full.

Tupe followed her glance. "Luck's on my side. The dunga I stole was running on empty."

No traffic to slow for. All green lights and no chance to fling herself out. She strained to hear a helicopter above the rattle and whirl of the air conditioner. She'd seen it often enough on the evening news, the police helicopter circling overhead, its searchlight pinpointing a getaway vehicle, Sarah's little yellow car easy to spot. Roadblocks erected. She'd get away then. Or get caught in crossfire as he left his mark on the world in a shoot-out.

"Gotta get rid of this car," Tupe muttered. He thumped his knee and the gun jolted.

She needed a miracle – a bullet ricocheting off the steering wheel, rebounding into him. She brushed at the tears misting her sight, clenched her teeth, cut off the sobs.

"You Tans all weak," Tupe sneered.

She gripped the steering wheel. Hold it together, her fear feeding him. Onto Pakuranga Road, past the sports grounds, past the college with the fancy brick pillars in its fence. Ahead, in the distance, lights flashed, coming towards them.

"Go left, into the car park. Stop by those trees."

She cursed the mall landscape designers who lined the street frontage of the car park with healthy, bushy shrubs. Tupe pulled her head to his chest, his hand hot on her neck. The tight hold muffled her cries. Police cars, at least three, flashed past, sirens fading, heading in the direction they had come from. To Richard and her father – were they still alive?

"Get going."

Back over the bridge, along the stretch, past the vast shopping mall she'd been to once, nearing the motorway interchange. Cars either side of her at the lights, neither driver looking at her. "Not the motorway, they'll expect that. Take the Onehunga exit," Tupe ordered.

Into an industrial area, dimly lit. Few parked cars, shop-front roller doors pulled down, graffitied. No people around. No one to remember the yellow car. *Why didn't I trust Finn, take up his offer to follow me back to Sarah's?*

Directing her through unfamiliar streets, Tupe peered out the window with the intense gaze of someone looking for recognisable landmarks. Reading the business signs out loud, making it hard for Tova to think. A good thing, better not to think.

Tupe cursed, ordered her to U-turn from Church Street into Mays Road. He had a destination in mind, but wasn't too sure how to get to it.

"Bet the cops go hassle my sister. Ha, she wouldn't help me if I gave her a million bucks. She sure as hell won't help the cops either." It took Tupe a good minute or more to stop snickering.

Most road signs were small, unlit, too hard to decipher before she'd driven past. Until she came to a big roundabout and he pointed her in the direction of Mt Albert Road. Each time she slowed at lights turning amber, he yelled at her to keep going.

An ordinary night in the suburbs, everyone sound asleep in bed unaware of her predicament. She was on her own. Without a clock in Sarah's car, Tova lost sense of time. She'd been driving ten minutes, twenty, maybe more. She doubted she'd be able to prise her fingers from the steering wheel even if it was possible to reach for her phone to check.

Tupe moaned about the car's lack of speed, its colour, no GPS, lack of a CD player. A small mercy, his taste in music no doubt as objectionable as Richard's, full of swearing and misogynistic lyrics.

Richard. And Finn.

Don't think.

Tupe checking over his shoulder, muttering. Tova looked in the rear-view mirror, hoping to see a police car tailgating. No such luck. He fidgeted, gestures wide and wild, stretched, tried to ease his long legs in the cramped foot space.

Does the gun have a safety catch?

33. FINN

Wiping vomit from his chin, Finn hobbled back up the driveway, the pain in his head stronger, and squatted by Richard, pressing two fingers into his neck, the pulse weak. Richard's arm flopped, unresponsive to touch. The crumpled body, the angle of the torso to his limbs and the slow-oozing blood from under his head where his skull had bounced on the cement were enough for Finn not to attempt a check for other injuries.

"Richard, can you hear me?" It was more for Finn to be doing something than an expectation that Richard's eyes would flicker. Mrs Tan, draped in a towel, pushed him aside. She knelt beside her son, her words foreign to Finn's ears and her cries heartbreaking.

The sound of running and Finn froze. Tupe coming back to finish Richard off?

Two uniforms, police officers running up the drive.

"Why did it take so long to get here?" Finn confronted the female who arrived first.

"We arrived within minutes of your call but had to follow orders." She stepped back from Finn and returned his stare. "Detective Senior Sergeant Harris left orders that he was to be informed first if anything happened at this address. We were waiting for his say-so to enter."

"What?" The word rushed out of Finn.

"We did a visual. Everything was quiet. I was on the phone, waiting for Harris to pick up. Then the screaming, and the body fell, and ... and the shot."

"He took a hostage." Blaming her.

"He had a gun," the constable said. "We backed off, took down the rego, rang it in. You need to sit down, you're hurt."

"Save it," Finn snapped as sirens, police and ambulance, muffled her excuses and the ringing in his ears. He pushed past her, dashed to the vehicle gates, figured they'd be on manual as a result of the fire. Adrenaline pumping, he forced them apart, the gates neatly sliding into the metal grooves along the inside of the wall.

"Get out of the way!" Finn yelled as the first squad car drew up in the driveway, although the ambulance had room to come up beside it. Finn waved the ambulance to come through and ran alongside it. "One gunshot upstairs, the other, fell, straight ahead, don't run over him." He wasn't sure if the paramedics heard but it made him feel useful.

Finn prised Mrs Tan up and away from the medics assessing her son, giving them space and relief from her keening.

More squad cars arrived. Another ambulance.

"Get Mrs Tan dressed, give her something to drink," Finn ordered the female constable hovering nearby.

"Find a neighbour to be with her. Or are you going to tell me you have to wait for Harris's command?"

Hands on her belt, eyes blazing, *do it yourself!* "Where will you be?" Suspicious, she expected him to leave the scene.

Which is what he wanted to do, dash off after Tova. Too many minutes had elapsed, too many ways for Tupe to head. Plus, he was unarmed.

With a barely disguised grunt of anger, Finn took to the stairs for the second time that night, back to the balcony. Malcolm Tan lay on a stretcher, a medic adjusting breathing apparatus over his face, the other tucking a blanket around him.

The medic stared at Finn. "Better let me look you over too, mate."

He took his time swabbing the wound. "You must have a hard head. The bullet grazed from your temple to behind your ear. Another millimetre, mate ... Here, let me help you get to the ambulance."

"I don't need to go to hospital. It's a graze, you said."

The medic sighed, probably used to uncooperative patients. "Have it your way, but get to your doctor sooner rather than later."

"Sure."

"Take pain relief every four hours. Dress the wound daily, watch out for infection. If nausea or pain persists, see your doctor." The medic ran each piece of advice into the next, giving it out as the everyday occurrence it probably was, handed him a strip of painkillers and patted him on the shoulder. OK, your life to throw away, the pat said.

34. TOVA

Once past Mt Albert, Tupe's directions became more timely. She didn't overshoot turns. He looked back less. "So far, so good." He tilted his head back and laughed. "The Boss is onto it – the cops are looking in all the wrong places."

But he was sweating and thumping the gun against his jiggling knee, frightening her more. "OK, New Lynn," Tupe read a luminous green road sign as she drew up at a wide intersection. Left to Titirangi, ahead to Kelston, right to Avondale. Tova silently repeated the directions in case she lived long enough to tell the police. A car drew up opposite, also obeying the road rules. Tova's finger touched the light lever, itched to flash onto high beam. Would the driver think anything of it? Would he be listening to the radio, hear on the news to notify the police if they recognised the car?

"Keep going," Tupe ordered. "Don't even look at them or I'll shoot them first, then you."

The moment passed, along with the other car.

A supermarket on the left, a girl's school on the right. She braked down a long hill, then stepped on the accelerator to increase power up the other side. No houses were visible on her left, but trees in the distance and a long, low wall and tidy lawn. She caught a glimpse of the sign: Waikumete Cemetery and Crematorium.

An image of her mother flashed in her mind. Tova wished she could talk to Areta, hold her close, be comforted.

The car laboured up the long, steep hill. The heater was inadequate to warm the deep cold of her bones. Without her jacket, she had only the T-shirt and thin sweater to ward off the night chill. She flexed her fingers to ease cramp.

"Reckon your father might pay to get you back?"

"Not if you killed him." It came out as a whisper, laced with tears.

"Oh, yeah. Bugger."

They were heading west. She had been out to the remote West Auckland beaches where people had been lost and their remains not found for years, if ever.

Tova blinked the tears away, her eyes stinging. Her mother used to smooth the hair from her face whenever she was upset. At every intersection, she anticipated flashing lights and a roadblock forcing the car to stop. Noises, real and imaginary, she hoped were the sound of an approaching helicopter. The few cars she'd seen, none had materialised into police cars.

They approached the deserted Henderson shopping area. She followed his directions onto Swanson Road, right into Lincoln Road. And into ribbons of fog. She switched on the wipers, succeeded in smearing the windscreen until the third swipe cleared an arc.

The sudden drop in temperature caused the inside to mist.

"This bloody fog might help us." Tupe brushed his sleeve against the window. "Yeah, get on the motorway. We'll go to Dargaville," as if they had conferred.

Dargaville was on the north-west coast, roughly in line with Whangarei, she was sure. Fairly sure. That gave her two hours, maybe more, to find a way to convince him he'd get away faster on his own. She'd promise to put in a good word for him, say he treated her well.

"I have mates there. They'll look after me." Out of the corner of her eye, she saw him look at her. "I'll trade you for a decent car."

Bile rose. She clamped her mouth shut, swallowing.

"You're a sour bitch like your mother. Can't you take a joke?" Tupe turned to her, mouth open wide, and laughed, teaching her how it was done.

"Shut up, don't talk about her like that." How did Tupe know Areta?

What possessed her to answer him back? Shock, her heart rate rapid, light-headed, nauseous. She shouldn't be driving.

Tupe feinted a jab at her shoulder, stopped short. "So, not as wimpy as your brother?"

A day ago, she would have corrected him, *half-brother*, distancing herself from Richard. Now, what she'd give to suck back every time she'd done that. When it mattered, up on the balcony, he'd tried to stop Tupe.

"What a dumb fuck. One simple instruction." Tupe shook his head theatrically, like the villain in a melodrama. "Wait at his place for Oso to call, but the idiot was at the Dunn house, sleeping the sleep of the recently shagged. Oso said that by the time he and Hemi realised Richard was there, things had gone arse up."

Why was he telling her? A tactic? Increase her fear so she'd obey him? Or because he really had no intention of letting her live?

"It's not as though you'll be telling anyone, is it?"

Tupe's cackle echoed in the enclosed space. "Jesus, the look on your face. Nah, I just need you long enough to make sure I get far enough away."

Then what?

He aimed a half-hearted kick at the radio. "The radio's crapped out, and you're no conversationalist." Tupe stammered the last word, unfamiliar with it. "Can't stand the quiet. Gotta have noise to keep us both awake – can't have you driving us off into a ditch."

The squirming and jiggling and constant chat. He was hyped and not coming down anytime soon. She wondered if he realised what he was saying. In a few hours, he wouldn't even remember.

"Juliette was a greedy cow, said she'd sell her seedy little brothels to him, then inflated the price. Even more stupid, she thought she was smart enough to cheat the Boss. He found out she was buying up apartments, putting in escorts. Muscling in on his lucrative territory. Everyone knows you don't cross the Boss. Oso was told to scare the girl, put the heat on Juliette to do as she was told. Jasmine didn't take to Oso barging in on her while she was in the bath. She didn't scare easily, and he didn't know his own strength. Oso said it was funny watching Richard try to dress the girl and fail, he was shaking and blubbering so much." Tupe shot a sly glance her way, expecting a reaction.

Tova imagined Richard, terrified, yet wanting dignity for Jasmine.

"I'm surrounded by fuckwits. Instead of figuring out how to blame Richard for the girl's death, Hemi panicked and rang his wife, who said dump the girl down on the beach, make it look like the tide carried her there. Hemi forgot to mention that Oso stabbed the girl. Bit of a giveaway that she hadn't jumped in the sea at Herne Bay and drifted to Te Atatu, don't you think?"

Her throat constricted, dried. She couldn't reply, even if she wanted to.

"Repeka told them to make it look like Mrs Dunn killed the daughter, then herself. That way, we accomplished what the Boss wanted, in a roundabout sort of way – no more trouble from Juliette Dunn."

"The Boss?" Her voice squeaked. Tupe had said it almost reverently.

Tupe ignored her. "Repeka's ideas could have worked. Dump the Dunns in two different places, use your idiot brother's car. Oso reckoned they were lucky that Richard didn't kill them all with his driving, he was shaking so much. Mrs Dunn was told Jasmine was in trouble out at O'neills. She realised too late it was a set-up. She tried to run, stupid bitch. Oso chased her down. Hemi had the jitters real bad by this time, and they dug a shallow grave. Idiots, can't think things through." He let out a cross between a laugh and a bitter grunt. "So much for Repeka's idea of a murder-suicide."

Tova tried concentrating on the white lines on the road but couldn't lose the image of Mrs Dunn's last moments, made vivid by Tupe's storytelling.

"Then Richard stuffed up over the car, didn't get rid of it as he was told. That bloody car could connect Hemi and Oso and the girl." Tupe sighed. "We had a good thing going, but the Boss was never satisfied. He wanted more, and more."

The Boss. "Don't oppose me," her father had said, his face set hard when Areta linked casinos and prostitution as reason enough to pull out of his investment. Areta opposed him and she was dead. Richard didn't toe the line, and he was most likely dead, too. The police and their constant questions about her father. Was this all Malcolm's doing? Then it all went wrong. The death of Oso, Richard's stupidity, Tupe taking what he could while he had the chance?

She pictured Malcolm by the bed, his eyes warning her. He'd freed himself, risked his life on the balcony, tried to stop Tupe as Richard had. *Actions speak louder than words.*

Tova struggled to inhale. Her eyes filled with tears of regret.

"What the shit's the matter with you now?" Tupe screeched. "If you're trying anything funny ..."

A van came up behind them, its headlights lighting up the inside of the car, highlighting the sheen on Tupe's face as he squirmed around to check. "Bloody tailgater. Speed up."

"The car won't go much faster," Tova reminded him.

"No shit." The rest of his words lost as he wrenched the steering wheel. The car rocked, slid, fishtailed.

"What are you doing?" Tova shrieked. A glance in the rear-view mirror and the vehicle behind veered around them on the left side, horn blaring as it sped down the motorway on-ramp, heading north.

Tova held on, swung the wheel back, an automatic reaction. Accelerate or brake in a skid?

"Stupid bitch, you'll get us killed," Tupe yelled back.

Killed in a rolling car suddenly more preferable to what his mates might do and the shallow grave they'd make her dig.

The car slowed, righted itself, stalled.

Movements jerky, fighting her stiff and aching limbs, fuelled by fear, Tova flung open the door, scrambled out, whimpered, willed it louder, and piercing, enough to wake the whole suburb.

"Think I'm stupid?" Tupe dragged her back, her knee scraping the asphalt. "I was ready for that, you stupid bitch. Now, drive before I think you're too much trouble."

Fingers trembling, she turned the key in the ignition. The engine fired. No such luck that the stall had been a last gasp.

"This car's shit, have to get rid of it." His knee jiggled and the gun jumped up and down. "Head back to Te Atatu peninsula and shut the fuck up, no more talking."

Te Atatu was on a peninsula; one way in, one way out. The slim chance of escape faded.

"Repeka started all this shit." Tupe broke the silence. His head bobbed up and down, decision made. "So she can fix it."

Tova gripped the steering wheel tighter. What would Repeka Hemona's idea of '*fixing it*' be? Tova instinctively lifted her foot from the accelerator.

Tupe prodded the gun into her ribs. "Fuck, you're nuts if you think jumping out is gonna save you. Now, just drive. Straight ahead." Apparently, no longer trusting her to remain docile, he kept the gun pressed into her side. His breathing was louder and his knee jiggled faster.

He was scared of Repeka, too. Why? "Is Mrs Hemona your Boss?" Did that explain his growing agitation? No, Tupe had referred to the Boss as 'he'.

"In her dreams. She thinks she's got all the answers. I'll let her figure out what to do with you."

"Let me go. Think it through. The cops know who you are. They'll find you." Tova cringed at her pleading tone, she spoke too fast. Slow down, give him time to think. "Don't make it worse than it already is. It'll be better for you if you let me go."

He turned to face her, his head on a slant. Was he really considering it?

"If you believe that, you're as stupid as your brother. Now, shut up. Take a right here. Keep going to the car park."

They bypassed the small shopping area, drove down a winding street. She had to get her bearings, visualise how close the houses were, where the paths led. Too dark for joggers. A mother up with a baby or an early-rising shift worker might hear her scream. Her heart rate increased. Her grip on the steering wheel didn't stop the trembling.

The headlights picked out the white parking lines, the metal rubbish bins, paper bags with the recognisable fast-food logo that had either escaped the bin or had never been captured in the first place. Tova turned off the engine, the lights cut out, the seaside car park enveloped in darkness, the light poles around the edge housing broken remnants of bulbs.

"Get out. We'll walk, check the place out first in case the cops aren't dumb." Tupe pulled her out the passenger side, the gear stick scraping her hip bone. Her yelp was lost in the night air and the rhythm of the waves on the shore. "Shut up, no one can hear you."

She stumbled. He yanked her up. She twisted her body to make sure he didn't feel the outline of the phone in her pocket. The throbbing in her shoulder took attention away from the agony in her side. The moon emitted enough light to make out the walkway. A dense angle of shadowy vegetation separated the reserve area from the nearby roads and homes.

The path divided. Tupe pinned her to him, shuffled into the trees, the hand smothering her smelt of sweat and gun metal and unwashed denim where he'd wiped his palm down his jeans. She wriggled free, breathed and gulped in a mixture of sea air and armpit odour.

Dew dampened her sneakers and soaked into the hem of her jeans which rubbed against her shins, coarse and clammy. The vegetation thinned, and the shape of a house loomed in front of her.

Tupe took a step forward, security lights flashed on and he pulled back, deeper into the foliage. Tova prayed for a barking dog, movement from the house, an opening door, a neighbour asking, "Who's there?" The lights flicked off.

Tupe stayed within the trees, oblivious to scratches and scrapes tea-tree branches inflicted on himself or Tova. He stopped, restrained her with a one-armed headlock and pulled out a phone from his jeans. She tugged against him; he tightened his hold. The call took a few seconds, grunts from him and what sounded like an angry retort from the receiver.

"This one." Tupe pulled her into a backyard, sidestepped a kid's bike abandoned on the ground. A sliver of light glinted below curtains covering ranchsliders. Tupe prodded her forward with the gun.

35. FINN

"You didn't chase after him, McIntosh?" Harris, sarcastic. Trust him to be the first senior officer to turn up. It wouldn't have surprised Finn to learn that Harris had been around the corner the whole time. His constable cornered him first as he came up the drive. Her words inaudible, accompanied with lots of arm waving in Finn's direction before Harris approached.

"No, sir. Vavau was armed. We attended to the injured and secured the site as best we could." Finn included the other officer. No point in throwing accusations around. Not yet. It would all come out in the internal enquiry.

"One of my men ascertained the Toyota on the side road is stolen. So we know how Vavau arrived here," Harris stated.

Another black mark against Finn for having failed to do that.

"My constable says Ms Tan gave Vavau the keys to the getaway car."

"Ms Tan is a hostage, not his accomplice. She had a gun to her head, giving her little choice. Sir." Finn let his deliberate pause convey his feelings.

Harris tightened his lips at the slight.

"Detective Pavletich cleared Ms Tan." Even though he wasn't too sure where his boss was with his latest thinking.

"Did he? That's a bad call." Harris eyed Finn up and down, noticed the state of him. "You ignored the medic's advice to get checked over, so you must be well enough to get to work. Clean yourself up and go keep that rabble out there quiet." He pointed to the growing number of spectators. "When I have time, you can give me your version of what happened." Implying it was sure to be lies.

"Sir ..." Finn wanted to be on the road, joining a search squad. The adrenaline rush still strong, heart rate up, sweating.

"This is my crime scene, McIntosh. You're in it, you follow my orders." Harris strode away, to the growing number of officials inside the Do Not Cross tape already cordoning off the vehicle entrance: uniforms, ESR staff, people on walkie-talkies and mobiles and holding clipboards.

Aided by torchlight and with the help of the house lights now blazing, Finn went looking for a tap, found one along from the back door, hose attached. He rinsed blood from hands and face, careful to avoid wetting the large bandage covering his ear, held in place by surgical tape. He swallowed two Panadol from the ten-pack the medic gave him, hoped they kicked in fast and dulled the throbbing gouge along the side of his head.

He joined the line of officers by the tape, blocking

the view of the body on the ground. The media could be stopped from climbing the wall. They couldn't be prevented from standing on the bonnets of their own cars and using telescopic lenses. One or two had collapsible stepladders. Old hands.

An official photographer arrived. Officers were suiting up in white coveralls; others were holding iPads, numbered scene triangles. They milled about, conversing, planning the scene examination. Two fingerprinters with their tool boxes waited to enter. Mrs Tan, in a full-length floral, silky kimono with matching glittering slippers, continued her wailing. A constable was failing to calm her down. Had Harris thought to find a translator?

Finn advised spectators to go back home, and avoided eye contact with the journalists, exasperated that they had arrived at the scene so quickly. He refused to respond to their questions and also to those from locals who, in spite of the low temperature and the fact that most of the action was hidden from their view, still waited, talking among themselves.

Harris appeared at his shoulder. "McIntosh, instead of standing around, go relieve my officer, she's keeping an eye on Mrs Tan until I can talk with her. There's a back entrance, don't go through the front, it's part of the crime scene." An afterthought. "Did you think to call a translator?"

Hitting a superior officer was a serious offence, Finn reminded himself. Veering left around the house, he rang Pavletich. Straight to voicemail. He disconnected the call before he said anything about Harris he might regret, pocketed the mobile. He entered the kitchen and Harris's constable hurried off, offering no transfer of information or thanks.

Mrs Tan got up from the table, refilled the kettle, lined up a cup, with saucer, placed a jug of milk and a sugar bowl beside them. Hostess duties ingrained.

"I'm Constable Finn McIntosh, Mrs Tan. As soon as possible, you'll be taken to the hospital." He didn't expect a reply, assumptions made because he had heard her speak Chinese. He checked his watch. Almost midnight and a few hours yet until the scene examination was complete. His mobile rang, the *Jaws* theme unmistakable.

"Where the bloody hell are you, McIntosh?"

Finn had never been so pleased to hear Pavletich.

"Kitchen, rear door access." Even Pavletich wouldn't be allowed to wander through the house during the forensic examination.

But it was Ngaire at the door a minute later. "You look like crap, Finny."

Snap. She looked straight out of a deep sleep, dark circles under her eyes and no time spent on combing her hair into its usual neat ponytail.

"Where's the boss?" he asked.

"Being briefed by Detective Harris. You tell me your version of what happened." She'd compare stories, check if they matched.

Finn moved to the back door and stood outside, out of earshot, but keeping Mrs Tan in view. The way she ignored Ngaire, and him, he was sure she understood English.

Ngaire followed, zipped up her jacket and snuggled into it. "Jeez, it's cold." She flapped her arms to generate warmth.

He skipped straight to the first gunshot, tripping over Malcolm Tan, seeing blood on his clothes. Glossed over his own injury: "It's a surface wound." He described

Tupe dragging Tova along the balcony and coughed to disguise the crack in his voice. Ngaire didn't do any of that shallow comfort stuff, patting his arm or widening her eyes in fake distress. As he thought how to recap the last few minutes, he experienced again the pain and fear on Tova's face, the pleading look she gave him as she disappeared down the stairs.

"Harris gave the order. No one to go near the house without his direct authority. Wasted precious time," Finn said neutrally, which belied the emotion below the surface. "So much for Harris's promise to cooperate with Pavletich."

"You do know that Harris and Pavletich are in the running for Inspector Smith's job? He's retiring soon."

Such matters were supposed to be hush-hush, to stop speculation and canvassing. It didn't surprise him that Ngaire knew the gossip.

"Are you implying that Harris put Tova at risk to get one up on Pavletich?"

"I doubt he'll see it that way. You know, resources stretched thin, or miscommunication, or ..." Ngaire obviously couldn't think of another reason.

"That bastard. I don't believe it," hissed Finn. Although he did. He took a step forward, ready to hunt Harris down. "If Tova's hurt, I'm going to ..."

Wright pulled him back. "Calm down. That *bastard* might be your next boss. With luck the roadblocks have worked."

"If that had happened, Harris would be crowing."

"Well, the experts will be onto it. There's nothing to do but wait."

Ngaire was right. An armed man on the loose in the suburbs, the Armed Offenders Squad would be on high alert, traffic details positioned at key points, roads blocked off. Tupe had nowhere to go. Finn's real fear was not knowing how a cornered Tupe would react: realise the senselessness of fighting it out and surrender, or choose to go down in a blaze of glory, taking Tova with him?

"I'll wait here, see if I can get anything out of Mrs Tan. Go for a walk, lurk in the shadows, whatever. Clear your head before you have to give your statement. I'll ring you if you're needed. And promise you won't do anything stupid."

What did Ngaire think he might do, run off after Tova? He'd been told to stay at the scene, so stay he would, but he had to be *doing* – back to the street, keeping an eye on the remaining few hardy spectators. Most had drifted off once the ambulances had driven away. His head felt tight, numb. Maybe he should have taken extra painkillers.

His headache worsened at the sight of Luke Unsworth, in uniform, approaching him.

"Yeah," Unsworth said as way of greeting and in response to Finn's frown of surprise. "Pavletich dragged Wright, Cranston and me along, talked it up, said our suspects were involved. We get here and he puts us on bloody crowd control. What's going on, McIntosh?"

Tempting, get it off his chest, expand on the summary he'd given Ngaire, rant about Harris. Something stopped him. If he was ever tempted to seek a confidante, it wouldn't be Unsworth.

"Don't know," Finn shrugged. True, if Unsworth was referring to what strategy Harris was adopting to apprehend Tupe Vavau.

Unsworth swore, not quite under his breath. "Bloody

hell," and he spun away from Finn, tugging his mobile from his pocket.

Unsworth losing his temper wasn't going to change anything. And if he was about to have a quick flutter, that was guaranteed to increase his stress level, not reduce it.

"Luke," Finn began, unsure of what he intended to say, feeling he should say something, offer advice or a warning, but his own mobile vibrated and gave off the door-knock sound, sign of an incoming text.

Come now main door, the curt text sent by Ngaire.

Finn walked up the drive, felt like he was on the road to doom. Pavletich and Harris stood out of the way of the forensic team and photographer still at work inside the entrance. Side by side, legs wide and arms crossed across their chests, they formed a blockade – no one in unless on their say-so.

Harris was so loud team members looked their way. "Your Westie hothead created this fiasco, Goran. His inaction let those two get away before roadblocks were in place. Better hope the Eagle spots them on the motorway."

"I'll deal with it," Pavletich said.

Finn stopped a respectful two paces away.

"Get yourself seen to, McIntosh, then go home. Be at my office tomorrow morning, we'll get your statement then."

"Sir? I want to ..." Finn spluttered out, ignoring his inner voice telling him to shut up.

"McIntosh. Eight am. Sharp." Pavletich clipped his words.

Harris thumped Pavletich on the back, and Finn interpreted it as sympathy for a colleague. *Rather you than me dealing with insubordination.* "You'll have my report by tomorrow afternoon." He eyeballed Finn as he left.

Pavletich accompanied Finn to his car and waited until he buckled into the driver's seat. "You sure you're well enough to drive? I can arrange for one of Harris's people to take you home."

Not bloody likely.

"Harris has it in for you. No authorisation, procedures of entry not followed, ill-prepared, your actions endangered others, not to mention allowing a suspect to escape. He even asked if you might be aiding and abetting Ms Tan. And he threw in a few remarks about your discipline charge at Counties Manukau."

Finn, about to object, thought better of it. *Don't react.* Not like the time he questioned Harris and ended up disciplined. *This time, be prepared.*

"McIntosh, I know who I'll believe."

Finn frowned, unsure who his boss meant.

Pavletich slapped the roof of the car. "You, McIntosh. Wright told me about the delay in help arriving. Sounds to me like Harris made a decision that's having repercussions. To be fair, we all have to make calls based on what we know at the time. I've known Harris for years – he's slick, he'll figure out a way to make himself look good. Too bad if it makes you look incompetent in the process."

Tired beyond exhaustion, Finn wanted a shower, more painkillers, curl up in bed, hibernate. He knew he wouldn't, couldn't. He'd find out the direction Tupe went, go that way.

Pavletich leaned down until at eye-level with Finn. "Vavau's ahead of the roadblocks. Harris is gambling on blood being thicker than water, says he will be making for his sister's place down Papatoetoe way, for a change of car, food, a place to lie low for a day or two. What do you think?"

Finn imagined Tupe's situation. He had a hostage. And a considerable head start. He needed to get the yellow car off the road, get another vehicle, preferably one not reported stolen. The first place the police checked would be Tupe's apartment, then family. Tupe was smart enough to figure that, so he wouldn't go to them. The same with his known city associates; he'd bank on the police going for the obvious first. He probably had mates all over the Far North but he'd have to get to them, so he needed to call in favours from someone on the fringe, someone who had reason to help him, feed him, get him a car, give him money if necessary. Someone unlikely to have any qualms about Tova Tan.

"Hemi Hemona. And in his absence, Repeka."

Pavletich slapped the car roof again. "We'll make a detective of you yet, McIntosh." He gazed back towards the Tan property. "Harris is stepping all over my investigation, and I don't want him to get wind of this, in case he's right and I'm losing my touch."

"Sir?"

"Think I'll call on Mrs Hemona. Tupe will be long gone, if he did go to Te Atatu in the first place. Repeka is in enough trouble already, she'll spill, tell us where to find him."

Finn undid his seat belt, opened the car door.

"Not you, McIntosh. You need rest. I'll go round up Wright, Unsworth and Cranston and return them to their warm beds, via a detour to Te Atatu. Don't worry, McIntosh, you'll get your chance one day. Go home; don't get caught speeding on the way."

36. TOVA

"Are you fucking mad?" The volume low, no more than a whisper, but Repeka's anger unmistakable. Bed-hair messy around her face, faded trackpants, baggy T-shirt and her usual intimidating glare. "Why's she with you?"

Suggesting Tova had a choice.

"A car and money, then I'm gone."

Tupe thrust Tova through the ranchslider into a space dominated by a long black leather couch and the largest TV screen Tova had ever seen. A wide bench separated off the kitchen, and an arch led through to a hallway. A strip of ceiling spotlights shed a soft glow across the sparsely furnished room. He propelled Tova to the kitchen bench, stood behind her, like customers waiting to order. "Anything to eat?"

Repeka slid the ranchslider shut, locked it and pulled the curtains. "Keep it down; you'll wake Jacob."

Pushed against the counter, Tova judged the distance to the hall, to the front door. Three against one if the kid woke up.

Repeka moved to the fridge, took out the makings for sandwiches. Tupe launched into his version of events, some of which Tova could dispute. He made out he'd fought off an army.

Repeka appeared unimpressed. She pulled out four thin slices of bread from a packet in the fridge, slathered on butter, then mayonnaise, dropped hunks of meat from a roast chicken onto two of them and slapped the other slices on top. Her palm squished the sandwiches flat, mayonnaise seeping out the sides. She sawed the sandwiches in half, leaving no doubt in Tova's mind as to her mood.

"Take the food and bugger off," Repeka said, pushing the sandwiches at him.

One bite and a third of the sandwich disappeared. Pellets of masticated bread and mayonnaise-laden chicken shreds erupted from Tupe, dropped to the bench. He scooped them up, shoved them back in his mouth.

"I need the toilet. Please." Tova clutched her crotch like a little kid.

Repeka moved plastic containers back into the fridge, rinsed utensils under the tap. Took her time thinking about it. "OK, don't want you pissing on my clean floor. Don't turn on any lights." Repeka signalled to Tupe, pushing the sandwich into his mouth like a starved man at a banquet. "Go with her, make sure she doesn't try anything."

"Jeez, woman, stop panicking," Tupe said with his mouth full. "No one followed us. The Boss saw to that."

37. FINN

Finn calculated he was ten, maybe fifteen minutes ahead of Pavletich, enough time to have a recce. He was already in trouble – another discipline breach on his record hardly worth worrying about – but for Pavletich, being forewarned that Tupe Vavau was or was not at the Hemonas' could be the one thing to tip Smith's job in his favour. A quick swipe and flick and his mobile was off: no way for Pavletich to check where he was.

He had to lift his foot off the accelerator several times as he travelled north on the almost-deserted motorway. It felt like hours since he'd sped away from Howick but the dashboard clock glowed 3:17. Tuesday already. He'd been on the road forty-nine minutes when he took the Te Atatu off-ramp, turned right on the green light and headed towards the peninsula.

If he was Tupe, what would he do? Not drive up to Repeka's door, that was for sure, but use the same walkway Oso and Hemi had used to dump Jasmine. Even if Tupe didn't have first-hand knowledge, he'd know it provided easy and, at this time of night, unseen access to the Hemonas'. So Finn followed Te Atatu Road almost its entire length before turning into Rewarewa Road, then first left into Dawnhaven Drive, to the small picnic area and car park at the end.

And there was Sarah's car.

Finn cruised up behind it, flicked his headlights to high beam and parked up. Tupe would be long gone but maybe Tova was there, hurt, unable to call for help. He took a moment before approaching the vehicle, watched for any movement from the shadows. Then, staying wide, he walked around it, peered through the windows. No one there. At the boot, he hesitated. He wouldn't put it past Tupe.

"Tova?" He knocked on the metal, listened.

Two strides back to his own car to grab the wheel brace, a lever to prise open the boot; he wondered if Sarah's car was unlocked. The Mt Roskill incident flashed in his mind, still contentious years later – a car parked at a crime scene, left untouched for days until someone thought to check. The sole saving grace, the woman in the boot declared already dead when she was put in.

The driver's door sprang open and Finn popped the boot release. With heartbeat rapid, fingers touching icy metal, he raised the boot.

Body-less, the cavity occupied by crumpled recyclable shopping bags. A second of relief, surpassed by the realisation that Tupe had taken Tova with him to the Hemonas'.

No gain by contacting Pavletich to tell him the car was empty. He'd be here in a few minutes, see for himself.

Wisps of fog came off the sea, adding to the gloom and shadows, changing the look of how he remembered the area. Torch beam on low, angled down, kept him to the path, forewarned him of low-hanging branches and a sudden plunge to the mud below. Where Jasmine's body had been found, he did a three-sixty degrees turn, the torch beam picking up no new body, not at the treeline, not in the water. At the path's junction he stopped, listened again. A vehicle heading his way. With torch off, he crept into the trees and shrubs at the back of the Hemona property and edged forward. No back fence, the treeline giving way to a few bedraggled shrubs, then the open backyard, an empty clothesline, a bike on its side, a line of dead plants in pots against the wall and a sliver of light along the bottom of the ranchslider.

Calculate the risk; cross the open space to get right up to the house or use the walkway, out of sight of the line of houses backing onto the reserve? The walkway presented the safer alternative. Finn backed out of the shrubs, kept his head down and entered the alley leading up to the cul-de-sac, the bulb end of Rewarewa Road. A metre separated the house and the wooden fence. Level with the back wall, he stopped, listened, sounds carrying in the stillness. Was that a television on or the murmur of people speaking? He strained to hear. Words indistinct, the rhythm too irregular for TV.

How long had it been? Five minutes, maybe a little more? Long enough for Pavletich to turn up, see his car, wonder where he was.

Tiptoeing until he reached the shrub line, away from the house and the possibility of his footsteps being heard, then into a run, he headed back to the car park. He broke stride at Jasmine's spot, mouthed, "I'm sorry. We haven't solved it yet, but we're onto it." The rhythmic wash of the waves against the wall his only answer.

He spilled off the path and into the headlight beam from Pavletich's vehicle, people getting out of it, all bracing themselves, ready to react to the person charging at them.

"Lights are on at the Hemonas'. I got close, heard people talking," Finn, puffing, short of breath.

"Likely to be Repeka and her son," Cranston said.

Finn had already wondered that, discounted it. Repeka and Jacob barely conversed in daylight. "Maybe, but ..."

They all talked over him.

"You had us worried, Finny; didn't answer your phone." Wright's relief evident.

"Bloody hell, McIntosh, you should be resting in bed." Pavletich's worry almost endearing. The moment passed. "First things first, McIntosh." Pavletich pointed to Sarah's car. "It's empty, I take it."

"Yes," Finn said, an admission he'd interfered in a crime scene.

"Still, this gives me leverage to get a full crew out here. Second, we don't know what we might be walking into so we wait for backup. Hope Harris hasn't commandeered all the dog handlers for the night." He opened his mobile, turned his back and walked several paces away to make the call.

Wright did as Finn had, walked around Sarah's car, peered in. Pulling her sleeve down to cover her hand, she opened the driver's door. Without touching anything, she checked under the seat, behind it. More clear-headed than he, leaving no indication of her presence to waste the forensic team's time.

"The boss's hunch that Vavau would head here was spot on," she said, admiration clear in her voice. "No blood, so Ms Tan isn't hurt, at least, not in the vehicle. What are the chances he dumped her along the way?" Ngaire put her hand on his arm. "By dumped, Finn, I mean he left her. She'd be a hindrance, slow him down."

A flash of hope, Ngaire, prophetic; Tova offloaded onto the side of a road somewhere, bedraggled, injured, but alive.

Finn knew Tova's chances were slim. Tupe, up until now, displayed more brains, leaving the brawn to Oso. But with Oso gone, and no time to replace him, Tupe had to do his own dirty work. Finn had already witnessed the extent of his cruelty to Richard.

"We'll get into the house, find both women with their throats slit and Vavau long gone," Unsworth said, mute until now.

"Was that necessary, Luke?" Ngaire asked and moved to Finn's side, closeness offering comfort.

It didn't work. Unsworth was probably right. But it wasn't like him to be so pessimistic. All night Unsworth had not been his usual cocky self. Whatever was going on in his life, he'd have to sort it fast before it impacted too much on his job.

"Luke, you've been wrong once tonight already, so I expect you're wrong this time, too. Pay up, and quit while you're ahead." Unsworth started to object, took in Ngaire's folded arms and fixed stare. He pulled out his wallet and withdrew a crisp twenty-dollar note and slapped it into her outstretched palm. "Thanks, Finn. Luke bet you'd be tucked up in bed by now and I said you'd be here."

Bloody hell, betting on him now.

Pavletich's call got their attention. "We're here." They crowded around and he swiped his finger across his phone, enlarged the Google map, bringing into focus the street they drove down, the car park, the harbourside walkway running behind the Hemonas' house.

"Repeka is too smart to leave," Finn decided. "She'll ride it out, play the victim, say Vavau turned up uninvited, threatened her if she didn't hand over car keys. We've got surprise on our side. I say we go talk to her." And see if Tova is there. He couldn't think beyond that.

"That sounds more like our Mrs Hemona. Running away isn't in her psyche, and I'd like nothing better than to confront her," Pavletich admitted. "She's got a lot of explaining to do, but until we know the house is safe, McIntosh, we do not approach. We wait for backup."

On cue, his phone rang. Pavletich listened, ended the call. "Shit. The action is still down South Auckland. No sightings of Vavau yet. They've got the Eagle up in the sky spotlighting every back road. Harris seems to have convinced the Area Commander that Sarah's car here is a decoy. Thinks Ms Tan drove him to where he had another car waiting, which is why we haven't found him yet. She drove to Te Atatu, left the car to sidetrack us. A tow truck is coming to secure it for forensic examination later."

"How can he think that?" Finn couldn't conceal his disbelief.

"I might have given him the idea, McIntosh," Pavletich said, avoiding Finn's stare. "Back at Howick, I told him some of what you told me about Ms Tan and the Hemonas. He already thought Tova and Tupe were connected: revenge on her father – he wasn't too clear yet on that – then them driving off together, he wonders if she's dumped the car close to the Hemonas to put them in the shit; payback for them sucking her brother into their dirty world."

Finn felt he'd been punched in the gut, winded. "I told him what I saw, Tupe dragged Tova off the balcony; no way did she go willingly." The image of Tova clear, her foot thrashing to get a hold of the railing, the fear, the plea for help on her face. He wanted to lash out, hit something, someone. Finn folded his arms.

"Conflicting reports, he said. He says we can't rely on your say-so that Ms Tan was abducted."

"The man's a ..."

"Delete that thought, McIntosh. You might end up working for Harris."

The sound of gentle waves sloshing against the beach wall, a distant barking dog, the rumble of a semi-trailer on the motorway – all sounds magnified in the still, cold night. Closer, Ngaire shuffled from foot to foot to keep warm, Unsworth played with the zipper on his jacket and Pavletich slapped his phone against his palm.

Think. Don't get distracted. "Let's say Harris is right, which means Vavau is kilometres away and no danger to us." Finn had their attention. "Tova is a fugitive suspect in a murder enquiry and is possibly holed up at Repeka's. That gives us cause to enter and search." He'd go with that scenario, if it got him into the house.

"I don't ..."

"Maybe not enter." Finn cut Pavletich off. "But put us to good use. We can gather intel, check vehicles, exits, dead ends, obstacles, make sure Repeka doesn't abscond." He sounded like a training manual. "For when backup arrives, make their job easier if they know the layout."

Pavletich didn't reply immediately. A good sign, meant he was considering Finn's idea.

"This is my case and I'll see it to the end. A recce of the street and house, get as close as you can without being seen," Pavletich said. "If I hear that Vavau has been located, or captured, I'll let you know. Then – and only then – go arrest Repeka on suspicion of harbouring a murder suspect. For all we know, Richard Tan or his father have died by now."

"And Ms Tan?" Finn tried not to linger on Pavletich's bluntness.

"We know she isn't Vavau's accomplice, but she still has to be cleared. If she's in the house, take her into custody." Pavletich peered at Finn's face. "You've had a rough night, McIntosh. Sure you're up to it?"

"I'll take Cranston." No way was he going to miss out. He fingered the bandage over his ear. It felt dry, the blood congealed by now. He'd pop two more Panadol, stave off the pending headache as soon as he got the chance.

"Unsworth, too. He's like a kid with ADHD tonight – do him good to work off all that pent-up energy."

"OK." Finn would have preferred Wright but he didn't suggest it, in case Pavletich had second thoughts and made them all hang around in the car park until backup arrived.

"Wright and I'll be on the walkway, keep an eye on the back of the house in case Repeka decides to bolt that way."

They made their way back along Dawnhaven Street, to its intersection with Rewarewa Road. Cranston was like an eager puppy waiting for its leash to be removed, keeping a few paces ahead, looking back. Unsworth stayed close. Finn ignored him, instead concentrating on storing information: stationery vehicles parked against the curb, in driveways, houses with high fences and gates protecting the inhabitants.

They turned into Rewarewa Road, the grass verge dulling footsteps. Cranston slowed. Unsworth pressed against his shoulder. Heavy cloud cover blocked the moon, and further into the street tendrils of fog drifted. No lights on in any house, the single street lamp near KK's home effective only in illuminating a three-metre circle under it.

Finn listened. If other squads were on their way, they were nowhere near yet.

"If Vavau's in there, let me have a go first," Unsworth whispered.

"That's not going to happen." Finn blew on fingers succumbing to the cold and wished he was in uniform like the other two with their police-issue gloves. He thrust his hands deep into his thin jacket's pockets.

"Talk to him, I mean. Negotiate." Unsworth sounded as if his idea was feasible.

"Don't be an idiot, Unsworth." What was he trying to do, sabotage his career? He must have displayed good sense somewhere along the line to be fast-tracked. "We'll go closer. Stay behind me," Finn ordered.

38. TOVA

Tova glanced along the hall. A deadlock and two slide bolts, top and bottom on the front door, hindered escape that way.

"Humour her, do it in the dark or she'll go mental." Tupe right behind her, pushed open the toilet door. Old-fashioned, a long, narrow space, louvred window high above the cistern.

"Even a skinny bitch like you is too big to slide through that." Tupe pointed at the window and then prodded her into the room. "One minute." He shoved the last of the sandwich into his mouth.

The door had no lock. Standing against it, her fingers shaky, Tova reached in her back pocket and dug out her mobile. Her fear that Tupe might see the phone's screen light was unfounded. The 'low battery' warning flickered, the brightness automatically dimmed to conserve power. She switched the phone to silent, cleared her throat and tapped in her password. Her fingers fluttered over the emergency call symbol.

Couldn't risk speaking. Hesitated. Text the police? She'd never heard that was possible, didn't have time to Google. Send Finn a text? She bit her lip. She had seen him on the dark balcony, the shot, him falling. Would he get it? She shivered. Mustn't think of Finn. Trembling, fingertips numb, she scrolled to Sarah's name, prayed the phone was right beside her bed, turned on.

Tova pulled her jeans down. She did need to pee.

@ hemonas tupe crazy tell police.

She pressed Send as she flushed the toilet. The phone battery had too little charge left to record. It didn't bear thinking what Tupe was capable of if he found it on her. She thought of dropping the phone in the cistern. Opening it might make noise he'd investigate. Raising the plastic toilet seat, she placed her feet on either side of the bowl and reached up to slide and push the phone out through the bottom louvre. She coughed again to mask the *plop* as it hit the ground.

"Hurry up." Tupe's fist thudded against the door.

Tova stepped out of the toilet's comparative safety. Tupe was already on his way back to the kitchen. Two bounds, maybe three to reach the front room and a window to freedom. She spun away, arms outstretched like a runner breasting finish-line tape.

Tupe's tackle dropped her and the sound forced out was more a yelp of frustration than the blood-curdling scream she intended. She kicked out in spite of the pain that shot up her side with each thrust. Tupe seized both legs and hauled her back to Repeka, dropping her in the centre of the room.

Repeka snorted, an aroused spectator at fight club, keen for more.

Tupe, teeth clenched, turned on her. "I'm in this mess because of you, so you deal with her." Nose to nose, like prize fighters upping the intimidation stakes. "Now I need a piss." He shifted the gun from his waistband, lodged it under his armpit and unzipped his fly as he ambled to the hall. At the toilet door, he flicked the light switch.

39. FINN

Finn signalled them to halt at the vantage point where the neighbour's high wooden fence ended and the Hemonas' wire fence began. Walking beyond it would put them in full view of anyone looking out from the front windows. Through the slithering fog, Finn made out the vehicles in the drive. Big men could be hiding behind them.

He took a peep. A light was on behind frosted, louvred slats high up in the side wall. He pulled back, bumped into Unsworth who stumbled against the fence, the thump echoing through the stillness.

Finn held his breath, counted to ten. No reaction from any of the houses. Maybe the noise not as loud as Finn thought.

Unsworth, on hands and knees, fumbled around on the ground.

Finn was about to haul him up, apologise for the collision when Cranston knelt, picked up a small dark object.

"Who were you calling, Unsworth?" Cranston said, and offered the object to Finn.

Unsworth made a grab at Finn's hand.

Finn retracted it automatically, keeping a firm grip on the slim mobile phone. He pocketed it and pulled Unsworth and Cranston back, beyond the neighbour's fence. "Keep it down. Noises travel. What the hell's going on?"

"It fell out of my pocket when you knocked into me. That's all. No big deal."

"It was turned on, Luke. I saw the screen," Cranston said.

Hell, the guy had it bad. They were on surveillance and he was checking a game site, maybe even having a quick flutter. "Do something about your gambling problem, Unsworth, before you end up losing your job." He couldn't ignore Unsworth's behaviour now; his lack of focus had the potential to put them all in danger. He'd have to report the incident to Pavletich.

"Give it back. You can't just take it." Unsworth leant in, plucked at Finn's jacket.

"What the …"Finn sidestepped, grabbed Unsworth's arm, swung it up behind his back and pushed him to his knees. Classic restraint, Finn surprised it had been so easy, given it was basic training.

"Gimme the phone." Unsworth's head down to the grass, voice muffled. His shoulders heaved.

"Cranston, keep him down." Finn removed his knee from Unsworth's back when Cranston took over. Finn looked around. No sudden lights on, no one at their front door. It had happened fast, and on the grass, no loud yells, the rustling of clothes and heavy breathing inaudible to the sleeping neighbourhood.

Finn stepped out of Unsworth's reach and pulled the phone from his jacket. A cheap, flip-style mobile. Finn hadn't seen one of that type in years. Police issue was smartphones and his own was similar. Not unheard of, people having two phones legitimately. But Unsworth's reaction was out of kilter with the offence of using a private phone while on active duty: a discipline notation, perhaps. Attacking a fellow officer was a whole different level.

Unsworth was on a projectory career path. Even he wouldn't be foolish enough to jeopardise that for a quick flutter, not in front of colleagues. A woman? Unsworth played the field with several women on the go at any one time. They did all the running, or so he said.

One way to find out. Finn flipped the phone. The screen was blank. He pressed the centre button, out of habit, not expecting the screen to light up.

"Don't, don't ..." Unsworth's whimper clear.

Finn checked the phone log. One listing, calls to and from VT over the last few days, several out, none received in the last several hours. One other listed, a call to VO three days ago. No other numbers, no listings in Contacts. No Facebook, or Twitter, or Internet icon.

Why have a burner? Prepaid, difficult to trace, easily discarded. VT and VO needed access to Unsworth without others knowing. Not used for gambling, phone calls only. Why try to use it in the middle of a stake-out?

VT and VO. Finn stared at the phone, felt sick. Tupe Vavau and Oso Vavau. Enforcers for hire. Unsworth's money troubles; nothing to do with university study and student loans; everything to do with gambling debts. Add in his odd behaviour the last few days and increasing agitation in the last few hours. Had he been told to do something his conscience struggled with?

"You borrowed dodgy money, didn't keep up repayments and next thing, you get a visit from a debt collector. Is that it?"

"I didn't tell them I was a cop. I don't know how they found out."

Those loaning that sort of money made it their business to know who they gave money to. His banker would have his ear to the ground, know who to pass on to whom, get a cut. Unsworth should know that, would know that if he hadn't been so desperate.

"What did you have to do? Tip Tupe off if we got too close to him?" Was it more than that? Finn thought over their efforts to work through the case: they'd been floundering, going round in circles, getting nowhere; it would not be too hard to plant or hold back intel to hinder the investigation.

"Honest, I gave them minimal intel only." Unsworth figured out what he was thinking. "Only to do with any of the Tans, but you didn't always keep us in the loop, going off on your own."

Blaming him now. Finn took another step back, lessen the temptation to boot him in the kidneys. Unsworth was well and truly busted, not just two officers as witnesses, but the phone as evidence. Where could he run to? Surrounded by sea, one road exit, with cops heading to the peninsula. If he was stupid enough to run, he wouldn't get far.

"Shit, Isaiah, take it easy, you're hurting me."

Cranston's response made his feelings clear. He lifted his knee off Unsworth's back, heaved him off his feet. But with a sudden thrust, Unsworth lurched, fell forward.

"I didn't think anyone would get hurt." Unsworth, unsteady on all fours, pushed himself upright, catching his breath. "I'll front Repeka, make her tell me where Tupe is."

"Like hell you will. We're going back to ..." Finn had no time to finish.

Like a rugby forward, Unsworth charged through both men, knocked them aside, arms flailing to fend off any attack. He sprinted down the street, into the fog.

40. TOVA

She had to talk her way free. Rushing Repeka was out of the question – twice her size, mean and angry with it. "You were at Areta's tangi, weren't you?" Tova asked as conversationally as she could.

"Appealing to my better nature? News for you, sweetie, I don't have one, not where your mother is concerned, the lying bitch." Repeka advanced, Tova retreated, keeping space between them. "You can't pick your family, can you? I bet you think that about your useless brother."

Had the fall killed him? She shuddered, remembering the thud as Richard hit the ground.

The couch blocked further withdrawal. Tova stood her ground as Repeka moved up to her, finger-stabbed her chest. "Hemi said Areta strutted around like she was better than everyone else, always going on and on about leaving that dump of a town and making it big in movies. They were kids, putting her in her place. Bloody drama queen, even back then, accused Hemi of attacking her, and exaggerated what happened. Hardly anyone believed her, anyway." Each point emphasised with a sharp prod, a double jab on the last.

"You mean ... he raped her?" Tova understood at last, making the link between Areta's indifference to her heritage, the snatches of conversations at the tangi, her father's disquiet at her declaration at the lunch, even the force of Repeka's fury.

"So she reckoned. He and his mates scared the shit out of her, that's all. He's her cousin, for God's sake. He wouldn't do what she said he did."

"She never told me ..." Tova said.

"Because it was all lies," Repeka said. "She buggers off, says she's not hanging around to be accused of making things up. Nothing was ever proven, but the rumours won't die and people still point the finger at Hemi. She ends up a celebrity rich-bitch who doesn't give a fuck about anyone else. Bloody short memories; the whānau fall over themselves to have her tangi. I wanted her to suffer but she goes and gets herself killed. I'm sick of Hemi being treated like shit, even now, all these years later. You and your stupid brother will have to do instead."

Tova's memories of Areta didn't fit with Repeka's, but those thoughts were knocked out of her mind by Repeka's 'gets herself killed'.

"Give it a rest, woman." Tupe stood in the doorway, zipping up his jeans, the gun poking out from his waistband again. "Give me the keys to the ute."

Repeka dangled a key ring. "I'll say you snuck in, took the ute, the keys were in it. Me and my boy were sound asleep, didn't hear a thing. Go on, get going." She pushed him towards the ranchslider. "If you're caught, bloody well stick to the same story. Oso and Richard killed the

Dunns, we had nothing to do with it. Oso can't argue, and the cops already think her idiot brother is a killer. They won't care as long as they have someone."

"Yeah," Tupe grunted in agreement. "It's the least Oso can do for us." His mouth drooped and he stared at Tova. "Can't blame Oso for her, though."

"Should have thought about that. Leave her alone, the Boss said. Kidnapping her is hardly obeying orders, is it?" Repeka rubbed her eyes. "She's a problem now. Dump her so she can't blab to the cops. Tell the Boss your Northland mates took her in exchange for hiding you. He might fall for it."

Tupe chewed at his lip, taking his time to consider Repeka's suggestion. "What's the Boss want with her, anyway?"

"Some sort of leverage over Malcolm Tan," Repeka said, "and you've gone and fucked it up."

If she ever got the chance to tell the police what Repeka and Hemi said, would they believe her?

"Can't blame me. That was Oso and Richard's doing." Tupe's indignation interrupted Tova's thoughts. "Anyway, what if your bloody Hemi dobs us in to save himself?"

"Don't you worry about Hemi. I'll be able to twist whatever crap he tells the cops," Repeka said. "Your worry is convincing the Boss you're not as big a fuckwit as Oso. Now piss off."

Her crude instruction incited Tupe. "Get me Hemi's rifle," he demanded. "I know he has one. Can't have you shooting me in the back as I leave."

"You stupid bugger." Repeka held Tupe's gaze. With a head shake, she moved to the kitchen, reached into the narrow space beside the fridge and pulled a rifle out.

Putting it to her shoulder, she pointed it at Tova, swung it round to Tupe, looking like she knew how to use it.

Tova's stomach churned. If hindered from leaving, Tupe planned to shoot his way out. Her legs wobbled like those of a newborn calf.

Tupe wrenched it from Repeka, pulling her forward. "Even Hemi isn't stupid enough to keep it loaded. Get me the bullets, all of them."

Repeka reached up, searching in the cupboard. Tupe watched her carefully and grabbed at the white box she brought out. Her gaze shifted, over Tova's head to the archway. "Jacob, get back to bed."

It was a trick, Tova thought, make Tupe turn round, give Repeka a chance to catch him off guard. Would it give her an opportunity, too?

The boy she'd seen the day before, leaning against the front door as Repeka was handcuffed, edged from the archway into the open area and closer to his mother. Tova willed him to make quick sense of what he had barged into and retreat, run to his neighbours, tell them a crazy man held his mother and a strange woman hostage.

"There's a dude in our yard," Jacob replied.

"How many?" Tupe stared down the hall as if he could see through walls.

"I dunno. Go see for yourself," Jacob said.

Tupe held the box of bullets and rifle in the crook of his arm as he strode towards the boy. "You're not so big I can't smack you one." He raised his free arm high.

Jacob ducked the swing and slid to his mother's side. Tupe overbalanced, the box tipped and bullets clacked to the floor. Cursing, Tupe brushed at them with a foot until he rounded them up, scooped them back into the box.

"Jacob, stop the cheek." Repeka, her tone a warning, slapped at him reaching for the leftovers.

His hand froze mid-air at the rebuke. Jacob followed her gaze, stared at Tupe with the rifle and the butt of the gun visible above the waistband of his jeans. He moved his gaze to Tova, like a statue in the centre of the room. "She looks like that Chink guy you brought here. The scared one." Jacob, like Richard, watched too many gangsta rap videos, imitating their staccato inflections, the sway of shoulders and the use of racist terms.

"You said you weren't followed," Repeka snarled at Tupe. She tried to pull Jacob back.

He squirmed to free himself and she cuffed him across his head. His lips moved in soundless curses.

Jacob had that air of disrespect and distrust for his mother that Tova saw too often meted out to teachers in the classroom. It came from years of unpredictable and unreliable boundaries, creating a survival mentality, a need to toughen up, to look after yourself. He wasn't intimidated by Tupe. The weapons didn't faze him and, although surprised, he was in no way troubled at the sight of her. She didn't dwell on what that meant. Jacob was young, twelve or thirteen, but he held himself and answered back with the confidence of one much older. She counted him out as a potential ally.

Thump, thump, thump on the door.

"It better not be that old fart from across the road again, accusing you of running a meth house," said Tupe. "Thought Hemi gave him what-for?"

Tova didn't know much about meth; it wasn't one of Richard's go-to drugs. She breathed in, unsure what a meth house might smell like. Saliva glands opened, and she inhaled the aroma of the chicken sandwich Repeka had made. She sniffed again. A whiff of body pong emanated from Tupe, aggression seeping out his pores.

"It won't be Weston, he knows better than to come on my property."

"Get rid of whoever it is." Tupe waved the rifle at Repeka, encouragement to do as he said.

"The Boss will have sent his men to silence you." She stabbed the air in front of Tupe with the confidence of knowing the rifle wasn't loaded.

"I'm too valuable. I'll do things for him no one else will."

Repeka's eyes flicked to Tova, back to Tupe. Something important was exchanged at that moment.

"If he tells me to waste you, don't think I won't." Tupe aimed the rifle at Repeka's chest. They were like kids in the playground, snowballing taunts. Tupe had the advantage with the rifle. He turned to Jacob, protected by the kitchen bench. "What did he look like?"

"I don't know. It's dark."

Tupe swooped. With one fluid movement he seized Jacob's T-shirt in a tight grip, hauled him across the benchtop, flipped him into a headlock.

Jacob gulped for air, fingers searching for a hold, legs scrabbling for traction. "Yeah, all right. One guy is in our yard, coming up to the door, two others behind him. Big guys, wearing uniforms, two of them, anyway."

Tupe let Jacob go and Repeka nudged her son behind her, shielding him, a mother protecting her cub.

"Thought you only had one bent copper at the moment," Repeka said. "He's brought a few mates, come to make sure you don't drop him in it. He'll shoot, claim it was self-defence. Should have gone when I told you."

The police. Saviours. Tova pictured the layout of the

house: ranchslider exit locked; toilet window too narrow and no door lock to provide precious seconds to wrangle louvres out; bedrooms at the front, either side of the hall, she guessed, with windows. No time to eenie-meenie her selection. Tupe's reflexes had already proved too fast, and she was no superwoman, outrunning bullets. The lone source of safety was the flimsy couch. She had to be ready to drop, roll and hunker down. Repeka's words resounded. With luck, they'd go for the standing targets first.

"How would he know I'd come here?" Tupe's forehead shone with sweat, his hairline damp.

"Whatever, you're stuffed, so piss off out the back." Repeka, in control. "Jacob, come with me."

The rifle levelled with Repeka's chest before she'd taken more than two steps. "Don't take me for an idiot. The boy stays with me."

Do as he says, Tova willed Repeka.

Repeka shrugged, but her gaze lingered on Jacob. "Have it your way. I'll distract them, you bugger off."

"Mum, don't go." Jacob's first word indignant; the rest, part whimper, suddenly anticipating the worst. Tova foresaw the same outcome and almost felt sorry for him. Except each time their eyes met, his lip curled, a silent accusation of blame and suspicion.

Repeka went through the arch, into the hall.

"Like I'm gonna trust you, bitch," Tupe muttered at her back, his cockiness returning. He sounded like an unfit runner after an uphill race, yet the most exercise he had done since dragging her into the house was to shamble back and forth, raise and lower the rifle.

"You're crazy," Repeka spat at him.

Yes, he is. All the more reason to do as he says.

With rifle prods, Tupe motioned Tova and Jacob ahead of him to follow Repeka. He kicked doors open, giving Tova fleeting glimpses into dark spaces that suggested storage and bathroom and bedroom as she and Jacob shambled, side by side, fear fettering her like a horse unable to break and run.

She stumbled, elbowed by Jacob as he sprang after his mother. Tupe, energised, his movements quick and powerful, cast the rifle like a fishing line, felled Jacob. Then stepped over him, leaned against the closed door Repeka had just gone through, his ear to it.

Tova tugged the stricken boy into the bedroom on her right and rolled him into the recovery position.

"Fuck off! It's three in the morning. I don't care who you work for." Repeka's smoker's voice reached them, her words far from conciliatory.

41. FINN

Finn signalled to Cranston as they chased Unsworth. Go wide, and to the right of the Hemona house, with a sight line into the alley; prevent Unsworth from doubling back. He'd grab Unsworth, force him to the alley and hand him over to Pavletich. With luck, and provided Unsworth didn't start resisting and yelling, they'd be gone before any of the neighbours heard a thing.

Unsworth was fast, too fast. He was into the yard, up to the porch, and his three loud knocks echoed into the night by the time Finn reached him, pulled him back.

"I screwed up, I know. It's over for me," Unsworth muttered. "The least I can do is put the hard word on Repeka."

Did he think that might earn him some leniency, a last-ditch effort to put things right? Chances were high Vavau was well up north by now. But they didn't know that for a fact.

"You're in enough shit, Unsworth. Get back to the fence and stay there unless I tell you otherwise."

The door opened. Repeka stood on the porch. Finn, arms out, palms open, making it obvious he carried no weapon, moved slowly forward.

"Mrs Hemona, we need to ask a few questions about Tupe Vavau. Invite us in, let's not put on a show for your neighbours." Finn, polite, stepped forward.

"You!"

Who had she thought they were?

"Fuck off! It's three in the morning." Repeka yelled loudly enough to wake neighbours, witnesses to the police on her doorstep in the middle of the night. Next step, a police harassment complaint. She moved to the step and checked left and right, and back again, assuring herself only three men were there.

"What's going on? I'll call the police." A man, silhouetted, backlit from the interior light, yelled out from a house across the road.

Unsworth shouted, "We are the police. Go inside, it's under control."

Instead of returning to his warm bed, reassured by the police presence, the neighbour was now joined by a woman. Before long, the rest of the street would come out to gawk.

"You can't come in. Go away." Her normal aggressive, self-righteous edge was gone.

"Mrs Hemona, we know Tupe Vavau has been here tonight. We can talk here or at the station."

"I can't leave. Jacob's asleep. Come back tomorrow." Her voice dropped. "Please." She wasn't one to shy away from confrontation with the police, and it wasn't in her nature to use the word 'please' with anyone. Tupe Vavau was inside, he was sure of it.

Finn, senses on high alert, gestured to Cranston and

Unsworth to withdraw, get back to the crest of the street. He started his retreat, keeping her in sight, walking backwards, hoping he didn't trip on the uneven ground.

A figure appeared behind Repeka and proved it. Tupe Vavau. "Take this message back to the Boss," he yelled into the darkness, at the same time dragging Repeka backwards, his arm around her throat.

"Get off me." Repeka tried to lurch forward and writhe out of his hold; he hauled back, a twosome tug-of-war. Vavau, far stronger, ignored her bellow of shock and yanked her back to the doorway.

Finn grabbed for her feet. She kicked out – whether in an effort to free herself or to strike at him was hard to tell. He dodged the kick, saw Vavau drop Repeka, straighten up and raise his arm.

"Get down!" Finn's skin tingled, as if spiders scurried over him. A whoosh of air passed by. "Unsworth, no!" He thrust out his arm, fingers touched fabric. The warning too late, Unsworth was well into his airborne tackle.

Vavau fired, jolting his torso backwards.

Unsworth spread-eagled, arms outstretched to break his fall. He bellyflopped onto the ground, a head shy of the first step to the porch. Elbows nudged forward, his fingers tapped the step. His head slumped and he lay still.

"Bloody good riddance, fucker. Think you others can take me? Come and try."

Finn was exposed: too far to sprint to the drive and the shelter of the wooden fence. If he made a break, he'd be shot, point-blank.

More shots fired, one pinged off the ute, metal and paint chips zinging past Finn's head. The ute. He had nowhere else to go.

Hunched over, Finn sprinted at the vehicle and rolled behind it, its thick wheel affording minimal protection. Where was Cranston? Finn crouched low, peered round the wheel, the high suspension allowing him a sight line.

Only metres away, he could see Vavau prod Unsworth's back with the gun, then bend down, tug at the unresponsive shoulder, let go. Unsworth's face hit the ground.

"Vavau. Police. Put the rifle down."

Swinging the gun from side to side in a wide arc, Vavau retreated to the porch. "I'll kill you all!"

Cranston skidded into Finn. It could have been the way he landed, or it could have been an embrace. Finn extricated himself from the white-faced man whose mouth worked like a fish craving air. He was about to throw up.

"You hurt?" Finn scanned Cranston's neck, chest, stomach, looking for blood, a bullet hole.

Cranston shook his head, thumbed in Unsworth's direction. "We have to get Luke."

"We'll be no use to him if we get shot, too." Finn prayed the neighbours recognised the sound of a gunshot and kept away from their windows. In this neighbourhood they were like as not to shut the door, avoid any involvement with the Hemonas, living for the day their neighbours moved on, or a Lotto win meant they could. Pavletich will have heard the shots, called for backup and the Armed Offenders Squad.

It would all take time, time they didn't have.

"We have to move before Vavau comes for us. We're easy targets here." Risking getting his head blown off, Finn eased up, tilted his head, less of a target. Vavau was still on the porch, the rifle low by his side.

Just then, Vavau turned back to the house, distracted by something.

"Now." Finn pushed Cranston ahead of him. Crouched, and hugging the fence, they scuttled on all fours like frenzied crabs, easy targets away from the comparative safety of the ute, up the drive to the footpath. Two long seconds to swivel round the corner to the protection of the wooden fence. Six seconds in total. More than enough time for Vavau to steady himself, aim and fire.

Finn stumbled, his palms scraped asphalt. Someone grabbed his shirt, dragged him.

All arms and legs and heavy breathing, he tried to run.

"You're safe, McIntosh." Pavletich's voice.

42. TOVA

She was sure she had heard a man say 'police'. Take the risk, rush out past Tupe, get to them before he had a chance to grab her? But he had the gun.

Working blind in the dark, she fumbled for the door knob, higher than expected, eased Jacob's comatose body aside to shut the door. No catch or latch or keyhole. Escape via the window but not until the men had gone, and without Tupe seeing her. Shattering glass would shred her before she died of gunshot wounds.

No way was she going to cower in the bedroom like a trapped rat. First, something to defend herself with.

Murky shadows loomed like giants until her eyes became accustomed to the gloom and she recognised them for what they were – oversized glossy posters of basketball players. Closed curtains, open shelving, a single clothes rack offering plastic coat hangers for weapons and a narrow bed, too obvious a hiding place. On hands and knees, she felt along the floor under the window, along the wall, hoping to touch a baseball bat or hockey stick. She'd settle for heavy rugby boots with studs. Under the bed, a jumble of clothes and gear, and she reached in.

Sharp spikes pierced her palm. It felt like she'd triggered a claw trap. The pain overrode the outside noises from Tupe, belligerent and manic. She had less than a minute or two until the house was invaded and the shooting started.

She clamped her teeth tight and yanked her hand free, hoping it retracted without detaching from the rest of her body. The mound of clothes heaved.

Tova leapt to her feet, hands out, defensive. Another Hemona to deal with.

"Don't hurt me." A boy unearthed from the jumble under the bed.

"You bit me." Fright made her defensive. She pressed the punctured skin, smudged droplets of blood.

The boy curled into himself and she stepped back.

"Sorry, I'm not going to hurt you. Look, the back door's locked, and I can't go out the front. Is there another way out?"

"Who are you?" The boy's voice quivered. "Are you with those guys out there?"

She shook her head, edged towards the door. No time for introductions. The bathroom must be near the toilet. Bathrooms had windows.

"Where's Jacob? He said he'd be right back." The boy hugged himself, didn't stop his shivering. "I want to go home."

The boy was terrified, unlike Jacob. Not a Hemona, then.

"He's ..." No time for explanations. "Look, is there another way out?"

Grunts and shrieks outside. Repeka's persuading the men to leave wasn't going well.

"The laundry door's not locked. Next to the toilet. I'm coming with you." The boy moved towards her, tripped.

"Wha-? Jacob?" The boy gently shook Jacob's shoulder, crouched closer as Jacob whimpered. "He's hurt. We have to help him."

Gunshots, and a thud, what sounded like a heavy object hitting solid ground, Tupe's yell. Tova flinched. *Escape, now!* Tupe enraged was capable of anything. They could carry Jacob. What if movement was the worst thing for him?

Her indecision was short-lived. The front door slammed.

Tova shut the bedroom door, pressed into it. The boy joined her.

Their combined weight was no match for Tupe. The door flung open. Tupe staggered in, Repeka in tow.

43. FINN

Beyond the curve in the road, a loose cluster of people in pyjamas and dressing gowns and trackpants and hoodies created a lopsided semicircle around the three men. Finn struggled to bring his breathing back to normal. What little food he had in him churned, his stomach like an agitator washing machine. Sweat trickled down his neck, although the chill factor called for polar fleeces. He shielded his eyes from bright torch beams.

"Unsworth down, sir. Single rifle shot at close range to the chest, no sign of life." Finn stated the facts, struggling to regain his breath, and resisted the urge to collapse into his boss the way Cranston had.

"Is an ambulance on its way?" Cranston craned his neck to see beyond them, as if expecting one to materialise from the darkness.

"It's the Armed Offenders Squad we need right now," Pavletich said. "If we can't get access quickly, be prepared for a retrieval, not a rescue." No time for emotion, be practical, his tone implied.

Cranston trembled, took a breath, another, short, shallow. Finn recognised the signs of a pending panic attack. "Breathe deep, Isaiah," he said, making no attempt to pretend Unsworth might survive – point blank shot, dead before he hit the ground.

A crowd formed. Finn wasn't surprised the gunshots hadn't stopped them from milling about in the street. In his experience, anything out of the ordinary brought people out for a look-see, believing there was safety in togetherness, in spite of common sense saying stay indoors until the all-clear had been given. A pyjama-clad woman held up a mobile phone, their run for their lives, no doubt, already uploaded to YouTube.

A few onlookers shuffled closer, and Pavletich pulled the two constables out of hearing range. "You're both stood down," Pavletich said.

"But ..." Finn began.

"As soon as backup gets here. Until then, I need you. Cranston, keep busy, get people up around the corner, find a suitable evacuation point. Get started on a list of the number of people in each house. We need everyone accounted for. Get Wright up here if she's not already on her way." Pavletich, training and experience to the fore, took command. "McIntosh, what intel have we for the AOS? Vavau has a weapon and isn't afraid to use it. Repeka Hemona and her son Jacob are in the house. We'll have to assume Ms Tan is there too until we know otherwise."

Finn had figured that but wished Pavletich had left it unsaid a little longer. "Why come here? Why stay? Vavau yelled something, sounded like 'take a message to the Boss'. What did he mean? He must have known we were cops." And Finn was still trying to get the order of events straight in his head. Had Vavau recognised Unsworth before he aimed?

"You sure, McIntosh? Cops?"

"Unsworth and Cranston were in uniform. Hard to mistake."

"Bent coppers?" Pavletich hid his face behind his hands, shook his head. "Or someone's got hold of old uniforms, fooled Tupe into believing they were cops? It's happened before. Do you think Malcolm Tan ...?"

"No." Finn cut him off. "If he knew Vavau was in the house, he'd know his daughter was there. I doubt he'd set the Vavau thugs onto his own son, too."

"You're right," Pavletich agreed. "Sounds like Vavau thought his Boss might want him out of the way; he's become a liability. Vavau is the link between this mysterious Boss and the Dunns. It's someone with the power to control a cop or two, and with a grudge against Malcolm Tan. What better way to get at someone than through their children."

"Your theory is the best we've got to date, McIntosh." Pavletich straightened up. "Bugger his lawyer who says we have to give Tan more time to recover from surgery before he can be interviewed. We need to know now who might want Malcolm ruined."

Distant sirens grew louder. Pavletich's head jerked up, the movement seeming to bring him to the present. "I'll get onto it, but right now, McIntosh, we deal with what's in front of us. You've been in the house. What do you know?"

"No landline. I've got Mrs Hemona's mobile. I'll get comms to send Vavau's if we have it on file."

"While you're on to comms, get someone to talk to Hemi Hemona. I want to know what the relationship is between the Hemonas and Vavau. We know Vavau is armed. Check out whether Hemona has ever been known to have a gun, legal or otherwise. The AOS need to know what they'll be facing. And draw up the layout of the Hemona house."

"I'll get the Kalgour boy, he'll know." Finn's nausea lessened, now that he had things to do.

"Get onto it, McIntosh."

44. TOVA

Tova gagged, sickened by the sounds. Her stomach heaved, the dry retching leaving her gasping. Where was the boy?

Tupe flicked on the light.

Tova preferred it dark, keeping her blind: to Repeka, propped in the doorway, blood oozing from her nose, thin rivulets merging into a stronger flow down her neck, staining her sweater; to Jacob, flipped out of the recovery position, onto his back, one arm covering his eyes; and to the small, pale boy, staring at her from the safety of the far wall, pressed into it like he was waiting to be absorbed whole.

"Fucked if I'll go down without a fight," Tupe snarled.

Tova held his gaze, stock-still in freeze-frame, determined to mask her fear. She suspected she didn't fool him.

Tupe looked from one boy to the other, then back again. Tova wouldn't have been surprised to hear him count out loud the number of teenage boys in front of him. He scanned the room to check that no one else had materialised. He gave up on the puzzle. "Open the curtains," he ordered Tova.

The distance between the doorway and the window was like a marathon obstacle course: skirting Repeka, averting her eyes from her bloody and broken face, stepping over Jacob's legs. She kept her eyes on Tupe until her shaking fingers held the pull cord.

"Not so fast. Wait," he ordered. "All of you, up against the window."

"Tupe, please. Repeka and Jacob are hurt, and let the boy go." He was too young to experience this. "You only need me."

Tupe grinned. "Aw, a bleeding heart, like your mother. Didn't do her much good. Won't do you any, either."

The boy let go the wall and scurried beside Tova. Repeka grunted and placed one palm on the floor as though to push herself up, indicating she knew what was expected. The effort proved too much and she slumped back down.

Tupe aimed the rifle at her, changed his mind and stood over Jacob. He prodded him in the ribs with his boot. The boy's body jerked. "You're faking it. I didn't hit you that hard. Get up or I'll give you something to moan about, don't think I won't." Using the rifle, he prised Jacob's arm away from his eyes.

Jacob stood, shrugged, a 'worth a try' gesture before joining Tova at the window. She had been easily fooled.

"Now, missy," Tupe said, "do the honours."

45. FINN

Finn's phone vibrated and he pulled it from his pocket. He didn't recognise the number.

"Answer the bloody thing, McIntosh," Pavletich muttered.

One swipe across the screen opened the call. "McIntosh."

"What's happening? Where's Tova? She sent a text and ..."

Finn placed the voice. "Sarah? Slow down. A text? From Tova?"

"I didn't know what to do. Tom said Tova was trouble and I was stupid to think I could help and he told me not to get any more involved. He's asleep and I thought about it and ... you left your card and ..."

"Sarah." Finn remained calm although he wanted to yell at her to stop snivelling. "Forward the text to me. Now. Don't worry, it's under control." He regretted those words as soon as they were said. Sarah would know he lied soon enough. The media were likely to arrive at the same time as the backup and the incident relayed ad nauseam on the news until a fresh disaster took precedence. It would have to be a catastrophic event affecting at least half the world to knock the brothel murders and their ever-widening sphere of cause and effect from the number-one spot. Bloggers had already saturated the Internet with their opinions on everything reaped from Inspector Smith's less-than-reticent media statements, feeding talkback radio rants about rising crime, Asian gangs and the casino a symbol of ever-dwindling family values. And police incompetence a standard fallback.

Finn signalled to Pavletich. Together, with heads down, they stared at the screen and waited for the 'knock-knock' of the text's arrival.

@hemonas tupe crazy tell police.

"Good. That's the confirmation we need. Ms Tan is in the house," Pavletich said. "And it's a hostage situation."

Good from the point of view that the Armed Offenders now knew how many people were in the house. Good that they confirmed one hostage, if not three. Good that resources were directed at the house and not diverted on a search for Tova elsewhere. Good that Pavletich was proven right.

Bad for Tova.

"Get those sirens off," Pavletich ordered as several police cars pulled to a stop.

Within minutes, the backup crew took up their positions. The cul-de-sac was cordoned off, and two police officers built like rugby forwards, arms outstretched, achieved what the sole officer had not. They moved the spectators back several hundred metres. Other officers were deployed on crowd control, house-emptying and sorting out an evacuation centre for people unable to return to their houses.

"Start interviewing them. Find out who knows the Hemonas," Pavletich said.

Two hurried off to clear the road of cars so the police helicopter could land if it needed to. One had instructions to direct Inspector Smith and his entourage to Pavletich as soon as he turned up.

Pavletich was handed a megaphone; he placed it at his feet. "Find a way to observe the house without anyone seeing you. Not you, McIntosh. You go find out what that boy can tell us. Get a move on, I want the intel by the time Inspector Smith gets here."

Finn hurried away towards the cordon before Pavletich remembered his threat to stand him down.

"We've been trying to get someone's attention." An officer at the cordon waved him over. "This woman ..."

Mrs Kalgour elbowed forward and fell into Finn's arms.

Finn's heart constricted. He led her away from the eyes and ears directed at them and shielded her from the man holding up his mobile.

Mrs Kalgour pulled her thick dressing gown together and wiped her face on a sleeve. "It's KK, he isn't in the house, he isn't out here. No one's seen him. He must be at Jacob's. There were gunshots, weren't there? That police officer won't tell me anything." She gulped in air. Anything else she may have been planning to say turned into a grief-stricken sob.

"Why do you think KK's with Jacob?" Finn, calm, feeling anything but.

"It's my fault. If anything happens ..."

"Mrs Kalgour. Tell me, then I'll be able to *help*." Finn put more weight on the last word.

"I told KK he wasn't to play with Jacob any more. KK said that was stupid, he saw Jacob at school and it was better if they were friends. He wanted to go and sort things out. I forbade it. He went anyway."

"When did you see KK last?" Finn spoke quietly, to reduce Mrs Kalgour's fear. And to quell his own rising dread.

"After dinner. About 7.30. He slammed his bedroom door and told me to leave him alone. He knows I hate that." Mrs Kalgour bit her lip and tears fell. "I didn't check on him before I went to bed."

"Mrs Kalgour, Nell, you know what kids are like. KK will be trying to get close to the action. I'll get the officers to look for him. Is there a neighbour who can stay with you?"

She clung to his arm and cried in earnest. He waved to the officer on cordon duty. "Look after her, will you? Get her a strong cup of tea."

The officer frowned as if considering whether to tell Finn to do his own babysitting. He didn't get the chance. Their attention was diverted by the five large black Nissan patrol vehicles, in convoy, rolling into the street and pulling up in front of the cordon. Several men, or women, it was impossible to tell, disgorged from the vehicles. They were kitted out, head to toe, in black balaclavas, goggles, Kevlar helmets, bulletproof vests. Some carried shields; all held sniper rifles. Two tracker dogs, on the end of thick leads, stayed close to their handlers.

I hope they rip Tupe apart, Finn thought. No, he didn't mean that.

"McIntosh, you're wanted." Wright tugged at his arm. "Pavletich needs you to do a visual identification."

Finn jogged to keep up with her, one foot in front of the other in sync with his pounding pulse. Identify who? He'd heard no shots, but it must be over. Vavau's weapon of availability likely a knife or machete, silent, lethal.

Instead of heading into the cul-de-sac, as Finn expected, Wright turned into a driveway on the opposite side to the Hemona house. "Your friend Mr Weston says we can use his front rooms to keep a lookout. Pavletich sent someone to negotiate with the people who back onto him for easier access. For now we have to go through a few backyards. The others made it without getting stuck, and I've run it twice." Wright let out a low chuckle. "There are no dogs but lots of gardens and shrubs."

And high fences. The first, a chest-high wire fence that he took at a run and jump, maintained his foothold on the damp and slippery top rail and lurched forward as he landed. Wright, several steps ahead, did an elegant, perfect up-and-over then straight into a run.

Finn trampled through garden beds and left muddy footprints on plastic furniture used as stepladders.

"Don't trigger the security light. I'm not sure if it's been disabled yet," Wright warned as they faced the last hurdle. A spotlight on his scramble over the thick, spiky coprosma hedge was the last thing Finn wanted.

"It'll grow back," Wright whispered as she led the way through a narrow gap, snapped branches evidence of those gone before them.

By the time he slunk up the back deck behind Wright, Finn's skin itched, his sneakers were wet and dirty and likely to leave marks on the carpet. No lights were on, and he edged along the hall to the front room, feeling for any table and photo frames perched on it before he knocked them clattering to the floor.

An officer he didn't recognise shushed him as he came forward. Finn hadn't made any noise. If he had, Finn doubted it would be audible to Vavau across the road.

"What took you so long, McIntosh? Did you bring the megaphone?" Pavletich, along with three other officers, crouched below sill height.

Finn nudged in beside his boss and peeked out through a gap made by his fingers in the wooden slat blinds that covered the window. He kept the answers to Pavletich's questions in his mind. It was a bit of an obstacle course. And yes.

Then he saw what they were looking at.

Straight at the Hemona house one hundred metres opposite, the body a dark shape near the front steps. The curtain across the front window pulled back, the room lit up. Finn had a clear view of three people facing the street, arms up, palms on the window.

Tova, centre, flanked by Jacob and KK.

46. TOVA

Tova, arms drooping, pressed her forehead against the glass window and concentrated on regulating her breathing. She wriggled her fingers to stir the circulation, relieve the pins and needles. She stretched her neck, worked her tension-taut shoulders.

With her eyes shut, the shape by the front steps was a roll of carpet, an odd-shaped log, anything but a motionless human. They wouldn't stay closed. As the sky lightened, she identified individual shapes – the splayed legs, the bunched jacket, the arm outstretched as though reaching for a lifeline. The face was turned away from her but she made out details of the police uniform. Constable McIntosh had been in casual clothes. Logic told her he hadn't had time or a reason to change. It wasn't him. Still, she ran her eyes up and down, double-checked. The hair was darker, the physique heavier. And she'd seen him injured, the gunshot, the fall. It couldn't be him.

Each time she let her gaze settle on the figure, she was sure it had moved. It was a trick of the changing light, the moving shadows. The body remained in the same place.

Tupe passed the doorway balancing a chair on one shoulder. The first time she saw him do it, she thought he was setting up camp in the doorway to keep watch over them. By his third pass with assorted household furniture, a stool, a side table, she grasped that the front entrance was barricaded.

He paraded up and down, talking to himself, swearing, punching the walls. He'd prop himself against the door frame, rifle held low, the gun tucked into the waistband of his jeans. He stayed long enough to ask, "Anything happening yet?" Then turned and disappeared from view.

She visualised his movements from the sounds. Three strides from the front door took him to the bedroom opposite. Two seconds and the TV remote clicked through channels. He cursed at the lack of news coverage, normal programmes still running, uninterrupted by the urgent tones of a newsreader. Two seconds more and he reached their door. Seventeen heavy footfalls took him down the hall and into the kitchen area. Sometimes he returned quickly, sometimes the fridge door opened, followed by the crrk of a ring tab pulled back. She'd seen Coke and lemonade cans in the fridge. There'd be a beer stash somewhere for Tupe to find. Other times, he was quiet. Tova imagined he was weighing up whether to make a dash for it, out the back, through the trees and shrubs, back to the car. The longer the silence, the more hopeful she became that he had scarpered, but each time she didn't hear the slow sliding back of the ranchslider, and each time she did hear Tupe's tread as he stomped back up the hall.

Seventeen steps back to their door. He'd lean into the bedroom, tell them to shut the fuck up - nothing wrong with his hearing as their whispering stopped at the sound of his approach.

Jacob did most of the talking, used to being the centre of attention. Perhaps hearing himself lessened the fear. "I know who you are. Your mother was that actress Mum hates; the one who got herself killed."

Tova couldn't clutter her mind with the reasons for Repeka's animosity. She'd think about that later, along with worry for Richard and her father. She needed to focus on the now.

But Jacob had an audience. "Your family took away the mana of our family, Mum said." He stepped away from her preventing further contagion. The move gave him room, elbows out, fists ready to block any blow Tova might throw.

Tova's gaze lingered on the truculent boy, his aggressive stance. They were about the same weight and similar height. She was fit but he looked stronger, fuelled by knowledge of his parents' frustration and belief that others were to blame.

Now was not the time, but what if the right time didn't come? Tova had to know. "What?" A quizzical eyebrow raise encouraged him to continue.

"Serve herself right, Mum said." He stood a little straighter, puffed out his chest. "Thought she was better than Dad and the whānau she grew up with. Lied about what Dad did to her. She shamed the whole family. And she never helped anyone back home, even though she was rich and famous."

Tupe was at the door. Jacob pressed his head to the glass, eyes closed. Dead on his feet or just pretending?

Tupe padded away back down the hall to the kitchen. Tova listened for anything that indicated help was coming.

Memories of TV sieges she'd watched, and how they ended, ran like movies in her mind. Tupe, tired of muttering and thwacking the wall, starts shooting, the police retaliate, storming the house. They'd go down in a blaze of bullets. Friendly fire, collateral damage popped into her head.

"She's to blame for everything going wrong for Dad," Jacob said. "That's what Mum said." Jacob turned his face away from her.

Areta never complained about anyone without reason.

"That was long before I was born."

"Doesn't matter. When she died, my mum was real mad, said her lies would never be undone now, and the only work Dad could get was with guys like Tupe."

"What does that have to do with me?"

"Mum found out that Tupe's Boss knew your family."

Tova worked out the rest. "She came up with a way to get back at us." Repeka no fool, go for the weakest link – Richard.

"Where the bloody hell are the cops?" Tupe's yell from the room opposite, interrupted her thoughts. "What's taking them so long?" The television volume boomed. Noise control was more likely to appear.

Ten seconds to get to the laundry with the pale boy. And Jacob, a kid spouting his parents' anger, but that was no reason to desert him.

The sky bleached from smoky black to pre-dawn grey. She shivered, imagined the cold seeping into the man on the ground. Shapes and shadows defined into fences, front yards and decks of the houses opposite as she and the boys stood facing out. She had expected police vans, armed men and dogs surrounding the house. But the cul-de-sac was empty and silent.

"I picked the wrong night, eh miss?" Up to now the other boy had been silent. He kept his eyes forward, his hands on the glass as Tupe ordered. "I thought I'd have it out with Jacob, get him to lay off me, stop lying. He had a new Xbox game and asked me to play. It was like he was sorry. I was going to sneak back home before Mum missed me." His smile was out of sync with the tears glistening in his eyes.

"I'm Tova. What's your name?" She turned towards him, the movement causing the already-thudding pulse behind her eyes to turn up the beat. It had been more than a while since she'd eaten or had a drink of water. Now wasn't the best time to be thinking of what she couldn't have.

"KK. Karl Kalgour," he explained. "No one calls me Karl, except Mum, if she's super angry with me." He bit his lip. "I guess she'll be real mad now."

Jacob stirred, flexed his fingers, then pressed his hands back to the glass. He didn't once glance over to his mother. But she detected the slight tilt of his head in KK's direction.

"She'll be more worried than angry," Tova assured him. He was holding up, keeping calm. She'd tell his parents how brave he was. *When* she had the chance, not the *if* that threatened to shout it down. "We'll be okay," she said. "The police will be working on a rescue plan."

Jacob let out a reedy snort, a deliberate 'yeah, right'.

She wanted to tell him to drop the tough-boy act, but with KK in earshot that was unlikely, even though the boys had barely acknowledged each other. She understood how stressful events changed people, altered the way they reacted. With each new trauma, her father's double life, her mother's death, its aftermath and her refusal to discard Richard, she had distanced herself from some friends, while others had dropped her.

It was hard to judge how much time had passed. An hour, more? The gunshots must have been reported by now. And the police wouldn't leave one of their men. They had to be out there. Conversation diversions for a thirteen-year-old boy? School, sport, video games? All so inconsequential.

Twice, escorting each boy to the toilet, Tupe's threats grew louder and more bizarre. "You escape and I'll shoot whoever's left! I'll gun down the cops! Your father will pay a ransom if the Boss hasn't taken his money already!"

She had to get them out.

47. FINN

It took too long. Pavletich speaking to the AOS team leader. "One officer down, three hostages, Vavau and Hemona not visible." Ordering two of the officers to stay in position and keep communications open.

More minutes following Pavletich back the way they had come, through hedges, over fences, back to the cordon. "Stay put, McIntosh. Don't move."

He had no intention of leaving. He'd join the gawkers if he had to.

He watched Pavletich with the team leader. Members of the unit were lined up by their vehicles, awaiting orders. Doing nothing.

That wasn't fair. Patience and planning were important or more lives would be lost.

"Negotiators are on their way." Pavletich returned to stand by Finn. "They'll try to make phone contact, resort to the loudhailer if Vavau won't pick up. Free the hostages first, Tupe surrenders, then retrieve Unsworth, that's the plan. It could take hours. Longer."

Finn knew the drill, and Pavletich's words provided a little comfort. Every second counted, each one feeling like a lifetime.

"You and Cranston are reinstated. For now. All hands to the cordon, so to speak."

"Thank you."

"Don't thank me yet. It could be hours of standing around when you could be back home, all snug and warm. And who knows what the outcome will be."

The negotiating team arrived, joined the growing number of officers inside the cordon, well out of view of the Hemona house. Muted sounds of talking drifted Finn's way but he was too distant to hear what was said. He kept his eye on the group, tried to read their body language.

"McIntosh." Pavletich waved him forward. "In five minutes, you're on. Reinforcements will take over the cordon, and you join the team surrounding the house. Go take a leak while you can."

Finn didn't require encouragement. He was back at the rendezvous point in under five.

"You're the eyes and ears around the house, the extra cordon," the officer giving the instructions said. "Those of you assigned to the front, one to each driveway, stay out of view of the Hemonas' house. The rest of you, cover the back and walkway side. If anyone makes a run for it, hostages or otherwise, they'll head for either of those exits. Stay well within the treeline if possible. Your job is to report any movement. At all times, all of you will be behind the AOS. Ready?"

Finn nudged his way to the group heading to the sea path, relieved he was included. Even if only to stand in a different spot.

48. TOVA

"Listen." KK stretched his neck to search the sky.

It was the most beautiful sound, the whoomp-whoomp-whoomp of a helicopter, faint and distant, then louder, closer, until it sounded overhead. The chopper circled, and Tova pushed aside the thought that it might be TV news muscling in to get prime video of the breaking news story. Mesmerised by the noise, her reaction to what she saw in her peripheral vision – Tupe at the door, the rifle pointed at them – was delayed.

The boys moved first, KK and Jacob repositioning themselves, hands firm on the window. Tova stepped between them and Tupe, her slight body offering insufficient protection. But if Tupe lashed out at her, the boys had time to get out of the line of fire.

"Tupe, it's over. Please let the boys go, they're kids."

Tupe cocked his head. Tova held her breath, willed him to focus on her request. "Maybe I'll trade the boys for a getaway ride." He grinned at his own joke and swivelled from side to side, limbering up, like a sprinter before a race.

"Mr Vavau. Police." The loudhailer whined, crackled, distortion causing an echo.

Tova sagged with sudden relief.

"Mr Vavau. Let the hostages come out and then we can talk."

Tupe cocked the rifle. One short blast. Then again.

Tova grabbed at each boy and tumbled with them to the floor, a tangle of arms and legs. Her chin crashed into a skull, her teeth jarred.

"Keep down," she said, although neither boy moved, made no effort to extricate limbs. They were right under the window, a dangerous position if gunfire shattered the glass.

The ringing in her ears had no chance to die away. Tupe fired again. Ceiling paint flakes and chips of plasterboard floated down like confetti. From her position on the floor, looking up, Tupe appeared giant-like.

"Mr Vavau? We need to know the hostages are okay."

"Get back to the window," Tupe ordered. "I'm not ready for them to shoot me yet."

On shaking legs, Tova stood, kia kaha repetitious in her head. Be strong. She said it out loud, put an arm around KK, did the same to Jacob and he didn't brush it off. KK copied the childlike bye-bye wave she gave in front of the window. Those watching needed to know she and the boys weren't hurt.

"Mr Vavau. Tupe. We can help you if you let the hostages go."

"The cops help me? Think I'm stupid?" Tupe yelled from his position near the door. Unlikely they heard him, but they couldn't mistake the sound of the shot he fired, nor the thud as it ploughed through the wood.

"Let us see Mrs Hemona. Is she okay?"

Tova watched Tupe stare down at Repeka. She lay slumped on the floor. Her eyelids flickered, a sign of life. She had wiped at her nose, blood smearing across her cheek. Her shoulders drooped, her skin waxen. Unlike Jacob, Repeka wasn't faking.

Tova turned back to the face the window, enunciated each word. "She needs to go to hospital." Had the police set up a camera, trained binoculars on the window, found a lip reader?

There was no sign anyone noticed. Maybe she'd watched too many television cop shows.

Tupe's eyes drooped, closed, near exhaustion.

Why waste sympathy on Tupe? If it hadn't already happened, it wouldn't take long for a reporter to uncover the link between her, Areta and Hemi Hemona. Her mother's life dredged up, rehashed, more assumptions added. *Raped as a teenager, no wonder she killed herself.* Like mother, like daughter. Mixing with the wrong crowd. Her brother was a druggie; it wasn't such a leap to wonder if she dabbled, too. One or two of her teaching colleagues, would they claim they were wise to her? *Too aloof, too quiet*, hands fluttering over their hearts in fake sorrow, *not surprising, given her upbringing*. And Tom, she could see him interviewed, basking in his fifteen minutes of fame.

No one would probe the assumptions. No cop or reporter did last year, so why would this year be different? But she stood a better chance of being believed with Tupe and Repeka alive.

"Tupe, it doesn't need to get any worse. Get help for Repeka. Tell the cops about your Boss. That's who they'll really be interested in." Did she sound convincing? She remembered his fear. "They'll protect you."

Could they? *Would* they protect him?

Still slouched against the door, eyes closed, Tupe snorted in disbelief. "Those cops will have orders to shoot me. You know the Boss gets rid of anyone who stands in his way."

How would I know that?

"They won't, not if we go out together." Tova's mind raced and clutched onto the one thing that had held Tupe back all along. Something about the Boss wanting her unharmed. *Who? Why?* "I'll explain you've treated me well."

"Yeah, maybe. The Boss has plans for you," Tupe grunted. "You and the Boss, you're not ... are you?" He shook his head, the thought was ludicrous.

"You mean her and that old bald guy, the one Dad was shit-scared of?" Jacob cut in, wide-eyed. "Gross."

Jacob's words snagged in Tova's mind; like coins in a slot machine, other snatches of information tumbled into place. Richard was obviously the *scared* Chinese man. "Who are you talking about?"

"The Boss. The Man." Jacob said it slowly, a mixture of awe and fear apparent. "Dad never said his Chink name right, so he called him Mr Joe."

Why hadn't she worked it out before? A second Chinese man, older, commanding respect. She rolled *Joe* around in her head with a little more 'sh' than the easier 'j' sound. *Mr Zhou?* No, she must be wrong. He was her father's friend.

"And I reckon his plans for you will no longer include me," said Tupe. "I'm a dead man. Gotta think ... which way?" He disappeared into the room opposite. The slamming of the door was final confirmation – he had come to a decision.

"He's going to start shooting." *At the cops, himself.*

Tova pulled the boys close, whispered, "Out the laundry door. KK first, then you, Jacob. I'll be right behind you." There were several things wrong with the plan: the door locked, Tupe shooting them as they fled, caught in crossfire. Too many more even to think about.

She couldn't leave Repeka behind. In return, Repeka would tell her about Areta. A fair deal.

She braced herself to counter KK's objection, too scared to go first, wanting the security of staying close to her. If it was possible, his face lost more colour, but he nodded. Tova pulled Repeka into a sitting position, grabbed hold under her arms, her back straining into the half-lift, half-drag.

A shot fractured the silence. A window shattered. Someone yowled. It could have been a dog.

It galvanised her into action. "KK, go, go." Where was Jacob?

Dismayed at Repeka's weight – it would take longer than ten seconds to drag her to safety.

More gunfire. Tupe taking potshots at the police. Or them at him.

Her load lightened. Jacob had his mother's legs. "That won't hold him forever," he indicated over his shoulder. He'd found his own use for Tupe's barricade. A jumble of chairs and tables blocked escape from the room Tupe was in.

She thought Jacob had fled. Or dashed across the hall to warn Tupe. She could have hugged him.

"Shit, hurry up. She's heavy," he said.

Tova and Jacob did a pull-push shuffle along the hallway. Repeka moaned.

The shooting stopped. Not a good sign. While Tupe was busy firing, he wasn't thinking of them.

Tova saw the opening, edged backwards into the narrow laundry, tightened her grip on Repeka. A few more steps to safety. She couldn't hold Repeka much longer, shoulders and fingers straining with the weight.

"Shit. Is it locked?" Jacob shunted into the space.

Tova turned to see what Jacob was looking at.

KK. Holding the door handle. He shook his head. "But what if the dogs are out there?"

Jacob met her glance. He, too, remembered his earlier statement.

Crucial seconds gone. A wave of despondency flooded over her.

The sound of furniture, falling, scraping. A door banging. Tupe shouting, lumbering down the hall.

"Go, go," Tova pleaded. "Now, KK."

Tupe's bulk swayed into sight, crashing against the wall. He thrust one hand out for support, the other waved the rifle at them. It steadied, pointed at Repeka sagging between Tova and Jacob.

"Can't have her live to tell lies." He drew the rifle to his shoulder.

Jacob dropped his mother's legs. Tova staggered with the extra weight. Her grip weakened. Repeka slid, and lay at her feet, whimpered.

Keep quiet, play dead.

Jacob flew at Tupe.

With practised ease, Tupe jabbed an elbow into his cheek. The boy's head snapped back. Blood spurted out of his nose. He fell to his knees. Tupe, with a scream loud and long, full of pain and anguish and disappointment, landed a blindside punch on the boy's head. Jacob dropped, out cold.

Tupe parted his feet to steady himself, the rifle gripped low by his side.

"Go, go, KK." Now would be a good time for the police to rush in.

Tova ran at Tupe. Not with the intention of knocking him out or over – she'd have little chance of that – but to push him back, get KK out, distract him from Repeka and Jacob.

She tackled low, elbows in, giving Tupe no limb to grab and fling her aside. Her head pushed into the soft flesh of his stomach, not lower, where she'd aimed. The rifle clattered to the floor. Freed of it, he grabbed her hair and yanked. She yowled, blinked to clear the sudden tears, gripped his arm, bit down and wound her legs around his. Writhing and twisting, she forced him to step back into the hall, away from their escape route.

"Get off, you stupid bitch!" Tupe jigged, slammed into the wall.

Screaming, she clung on.

"Vavau, let her go, Vavau!"

Large black shadows appeared. Not shadows, men in black.

In one movement, Tupe scooped up the rifle and loosened his grip on her.

Tova kicked away from him, slid to the floor, curled on her side, foetal position, arms drawn in to protect her chest, head tucked down to shield her face.

"Put the rifle down, Vavau. Last warning. Put the rifle down."

"Like hell."

The noise deafened her. She couldn't hear, but she could see, peeking out from splayed fingers, like cheating at hide-and-seek.

Tupe shuddered, buckled. Rank sweat drops trickled onto her cheek, her neck. She raised her arms to break his fall. His T-shirt darkened. Her palm, wet, slipped, and her wrist bent back. He toppled, pinning her to the ground, the breath crushed out of her.

Echoes and boots clomping and men shouting. Was that Tupe whimpering, or her? Relief as Tupe's body was lifted off. She gulped for air.

Someone knelt beside her. "Stay still."

"The boys ... Repeka?"

"Where do you hurt?" It sounded like Finn.

All over. Her ankles were bruised from bashing against the railing, her hip ached and her ribs pulled each time she moved. Her face felt hot, puffy, and a new pain cramped her hand. Liquid trickled down her neck. Conscious of it now, she tried to move her fingers to point. "Is that blood? It's not mine, is it?"

49. FINN

Finn gave a summary of events as he recalled them while a medic checked him over and then Smith appeared, suspended him from duties and sent him home with strict instructions to confer with nobody. He'd be told when they were ready for him. The initial investigation would take time; double-checking the chronology of events, ballistic reports – who shot whom, and medical reports of the three deceased.

At home, he tried to rest but sleep was broken with the same dreams: Tupe Vavau falling onto Tova; Repeka's lifeless body lifted on the gurney; and Unsworth, so still on the cold ground.

He stared at the TV, but took in nothing of the moving pictures in front of him. He cooked some sausages, added a baked potato, but one bite into the meat and he felt sick, swallowed hard.

He waited, sat on the couch, head in his hands.

The summons came less than twenty-four hours later. Get yourself to District Headquarters. All very formal, even though that was Henderson, his own station. He considered slinking in the back way, but he took a deep breath and entered through the main entrance. One officer at the counter was too engrossed in his computer screen to notice him, but he received a surprised look, then a smile and thumbs up from the other.

He was made to wait, cooped up in a soulless interview room until two police investigators arrived to question him, one with the thickest, bushiest eyebrows Finn had ever seen, and one with a leaning-towards-garish polka-dot tie. If they had introduced themselves, Finn hadn't heard. They both wore gold name badges with small black lettering on their lapels. To read them, Finn would have had to get up closer.

"A preliminary chat, Constable McIntosh, that's all, go over your statement, check your timeline of events, see if you've remembered anything else. Just making sure it's complete for the full internal review. Everyone involved is being consulted. Standard procedure when deaths during a police operation are involved," Tie Man said.

"Yes, sir." Finn was well aware this was far from a casual chat.

"We have your statement." Shaggy Eyebrows flicked through a folder on the table, the sound of the loose pages turning over amplified in the quiet. Finn had said as little as possible the previous day, and his written statement laid out only the bare facts, so the folder must hold his service record, too.

"Seems you were faced with a difficult situation. Poor lighting, minimal intel," Shaggy Eyebrows said.

A statement, not a question, so Finn remained silent. He was familiar with the tactic. Imply sympathy, sit back and wait for him to say too much.

"Let's start by talking about Constable Luke Unsworth," Shaggy Eyebrows said.

Let's not.

"With Vavau and Repeka Hemona deceased, obviously we won't be able to triangulate events from their viewpoint. We'll have to rely on Constable Cranston's and your accounts."

Obviously. A non-too-subtle warning that the two stories better match?

"You say here Unsworth ran towards Tupe Vavau. Can you elaborate?"

"That's what it looked like to me."

"Why do you think he did that? Against your order to wait."

"Everything happened so fast." Finn had spent hours reliving those moments. Came up with one clear reason for Unsworth's action.

"So it's possible he was aiming to divert Vavau's attention. Took a risk to save his fellow officers. Heroic, you might say," Shaggy Eyebrows said.

More like suicidal. But Finn could guess how they wanted the public story to unfold.

"You haven't mentioned the disagreement between you and Unsworth prior to events at the Hemona house."

They'd interviewed Cranston already.

"So you knew Unsworth was emotional, under pressure. Yet Pavletich, and you, kept him on active duty."

"It wasn't like that." Surely Cranston had said the same.

"Yes, well, there will be a full investigation into Constable Unsworth's background in an attempt to comprehend his motives," Tie Man said, his accent soft and pleasant, a surprising contrast to his loud tie.

"Yes, sir." Finn could only trust that a full and objective investigation would be carried out. He didn't want Unsworth vilified twice over; dead and reputation in ruins. But he sure didn't want *a hero of the hour* PR whitewash either. Especially not one that made scapegoats out of Pavletich and him. What he did want, and expect, was the truth to be known, and Tova exonerated.

Shaggy Eyebrows turned another page. "Take us through how you ended up inside the house, obstructing an AOS operation."

Finn, too, had been through interview training, had enough experience behind him. Change tack, up the pressure, see where that led.

Finn tried to remember exactly what he had written down. Stick to that as much as possible. "A number of officers, including me, were ordered to surround the house, from a distance, in case anyone made a break for it." Omitted from both written and spoken accounts, his manoeuvring to be stationed nearest the side door.

"The AOS entered the house. KK, one of the hostages, stumbled out, disoriented. I pulled him away from the door, handed him over to the officer behind me. I heard the AOS yell, very clearly, telling Vavau to put his weapon down. Then shots were fired. From my position I could see Vavau had fallen on top of one of the hostages." Before he was even conscious of moving, he was through the door, kneeling beside Tova.

"The AOS focused on Mr Vavau, pulled him off the hostage. I ascertained that the hostage was hurt, and called for paramedics. At no time did I interfere with any AOS member carrying out their duty."

"Ah, yes, Ms Tan. We haven't been able to interview her yet."

Meaning? Were her injuries worse than they had looked?

"The doctors are being cautious," Tie Man explained. "As are we. Until we know her exact involvement, she's under guard in hospital."

"What do you mean, her involvement? She was a hostage." Finn's voice rose, heat spreading up his neck.

Tie Man held up one hand. "This seems a good time to move on. What we need is a clearer understanding of the bigger picture." Tie Man pushed his chair back from the table, stretched his legs out in front of him.

For all it looked like Tie Man was in casual chat mode, Finn sat up straighter, alert. Tie Man was in charge, and he was about to get serious.

"Preliminary interviews with those officers at the Howick scene suggest that Goran Pavletich disagreed with the strategy suggested by Detective Senior Sergeant Hammond Harris, the officer in charge of the incident at the Tan home," Tie Man said.

"I wouldn't know about that. I was on crowd control." And from what he remembered, no one else was close enough to hear Pavletich and Harris when they were talking.

"We have an allegation that Pavletich endangered your life. First, he reinstates you to duty after the shooting at the Tan house, and second, your injury puts you at risk. No one could expect you to carry out your duties in that condition."

"A few painkillers did the trick." Finn, too late, tilted his head away from them, but they would already have seen the raw, red, broken skin around his ear. Fresh air, he'd remembered from somewhere in his childhood, was good for healing, so he'd removed the bandage.

Harris had to be behind this approach, using whatever contacts he had to guide the line of questioning. Discrediting Pavletich was one sure way to defend his own decisions. Pavletich's instincts had been good, but the hierarchy would never publicly state the ends justify the means. Harris would end up with a commendation, Pavletich more likely be slapped with a negligence charge.

"Do you think Detective Senior Sergeant Goran Pavletich was acting outside his authorisation?" Shaggy Eyebrows asked.

"He was doing his job, sir."

"I'm sure he believed he was. Nevertheless, his actions will be a subject of the enquiry."

Normal procedure under the circumstances. But he was certain they had formed their opinion by now.

"You transferred out of Counties Manukau because of difficulties with Detective Senior Sergeant Harris. Is that right?"

Tie Man's change of tack unsettled Finn. Gunning for him now, linked with Pavletich, both with reasons to be disaffected with Harris.

Shaggy Eyebrows openly looked at his watch.

"Giving us a hint, eh, McIntosh?" Tie Man laughed. "Right, that hour went fast. Go home, rest up." He stood, nodded to his colleague and left the room.

That was it?

"If anyone asks, the meeting was to check facts on your statement." Shaggy Eyebrows busied himself with straightening loose pages, squaring them off, before placing them back in the folder. "Which could do with some fleshing out, by the way."

"OK." Finn had entered the room under that impression, but it soon became clear that the two interviewers had another motive. Had Tie Man left his underling to deliver the warning – play the game our way?

"This is a heads-up." Shaggy Eyebrows lowered his voice, "Strictly off the record."

"OK," Finn repeated, more slowly.

"Harris's behaviour over the last few years, has, let's say, raised a few red flags. There's the suggestion that he may have misled this investigation, among others. He's being investigated, so don't hold back on details."

A beer in hand, Finn slouched on the couch but the TV news programmes were hard to stomach, saturated with the siege. The latest feed running along the bottom of the screen: Knock-on Effect of Brothel Murders, the newsroom crew likely running bets on who came up with the best puns.

Solemn newsreaders, footage of the street and house segueing into images of bodies on gurneys and stills of Areta, as journalists were fed more information and made more connections. Juliette's business, her character and mothering skills maligned at length; *We're sorry she's dead, but ...* Neighbours who had offered little to police had plenty to say to reporters. Inspector Smith interviewed, several questions asked about the police officer's death. A PR fail if Smith's ums and ahs and avoiding the camera were any indication.

Finn headed off to the gym rather than watch the celebrity panel sound off on police ineptitude.

With each stroke as he swam up and down the pool, waterproof Band-Aids living up to their promises, he wished he'd stopped Unsworth. With each laboured breath on the treadmill, he thought of ways to help

Pavletich. As he lifted more weights, he wondered how the boys were.

Richard's injuries severe, and Malcolm Tan with a gunshot wound. Different needs meant different care required. Both of them suspects in a murder case, they would be kept separate from Tova and the boys, crucial witnesses. And under guard until Zhou was found.

By mid-afternoon the need to know was like an itch he couldn't reach. He created distractions, mowed the front lawn before the drizzle defeated him, had a beer, thought about cleaning the whole house, accomplished a half-hearted effort on the bathroom. By dinner time, the itch was unbearable. What was happening with Tova? KK and Jacob, too. No one had said he couldn't visit them. But where were they?

Process of elimination. They wouldn't be taken to a public hospital, too open, and too difficult to secure. The clinic on the North Shore. Or the one in South Auckland. Both private, but used by police when the person needing care also needed to be under anyone's radar.

He'd try the North Shore first, it was closer and he'd go in uniform. Someone there might at least tell him if they were on the premises. He didn't need to speak to Tova, he just needed to know she was okay.

He powered up his laptop and searched for the private hospital. The images were of handsome doctors and attractive nurses and modern, pastel-coloured rooms, making it appear exclusive, a haven for the rich undergoing elective cosmetic surgery. There was no floor map. Finn had never been there but he assumed security would be tight: automatic doors with night locks and the whole complex covered with security cameras.

Was it worth the trouble to get there, be caught – and for what? Tova might not even be there.

By midnight, he was in his car and crossing the Harbour Bridge. He exited at Wairau Road and fifteen minutes later he'd parked two hundred metres beyond the hospital entrance. He walked back. No obvious police presence, no marked cars, no uniforms on the door, but there wouldn't be.

The automatic doors opened. No one was on reception but he did notice the cameras and kept his head down. Anyone checking security camera footage wouldn't be fooled.

Patients' rooms would be in the back wing, so he took the stairs, ignoring the chant of each footfall, 'Stop now. Go home.'

The best bluff was one based on truth with enough detail to sound convincing, delivered with confidence. He had his story ready in case he was stopped: he was known to each of the victims, he was on the incident team and he had an urgent question to ask the patients. Yes, it was late, he'd been busy until now. This investigation was 24/7.

Small whiteboards announced if the rooms were occupied, the names of the patients, their doctor and the nurse in charge, written in black marker. It occurred to him that if Tova and the boys were there, they would be at the far end, beyond the gauntlet of the nurses' station. A little added security.

The corridor was lit by low wall lighting, enough to see by, not bright enough to disturb the sleep of patients, and most doors were closed. No one accosted him as he tiptoed from room to room, the carpet muting his approach.

The nurses' station was empty. The night nurses were probably busy with a patient, or maybe exclusive hospitals suffered staff cuts too. He counted the whiteboards he could see - three each side of the corridor. Plus the visitor toilets, one MALE, one FEMALE and a door at the end, with EXIT glowing green.

The first door beyond the nurses' area was ajar, no name on the whiteboard, the room in darkness, but he could make out the bed nearest to him, the mattress rolled and sheets and blankets folded on top of it. The bed by the window held a thin body clad in patterned pyjamas. Watery moonlight came through the uncurtained window. Finn recognised KK, spread-eagled over the covers, the sheets jumbled around his feet, kicked off to cool down in the room's artificial warmth.

Finn stepped into the room. KK's lips upturned. The resilience of the young, able to dream sweet dreams in spite of the ordeal he had experienced. Along the windowsill Get Well Soon helium balloons rose like stalagmites among the row of corny greeting cards. He tiptoed out, not wanting to wake the boy.

The next room identical, two beds, the one by the door unoccupied, Jacob in the other. He was flat on his back, the sheets pulled up to his chin and taut across his body, restricting movement like a straitjacket. The bed's safety rails were raised. Tubes led from the machine beside him, one in under the covers, one into the loops around his ears and into his bandaged nose. An IV drip stood like a sentinel at the head of the bed. He breathed through his mouth, a wheezy sound, his lungs struggling to do their job. Finn wished he'd thought to bring a card or flowers. Jacob's room held no evidence that anyone cared. Had anyone told the boy his mother was dead?

Passed the visitors' toilet, the door to the next room was shut. No name on the whiteboard, but it had to house Tova. He peered into the darkness through the narrow viewing window, cupped his hands around his eyes to block out the corridor lights.

A hint of smoke made Finn turn. He expected a nurse behind him, returning from a cigarette break, demanding to know what he was doing, her words a soft hiss so as not to wake the patients.

The first thump to his jaw knocked him sideways into the door. The second punch a direct hit into his ear. He dropped to his knees. Head pounding, vision blurring, he rocked away from the jean-clad legs and black boots and tried to stand.

The kick into his side felled him.

50. TOVA

Tova jolted awake. A loud thud had jarred the silence of the empty ward. She rolled onto her side, protecting her arm, and clamped back the moan as her ribs compressed. Bruises pressed into the sheets.

The privacy curtains around her bed were drawn. The jittery night nurse must have returned once she slept and closed them. Open, the curtains provided a clear sight line to the other bed in the room, its side table and visitor's chair, and revealed that no one hid in or under them. The lights in the corridor were like floor lights in an aeroplane, guiding the way to safety.

Detective Pavletich had reassured her earlier. "With Zhou's resources, he's long gone. Can't find him anywhere."

"Why the guard outside my door, then?" Tova had asked, looking at the uniformed guard, less like a front-row forward and more like someone's amiable grandfather.

"He'll keep journalists away until our interviewers are satisfied you've told them everything," Pavletich said.

A man stood at the end of her bed, dressed in a dark polo shirt, leather jacket and jeans. Her mind played tricks in the gloom. It couldn't be Victor Zhou, never out of his dark-grey suit, white business shirt. Another doctor, so late? He'd come about Richard or her father, to tell her the worst. She wriggled to sit up, bunched pillows behind her for support, felt less vulnerable.

The man moved his head. That slight bow.

She groped for the buzzer.

"The call button has been disconnected," Victor Zhou said, dispassionate.

"How did you get in?" Tova's mind raced. "The nurse will come to check soon."

"She drove a hard deal," Zhou said, admiration in his tone. "Her student loan paid off up front in exchange for an uninterrupted fifteen minutes with you."

The nurse who had never engaged in time-passing chatter while dispensing medicine, taking her pulse and blood pressure, avoiding eye contact. Not a mark of respect, Tova now realised, but a way to remain detached.

"There's a guard?"

"He won't help you."

The thud – the guard less cooperative than the nurse.

"Nor will that officer. My new assistant is dealing with them." Zhou waved in the direction of the door.

Tova struggled to understand. What officer?

"There'll be more police here, then," she said. "It's too late, anyway, I've told the police everything that Tupe and Repeka told me."

"There are no more police here, Tova. They, like everyone else, underestimate me. My police friends keep me informed, and I help them. That's how the world works. You're not as clever as your father thinks if you haven't figured that out yet."

Had she heard correctly? Police friends?

"And who will the police believe? Two dead, low-life criminals and you, with all your baggage, or me, an upstanding citizen?" Zhou's snicker a satisfied 'checkmate'.

Tova eased off the bed, feet touching the floor, muscles aching with the sudden weight. It felt important to stand to confront him, keep him talking. Someone must come to check why the guard hadn't made one of his regular phone-ins.

"Stay where you are," Zhou demanded from the end of the bed, out of reach. Like Napoleon, one hand inside his jacket.

A bluff? In her weakened state, any punch or kick as ineffective as striking him with a feather. Stall for time, let him talk.

"You will listen to me, and come to ... appreciate the consequences of your father's actions." Zhou stood tall, shoulders back.

"I thought you were my father's friend." Tova clutched the bed for support. She wasn't sure how long she could stand.

"Once, I believed that. Both born and educated here, but we were not always trusted by others, so we promised to help each other. Many of my clients did business with Malcolm, and vice versa, and we did well for ourselves. But when I needed his backing on my vision for the new casino development, he reneged."

"It went ahead, didn't it?" What did Zhou mean, needed his backing? Tova had lived through the constant arguments about it: her mother vehemently against the project; her father telling her he was a businessman, doing business. The whole city had seemed divided; those on the 'go-ahead' side, citing improved entertainment facilities for the city and tourists, those against complaining of the twin social ills it would encourage – gambling and prostitution. Since Areta's death, Tova realised she had not followed any of the news about it.

Zhou dismissed her question with a wave of his hand. "Not using the initial plans and not with me at the helm. More than money, I lost the respect. Many clients have deserted me. Malcolm lost nothing. I lost everything."

The absurdity of his statement stunned Tova. She thought of the reason for the regular lunches with her father. He had never mentioned any of this. But when would he have? She never gave him the opportunity to talk of his business.

"It was a one-in-a-lifetime opportunity. Few New Zealand investors were willing to commit to such a large development. I was able to bring together like-minded business investors, and we could have done it without requiring any other outsider finance. Quite a coup, in the business world. Your father's money and his support was all I needed. His local construction experience and business standing in the community was the cornerstone of the project. He was interested, then Areta got to him and he ... wavered. Your father was weak, mixing business with his private life. I could not tolerate her influence over him any longer."

Blinded by her dislike of his ingratiating manner, she had never seen it before, that glint of arrogance, of superiority. His callousness. Like a slow dawn rising, light increasing, understanding grew. His power over Malcolm usurped, his plans thwarted.

"So you killed her?" Impossible to stop the tears flowing, Tova brushed at them, sniffed them back. She hated showing weakness in front of him.

"That was not the original intention. I tried persuasion, even bribery. In the end I sent Oso ... as an inducement," Zhou said. "Areta would not listen to reason."

Justifying Areta's death was her own fault. Chilled to the bone, in spite of the warmth in the room, Tova shuddered. To lie back down, pull the covers up, close her eyes, let the realisation of her mother's death wash over her, despair in solitude at her loss – that's what she craved. Time for that later. Now, she had to focus, listen.

"Free of her, I hoped Malcolm would regain his business sense, but Areta's death served to seal his decision. He pulled his financial backing out of respect for her wishes. He planned to use those funds to compensate people affected by the weather-tightness issue in his apartment buildings." Zhou massaged his temples as if that might help him comprehend such a business decision. "As soon as the investors heard, they grew nervous and withdrew their support. I had funded the initial planning. I lost all my money. Your father has come out of the failure unscathed. His businesses are intact, whereas I am in debt. He still had his dream, ridiculous as it was." Zhou spat the words out.

"His dream?" What was he talking about?

"That you would forgive him, that Richard would grow out of his juvenile ways and the three of you join together to expand the Tan empire. Little chance of Richard contributing much now."

More fell into place. "You persuaded our father to let Richard leave home, then made sure he had easy access to drugs. That was your doing, wasn't it?" That would certainly cause Malcolm much heartache.

"I can't take credit for the original idea," Zhou said. "That was Repeka. Tupe recruited Hemi for the Dunn job, Repeka figured out the connections, and she saw an opportunity to get a little revenge of her own. I just helped it along."

Annoying but harmless, she would have said of Victor Zhou a few days ago. How could she and her father have been so wrong?

"What did the Dunns have to do with us?"

"Juliette provided a way for me to recoup some of my money and get back in with the financiers. One way – control the lucrative, exclusive escort business supplied to the casino. Corner that, I make a lot of money and I gain a way back into the inner circle of financiers. But she was like your father, went back on her promises. First, she thought she could trick me into paying a higher price for her businesses than they were worth. She said she was getting right out of the brothels, wanted to buy a more reputable business, thinking of her precious daughter's future. Then I discover she was setting herself up in competition, contracting the best girls, putting them into apartments around the casino. Unlike your father, Juliette didn't have the decency to be honest with me. Scaring the daughter was meant to encourage Juliette to keep to our original deal. The girl resisted."

Warning her.

How many of the fifteen minutes had they used up? "Someone will be here soon," she said. Other nurses. Anybody. Tova glanced up. The rings holding the curtain looked flimsy. A quick tug to bring it down, throw it over him, catch him off guard, give her time to reach the corridor or at least the buzzer by the next bed. There was a chance the nurse hadn't tampered with it.

Zhou checked his watch. "I'd better get down to business, then. All you have to do is sign."

"Sign what?" Something Zhou had said earlier played on Tova's mind. She needed to think about it to get it clear. Hard to accomplish with Zhou a bed length away. Her father had already suffered a great deal: the death of Areta, Richard fighting for his life, being shot, even the loss of his cars.

Malcolm lost nothing. That's what Zhou had said. He wasn't talking about people.

"Your father's will leaves control of his businesses to you. His way of making things right, in spite of how you treat him. You will sign it over to me. If you don't, your father will suffer complications from his gunshot wound. Fatal complications, you understand. You know I can arrange that."

"You're not making sense. I sign, you get everything but not until he dies. If I don't sign, you will kill him, even though you end up with nothing."

Zhou sighed, his exasperation at her slow thinking obvious.

"What if you're caught? A good lawyer will make the deal invalid." Tova fired the words out. "What if my father runs the business down until there is nothing left?"

Zhou smiled. "It is in the interests of my police friend to make sure I am not caught. As for the other possibility, if that happens, I will have the satisfaction of knowing I got the better of Malcolm, and he will know that, too." His hand went to the inside pocket of his jacket.

"No!" Tova yelled. She lunged. Supergirl stopping a bullet.

51. FINN

Finn came to on the hard floor. Where was he? He opened one eye, squeezed it shut against the harsh light, a torch shone right at him, the eye movement alone enough for nausea to rise. Morning already?

No, fluorescent light.

Deep, slow breaths, not remedy enough against the worst hangover he'd ever had, worse than the bender when Emily left. Lie still, sleep it off.

Where was he? Finn struggled to his knees, a woozy, dizzying, unsteady manoeuvre, grabbed the rim of the basin. Basin? The last thing he remembered was peering into Tova's room. A gentle press to his ear and his fingers came away bloody, the scab scraped off. Eyes slit against the harsh light, he saw bloody streaks marring the white flooring, wall-hung urinals – and a boot, at an unnatural angle, poking out from under a cubicle door. A few seconds of ignorance before he put the incongruent images together. He was in the hospital bathroom.

Finn pressed the cubicle door, pushed again against

the obstruction, squeezed a gap wide enough to peer round. An older man, slumped against the toilet bowl, legs splayed like a discarded doll. A red string line ran from his temple, across the edge of his eyebrow, down his cheek, creating a tiny pond in the corner of his mouth. Apex Security, stitched into his jacket breast pocket, rose and fell with each shallow breath.

The jolt as he remembered the punch to his head, to his side. Explained why he felt like shit.

Tova.

Back out, turn, head for the door. Too fast. Finn held on to the sink rim to steady himself.

Shit, shit, shit. What if the guard choked on his own blood? Back to the cubicle, Finn tugged at the man, slid him to the floor, pulled him to the centre of the room and into the recovery position. He patted the man down, remembered the panic button issued to the guard and the nurses. Nothing.

Finn reached for his mobile, shoved into his back pocket. Gone.

Colder air fanned over Finn's hot skin. He spun round. The bathroom door eased shut. KK, as pale as the bathroom tiles, stood there, feet straddling the blood trail.

"Thank God it's you, KK." Finn rushed to the boy, held him by the shoulders, a plan clear in his mind. Can't leave the boy in the bathroom. What if the attacker returned to finish off what he'd started? Can't send the boy into the main corridor or across to the other wing or down the stairs. His attacker could be positioned there, preventing anyone entering or leaving.

"Get into the nurses' station. Climb over the counter if the door's locked." Finn did his best to tone down the urgency, tried to visualise the office from his brief glance earlier. "Ring the panic button." There was sure to be one. "Under the main desk. If you can't find it, ring emergency. Tell them there could be an active shooter in the ward. Then hide in there. Stay out of view until I come back for you. Do you understand?" Simple instructions, giving KK no choice. Do this, then that. KK, the automaton.

"Wha- ... what are you going to do? You're hurt." Good sign, KK's brain was connecting, thinking.

No time to explain. Finn eased the door ajar, peeked out, a quick glance left, right, the corridor empty. For now.

He turned KK in the direction of the nurses' station. Three, four running steps away. "Remember. Ring for help. Go."

Two, maybe three agonising seconds watching KK run, scale the counter, arms and legs scrabbling for a hold. Finn scooted across the corridor, shouldered through Tova's door. Saw the body outlined against the curtain around the bed, the curtain fluttering. As he dived at the figure, a shrieking alarm drowned out his own battle cry.

52. TOVA

In Zhou's hand, not a gun, but a long white envelope withdrawn from his jacket pocket.

The door crashed open, an inrush of air billowed the curtain, a siren shrieked, the envelope coiled in the air, and a dark shape rushed at Zhou, pushing him against the bed.

Tova grabbed the curtain, pulled down hard and cried out with the shooting pain up her arm. Zhou clutched the safety rope of material raining on him. It ripped. He fell, kicked out and upended the bedside chair. She seized it, swung it around like a lion tamer fending off an enraged beast. Zhou and his attacker were down, a writhing tangle of arms and legs, like a fallen rugby scrum.

Get out. Get help.

She held the chair like a protective shield and circled the thrashing legs.

Whoever had charged in pummelled Zhou. Or was that Zhou's arm?

Hard to focus, the shrieking alarm setting her teeth on edge.

The mass rolled towards her. Zhou, thrashing free, his assailant, face averted, grabbing for Zhou's leg.

Keep Zhou down. She thrust, jabbed, but the tangle roiled and churned.

Something gripped her arm. She yelped, spun round, swung at her attacker.

"Tova, it's me, KK. Stop or you'll hurt ..."

And the chair connected.

53. FINN

The café near the hospital was almost empty after the lunch rush and not long until closing. It had been Pavletich's idea to meet there before heading to the hospital, their first opportunity to catch up. The two customers at a window table had given him the once-over, a uniformed police officer with a bandaged head not a common sight.

Three mugs of coffee and three plates with large muffins, plus the standard salt and pepper shakers and the miniature bucket holding knives, forks and napkins, meant there was no room for Finn to put his elbows on the small round table. He leaned back, stretched out his legs, presenting an obstacle to anyone walking past to go through to the toilet.

"The reporter has forgotten that Juliette was a human being and that Jasmine was murdered because her mother made a bad business decision. The only justice seems to be that both Vavaus are dead, too." Wright leaned over Pavletich's shoulder. Too busy reading the front page of the newspaper he held, she had yet to start on her food or drink.

From his position, Finn couldn't help but see the huge headline: 'Casino Link to Brothel Murders'. He bit into his muffin, found it dry and tasteless, wished he'd gone for the last lemon slice instead.

"I bet this unnamed neighbour is Mr Weston," Wright said, her finger pointing to the print. "He makes out both boys were local hooligans, roaming the streets looking for trouble." She tut-tutted. "That's unfair on KK."

Finn sighed. He didn't want to hear what some ill-informed reporter said. He wanted to see Tova.

"Ignore it." Pavletich rolled the paper into a tube which he then tapped against his knee. "Until the full press conference later this afternoon, the press hasn't had much to go on, so they've got to fill the blanks with something."

Those blanks – backstory about the Tans, gossip about Areta, innuendoes about Juliette Dunn and sordid details about the Vavaus and Hemonas. And too many snide digs about police incompetence. Finn sighed again and took a sip of coffee. It was cold.

"You said Smith will be the spokesperson. Think he'll put them all straight about Ms Tan and Detective Harris?" Finn's tone suggested he doubted it.

"Ms Tan will be vindicated, certainly. As for Harris, we'll have to wait for the full enquiry." Pavletich leaned in, even though no one was within earshot. "A handful of officers knew that you were at the Tan house before the firing started, McIntosh. As soon as that information appeared in online news sites, it was a process of elimination. The leak didn't come from us. I doubt any of Harris's people would dare be so insubordinate as to speak to a reporter. That left only Harris who had the information and the means." Pavletich paused. Both Wright and Finn sat up straighter. "So I had a chat with someone who had reason to make things easier for himself by enlightening me."

"Hemi Hemona," Finn guessed.

"Spot on, McIntosh." Pavletich didn't seem to mind his punchline ruined; he sounded impressed. "Hemi provided detailed corroboration to Ms Tan's information about Tupe's work for Victor Zhou, in exchange for leniency. His way of getting back at Tupe for what he did to Repeka, and to Zhou - Mr Joe to him - for getting him involved in the first place. Hemi's biggest regret, that Tupe wouldn't end up in jail to be dealt with by his cuzzie bros."

Pavletich wiped a hand across his forehead. It didn't iron out the creases. "Best of all, we have it on record that Hemi clearly named Detective Harris as being Mr Joe's well-paid Howick cop friend."

"I heard Harris has already spouted bullshit about infiltrating the local gangs run by influential Chinese businessmen, allowing them leeway on petty crimes in return for intel on the bigger stuff." Finn snorted. "Leeway! Backhanders, he means."

"Like I said, McIntosh, there'll be a full enquiry. We'll have our say."

"Harris is smart, though. He'll spin it, twist whatever Zhou claims. He'll weigh up the odds and gamble on some hotshot lawyer arguing his unblemished career, work stress, undue pressure due to staff shortages, you know the sort of thing. He should go to prison, but I know what will happen; they'll let him retire into obscurity."

"Oh, Mcintosh, ye of little faith," Pavletich grimaced. He smeared his last piece of muffin with butter, took a large bite. Crumbs fluttered from his mouth as he spoke. "You're probably right, especially as we aren't squeaky clean. Our evidence may not be given the weight we'd like."

Ngaire pushed her untouched coffee mug away from her. "You mean he'll use Finn's being at the Tan's house and not stopping Unsworth and sneaking into the hospital, as an argument for Harris – like, Harris needed to resort to lateral practices, given the calibre of officers he sometimes had to work with."

Finn didn't need her to spell it out.

"Something like that, Wright," Pavletich agreed. "Which means no promotions for us for a while. No matter the reasons or the outcomes, the higher-ups don't take kindly to officers operating outside the rules. Sensible decision of yours to take leave, Wright."

Finn looked from Ngaire to Pavletich. He'd missed something.

"Don't worry, you'll be busy, McIntosh, training up a new partner." Pavletich nodded towards Ngaire's untouched coffee and muffin.

It took Finn a moment. "Are you ...?"

"No, the boss is ahead of himself," Ngaire's eye roll suggested she didn't mind too much. "This case has made me think of my priorities. I'm taking a few months off, see if that helps ... things to happen."

"There's a sweepstake on the reason you're going." Finn smiled. He had a chance of winning this one.

"On that note," Pavletich checked his watch, stood up, "we should be allowed in to see the patients now."

54. TOVA

"I'm sorry, Ms Tan. I thought you'd be safe here," Detective Pavletich said.

"He's caught now, and I'm fine."

She sat in a chair by the window. Different, but identical room, her previous one cordoned off, being dusted for prints. Pavletich leaned against the window sill, Constable Wright and Finn stood at the end of the bed. Tova wanted to ask how his head was. The bandage was impressive.

"I'm sorry, too. I had no idea Victor Zhou was so angry with my father." If she had known, would she have suspected his anger could lead to murder?

"You have nothing to apologise for, Ms Tan," Pavletich said. "Your calmness under pressure at the Hemonas saved Jacob and KK's lives, and the fact that you had the presence of mind to get so much information out of Zhou will help the investigation."

Calm? Had she been? The adrenaline must have masked the pain. Now she was conscious of her arm, heavy and hot in its plaster. Sitting down for too long cramped her muscles.

"I know Inspector Smith called in earlier, so you probably know we're off the case." Pavletich indicated towards the other two officers.

Here it came, the apology. Nothing we can do, out of our hands.

"In spite of that, my officers and I will do everything we can to assist the investigation into Detective Harris's involvement with Victor Zhou."

"He means, your mother's case will be reopened and independently re-investigated," Finn clarified.

Had she heard right? They were both smiling, waiting for her response.

"Thank you." It was a start. She believed they would keep their word. She held on to the armrest to rise from the chair. Finn rushed to her side, assisted her. She only wanted to ease tightening muscles, but Pavletich moved in, gave her a tentative hug, patted her back with light, hesitant touches.

Tova drew away first.

"No, thank *you*. All the best, Ms Tan. Come on, we'll go see the boy before he gets discharged."

"May I speak to Constable McIntosh for a moment?" The words out before she had time to think.

Wright pulled Pavletich out of the room.

"I haven't been very nice to you, have I?" Tova hurried on before she could change her mind. "I didn't trust you. If I'd been more open with you and listened, maybe we could have figured it out and stopped Zhou before … Anyway, I'm sorry, and I want to thank you for not giving up."

He smiled. "I'm relieved you now know that most cops aren't bad."

She couldn't help smiling, too, but said, "I'll reserve judgement. I'll be meeting plenty more over the next few months, I expect."

"The wheels of justice move slowly, I'm sorry."

"And there's Richard and my father."

"How are they? Being off the case, it's harder to get any inside information," Finn said.

"I haven't been able to see them yet, but Richard will require care for a long time. My father will recover." Tova paused. "Richard's mother came here. She told me. She's finding it hard, too. About Zhou." What had she said? That Malcolm's physical injuries would heal, but she wasn't so sure about his mental state. It would take a long time for the betrayal to fade.

"Sarah's told Tom to go while she thinks things through. I can have my old room back," Tova said. "When Richard is well enough to be moved to the rehab spinal unit at Middlemore, I'll be able to catch the train from Newmarket straight there." She chewed at her lip. "He can't go to prison. His injuries will be taken into consideration, won't they?" Would the police argue leniency for Richard, or was that too much to hope for?

Finn didn't reply. He looked away.

55. KK

KK's mother raised the bed, repositioned pillows, and rearranged him. He'd been washed down, stitched up and checked over by nurses. With a feather-light touch, she brushed his fringe aside and tapped the bandage above his eye. She asked if he needed another painkiller. Stop fussing. She filled his water jug, adjusted the bed sheet, pulled it up above his waist. KK kicked out, an impatient jerk of his foot, wanting the attention, not wanting it. She'd brought him his rocket-ship-patterned PJs.

"I thought these were your favourites," she had said, sighing.

Used to be, but somehow, in them, he slid back into little-boy mode where it was okay to be scared. On the upside, he had almost outgrown them, the pants rode up and revealed his grazed shins, gained when dragged to safety from the Hemonas' laundry.

With stitches in his eyebrow added to the grazes, he felt less of a fraud.

People at the door. KK dropped the car magazine he was pretending to read.

It wasn't Tova, or Constable Finn. The detective and the female officer introduced themselves, shook his mother's hand, then his.

"Thank you for your part in capturing Victor Zhou, young man," Detective Pavletich, said, rocking to a rhythm only he could hear. He rolled his silver watch round and round his wrist without glancing at it.

"He might have been killed," his mum said. She swiped at tears and patted the bed sheets.

"You were very brave, I hear." Constable Wright, propped against the window ledge, smiled at him. "Constable McIntosh said he couldn't have held Zhou down much longer. You followed his instructions and help came at the right time."

"It was lucky you needed the bathroom when you did," Wright said.

That's what he'd told the officer who had interviewed him earlier. He hadn't mentioned that he'd woken, and the room was much lonelier in the dark. He'd gone looking for someone to talk to.

He looked in on Jacob but, like all the other times, he retreated. Like earlier that day when a nurse had tried to usher him in. "Do Jacob good to hear a friendly voice."

KK had seen the bodies. What if Jacob woke, asked about his mother?

Tova's door was closed. During the day someone was always with Tova - police, nurses, doctors, her friend. Night was probably the only time she had to herself. The security guard wasn't in his chair. Must be stretching his legs somewhere.

No one was at the nurses' station. Going back to his

room didn't appeal. He detoured to the men's toilet. Not for a piss but for the long mirror above the basins, check if any new bruises had surfaced. And to take advantage of the first moments alone to squeeze the fresh chin zit.

He remembered all that clearly. The next bits were blurry, like watching events unfold through a rain-spotted windscreen: the guard on the floor, blood on Finn's face, the strength of Finn's hands on his shoulders, the solid cool of the counter on his legs as he scrambled over, his shaking fingers pressing the alarm, *hide, hide* echoing through his head and the chill that tremored through his body. But he was up, back over the counter and into Tova's room. Finn was hurt and needed his help. And he wasn't about to leave Tova alone this time.

And then in Tova's room, shouting and pulling at her before she knocked Finn unconscious.

"Tova almost knocked me out with the chair." KK fingered the cut above his eye. "Crazy mad until she realised it was me."

"Did I do that?" Tova, from the doorway. She smiled.

He grinned, felt it was wide enough to crinkle and crack the skin.

"I'm so sorry I threw the chair at you. And after you helped save me." She perched on the end of his bed, her arm wrist-to-elbow in fresh plaster, the skin above a translucent blue of bruises.

Constable Finn came in behind her, one side of his head shaved and a wadded bandage taped over his ear. It would hurt when the hair grew and the bandage had to come off.

"It's only a scratch." KK wriggled his toes, manoeuvred the sheet over one leg but made sure the raised welts remained visible. "How's the guard?" he asked, to stop from leaping up, stitches and all, and giving them both a hug.

"He'll live," the detective said. "But thank goodness Zhou's new man wasn't the calibre of Tupe. Willing to throw a few punches, but no stomach for anything more. He handed himself in when he heard the second man he hit was a police officer."

Detective Pavletich used a rolled-up newspaper like a drumstick on the bed. KK's mum placed her hand on his arm, a signal to keep quiet. Sounds around them amplified, a food trolley wheeled past and a phone rang in the nurses' station. "There's a press briefing later," Pavletich said. "You'll be mentioned, KK, and how you helped the police capture Victor Zhou."

KK's smile wavered. He'd be in the paper, on the news, the centre of attention at school, kids crowding around him, wanting details. He'd want to repeat saving Tova and Finn, they'd want the gore. It was hard enough already trying to unsee the image of the dead constable, outside in the cold for hours and no one able to help him. His mates would clamour for a blow-by-blow recount of what happened to Jacob. He could see some of them now, acting out the scenes he described.

A doctor and nurse arrived. One final check, forms to fill in, painkillers to take home with him.

Tova and Finn and the officers shuffled in that way adults do when the meeting's over but no one wants to be the first to go.

"Looks like we're in the way. We'll be going," the detective said. He tapped the newspaper on KK's foot. "You, young man, are quite the hero."

KK continued grinning, long after there was only his mum in the room.

"Will I see them again?" asked KK.

"I expect so. As they learn more, the police will want to check facts with you. There'll be a trial, eventually." His mother tidied magazines and took out the few clothes in the bedside locker, placing them one by one into the overnight bag on his bed, smoothing them down lovingly.

"No, I mean, Tova and Constable Finn."

"Well, judging by the way he was looking at her, maybe they'll invite us to their wedding."

"What?"

"Nothing."

"You haven't mentioned Jacob." His mum had insisted he sit in the back, belted in, cocooned with pillows, a fragile package. Roadworks at the Point Chev interchange slowed the traffic to a crawl. "His dad will go to prison," she said. "He's without his mum. He does have relatives in Tauranga, I suppose but …"

KK stopped, images and sounds and smells flashed in his mind, Jacob and Tova talking. "Tova's related to the Hemonas, somehow." It didn't bear thinking about.

"Jacob will need hospital and doctors for a while, and physiotherapy. Those services are easier to access here in Auckland. The police will want to speak with him again, too. There will be so many other changes in his life. He needs to be somewhere familiar."

He locked eyes with her in the rear-view mirror. Nine days ago, he and Jacob rode their bikes to the beach. How many lots of nine days had he had with Jacob over the years?

"Mum, you're not thinking …"

He sat up straight, tossed pillows aside, ignored his mother's protests. A breeze worked its way down the harbour, pushing the clouds away and stirring up the white caps glinting in the feeble sunshine. He missed the soccer game. He'd play next week. Jacob wouldn't, off for the rest of the season at least.

"Kia kaha," Tova had whispered at the window in the house. KK understood. He'd wanted to say it back to her but his mouth had been too dry. And he'd been terrified when he'd walked in on Finn in the bathroom. Wanting to run back to bed. But he overcame his fear, as Tova had.

"OK, Mum, just until he's better."

About the Author

Jeannie's career in the secondary education sector has given her a great source of material, some of which ended up in crime-centred short stories and some in her published YA novels *Such Good Mates*, *Impact* and two short readers, *Being Theo* and *A Few Minutes*.

She was the recipient of a New Zealand Society of Authors manuscript assessment, the result of which, this novel – *Caught Between* – was one of three works shortlisted out of nearly two hundred entries in the inaugural Michael Gifkins Prize for an Unpublished Novel 2018.

Jeannie lives in Auckland and, when not writing, she enjoys swimming, travelling and reading anything and everything.